The  of

Arandella

Tales of Gwilldonum, Book One

J. D. McBride

Cover art by Alyssa McBride
Back cover photograph by TM

ISBN: 9781522016694

PART ONE

CHAPTER ONE – A Way Through the Well

Beginnings can be elusive things, but Beth DeVere was once heard to say that the great adventures of her life began on that autumn Tuesday when her aunts, unexpected and largely unwelcome, arrived on the doorstep of her two-story rural home and rang the bell.

An inauspicious beginning for great adventures, certainly. Nothing in the oddly dated appearance of the middle-aged women hinted of the extraordinary, no flicker in the stern expression of one or the determined look of the other suggested that adventure might hazard an appearance anywhere within a hundred miles of the pair of them. The ladies brought with them no news of great import to share, no object of mystery to reveal. But their arrival did send twelve-year-old Beth and her best friend Luke McKinnon out the back door of the DeVere house at just the right moment and in just the right direction.

And that was what mattered.

Listening from the upstairs landing once the fateful bell had rung, Beth groaned softly when she recognized her aunts' voices mixing with her mother's in the entryway below. Beside her, Luke leaned close, grinned mischievously, and whispered, "The secret stairs?" The suggested escape was too tempting. Before anyone even thought of calling up to her from downstairs, Beth was moving silently over the old hallway floorboards that creaked for anyone else.

The secret stairs, in Luke's opinion, were the coolest thing about Beth's house. Unless maybe it was that mega-sized telescope in the attic, which was also pretty cool, or the tattered old book with weird symbols he and Beth had found that one time (it wasn't there the next time they'd looked), or . . . Come to think of it, there were actually quite a few cool things about Beth's house.

In any event, the "secret stairs" weren't all that secret, though Luke enjoyed calling them that, but the cool thing was that you had to open a trapdoor in the floor to get to them. Then, you could climb down from the second-story storage room and go all the way to the basement, or you could stop at the main floor landing, cut across the little pantry by the kitchen, and then go right out through the back porch without any surprise visitors in the front rooms knowing you'd been home . . . . Should you ever *want* to go out through the back porch without the surprise visitors knowing, that is. Like today.

Beth was already in a strange mood, Luke thought, and he knew that a friendly little visit with the aunts wouldn't make it better . . . because those two were totally *weird*!

Once outside the house, Beth said a little defensively, "I just don't want to deal with them right now."

"And why should you, is what I want to know!" answered her best friend in a much heartier voice, wisps of his dark hair dancing a little in the late-afternoon breeze. "You do the good-niece thing often enough. Take a break. Besides," he added practically, "if it's important or anything, your mom'll guess which way we're headed and she'll call you back; and if not, she'll probably be glad you got safely away. In fact," he added, inspired, "I wouldn't be at all surprised if that's why she was talking to them in such a loud voice just now. I said to myself at the time, 'Beth's mom sure is talking in a loud voice; must be trying to give us some kind of a hint.' A whole lot more subtle, you know, than just calling up the stairs, 'Beth, get out fast! Your aunts are here and it looks like they're really going to be a pain today'."

Luke enjoyed words, both silly ones and clever ones, and nearly always knew which to pick to make Beth smile. The fact that she never thought him *too* silly or *too* clever was one of the things that solidified their friendship, despite the difference in their ages (he'd been a teenager for nearly a year and a half already and she still had about a week to go before hitting that milestone).

Predictably, she smiled crookedly when she answered him, tilting her head to one side. "Hmmm. *That's* strange. *I* don't remember my mom talking in a loud voice." Still, her mother knew how hard it could be to deal with the aunts (and their endless, nit-picking criticisms!) and probably wouldn't mind in the least if her daughter managed to escape them today, because, as it happened, Beth's mom was one of the other cool things about Beth's house. "OK," she decided. "We'll just pretend they're not here."

"Yeah, whatever, but let's pretend it a little farther away . . .

2

like, out of view of the house," suggested Luke, not a great fan of the aunts himself. Pointing a straight arm toward the open field ahead, he announced in the deep and measured tones of a television broadcaster, "Down the hill and into The Thinking Place!" Then off he marched like a soldier doing drills; he looked ridiculous, but only Beth was there to see, so he didn't care.

The marching soon gave way to a more casual gait as the path grew uneven. The trail itself was clearly marked, Beth having beaten it down severely over the last few years. No one else ever came that way, as far as she knew, excepting the times that Luke accompanied her.

Near the southwestern corner of the DeVere back field, "The Thinking Place" (as Luke alone called it) was Beth's own special retreat. High, gateless stone walls (now ruined) had once enclosed a garden there, though why someone should have so entirely closed off the small garden in the first place no one could guess. Despite long neglect, the place remained quite pretty, in a wild sort of way. Most of the garden's coloring now came only in shades of green and brown, but hardy, flowering weeds sprinkled yellows and white about, as the seasons allowed. A lone rosebush, stubbornly survived from an earlier time and resolutely holding its bloom past the expected season, boasted a striking crimson hue. Some years back, redbud seeds must have discovered their way down the hill to settle into a new home, for a young tree had been growing along the broken eastern wall of the garden and had finally, in its vigor, managed to upset the stone remnant beside it. The western side of the wall had all but vanished years ago, leaving only its foundational blocks to hold their line steadfastly.

Though it was unkempt, abandoned, and rather ordinary-looking, except when brightened by the redbud's blossoms or the dark roses, Beth loved this place with a deep-rooted passion. For her, it was more alive than any tended garden she'd ever seen. For her, it was magic.

And most magic of all was the broken-down, dried-up, filled-in well – even older-looking than the ruined walls – that still managed to dominate the erstwhile garden. That well knew such mysteries as she could only guess, could tell such stories as she could only imagine, and – late on a quiet evening, when no one was around to know – could even come alive with bright scenes and stirring tales, faint music and invisible dances that would rise up from within it as cool, refreshing water must once have done.

Or so Beth imagined it.

For her, this was a place where anything might seem true.

She avoided calling it "The Thinking Place" (though it was true that she often came here to think in peace), but when she had first decided that it was okay to bring Luke along, he had asked at once what name she had given the place. "Secret places have to have names," he'd informed her without hesitation. "I'm pretty sure it's some kind of rule, and I know how you feel about that whole *rule* business." Beth couldn't think of a name, though it was such a meaningful place to her. Calling it "The Magic Place" would somehow diminish the magic, she thought – and sound silly. It was an imagining place, of course; when she read favorite books while sitting with the cooling stones of the old well against her back, Beth could almost feel the action of the stories come alive. But neither "The Imagining Place" nor "The Reading Place" seemed quite right either, and she'd had nothing to suggest that would say all she wanted.

So Luke had dubbed it The Thinking Place.

Today, though, it was The Escaping Place.

Luke didn't blame Beth for avoiding her aunts. As far as he was concerned, their pendulum seemed to swing between a little eccentric (as in, "They're just a little eccentric, dear; be polite") and kind of creepy (as if Twilight Zone music ought to play in the background at their approach). Besides, Beth had been in a strange mood herself for the last few days. He couldn't figure it. What was that word? *Fey.* He'd looked it up once, a long time ago, but hadn't ever had just the right moment to slide it into a conversation. But now, it fit Beth. It fit because she'd been getting this faraway, lost look, like she was waiting for something to happen or maybe like she was under some kind of spell. Not that he believed in spells, of course. And not that she'd been acting that way all the time – but once in a while, she'd get that look. Like now. Kind of spooky.

But that was OK, because they were friends – *real* friends – whether or not one of them was getting all spooky and weird.

That had been the best thing for Luke about moving from the California coast to the rural Midwest – finding such a good friend right next door. Of course, out here in the middle of nowhere (which is how he still thought of his new home), "right next door" still might mean you had to walk for a couple of

4

minutes to get there. Luke had hated the idea of moving to the country. *Farm* country! He'd been just short of thirteen back then, the same age Beth was now, and certain he'd never find friends to replace the ones he'd left behind . . . so he'd scarcely seen the point in trying.

Luke had first run into Beth early on when he'd been out exploring the neighborhood (if you could even call it that). Before noticing her, he'd seen her maniac little dog, yipping and yapping and zigzagging around in tall grass, trying to catch a butterfly or something. He told himself he hated yippy little dogs, but the fact was that he'd never before given them much thought one way or the other. He was merely in a sullen mood and prepared to dislike everything about his new surroundings. Then, a little farther off, a dozen yards in from the road, he caught sight of another dog – some sort of collie, much more his type – its head cocked, looking in Luke's direction. It was lying in the grass but looked alert, seemingly standing guard over the girl stretched out on a blanket beside it and propped up on one elbow. Engrossed in the large open book laid out before her, long brown hair falling like curtains around her face, she hadn't noticed Luke's approach until her dog had. "Hi!" she called out then, looking up with a bright, friendly expression.

Luke acknowledged the greeting with an upward jerk of the head and nearly continued down the road without speaking. Almost at once he thought better of it, though, and turned in the girl's direction instead. He supposed he might as well find out from her what other kids lived around there. Other kids that were *boys*, that is. And didn't look like they were about ten years old! Maybe she had an older brother or something. Not that Luke would necessarily *like* the older brother. Probably he wouldn't. At all. But he might as well find out.

It turned out that the girl, Beth, was an only child and that the only other boys on that stretch of road were either a lot younger or a lot older than Luke, but there were two "really nice" boys his age over on Wildeberry Road, wherever that was, and then "lots more" if you kept heading on towards town.

Great!

On the verge of turning back, he couldn't help first checking out the title of the open book. He stopped short, surprised, when he realized that it was one of his favorites. Back

5

home, only a couple of his friends were much into reading, and none of them had gotten through this particular book (though they'd seen the movie enough times) because it was just too long and difficult. Luke noticed that the girl hadn't gotten very far either, and he commented on the fact with satisfaction.

"Yeah, I'm only on the second chapter," she answered, "but I've read it before." Then she added with evident interest, "Have you?" Partly he wanted to say, "Yes, and I love it," and then ask who her favorite characters were and what sections she liked best and whether she liked the ways they changed things for the movie and . . . all sorts of things. But partly he wanted to go on feeling mad about how he'd never find anyone to talk to. It was that part that won, for the moment, so he simply said, "Yeah," and moved away. ("It was because," Beth told him later, when they'd become real friends, "you thought you were way too cool to share your clever ideas with an eleven-year-old kid like me – who was even a *girl*, of all things!" "It wasn't that," he'd answered . . . but maybe it was, partly.)

But that had been forever ago. They kept running into one another over the summer, and their families got acquainted, and it didn't take long for Luke and Beth to discover how similar their tastes in books were and how similar the turnings of their minds. The discovery pleased them both but surprised Luke more. He found that he enjoyed involved conversations with Beth not only when they agreed but also when they didn't. Not that he hadn't liked a good debate in the past . . . but that was because he knew he could be quick and witty with words, when he felt like it, and he generally counted on winning any argument with any other kid (and he felt pretty good about his arguments with adults as well!). It was the winning he'd liked. Luke was more intellectual, better read, and, frankly, just plain smarter than most of his old friends. And he knew it. And even though those qualities set him apart from others in ways that weren't always comfortable, he did let them shine through from time to time. (Not *too* often, of course; just at choice moments.) In Beth he found if not an equal match (he never saw a reason for examining *that* question too closely), at least a good one. With her, he enjoyed arguing out points whether anyone won or not. She had interesting ideas. Her way of looking at the world was different from his, but disagreements never interfered with their friendship. So, he'd found a good friend after all. A better one, in fact, than any he'd left behind in California, though that idea hadn't yet occurred to him, even now, nearly a year and a half later. He and Beth could tell each other (almost) anything.

Beth, for her part, had always made friends easily, but had never had a best friend before. Not really. About a year after meeting Luke, she realized that that had changed, though she couldn't say exactly when. She felt so at ease talking to him – trying out ideas without worrying what he'd think, letting show how much she knew about a subject without being afraid it would seem like showing off, admitting when she felt clueless or all mixed up about something without wondering if he'd think less of her or be . . . *disappointed* in her. She and Luke could tell each other (almost) anything.

But today something was up with Beth, and she wasn't saying what it was, and Luke couldn't figure it out. So, when they got to the Thinking Place and had found not-entirely-uncomfortable places to sit – Beth on an old stone bench and Luke on the ground, leaning against the redbud tree – he asked.

"What's up?"

"Nothing," she responded casually. "I just didn't feel like—"

"Hmm," he interrupted. "*Nothing.* Let's just pause for a minute and see if I believe you; and the answer would be, u-u-uh, no. So, what's up? And I don't just mean in the last ten minutes. I mean for the last few hours – *days,* maybe."

"Oh!" She was surprised. "I don't know. I mean— It's just—" She stopped and Luke waited while she organized her thoughts into the right words. Beth liked that about Luke. Even though he could talk in circles fast enough to make an acrobat dizzy, he could also wait a long time while she thought something out. Well, a minute or so, at least, which was more than people usually did.

"Two things, I guess," she began, after a moment. "And one actually does have to do with the aunts." That was the easier thing to talk about. "They're really creeping me out."

"So what else is new?" Good old Aunt Julia and Aunt Claudia were on the odd side even by Luke's standards, and his own family background left him with a high tolerance for oddities. But it wasn't that, so much, that bugged Beth; the aunts were always jumping on her about the littlest things, criticizing and

7

correcting, treating her views with condescension, or trying to make some monumental life lesson out of the most insignificant things (to a lot of people, the last part wouldn't sound so bad, but Luke had had a grandmother who did just the same thing – so he got it about how aggravating that could be).

"No, I mean it's worse. Or maybe I've just been noticing it more, but it's the way they look at me sometimes when they think I don't know. Everything's normal – or normal enough – and then I catch one of them staring at me, and it's like . . . I don't know, like they're trying to figure me out. Or like they know something about me that *I* don't know. Or . . . maybe like they're waiting for something to happen."

"Something like . . . what?" Beth halfheartedly shrugged, so he went on. "Spontaneous combustion, probably. I'm pretty sure that's gotta be it. . . .What? You don't think so?" Luke responded to his friend's expression. "OK, so maybe," he suggested with feigned enthusiasm, "they're waiting for you to transform into some pint-sized amphibian *right* before their eyes and hop away to a really sleazy lily pad on the far side of town? Something kind of like that, you're thinkin'?"

"Yeah, right, it *could* be that, or maybe something a *little* less insane . . . You know, mostly I think they're just kind of 'off' about stuff, but sometimes . . ." Beth paused, sighed, then began again. "It's probably not true, but sometimes it feels like they're just waiting for me to mess up . . . like my dad, I mean. You know, when I was little I thought he was perfect," her voice caught a bit, but she kept going, "and my mom always talks about him like he was great, but even she admits he was sort of a wild child when he was younger. . . . Did you know?" They hadn't ever talked much about her dad.

"Yeah, I've heard a thing or two." Luke's mother, Dina, whose idea it had been to move to the middle of nowhere in the first place, never seemed to invest much effort in befriending "the lovely local ladies," as she called them, yet she always managed to discover whatever they had to offer in the way of interesting gossip. From what Luke gathered (it had never crossed Dina's mind to keep the gossip she'd learned about Beth's family to herself), the local take on Beth's dad in his younger days didn't stop with "wild child" – it included "black sheep" and even "juvenile delinquent" (also "gadabout," but Luke wasn't entirely sure what that meant). He apparently did his share of joyriding and that sort of thing, with maybe a little petty theft thrown in for good measure, though the ladies seemed divided on that point. The big thing was that he kept running away. One time he got tracked down at Union Station in Chicago and another time he made it as far as Kansas – he was headed to California, apparently. Well, Luke couldn't blame him for that. He himself had thought more than once about taking off to head back to his "real" home on the west coast. In fact, Luke pretty much thought he and the teenaged version of Beth's dad would have gotten along pretty well. He couldn't blame him for wanting to get away from Fairspring, Indiana.

But he did blame the grown-up version of the guy for leaving Beth and her mom behind. He absolutely blamed him for that.

They'd both been quiet for a moment. When Luke spoke, it was in a brisk and matter-of-fact manner, as if settling the question once and for all. "Well, I don't know why your dad took off and you don't either, but I can tell you this for sure – *you* are just not the messing up type and you're less like a wild child than just about anyone I've ever known. *You're* not taking off anywhere. You're a staying-at-home, keep-me-away-from-wild-adventures kind of a girl, if ever I—" When he saw the change in her expression, he thought maybe he was going too far. "Well, what I'm saying is this: *you* won't be running off anywhere because if you did you'd be leaving me alone out here with no one but the kidlet and my alpaca buddies to talk to." (Luke's parents, assisted to varying degrees by Luke and his younger sister – also known as "Bug" or "the kidlet" – ran a small alpaca farm. The idea for this enterprise had come to Luke's mother suddenly when the family was living in southern California, where they'd never even seen an alpaca, and she had happened across a fateful magazine article on just that topic. Dina McKinnon had a penchant for seizing Great New Ideas – like starting one's own alpaca farm – and this idea had actually stuck. Within eight months, the family had packed up and moved to Indiana.)

"You *do* have other friends," Beth said, relieved to steer the conversation in a new direction since she was having second thoughts about discussing more important and personal things.

"Yeah, *duh*! Who wouldn't be crazy about me? But you're

right here and everything. So if I had, like, an hour to kill and wanted to hang with somebody and you weren't around, I'd have to . . . I don't know, make an effort or something."

Beth made a half-amused, half-disgusted sound. "Wow, thanks!" There was a pause then as they both considered that Beth had said *two* things were bothering her, but just as Luke was thinking he ought to ask about the other thing, and Beth was wishing she hadn't mentioned that there was one (because it was ridiculous, what she'd been thinking – absolutely ridiculous!), something strange happened. "Look!" Beth cried, springing off the bench and rushing to kneel by the old well to stare hard down into it. "Did you see? The water? There was water in here."

Bewildered, Luke moved closer, took a look, and said, "Nope. Dry as the proverbial bone. Nothin' there besides dirt and crumbly leaves."

And there *wasn't* anything else there.

But there *had* been. Beth *knew* it, and the thought made her skin tingle. For days she'd been having the most peculiar feelings (*that's* what she'd been considering telling Luke about) that seemed increasingly centered on the well. She'd felt drawn here. Or she felt a premonition. Or something. She didn't know how to put it, but now that something had actually happened – something bizarre, something impossible – she felt *relief* more than anything else. Relief and excitement.

It had all been so weird this past week! Again and again she'd felt almost as if the well *wanted* her, which she knew was just crazy. Nothing ever happened, nothing was different from the way it always was. Nothing except her feelings. But now she'd seen water in the well. Not a muddy little puddle, carelessly left behind by a sudden autumn shower. A full, deep water. She knew that, though she'd seen it for only an instant. And for that instant, she'd believed.

In magic.

"I was sure I saw it," she said aloud, her voice breathy and strained.

Luke lowered his voice and spoke into his fist, saying, "Breaking news! Elizabeth DeVere of Fairspring Township enters," his tone dropped an octave, "*the Twilight Zone.* Sees water where there is none. Details at eleven, ten Central."

"No, I mean that I *really was sure.*" She spoke quietly but stared at him intently, as if trying to tell him more than the words alone conveyed.

What's the big deal? he wondered. *She made a mistake, that's all.* But aloud he merely said, "A trick of the light."

Beth murmured, "I guess so," but that wasn't what she was thinking. How could she tell him what was really in her mind? It was such nonsense. But . . . if she didn't tell him, if she pretended it hadn't happened . . . Impulsively, before she could change her mind, she blurted out, "It was like magic." She'd looked down while she said the words, but as soon as they were out of her mouth, she turned toward Luke again, expectant.

There must have been a breeze then because Luke shivered suddenly. "You're kind of weirding me out here, Beth," he said after studying her face for a minute. "Magic water? That dirt is dry! It had to be some kind of optical illusion, that's all. A trick of the light," he repeated, though he couldn't quite see how the trick could be managed, there in the heavy shade. But what else could he say? There just wasn't anything there and it couldn't have been there one minute and then seeped away entirely the next, not leaving the dirt as dry as that. Uncomfortable, he tried to change the subject back. "So, anyway, about the other thing you were going to—" A distant but distinct voice calling Luke's name interrupted him, and he responded with a groan. "Great! It's the kidlet. Think if we're quiet she'll give up and go away?"

"I know you're out there somewhere," his younger sister called in a sing-song voice, from slightly closer this time. "I saw your bike in Beth's yard. Mom says you'd better not be late again."

Luke looked at his watch. "Rats! Forgot. Got to run," he said, already getting up and brushing off his jeans. He started to move away, adding, "You coming?"

"N-no, I guess I'll stay here awhile."

"OK. Later." He hesitated, though. Beth was just sitting there, staring at the well. So weird! "It was nothing, Beth. Some kind of optical illusion . . . and, uhm, anyway . . . I guess you can just finish what you were going to say about the other thing some other time . . . right?"

"Sure," she answered meaninglessly.

Later that night, Beth sat in her room, ready for bed, but not ready. Her head was spinning in thought. What a strange week it had been! And it was getting worse . . . or better. Stronger, at least; the feeling was getting stronger; the feeling she'd been having for days that there was a real – oh, she might as well just face it! – a real *magic* around the well. And today there'd been water. Magic water? It *had* to have been because it was there and then gone . . . but she couldn't believe she'd said that out loud to Luke! He must think she was a nutcase. The whole idea was insane. Really insane!

But exciting!

She used to believe that the old garden was truly a magical place, but she was younger then. And later, after her father left them and everybody worried about her so much, she'd go there and think about him and pretend that the well was a wishing well and that she could wish him back if she tried hard enough. But she'd known it wasn't real.

This feeling – the one that had been growing all week, the one she'd felt so strongly this afternoon – was different. The feeling that there was something in the garden. A presence, or something, but not a scary presence; she *wanted* it to be there. It, whatever it was, was drawing her, calling her. She wanted to ask Luke what he thought about that – about premonitions and psychic experiences and. . . . No, about magic. She wanted to ask him if he could maybe, possibly, somehow, even just a little bit believe in magic. And she didn't want to – because of the look he'd had on his face when she'd said the word today.

"And also because it's crazy," she told herself firmly, settling into bed and pulling the blankets close to her chin. I *don't even believe in magic . . . I'm pretty sure*. But she'd seen the water, no matter what Luke said. And then it vanished. *So I guess that makes* me *crazy*. But she wasn't crazy, and she knew it.

She went back and forth like that for some time, alternately believing and not believing that something strange was happening in the old garden and that it had to do with her. But whenever she pictured the water in the well, she believed. She had seen it; she *knew* she had. And there was something strange about it, but she couldn't quite say what. If only she could see it again.

After Luke had left, she'd stayed for nearly an hour, waiting and watching. But nothing had happened. And later, after dinner and chores, while her mother was in the shower, she couldn't help grabbing the flashlight by the back door and going one more time to check. Nothing, of course.

Of course there'd been nothing! But even as those words repeated themselves in her head, she could barely keep from throwing back the covers and slipping on shoes to go out one more time, pajamas and all. *But that would be a stupid waste of time,* she told herself firmly – about eight seconds before doing exactly that.

When Beth let Augustus and Cicero, the two DeVere dogs, out first thing the next morning, she took a few extra minutes to run down and check the well before going back into the house. After morning lessons in math, history, and Latin (she was homeschooled), she picked at her lunch for a while, said she wasn't hungry, then went out again. The feeling was growing in her that the water would be back, and she didn't want to miss it.

A little after 1:30, she was picked up by Aiesha Perry's mother, who drove Beth, Aiesha, and two other girls into town for a gymnastics class. It wasn't one of Beth's better days; the instructor told her more than once that she wasn't concentrating.

She got dropped off at home just after 3:30, changed clothes, grabbed a book she'd been reading, exchanged about ten words with her mother, then headed down to the old garden and well. Beth had enjoyed the first part of her book immensely, but today she looked up from the pages often, lost her place repeatedly, and started a particular paragraph four times.

She must have seemed anxious that evening because her mother asked if she felt well. Beth answered that she was fine and then went upstairs to bed early, though her mother heard her go back down for something an hour or so later.

The next morning was much the same, except that Beth and Luke rode bikes over to Josh and Jordan Loo's house for an 11:00 science class. Their friends' dad taught at the nearest community college but offered one course each semester to the kids in the homeschool co-op. Luke came home with Beth for lunch, since Thursday was the day Beth's mom taught an archery class in the DeVeres' east field, weather permitting.

Archery was Luke's favorite class, and he was exceptionally adept with a bow; Beth, though not *quite* as skilled, did nearly as well and enjoyed the sport at least as much. She'd been better at fencing, last spring, but hadn't found it as fun. She'd been hesitant about taking that class in the first place, so her mother (whose suggestion it had been) just happened to mention the plan in front of Luke's mother, who immediately saw it as another Great New Idea (though not quite as life-altering a one as starting the alpaca farm had been). Luke was signed up immediately and Beth decided that taking the fencing class wouldn't be so bad after all.

Archery was a different matter entirely. Beth loved the idea from the start, lots of her friends signed up, both Beth and Luke found that they had some natural talent for the sport, and Beth's mother proved to be an excellent archer and instructor. "Whoa!" Luke had exclaimed during the first day's demonstration. "Who'd've guessed your mom could do something like that?" He'd been speaking quietly, but Beth's mother must have been particularly good at hearing as well because she immediately turned to flash him a smile.

For today's class, as for most, Beth and Luke were stationed next to each other. Both were aware of the unfinished conversation between them; neither made an attempt to continue it, choosing instead to make occasional trivial comments and to concentrate on archery. Or at least Luke was concentrating. He was doing especially well and seemed extraordinarily pleased with himself.

"Whoo-hoo! Nailed it!" he called out, not for the first time, after a particularly good shot.

"Do you have to say that every time you hit the bullseye?" Beth surprised them both by sounding genuinely irritated.

"Nah, I don't have to. But I really *like* to." He grinned, lowering his bow. "So, let's see your best shot."

She took aim, wishing he weren't watching, and released the arrow before she meant to. It was a spectacular miss. "Oops," was all Luke said, turning away with exaggerated movement as if pretending (badly) not to have noticed. After that, he kept quiet. He hadn't really meant to bug her, after all; he was just fooling around.

Beth couldn't keep her mind on what she was doing. The class was nearly over and all she'd been thinking about was how she *did* want to and *didn't* want to talk to Luke about magic, or at least psychic experiences. She had even come up with an approach and had imagined the conversation part way through. They'd had an involved after-class discussion once about twins who seemed to have some sort of psychic link, and they hadn't come to a very

14

satisfying explanation for how that could be. She thought she'd start with that and move on to psychic connections more generally, then magic (maybe), then the well in particular. She had it all worked out. She knew just how she'd start. She'd talk to him as soon as class was over and everyone else had gone.

"See ya," he called to her about fifteen minutes later, after they had put their equipment away in the shed, as he headed toward the front road with Josh Loo at his side.

"Yeah," she answered with a weak smile and something resembling a wave. As Luke and Josh headed toward the bikes at the front of the house, Beth turned toward the back, on her way to check the well one more time.

"You're sure you don't mind?" Beth's mother asked a few hours later. "We could probably drop you at Luke's house, if you wanted." She knew that having someone – anyone – come to their own home would feel to Beth too much like having a babysitter. It was, after all, only a matter of days until her thirteenth birthday. "Why don't I call over there and see? Just so you have some company. This co-op meeting is bound to last for hours. Last time it seemed to go on forever!" Beth had stayed alone in the house before but usually for short periods and nearly always in daylight, since her mother rarely went out in the evening. It was nearing dusk and would be fully dark long before her mother was likely to return.

"No, I'm fine. And you know Augustus is a great watchdog." As an afterthought, she added, "And Cicero is . . . well, a dog, at least."

Her mother hesitated. True, those two animals could practically wake the dead if they put their minds to it, and she had always believed their home to be especially safe, somewhat isolated though it was. Still, Beth's own uneasiness of the past several days had not left her mother unaffected. "You know, Beth, I don't really need to—" At that moment, her ride pulled up in front of the house and honked. *I'm not being reasonable,* Joy DeVere told herself. *I suppose the real problem is that I don't want to accept that she's growing up and away from me. The rest is my imagination.* "Well, all right. You can always call and of course I won't be far. It wouldn't be a problem for someone to bring me right back if—"

"Bye, Mom," interrupted Beth. She gave a quick parting kiss, and the simple action brought a surge of sentiment to both mother and daughter. *She's still got such soft cheeks,* Beth thought fondly ("the softest in the world" she used to say), while Joy DeVere reflected, *She won't always do this each time I leave.*

Twenty minutes had passed since her mother's departure, and Beth had barely kept still. She wasn't particularly *doing* anything, she just wasn't keeping still.

It wasn't the fact that she was alone in the house that made her restless, though that may have made her more alert. She had already decided not to go down to the well tonight. Every time she went, nothing happened. And besides, it would be dark soon, and she really shouldn't go out after dark with no one home in case something happened – like if she tripped and got a little hurt, or something entirely normal like that. And the wind was kicking up, and it sure looked like a storm was coming, no matter what that weather guy said, so if she wanted to go at all, which she didn't, she'd really have no choice but to do it now. Right now.

But she wasn't going. The whole thing was ridiculous. The idea of a supernatural message knocking on the door of her psyche, the idea that something magical was happening in her own backyard, the crazy idea that she'd seen water where there wasn't any, where there *couldn't* have been any, the idea that any minute an incredible Something might happen right outside her house and that it had to do with her, that it was *calling* to her even, the idea that something strange or wonderful or magic was about to happen, and that she'd miss it if she didn't go right this instant, right *now* – *that's* what was totally ridiculous!

She grabbed her sweatshirt.

At the outside door, she had to push back the dogs, who wanted to come along. "Not this time," she told them. A moment later, walking briskly, feeling the cold wind, hearing (she was pretty sure) her own heart beat, she wondered what had compelled her to say that. Bringing the dogs along might have been a smart idea. But she wasn't going back for them now.

Instead, she fixed her attention ahead. She knew where she was going, knew every step to take. She'd be at the well in two minutes, see that there was nothing there, then be safely back in her house a few minutes after that. She didn't look down at the path

16

she'd followed so often, barely registered the fact that the dogs were barking loudly from behind the kitchen door . . . didn't realize in the least that someone was following her – following and gaining quickly. With an anticipation that was nearly electric, she reached the low remnant of the garden wall, stepped purposefully over, hesitated for the briefest instant, then rushed forward to kneel before the old ruined well.

Behind her, someone arrived just in time to see her reach down into it. Beth seemed to say something. And then she vanished.

CHAPTER TWO – On the Other Side

In the land of Gwilldonum, in a lush meadow nestled in amid thick surrounding woods, the ruling Council of Ten had assembled at its traditional meeting place.

The meadow was known as Arystar's Green.

Here, leading representatives of the land had met since time out of memory whenever great matters called them together. Here, questions of war and peace had been decided, heirs to the throne had been anointed, and kings and queens had made vows of allegiance to their country. Here, the history of Gwilldonum lived and breathed.

And here, on the last afternoon of his life, the council member Rane of the Brenmarch sat among his compatriots on the very stone bench he had always chosen, the one that gave him a good view of the rest of the council while keeping his own face somewhat obscured. He did not remember the bench being quite so uncomfortable in his younger days . . . but then, in his younger days the honor of being named to the Council of Ten, esteemed advisors to the good king of Gwilldonum, had so filled his mind that he had little attention left to pay to the state of the poor old bench. To assemble with the others at Arystar's Green, to be consulted on questions of import, to have his own counsel heard and considered by King DarQuinn himself . . . what mattered the nature of a cold stone slab when set against such things?

If only the king were still alive, standing before them now! Or if his daughter, Arandella, had lived long enough to take the throne after him! A fine queen she would have made, holding her own through the dark time, had her life not been cut even shorter than her father's.

But then, if either were here now, there would be no need for this meeting and he, Rane, would be back in the Brenmarch region where he belonged, living a life that brought warmth to his

18

heart. A twisting ribbon of thoughts about his homeland as it ought to have been ended with his mind drifting to the comforting past, as it increasingly did these days – not because he was so very old, but because he was so very, very tired . . .

His mind snapped back.

The Council of Ten.

Lady Gweynleyn occupied the seat of honor in the circle of council members. Since the death of the king, the Council of Ten had had, in theory, no single leader, but in practice, the council looked to its senior member, Lady Gweynleyn, for leadership, approval, and, as was sometimes necessary, arbitration. Thus it had been for the many years that Gwilldonum, its throne empty, had been ruled by the council.

To her right sat Harac, a warrior of renown and the son of great warriors. A stocky, russet-haired dwarf whose expression rarely lightened, Harac was gruff and suspicious and not as refined as some of his fellow council members, but Rane knew that he would trust Harac with his life.

Quillin Qu'en of the Meadowlands was of a different sort. He seemed a jolly fellow on the surface, but his tongue could be sharp and he enjoyed needling those who displeased him at any given moment. Sometimes Harac fell into that category.

Cassian Maris, by contrast, appeared a genuinely content and pleasant person with rarely an unkind word to speak. He represented the people of the coastlands, known for their satisfaction in their simple ways of life.

Rane found Jeron Rabirius, the lord of the city of Greyvic, as admirable and nearly as likable as Cassian Maris. Jeron was an excellent leader, though rumor suggested that in his home his many daughters ruled *him* rather than the reverse.

Rane did not know or understand as well the council members from the deep woods – Daasa of the Westmarch (a faun), Blom (a chameleon-like creature known as a nightling) or Merk of the Nether Woods (a half-human darkwood-dweller). There were no fauns or nightlings in the Brenmarch (Rane's own region). There *were* many half-humans of different sorts, and Merk had been a council member for even longer than he, Rane, had been . . . but still, Rane could not be confident of understanding him.

Terilla of the Gilmarch was the newest council member, and Rane did not know her well either, though she seemed a pleasing sort. She served the council as her father before her had.

And he, Rane, made the tenth council member.

There were others present, of course – attendants, messengers, interpreters . . . and one tiresome ambassador!

Gaarius served as ambassador from the neighboring country of Ferinia. He had brought an odious request from his rulers to their great ally to the south. Neither he nor the position he represented was generally welcomed by the council. The situation was dire enough without them!

The question at issue was nothing less than the future rulership of Gwilldonum! Though the Council of Ten had ruled for more than ten years, Myrmidon Tork, a very distant relation of the last king, had recently petitioned the council to be allowed to address the Great Assembly at Greyvic and make the case that *he* should be crowned as Gwilldonum's newest monarch.

The council met the idea with contempt. The Torks were harsh rulers in their own nearby land and were no friends of Gwilldonum. It was, after all, Myrmidon's older brother who had waged war against Gwilldonum a dozen years earlier – the war that ended the life of the beloved King DarQuinn. Every council member recalled vividly the destruction the Torks had brought to their homeland.

And yet . . . over time it became clear that there were some Gwilldonians so anxious to have a king again that they would even consider a Tork on the throne and wished at least to hear the proposal. There were even reports of some who actively supported the idea. Finally, the neighboring country of Ferinia had hosted a delegation from the Torks and, consequently, sent its ambassador to announce support of the Tork proposal!

Time was short. The Great Assembly would take place at the end of the annual festival at Greyvic, a large city on the northern border. The date was approaching rapidly. The council had to decide: would Myrmidon Tork be permitted to enter Gwilldonum and address the assembly as he had requested? For the sixth time in as many days, council members and attendants, had gathered on Arystar's Green to attack the issues. Restlessness had grown, and no consensus had been reached.

In the midst of a tension that was nearly palpable, one husky voice announced with gusto, "I say we keep 'em out with the points of our swords! *I*'m not afraid of a good fight!"

It was Harac, the dwarf council member, who had spoken.

In response to his heartfelt exclamation, assenting voices rose through the assembly but lost themselves at once beneath the bellowing of the well-fed, pug-nosed, bushy-haired council member, Quillin Qu'en of the Meadowlands. "Ooof! You're always wantin' a fight, Harac!" He spoke in the lilting accent of his region. "Did not your dear mother e'er teach you any other tune but that?"

Harac (whose mother had indeed been a great warrior) began to rise in angry response, but he was stayed by the hand of the council member Terilla, who answered Quillin, "Harac may be right in this. You know that I am not one to rush easily into war. All of us here are of an age to remember the Tork Invasion well enough. My own father perished in its last days, in the same battle as the king. Some of us are from regions scarcely recovered from the devastation, even now. But we may have no choice."

"We can choose to wait a while longer before taking such a heavy decision," intervened the calm voice of Lady Gweynleyn, the most widely-respected council member. Renowned for the loveliness of her person, the lady was even more esteemed for her wisdom and her steady, guiding hand.

Harac himself admired Lady Gweynleyn exceedingly, but patience was not his greatest virtue. His booming voice responded, "*Wait?* All respect, m'lady, but that's all we've done, is wait! The enemy is lined up at our gates, and we're on the verge of inviting the blasted lot of 'em in for supper!" A mix of voices sounded in agreement, though a careful ear would have discerned the ripple of dissent. "How much longer are we to wait? The moment of decision is on us." Again, voices (greater in number now) agreed.

"If I might address the council for a moment," came a seemingly demure and occasionally squeaking voice, "perhaps I will be able to clarify this dark and difficult situation." This offer originated with Gaarius, the disliked Ferinian ambassador sent to plead Myrmidon Tork's case. He was a tall, angular creature with an elongated nose, dark, darting eyes, and shoulder-length black hair accentuated by narrow braids and silky ribbons. The rich attire that hid his spindly limbs stood out in the simple sylvan surroundings. Only Lady Gweynleyn wore finer threads than his, and hers had been spun in an age when fairies could still be found in the region. "Naturally I have the highest respect for each council member here," continued Gaarius, "and I have great confidence that the decision you make in the end will be a worthy one—"

"Fine!" cut in Quillin Qu'en's voice, disgusted. "An admirable position t'take, t'be sure. So why don't you leave it at that and sit yourself back down again." Murmurs of assent rippled around the circle, but the prim voice persevered.

"There is a proposal before you, a proposal put forth by Myrmidon of the Torks, a direct descendant of William the Aethling, of ancient and beloved memory – a proposal that may well usher fresh and strong leadership to the throne of your land." The Ferinian ambassador was interrupted yet again, this time by a mix of voices and animal noises sounding together. He spoke louder. "Now, it is perhaps true – I do admit it – that the Tork clan has in the past shown itself to be a harsh leader of its subjects, and certainly the memory of the ill-begotten invasion of years gone by has left a bitter taste, but the lord Myrmidon Tork has been a guest of Ferinia these many weeks and has been judged quite charming by the very *best* families, who, I assure you, are *quite* discriminating—" The surrounding noise, far from subsiding, increased to the point that Gaarius' words lost themselves within it. Rather than intimidate him further, however, the opposition braced Gaarius' resolve. In a stronger voice, he spoke out. "*Have* I not full rights of ambassadorship? *Do* I not have the right to be heard?"

A reluctant quieting was followed by Gweynleyn's weary answer. "Truth, Gaarius, as ambassador from Ferinia you hold the right to be heard, though you can have no doubt of the reception your words will receive. Your position is well known." ("*And* roundly detested!" murmured a new voice.) "Nevertheless, speak."

"Thank you, gracious Lady Gweynleyn," answered Gaarius with a low bow and a satisfied but unnatural smile. "If I might recommence . . ." His long, bony legs walked him into the midst of the circle of council members, and he began to speak in a lofty voice over more than one low groan. "The throne of Gwilldonum has too long sat empty. For too long, you have had no *princeps*, as your people call your monarch, to lead this fine land. We must all agree that the time has come for that circumstance to change . . ."

Rane's head lowered and rocked gently from side to side. Along with every other person present, he knew what was coming: the argument that the widely-despised Myrmidon Tork ought to be given permission to come before the Great Assembly at Greyvic to make his case for assuming the throne.

The air over Arystar's Green was heavy with impatience, despair, and regret, and Rane was not the only council member who longed for the bygone days of King DarQuinn the Good!

How different the spirit of that council meeting might have been if any of its members, their attention turned to the situation in the north, had been able to discern the events unfolding less than three days' journey to the south! The scene, to begin with, was a simple one: beside a pool of settling water knelt a girl, arm outstretched, as still and silent as if held by a trance. Then a tremble ran through her, jarring her to attention.

The fierce shiver that overcame Beth, whether caused by a change in the air or by lingering magic, was peculiar and wonderful . . . and it left her a bit frightened.

Or more than a bit.

She knew instantly that the magic of the well had come fully alive, knew that she had been carried away from everything familiar, knew that she was *Somewhere Else.*

She still knelt, fingers extended to the water, but . . . nothing around her was the same. The dark had lightened, the noises had quieted, and the water, no longer confined by her cherished well, spread out in a small enchanting pool before her. Keeping fingertips dipped in the water, as if moving them might break a spell, she cautiously raised her head.

Wild beauty met her eyes. Thick greenery emerged from a backdrop of shadows – large ferns of striking hues and solid trees that seemed, despite their size, youthful. Everything seemed so . . . *fresh*, as if it had just been born, which she knew was absurd. Still, it was *unnaturally* fresh here, she sensed. Unnaturally *quiet.* A lovely spot, but an eerie one.

Beth shivered again and drew back her hand from the cool water. The spring water glimmered, then settled again, and Beth saw her own *un*settled reflection in it. She was relieved to find no one else's looming above hers, and yet . . . she had the uncanny feeling that she wasn't alone.

She braced herself before standing and turning slowly to survey her surroundings, seeking any sign of movement or life between the rifts of the greenery.

She saw none. Or maybe—

She caught her breath in a gasp!

Then, relaxing, she exhaled. Nothing after all – only a strangely-formed plant, almost human in shape, distorted by the shadows to look like a person.

But as it happened, the plant had heard her gasp and when it turned and moved out of the shadows and had, of all things, a *face*, Beth gasped again. She didn't scream (she couldn't) and she didn't back away; she barely breathed. Simply staring, fixed in place, she took in the sight.

The thing was indeed some sort of plant-creature, though also humanlike and dressed. Leaves and stems emerged from every opening of simple earth-tone clothing, and a tattered hat half marshaled the leafy mop that crowned an elongated green head. Before Beth had a chance to examine the face beneath the hat, however, her eyes were caught by a gleam farther down. A streak of light caught the metal blade of a knife – a knife clutched by stemlike fingers and twisted loosely in Beth's direction.

Fear grasped at Beth and her eyes darted reflexively to the plant-thing's face, but the expression she saw there was not frightening, only strange. A smile curled up one side of the fibrous, nearly-lipless mouth. When the creature spoke, its voice, though suggesting urgency, was jarring in its timid friendliness.

"Here at last, then. Not much time," the plant-creature pronounced in choppy but not unpleasant tones. "Door's closing." Before even finishing the words, it had slid the knife into a sheath, tossed some sort of fruit rind into the bushes, and snatched up a knapsack previously hidden from view. "C'm'on, then. It's *closing*," the thing repeated, motioning toward a sight even stranger to Beth than the plant-person itself.

Turning in a direction she hadn't previously looked, Beth saw the same sorts of trees and shrubs that surrounded on every side, but there seemed to be a *hole* in these. Not in each one, but in the entire scene, as if all the trees and plants were merely a painting on a canvas and one section of the canvas had been ripped out, revealing a dark void behind. But the rip, if you could call it that, was skillfully done, forming a perfect oval opening – an opening that was gradually shrinking.

The plant-thing moved toward it and, a bit awkwardly but without real difficulty, stepped through the hole to the other side, beckoning to Beth to follow. It was too dark to see what lay beyond the creature, and the opening through which it had climbed was growing steadily smaller. Soon, it would be closed.

There are moments in life when time appears to jump off its track. It seems then that you can think a thousand thoughts in what you later realize must have been seconds. Standing and staring at the shrinking hole, the stranger awaiting her expectantly, Beth experienced such a moment. Though little time passed, a rush of thoughts coursed through her mind like water toward the falls.

She pictured her home, the back field, her garden, the well – all so familiar – and then this new pool of water behind her, her sole connection to her world . . . but at the same time she couldn't help but feel the pull of the unknown world ahead, a world filled undoubtedly with wonders and curiosities, adventures and dangers. She had an instant to decide. A single moment that could change everything, that *would* change everything. A moment unlike any she had known or imagined. Except . . . she *had* imagined this moment before. Not the exact scenario, but this moment of great decision. The beginning of true adventure. In imagining such a thing in the past, scenes from favorite books had appeared like movie clips in her head. The kids in the books she loved always chose adventure when they could (well, they would, wouldn't they? Not much of a story otherwise!) – but would *she*? Would she really? Though imaginative, adventuresome, and – without knowing it yet – rather brave, Beth managed at the same time to be a sensible and circumspect girl. As much as she'd dreamed of strange and wonderful (magical) adventures, she'd wondered if she'd actually seize the chance if ever she came face to face with it. There'd be so much to consider . . .

In the event, however, there was little time for considering. Though a myriad of thoughts had raced through her mind, it had been only a flickering of her brain that had recognized this instant as the great moment she'd imagined in the past. Seconds passed, she had seconds to decide. The opening was disappearing. If she didn't move. . . An instant to choose. . . She could go . . . or not.

Swallowing hard, hoping harder . . . she went!

She nearly threw herself through the hole, then tumbled to the rough ground on the other side, jerking her head up in time to watch the last bit of the opening vanish away behind her. She found herself staring at the flat, solid face of a rock wall. There were patterns of deep scratches carved into the rock, but no opening. Beth had no chance to reflect on the carvings, which seemed to be some sort of writing, not much chance, in fact, to think anything beyond, "*What have I done?*" before stem-fingers grabbed hold of her sleeve, pulling her up and turning her around. "Best be moving," Beth heard. "They'll be waiting. No saying what trouble we'll find along the way." With those ominous words, the plant-creature released Beth's arm and set off at a pace as quick as due caution allowed. After an entirely understandable hesitation, Beth scrambled to catch up.

Beth didn't know how long they'd been walking (at a brisk pace first, then more slowly as she'd found it hard to keep up) when she stumbled and started to slip off the narrow dirt path they followed. The plant-creature made a quick grab for her, but Beth – she couldn't help it, it was just a reflex – jerked away. It was the first time the stem-fingers had touched her flesh, and their cold, skeletal feel repelled her. The jerking movement took less than a second, but its force was enough to knock Beth further off balance, and one foot slid several inches down steeply-sloping ground.

Luckily, the plant was quick enough to grab again, this time with both hands, and strong enough to steady Beth while she regained her footing. Beth murmured her thanks automatically, though she knew she couldn't have fallen far – the terrain evened out again after a couple of feet – but then she followed the gaze of the plant-creature past the short slope to a tangle of vines below. When she saw the multitude of thorny, oversized, wormy creatures weaving through the vines, she shuddered, exclaiming, "Oh, thanks!" and then, with greater feeling, "*Thanks!*" It was incredible how many of the creatures there were – *hundreds* – in the very spot she would have landed! *Eeew!* Luckily, they confined themselves to the vines and no strays left the colony to make their ways to the pathway above.

"Spiked slithers," the plant announced. Then she (Beth had decided, rightly, that the creature was probably a "she") made a face, saying, "Not nice. Not at all!" She turned to resume their journey.

Beth started to follow but said wearily, "Do you think maybe we could stop a while? And could you *please* explain where we're going?" It wasn't the first time she'd asked.

Beth had tried early on (in her initial panic at the thought that throwing herself through the shrinking hole was the most foolish thing she ever had done or ever was likely to do no matter how long she lived) to explain that there'd been a mistake, that she wasn't whatever person the plant thought she was, that she really ought to go back, and that she was very, *very* sorry if she'd caused any sort of problem at all. . . but the plant had responded with confidence, "No, you're the one; they sent me for you. Better be movin'." A little later, when they had stopped to survey the width of an open meadow before briskly making their way across, Beth had started to ask, "Would you mind explaining—," but her companion had said, "Not the right time," and then again, since the path seemed clear, "Better be movin'."

Beth had given up for a while. She could hear Luke's mocking voice in her head, "*In for a penny, in for a pound.*" The old-fashioned saying was a favorite of his mother's. It sometimes seemed, in fact, to be the main creed by which Dina McKinnon lived: If you're going to do a thing at all, you might as well throw yourself into it entirely. Until the next thing comes along, that is.

In for a penny, in for a pound. "All right," Beth agreed. "Since I wouldn't even know how to go back if I had to, I guess I'm in!" Once she'd made that decision, an enthusiasm she'd held in check began to fill her. "This is a real, live adventure," she thought with a thrill, "and if I run away from it, I'll always wonder what would've happened."

From that point, the journey excited Beth, though no particularly exciting thing happened. She and the plant-person simply walked, mostly in silence. They walked through heather and over rocks, in sunshine and under shady trees, on pathways (occasionally) and on rough, pathless ground (more often). After about an hour, they crossed a shallow stream where plentiful, colorful fish blissfully ignored their trespassing.

Then they walked some more.

They occasionally saw a barn or farmhouse in the distance, but no people (plantlike or otherwise). The wildlife caught Beth's interest – unusual birds and occasional animals that kept their distance but didn't seem as frightened by the travelers as she might've expected. Some resembled animals of her own world, a few were fascinating in their difference, but there was little time to observe. They kept walking.

It was daytime, not evening as it had been at home, nor was it like the place where she'd first arrived, by the pool, where it seemed to be neither night nor day. Here, a late afternoon sun lit a brightly-colored land, and as exercise warmed her, Beth removed her sweatshirt and tied it around her neck. The air that filled her lungs was clean, invigorating, wonderful.

Even so, she had begun to tire, and the two travelers had gradually moved into darker places and thicker woods. No bright hues here, and the back of her guide's mud-colored jacket had been Beth's main sight for a good fifteen minutes. She'd been walking mechanically, fatigue pressing on her, when she'd stumbled and nearly slipped into the nest of spiked slithers. Her legs were tired and she still didn't know where she was going; it seemed high time to do something about both of those circumstances, and so she'd asked for a break and an explanation.

In response, the plant-creature looked about warily, and Beth's eyes followed hers. Having paid little attention to her surroundings during the last stretch of walking, Beth hadn't noticed how sinister they'd become. Menacing shadows loomed all about and an eerie quiet settled around the travelers, now that they themselves were keeping still. "Not the time, not the place," the plant answered cautiously. She began to walk again, but added over her shoulder, "Soon."

Beth, feeling the creepiness of her surroundings, agreed and decided to press one point only. "I don't even know your name."

The plant stopped short and turned, causing Beth, who had started to follow, to bump right into her. "No?" She searched her memory. "No!" she decided. "It's—" then she said something long and Latin-sounding before ending with "of the Nethermarshes."

"And I'm Beth," said Beth, struck as never before by the brevity of her name. "Elizabeth DeVere, I mean. Of Fairspring Township in Carson County, Indiana. Of the United States. And. . . could you please tell me your name again?"

A short laugh escaped the plant's fibrous mouth and the sound of it made Beth jump. A "backwards" sort of laugh would be the best way to describe it, where air is inhaled rather than exhaled. Very odd.

"Aynyxiacichorium. A walkabout name," explained the plant almost apologetically. "Of the Intybus clan. Of the Nethermarshes. But most of your kind call me Aynyxia."

"OK. Aynyxia," Beth repeated. "And just plain 'Beth' is fine for me." She didn't know what a walkabout was but decided to save that question for another time. Warning sounds having registered in the back of her mind, she'd gotten a sudden feeling that she and her companion were no longer alone. A pressing desire to move on overtook her.

"Then, *Beth*," Aynyxia repeated, turning back toward the path, "we'd best—" She stopped abruptly, interrupted by a piercing scream.

Beth, though half-paralyzed, was nearly certain the scream was coming from her own mouth.

Meanwhile, the council meeting had continued, though without progress. Gaarius had droned on for a while, some of the council members listening more politely than others.

Quillin Qu'en was one who made little effort to feign interest or respect for the Ferinian ambassador. "A traitor t'the Southlands, that one is," Quillin whispered to the council member on his left during the offending speech, "saying we ought have a *Tork* on the throne!"

"Truth," his neighbor agreed in a whisper; then, listening a moment longer to Gaarius' words, he was inspired to add, "Or, could be just a fool and a coward. Take your pick. At any rate, disloyal to the house of King DarQuinn though he may be, he seems not to have broken his vow of secrecy concerning this council meeting— though he is carefully watched."

"He shouldn't be here at all!" Quillin spoke in a whisper, but with a strong voice nonetheless.

"I do not trust him myself, but we could not bar him from the meeting without losing the support and goodwill of Ferinia."

"Already is that lost for us," Merk of the Nether Woods, on Quillin's right, joined in gruffly. Merk, whose ashen face was framed by coarse fur rather than hair, was a darkwood-dweller of fierce aspect. Most of his fellow council members believed his rough exterior sheltered a benevolent spirit, but a few made a point of keeping him at a safe distance. As a rule, his wit was not considered sharp or quick, but on the point currently at issue, his opinion was sound, even astute. "Ferinians will throw in lot with Torks before we have done talking of it. And good riddance to them all, say I, Merk of the Nether Woods!" As he thumped his chest to emphasize the words, his deep, indignant voice carried through the cool air to catch the attention of Gaarius, who stopped mid-sentence and glared at the three disruptive council members. His gaze soon dismissed two of them and narrowed in the direction of Quillin, whom he judged to be the instigator of the disturbance. "Perhaps you have a subject to raise that you consider of more importance than the future of the Southlands," Gaarius said in a tone not unknown to schoolmasters the worlds over.

"Me deepest apologies t' you, y'graciousness," answered Quillin cheerily, with a bow of the head and a much more pronounced accent than came naturally to him. He could speak in the tones considered most refined whenever he wished it, but at the moment, he did not wish it. "Wair you sayin' somethin' new, then, or was i' jes' more 'n' more o' the same? I cannot tell!"

No response came quickly enough to the outraged Gaarius, and Lady Gweynleyn took advantage of the fact to call for a break in the proceedings. "I believe a respite is in order." She rose.

"But nothing has been resolved!" a voice protested.

"Truth!" agreed another, and "Aye!" joined in a third.

"Then, pray continue without me," the lady answered. "If you wish, I will leave my attendant in my stead; you have no need of my person."

"Stay, Lady Gweynleyn." Rane of the Brenmarch spoke for them all. "We have need of your wisdom and your calm."

"I am greatly fatigued," she answered with a weak smile. Indeed, they could all see now that she was. "The burden on us is great, but we do not have the means of discharging it at this moment. If I may, I suggest that we take rest while we are able. We are secure here and the watchers will alert us if there is any report." After a general though somewhat reluctant agreement from the others, Gweynleyn turned and moved toward her tent, followed at once by her attendants, who had been waiting apart.

Aynyxia understood the situation at once. Beth had been bitten by a fanged tree-rat. Approaching unseen and springing from the shadows, it had landed on Beth's back, gripped her shoulders with sharp claws (luckily, her sweatshirt gave her some protection), and sunk an oversized front tooth into the exposed flesh above the girl's collarbone. Though called a rat, the animal more closely resembled a cross between a large bat and a flying squirrel, only bigger – not that Beth was in a position to observe one. She knew only the severity of the pain.

In a flash, Aynyxia's right hand unsheathed her knife and her left swept up a stick from the ground. Instantly she was behind Beth, striking the rat's head with the stick then plunging the knife into its belly. The beast had turned its fearsome face at once, a streak of Beth's blood visible on its fang, and would have flung itself next on Aynyxia had her thrust been less sure. In an instant, the plant-girl flung the monstrous creature back into the shadows whence it had come. Swiftly wiping her knife on tree moss, she asked her companion urgently, "You can move your neck?"

Beth, who'd held herself stiffly since the first instant of the attack, let loose her breath, carefully bending her head forward and answering shakily, "Yes."

"Move, then!" Aynyxia responded, acting on her own advice. "Bound to be more."

They moved. They ran fast.

But they couldn't run fast enough.

There were more. Many more.

On Arystar's Green, the Council of Ten had officially adjourned its meeting, but small groups formed here and there as various council members and attendants carried on their own discussions – a few privately, inside tents, but most of them out in the mild evening, around campfires or in close proximity to welcoming barrels of ale.

"Why this urgent need for a king?" Rane of the Brenmarch was demanding of the Ferinian ambassador Gaarius, who had stopped to share a drink with the small company from the Brenmarch region. "The decisions of the council have served us well enough to this day." To have a *princeps* at Arystar again would be a fine thing indeed, judged Rane, but not if it meant settling for the likes of Myrmidon Tork on the throne!

"Truth, the council has been strong in its time," Gaarius agreed heartily, "but there has been none to lead it these many years. It has been *ten years and more* since the death of King DarQuinn and still there is none to hold the scepter of Gwilldonum, to sit in the seat of the ancients."

"There will be again," Rane answered with confidence.

"But when? And how much longer will the good peoples of Gwilldonum wait? How much longer *can* they wait? Even if all the borders could be secured – and that has not been managed, has it?

– all would still not be right with the land, which cries for a rightful leader. You cannot deny it. Your kind till the ground, do they not? What fruit have your fields given this year and last and the year before that? Is the yield not poorer with each harvest?"

"He speaks true," joined in Veen, one of Rane's attendants. "The crops have not been worse in my father's or my father's father's time."

"Has it not always been so when the seat of the *princeps* remains empty?" Gaarius responded with a patronizing smile.

"I'll not see Myrmidon Tork on that seat!" Rane stated decisively, rising.

"But, Rane," countered another of the Brenmarchers, "he *is* of the royal family."

"The *twisted* line of the family, may they be cursed forever. Now, I'll hear no more of this talk." He left then . . . but his two companions remained with Gaarius.

As Rane wandered wearily about the encampment, he listened to the conversations around him, sometimes stopping for a moment but never joining in.

"So we've come round to this again," he heard the new council member say. Terilla. A tall, willowy sort of woman with intelligent eyes and an engaging manner. He'd met her father, who had perished in the same battle that took King DarQuinn. That had been a sad day indeed! "It will be war in the end," Terilla continued in a resigned tone, "and the only question remaining is who will strike the first blow."

"The Great Wood of the Westmarch is ready!" announced Daasa, the proud faun representative of that region.

"There is no doubt of it, worthy sister," Terilla answered, "but the same cannot be said of many of the others represented by this council. We have been greatly weakened."

"Not so weakened in body or in spirit that we would let that fiend rule the land of our ancestors and the land of our children's children!" An ancient oak hid the speaker from Rane's view, but the voice and opinion were unmistakably those of the dwarf council member, Harac. "We here will stand against the Tork and his accursed followers as long as we have breath, will we not?"

Rane did not wait for the answer. With a certain despair in his heart, he moved on to where a larger group was gathered but where one voice dominated – the voice of Therin Mandek, Captain of the Council Guard, who must have returned that very hour.

"Truth, all those here who are of noble sentiment" – at this point, though Rane could not see it, the captain sent a meaningful look across the clearing in Gaarius' direction – "would defend the Southlands against Myrmidon Tork even should he bring every last creature of the Wastelands with him. But I have seen with my own eyes and heard with my own ears how his support grows stronger in our land. If war is declared, who will stand in the fiend's ranks? Some of our own, that is who."

There followed an animal's guttural sounds; Rane could neither make sense of them nor see the speaker, but a "friend of the wild" (as the interpreter-representatives had come to be known) immediately conveyed the meaning: "Then they are traitors."

"They are poor and hungry and frightened!" Therin answered with frustration and a rising voice. "They do not know where to turn. Have *we* managed to give what Myrmidon grandly promises? And if in their ignorance and foolishness they choose his rule, evil though it may be, over the starvation they foresee for their children, *will* we draw our swords against them in payment?"

There was no answer to that.

Tree-rats seemed to be all around Beth, mostly in branches above, ready to swoop, but some already on the ground, moving slowly, as if enjoying her distress and wishing to prolong it. Her eyes darted from one to the next but kept returning to the nearest creature. Though a good ten feet away, its gruesome face seemed inches from hers; its flooded, beady eyes, its great yellowing fang, and its open mouth dripping thick, olive-green saliva were magnified in her vision. She imagined she felt its hot breath reaching her.

She had lost sight of Aynyxia but had the vague impression that her guide had scrambled to safety among the rocks. Beth wouldn't have minded a good hiding place herself! Nothing foolhardy about her! Heroics could wait for some other day.

She had a stick in each hand, brandishing them as if that action could help much against a dozen of the beasts. Two, three, maybe four would be on her before she could fend off the first.

Really, she never should have come here!

CHAPTER THREE – Night Falls

Therin Mandek was no coward. He had never shown fear of battle or of death, not since childhood when he feared those things on behalf of his beloved father, Risardas. Risardas Mandek had served as Captain of the Guard before Therin, but in those days it was the royal, not the council, guard. It was now more than ten years since Risardas had died at the side of his king, DarQuinn the Good, when the royal company was ambushed by invaders from the west. Though of a tender age, Therin had fought in the same war, already bearing his arms well. He was an exceptional fighter and it surprised only a few when, after the invaders had been pushed back and order restored in Gwilldonum, the young man was named to succeed his father as captain. Since both the long-widowed king and the king's only child had died by then, Therin vowed his allegiance instead to the Council of Ten that was to rule in the absence of a *princeps*.

A warrior, he knew what war could do. He knew what it had done to himself and to his mother, who survived her husband's death only by a matter of months. She did not live to know that her son had taken his place.

Still, if truth were told, battle thrilled him as nothing else could. Nothing compared to the rush of excitement, the heightened vitality of riding into combat, outcome unknown. But this battle – nay, this war – that was brewing about them was a different matter. He feared it would become as much a rebellion from within as a menace from without. He had slain many an enemy, but had never yet found an old friend at the sharp end of his sword. Would that day be on him soon?

Myrmidon Tork was no son of Gwilldonum and had only the slightest of claims on its throne, as far as Therin was concerned. But for some, his claim was enough. They wanted a king, even one of the cursed, exiled line, and it seemed that every passing fortnight saw more who were foolishly willing to throw in their lot with him, should it come to that. And if the pernicious Torks prevailed, what would become of Gwilldonum?

There was still hope, though. Hope, but little time.

Arriving at the council's encampment, Therin had stopped when greeted by a friend and had briefly joined a discussion on the state of affairs, but he soon excused himself to seek out the lady Gweynleyn. He found one of her attendants, Mariza, seated outside the lady's tent. At his approach, Mariza worldlessly rose and disappeared into the tent. An instant later, Gweynleyn was anxiously approaching the captain.

"What news have you for us?" she asked without preamble, searching his face with a mix of hope and fear.

"None that is good, but none that will cause you great surprise either. My report, such as it is, can wait until the morning's council. But what of you here? The escorts have not returned, I gather?"

"They have not, though word has come that Rowan is on his way back."

"Alone?"

"Alone."

"No word of the others?" *Three* escorts had been sent out, each in a different direction, but all in secret and alone.

"None."

After a pause, Therin said with feeling, "You should have permitted *me* to go."

"It was not my decision alone," Gweynleyn answered evenly. "The council commissioned the escorts."

"Truth, but the council sways where you will."

"If such only *were* the truth," the lady answered with half a smile, "our proceedings would occupy a sliver of the time they now do and would exhaust us so much the less."

"A walkabout!" he exclaimed, returning to the point. "You – you and the council that sways not at your will – sent such a creature on such a mission!"

"But you, Therin, have cause to know the worth of this *particular* walkabout, do you not?"

"I do," he admitted, "and truly she is worth more alone than the rest of her clan together, but I flatter myself that I possess a skill or two she does not."

"So you do, and so have you earned your rank. But how if you were observed – you, the Captain of the Guard in the central regions at such a time as this, when all attention is drawn to the north and west? To what purpose could such a journey be? You would draw suspicion – and followers – at once. No, the risk would have been too great. We cannot always tell friend from foe in these days, as you are aware. It is enough of a danger that every council member and half their attendants now know of the business. . . . But come," she said in a coaxing tone, "you have heard this argument before. Let us not quarrel over it now."

After a pause, Therin sighed in unaccustomed defeat. "You are right, my lady. Indeed, let us not quarrel at all." He took her hand and raised it. Pressing it to his lips, he looked into Gweynleyn's eyes. When at last he lowered her hand, he still kept hold, saying tenderly, "It is not only the proceedings of the council that exhaust you, is it? Will you not speak with me of it?" He could not understand the ways of her kind, but his desire to share her burden in some way, by any means he could, was deep and true.

"I will not," she answered firmly, withdrawing her hand; then, fearing that she had spoken coldly, she added, "my friend." She hesitated, torn by her own conflicting desires, then turned away from him and back toward her tent, "Let us speak again in the morning. I wish to retire now, and you have duties of your own."

He stood looking after her for a long moment.

If Beth had known her better, she would have realized that Aynyxia had not gone into the rocks to hide. In fact, the plant-creature was hunting for, and then quickly found, a rock that had qualities much like those of flint. With the steel of her knife, she instantly got a spark from the rock, though it took longer than she liked to move from leaping sparks to full flame on the brittle fingers of a cast-off branch. Though some sound resulting from Aynyxia's efforts made its way to Beth's ears, Beth did not recognize it for what it was and felt herself quite abandoned.

With seconds passing like minutes, Beth gripped her stick weapons fiercely. Her glances darted about the shadowy areas that surrounded her but kept returning to the tree-rat directly ahead. The creature inched across the ground toward her. It was significantly larger than the others, Beth realized; perhaps it was the leader and the rest would stay back until it had made the first attack. Under the circumstances, this was a remarkably clear-headed line of thought – but it wasn't an entirely dependable one.

Behind and above her, another oversized tree-rat was poised to make its move and was not content to defer to another of its kind. As it began its leap, Beth heard the scratch of its claws against tree bark and she turned suddenly. Seeing the creature's ugly face headed straight for her, she leaned back and swung hard with one of her sticks.

Thwack! It was a good hit, and for an instant Beth felt a rush of relief and satisfaction. The tree-rats, though fierce animals, were still ultimately a lot smaller than she was, and her force had sent the thing flying. That one did not return. But there were others, and Beth heard several move at once. All relief vanished and she began swinging wildly with both arms and little hope.

Any moment, she was sure, she would feel again the searing pain of a fang piercing her skin. But the pain didn't come and the scrambling noises of the little beasts soon faded and then ceased. When she opened her eyes (not registering until that moment that she had closed them), the first thing she saw was the makeshift torch that Aynyxia was waving about.

"Fire's what scares 'em most, you know," Aynyxia said, throwing down the tiny burning bundle once it had done its job. She did not stamp it out with her bare root-feet, but let it fizzle away in the dirt.

Beth was more grateful than she had ever been, but she didn't then realize just how bravely Aynyxia had acted, for plants – at least those that have not recently "soaked," as the walkabout plants called it – have a strong and healthy aversion to fire. Having moved along quickly for some time, mostly in the sunlight, with no lengthy stop at a stream or pool, Aynyxia was too dry to approach any flame unless out of great necessity. Even so, her manner remained casual, as was her way. "Probably won't be back," she said, picking up the pack she had dropped earlier in the confusion.

She also retrieved Beth's sweatshirt, which had been tied around Beth's neck and then somehow ended up on the ground. She held it up in such a way that Beth could see two large tears in it – one through a sleeve, one across the bottom of the back. "Fangs," said Aynyxia. "Might have thought this was part of you. Maybe tried to get blood out of it. Disappointing for them," she added, laughing her strange laugh and tossing the ruined piece of clothing to Beth. "Find you something else, something better for cold nights." They had begun to walk. "No weapon?"

Thrown by the abrupt change of subject and not entirely sure she'd understood, Beth asked hesitantly, "You mean, do I *have* a weapon? No, nothing."

"Take care of that, too. Not far now. Knife? Sword? Bow?"

"Oh! I don't know." She thought as she walked briskly, adrenaline having renewed her energy. "I've done a little fencing, but the swords we use are pretty light. I expect anything you have here is heavier and I don't know that I could manage it very well. And I've never used a knife to . . . to hurt anything before. I'm pretty good with a bow. Not *hurting* things with a bow; I didn't mean *that*!" she added quickly. But then she pictured the tree-rats and said half to herself, "I think I could, though, if I had to." She couldn't believe she was saying that! She wouldn't have said it a week ago. Or this morning? Was it only this morning – this *evening* even, in her time – that she had been at home? How different she was becoming already! Being bitten by a fanged tree-rat could do that to a person, she supposed.

They were out of the wood now, but not back into bright light. A graying dusk was settling. "C'mon," Aynyxia said. "Know where we can get what we need."

"What do you at this hour of the night, friend?" Cassian Maris asked, surprised, as he paused while passing though the Brenmarcher camp.

"I return to the Brenmarch," Rane answered his fellow council member. "We leave in the instant." One of Rane's attendants, a sullen female with eyes that darted about, was packing the last of the party's belongings into a cart while another inexpertly attempted to secure the mule that would pull it. Rane was readying his own animal, a fine pony, for mounting.

"Leaving the council meeting?" There had been some discussion throughout the assembly about disbanding the meeting and advancing to Greyvic as a whole, but it was a surprise that a member should be leaving the council altogether and returning home with his companions.

"Aye, there is little I can do here – little save wait – but there is much to be done at home. A messenger arrived not an hour ago," Rane explained, motioning to a figure resting in the shadows. "His report disturbs me greatly, and I fear the situation can only have worsened by now. Support for the enemy grows strong in the Brenmarch, it seems."

"Truth? How can this be? My *own* people tend towards complacency and unwisely deem themselves removed from any threat posed by the Torks," – Cassian hailed from a region that considered itself securely nestled between a protective range of low mountains and a long eastern coastline that had seen no enemy ship for generations and generations again – "but *your* people, settled on the very threshold of the Western Waste as they are . . . your people last of *all* should turn to Myrmidon. They know the cruel ways of his kind, who have raided yours at will these many years."

"It is so. But all is now forgotten in the glow of grand promises, it seems. I cannot tarry. I know where I ought be. I will not see my homeland fall into the hands of the Torks." If, at that moment, Rane had caught the sly looks his Brenmarcher companions exchanged in the dying firelight, he would have found cause for concern, but his back was to them, and he continued to address Cassian. "Explain my cause to Lady Gweynleyn, will you? And convey my respects. I did not wish to disturb her rest." Thoughtfully, he added, "Whenever it is dark for Gwilldonum, she feels the weight strongly."

"Aye, I have seen this in her also," the other council member agreed. "I will speak to her for you in the morning."

As it would happen, however, this promise would prove of no use, for even without Cassian's assistance, news of Rane's departure would spread along with dawn's light through the whole camp and more than one council member would soon consider following his example. Yet none would know, in those early hours, that Rane's lifeless body then lay only a few miles away, concealed by thick, sweet-smelling jackberry bushes that grew wild along the road west.

About a quarter of an hour after leaving the wood where they'd encountered the tree-rats, Beth and her companion stopped for something to eat in a wide flowering meadow. Aynyxia brought some bread out of her pack ("*Knew* it would be one of your kind I'd find," she said proudly, "and they're always wantin' bread") and shared her canteen of water ("I'll probably get all kinds of weird germs and die," thought a hungry, thirsty, exhausted Beth, taking a good long drink). They also ate wild berries and something that Aynyxia called a tanga, though Beth had only a few bites of the latter, finding it too sour to enjoy.

Sitting there in the meadow, Beth would have asked the many questions she'd been holding back, if only she hadn't been so very hungry and so very tired. She ate, she drank, she rested her feet, and she leaned back in the wild grass, half closing her eyes. Almost at once her eyes opened wide again, and there was one question she had to ask, though the answer seemed evident. "There are *two* moons here?" Maybe fatigue and the dim light of dusk were playing some trick on her.

"Sure," Aynyxia answered simply. "Closer one is Korisye, little one there is—" she hesitated a little over the pronunciation, "—Er-ras-ti-sye." She talked for a while, in her choppy way, about the moons and the constellations. Beth found it interesting but soon closed her eyes while listening. "Can't sleep now," Aynyxia said next (actually, it was several minutes later, but Beth had drifted off). "Not long, though." As she made herself stand back up and start walking again, a sleepy Beth reflected that she and Aynyxia probably had different ideas about what constituted "long." She'd already had much more exercise than she was used to in a single day and wasn't sure how much farther she'd be able to go.

Thankfully, almost at once they reached an honest-to-goodness road, and Aynyxia indicated that they were nearing a place where they could get supplies and safely pass the night. The combination of these circumstances boosted Beth's energy. The relatively even, clearly-cut road made the walking easier for her, and her senses became more alert at the thought that she might soon see signs of civilization – a town with lodging. She was quite curious about it. But as they walked, it didn't look like they were getting any closer to a town, except that twice there were other travelers that passed them; Beth had no way of seeing, though, whether they were plant-people like her guide or some other type of creature, because Aynyxia led her off the road and out of view when she heard, the first time, the sound of approaching voices and, the second time, the noises of a cart's wheels and an animal's hooves laboring along the road.

At last, when Beth felt as if she couldn't go on, Aynyxia said, "This way," and took her off the road for good. Beth couldn't see a path, even though the moons were bright by then, but Aynyxia found her way well enough.

Beth realized she'd been mistaken. She had assumed they were aiming for a town or village where they would spend the night, maybe at an inn, but there was no sign of such a thing. She soon could make out, though, the shape of a single cottage ahead, light escaping through two arched windows.

"Gribbs live here," Aynyxia softly informed her as they neared the cottage. "Bet you haven't met any like *them* before!"

"Well, *that's* for sure," thought Beth, "*whatever* they are."

"Better keep back," Aynyxia told her with a wave of the hand.

Moving into the shadows and positioning herself behind an oak tree, Beth wondered what sort of creatures *gribbs* were. But mostly she wondered if they had comfortable beds with big, soft pillows.

When she heard the door creak open, Beth couldn't help peeking around. At first, she couldn't see anyone there.

Then she could.

"We should've finished him off!" Veen, the sullen Brenmarcher who had loaded the cart earlier that evening, addressed Gort, the traitorous messenger from their homeland. It was Gort who had reported to Rane hours before and encouraged an immediate departure, despite the lateness of the hour. The moons were full and would light their way along the Great Road for hours to come, he insisted, and the situation was urgent enough that they could not afford to lose that time. Now only three traveled the road home, Rane's companions having left him unconscious and mortally wounded a few miles back, no more than an hour's distance from the assembly at Arystar's Green.

"Let it be, will you?" Gort responded roughly. "I told you. The way that blood was spilling out" – the youngest member of the group cringed involuntarily – "there's not a chance he'll hang on until morning. And who's likely to find him before that?"

"*You think someone might find him tonight?*" demanded Dosst, the youngest, in a panic. A weak yet ambitious character, Dosst knew himself to be morally superior to his older companions, in general as well as in this particular instance; he had, after all, merely provided a distraction and then kept watch while the other two had made their attack on Rane; he had never touched the man himself; still . . . not everyone could see these things as clearly as he. It wouldn't do to find himself in serious trouble over this. It wouldn't do *at all!*

"Stop it, the pair of you!" answered Gort angrily. "He's probably dead already, and it'll look like an accident anyway. Thrown by his pony, he was. Right, girl?" He patted the animal in question as he said this; Gort's own pony was tied behind the cart while he rode Rane's finer, better-rested one. "But *if* I hadn't kept your knife out of his heart, Veen, some fool might have stumbled across him and sent a patrol out looking for murdering bandits along this very road. We're too close to Arystar to take that kind of chance. The council will figure it out in time, but we'll be safely home by then – and just *let* them try to come after us there! So leave it alone or *my* knife will be making its mark across *your* throats!" He sneered in such a way that his companions half believed him.

"Tell us more about what will happen at home," suggested Dosst nervously, not liking the direction of the conversation. "How will the new leadership be arranged?" He was always quick to nose out the source of power and attach himself – tentatively, of course – when he found it. With Rane dead, the way would be open to those Brenmarchers who sought alliance with the Torks . . . and to those, like himself, who were willing to lend their allegiance in whatever direction seemed most expedient. "And do you believe that we and the Ferinians will be able to break off successfully from the Southlands, as some have suggested, in an alliance that will be just as mighty? Or do you think that Gwilldonum itself will eventually accept Myrmidon Tork as *princeps*? . . . What will be the future of it all?" The last question he asked somewhat thoughtfully because he actually had a genuine (if callow) interest in politics and history even apart from his personal ambitions. Under the mentorship of someone like Rane, Dosst might possibly have developed into a halfway-decent being who did some good for his people. *Possibly.*

Gort made a disdainful noise and glanced toward Veen. Had sufficient moonlight reached them at that moment, they could have shared their contemptuous looks. Instead, Gort packed all the contempt he could into his voice. "What do I care for any of that? Here's how I see it. As a poor-relation dependent of Gwilldonum, what have we Brenmarchers always got? The worst of everything, that's what. When the Torks have got it into their heads to invade or just do a bit of wild raiding for the mere pleasure of it, what's the first region they come to? The Brenmarch, of course. Who got the worst of it from the Great Tork Invasion of our mother and fathers' time? Again, the Brenmarch! And we're still paying the price. So we give up the council's protection and take Myrmidon's instead. What do we gain? No more invasions, no more raids. What do we lose? Nothing! And if the Ferinians have thrown in their lot as well, so much the better. We'll have no trouble from that direction either."

"And Myrmidon does have some claim on the throne. That in itself will help bring things to right in the Brenmarch," Dosst added in a voice that he hoped would communicate his authoritative knowledge.

"That's more than I know or care about," said Gort dismissively. "The old ones half-dead and the young fools like your high and mighty self always think that the Right One holding the scepter will make the crops richer and the fishing holes fuller and no doubt the blessed sunshine brighter, but I'll believe it when I see it, myself."

"But have we not always been told—"

"Shut-up-your-stupid-mouth-and-give-us-some-peace," spat Gort.

A long silence followed the remark. In the darkness, Veen smiled – for a change.

So, these were gribbs – or, the Gribbs, rather. Marcus and Gerta Gribb, to be precise. The first thing Beth noticed about them was that they were short. Very. Not even four feet tall, she guessed. The second was that they seemed (though Beth tried not to stare) to have no necks between their oblong, pudgy heads and their equally pudgy bodies; when they turned their heads to look about, which they did frequently, they reminded Beth of owls; their hair looked as coarse as rope, and their wide thumbs seemed to be coming out of the wrong places, but apart from these things, they appeared more or less human. Their clothes looked like ordinary, old-fashioned country clothes to Beth – a long dress covered by an apron for her, a worn workshirt and gray pants held up by suspenders for him. Their faces were cheerful and their manners welcoming.

"A warm wash and a warmer meal is what you need, by the looks of it," Gerta kindly told Beth once they were inside the cottage. "Business can wait a moment," she warned her husband, who had opened his mouth to speak. "You'll be passing the night here then, will you?" This question was addressed to Aynyxia, who nodded in response. "I thought as much, I did. We're quite ready, dears." Gerta invited Beth to take a seat on a surprisingly large chair. "We're in the trading business," Gerta explained, "and deal with all sorts. We like to accommodate the customers, we do." True enough, the main room of the cottage was crammed with mismatched furniture of various sizes and types, though one cozy corner with two miniature armchairs seemed reserved for the use of the owners. (Beth eventually understood that the rather large room served both as the Gribbs' personal living space and as a showroom of sorts for a wide range of items. There were odds and ends everywhere, cramming shelves and filling corners. Rummage Sale Decor, her Aunt Julia would call it disapprovingly, but Beth liked it.)

As Gerta fussed about with a pot by the fireplace, Aynyxia took advantage of the light of an oil lamp to examine Beth's wound from the tree-rat's bite. "Nasty-looking, that is," Marcus voiced his opinion, "but not too serious. I've got an ointment that will clear it right up," he said, moving to get the item in question. "Just half a denarius for the whole bottle for a good customer like you."

"*Marcus!*" exclaimed Gerta from the fireside.

"Oh, all right, Woman," he grumbled. In a hearty, generous voice, he said to Aynyxia, as if the exchange with his wife hadn't taken place, "On the house, it is. A goodwill token, you could say."

The ointment, which Beth expected to sting, actually felt good against her skin. Her neck, which had been sore and beginning to itch, began gradually to improve. A warm, wet towel that wiped the grime away from her face and hands felt nearly as good as the ointment, and a mugful of steaming cider poured from a pewter jug was better still. Next came hot soup and a hunk of bread, but Aynyxia and Marcus (or "Gribb" as almost everyone but his wife called him) slipped away to settle the matter of supplies.

At one point, when those two had taken lanterns to go rummage through a storage hut behind the cottage, Beth was gladly consuming her meal while Gerta looked on thoughtfully. "Well, you're not what I expected, Child, and that's for might certain," Gerta said at last. "But I'm the last to make the mistake of thinking size determines worth, I am. And youth . . . well, youth has gifts of its own, doesn't it, dear?" Beth, taking in these words, couldn't help but wonder what sort of person they *had* anticipated. *Well, someone older and bigger, obviously!* And then, with some anxiety, *What is it they expect of me?*

Gerta, believing she had guessed what Beth was thinking, leaned in closer to say, "We know why you've come, we do." *Then you're way ahead of me!* thought Beth, but she prudently kept quiet to see what she could learn. "Not supposed to, of course, but we have our ways of finding things out, we have." Before she could say more, the door opened to let Aynyxia and Marcus back into the cottage, and Gerta jumped up and busied herself with clearing off the table. As soon as she had done so, Aynyxia happily set down a used but very fine-looking bow, newly strung, for Beth to see. A quiver of arrows hung over her shoulder.

"Think that'll do?" she asked with beaming satisfaction.

Beth couldn't help but admire the bow before her. It was so handsome and so delicately carved that it seemed more a work of art than an actual weapon, and yet something indefinable made her certain it had once belonged to a great warrior-archer. She took the piece in her hands, raising it and pulling steadily back on the string. She'd thought it would be the wrong size for her – too big for her to manage well – but it felt right. *Exactly* right.

Weeks or maybe months later, when she reflected on the early days of her adventure, Beth thought that this moment, when she took up the bow, was the first in that remarkable day when she truly believed that she was exactly where she belonged. For an instant, she felt as if she fit this place just as the bow fit her. Exactly right.

Aynyxia went over the other items she had acquired for Beth – a jacket, a hat, a small pack of miscellaneous practical items, and a short dagger to keep close "just in case." Gerta promised additional foodstuffs in the morning but suggested the travelers get themselves straight to bed, as she could see how tired Beth was.

Toward the back of the cottage, Gerta showed them a ceiling trapdoor that hid a cozy attic room – a wooden ladder would take them up (and then be hidden away for the night), a rope ladder from above could let them down when necessary. The attic had no windows, but three discreet vents allowed fresh air to circulate. "You'll be rightly safe here, you will," their hostess told them. "Don't you worry. And if you do hear any trouble going on below, you just keep yourselves quiet and everything will be fine." Beth supposed that she should feel assured by the words.

Inviting beds had already been made up for them, and Beth was anxious to curl up in hers as soon as possible. There remained, however, the embarrassing matter of "bathroom" needs to raise, but before she could figure out how to do so, Gerta gave her a few discreet words on that very subject.

Not much later, Beth was settling in between a surprisingly comfortable blanket and a mattress stuffed with corn husks and sate leaves. Aynyxia, however, was not ready to retire for the night. "Going to the stream," she told Beth. "Got to soak a bit before moving on in the morning. I'm a plant, you know."

Yes, Beth thought – and she couldn't help smiling into the darkness – *I know.* She pictured again Aynyxia as she had first seen her, a plant that looked liked a person, coming out from the shadows by the pool, and could scarcely believe that they'd only met that day, mere hours ago; she remembered the strange feel of the stem-fingers that had tried to grab her when she stumbled, and she was part-puzzled, part-ashamed that she had recoiled from the touch. Now, she trusted this strange creature completely. And she did feel safe (pretty much) snuggled in this bed despite the strangeness of everything, the talk of trouble, and the acute watchfulness of the three unusual creatures she'd met so far. It didn't even disturb her, at that particular moment, that she understood so little of what was happening.

She had learned a few things along the way. They were in a country called Gwilldonum, which was facing some kind of crisis. There was no king or queen and that seemed to be causing a problem, though she wasn't quite sure why since that had apparently been the case for some time. She gathered that there were spies or agents or some sort of troublemakers they'd have to watch our for, not so much in the sparsely-populated region where they were, but more in the northern areas where they would soon be headed. Someone – or, rather, some group of someones – was waiting for her . . . but that's where her understanding gave out. She didn't know what her own part in this was supposed to be, though apparently it was something very secret.

Tomorrow she would know more, no doubt. For now . . .

She began to drift off but roused a bit when she heard voices below. The trapdoor was still open, and the conversation was clear.

"Thought you were headed to the stream." That was Gerta's voice.

"Was," answered Aynyxia, "but thought I'd better return the angeli first."

"I knew you'd be wanting her, so I've got her right here. . . . Ah, such a beautiful little bird."

"Gert's rightly taken with her, she is." That was Gribb's voice. "Thought she might not give her up when it was time."

"Go on with you, Marcus," Gerta answered in a mock scolding tone. "Now, what do you want the note to say?" she asked in a businesslike voice. "Gribb has a very neat hand, as you know."

"'Nothing to report. Returning straightaway'," Aynyxia said carefully.

After a pause, Gribb repeated in a puzzled way, "'Nothing to report?' That's what you'd have me write?"

"Yep."

He sighed. "As you say," he answered, puzzled. It was quiet; he must have been writing. "'Nothing to report. Returning now'," Gribb read back. "Will that do? Couldn't spell 'straightaway'."

"Yep. Thanks."

"Strange sort of a message all the same," Gribb replied, a question in his voice.

There was no answer, however, merely sounds of movement and then the opening and closing of a door.

Must be something like a carrier pigeon, Beth had decided. *And it* is *a strange message. . . .* But that's as far as she got. It had been a *very* long day.

She closed her eyes, and her mind let go of the conversation she'd just heard and began instead to replay some of the pleasant scenes of the day, though in a jumbled-up order: the two moons, a lovely meadow, Gerta by the fire, interesting wildlife in the forest, the beckoning water in the well . . .

Beth was asleep.

CHAPTER FOUR – The Kritt Pass

Beth's first morning in Gwilldonum began poorly and went mostly downhill from there. She awoke sore from the previous day's exercise, and the fair weather had passed, a blanket of gray having spread in every direction above wet ground. Though gone for the moment, rain threatened an immediate return. Despite having enjoyed a long sleep, Beth wanted nothing more, after her hot breakfast, than to climb back in bed and slip away into pleasant dreams rather than to prepare for another long trek, this time in the mud. She found the Gribb cottage comfortable and homey (despite its being crowded with so many, many things), and she was sorry to be leaving the amiable couple so soon.

"Going by Greenwood and then down the Great Road, are you? Or will you go by way of the Dayrn?" Marcus Gribb asked Aynyxia while she and Beth gathered their things.

"Not one, not the other," Aynyxia answered. "Going through the pass."

"Kritt Pass?" His odd little head wobbled. "I suppose you're wanting to cross the Tinker's Bridge and cut to the Great Road from there, you are. Well, best of luck to you. Never go that way myself if I can avoid it." Beth couldn't help but wonder why, and her concern must have shown for Gerta's next words were clearly intended to reassure her.

"Don't you worry 'bout the pass, dear. Your Aynyxia knows every little creak and crack in it, she does, and you'll be glad for the shortcut. Just keep moving, of course, and you'll be fine. . . . It's really not as bad as folks say, though it's not to our liking, Gribb's and mine." She patted Beth's arm.

"I'll tell you what," Gribb said as if the thought had just occurred to him (though he'd been planning something of the sort since the night before), "I'll go with you as far as our old nag and wagon will take us, I will, though that won't save you much more

49

than an hour of walking time, for the road itself has too much sense to go close to the Pass." Aynyxia gratefully accepted the offer and Beth was pleased at the delay before she'd need to force her legs to keep moving again. She wasn't sure how much they were supposed to walk that day, but whatever it was, an hour less of it sounded good!

Marcus and Gerta soon led their visitors out a side door and into a yard that was nearly as cluttered as the cottage, but by bigger items, most of them in disrepair, giving Beth the impression of a junkyard. Scattered about were wooden chairs with broken legs, a small cart missing a wheel and another with no wheels at all, what looked like a water pump handle, and a number of items Beth couldn't identify at all. Some things were shaded by a large canopy for whatever shelter that might give them from the rain, but the rest took what nature sent them and survived as well as they could.

When the Gribbs led Aynyxia and Beth around to the front of the cottage, the view was entirely different. A beautifully manicured garden, bordered by a foot-high picketed fence of pale blue, graced the Gribb home and gave it a fairy-tale look. Beth had not noticed in the darkness of the night before, but now she could see a dozen types of flowers growing in perfect patterns. Even the cover of a dreary sky barely dimmed the luster of their colors. Peering closer, Beth could see miniature benches and chairs, only inches high, placed on tiny pathways that twisted among the flowers; next, she discovered a small fountain and beyond that a tiny cottage. She craned her neck to get a better view, before exclaiming, "It's *your* cottage! It's a miniature of your home!" She looked at Mrs. Gribb, whose face beamed and eyes moistened with pleasure.

"Gert's pride and joy, that garden is," exclaimed Mr. Gribb.

The sight of the garden made Beth reluctant to climb up on the wagon bed to go. Here was a pleasant and safe spot, and she was sorry to leave it behind. She was sorry too to bid farewell to Gerta Gribb, who hugged her tightly, and, later in the morning, to Marcus Gribb, once he had deposited his guests as close to the Kritt Pass as the road would allow his little horse and wagon to go. The old married couple had been as warm and welcoming as their charming little home, and Beth wished the visit could have lasted longer.

Still . . .

Adventure lay ahead, she told herself as she turned her back to the road and followed Aynyxia along a rough path. She, Beth DeVere, was on an adventure – an incredible adventure – in a strange land. She had a dagger hanging from her belt and a bow and quiver slung across her back! And . . .

She was following a plant!

In the mud.

To go . . . somewhere.

And see someone.

About something.

At Arystar's Green, the morning was eventful and difficult.

By early light, news of Rane's departure began to spread, soon accompanied by the report that Jeron Rabirius of Greyvic, a council member who had been uneasy for some time about his absence from home, would not delay his departure another day. Cassian Maris, the council member from the coastal region, agreed that since Greyvic was where they all must be before long, the sooner, the better.

In this atmosphere, Therin Mandek made his own report to the assembly. He confirmed what by now was generally suspected, that the Brenmarch could not be depended on to back the Council of Ten if the latter were to take a firm stand against the Torks. Further, the Dayrn Valley region, while *willing* to support any council decision, including a decision to take up arms, seemed ill-equipped to do so. Indeed the region was more likely to need significant numbers of troops sent in for defense than to be able to put their own motley troops at the council's disposal. Lastly, a handpicked guard was camped along the Ferinian border, watching it carefully and waiting on Therin's presence to escort the Tork "guests" from there to the city of Greyvic, assuming that the Council of Ten agreed to permit Myrmidon to address the festival assembly as he had requested. The Tork leader would be accompanied by his captain, an advisor, and a company of only twelve soldiers or other attendants, if the council approved the plan.

If this were not enough to consider, by late morning the council members learned the stunning news of Rane's death – or assassination, as it was supposed. By a stroke of fortune, the Brenmarcher's body had been discovered early in the day by

Arastius Emmon, a man of learning, who recognized that death had not come by accident. Arastius often served as advisor to the council member Merk and had in fact been on his way to Arystar to join the meeting in progress there when he sighted the body near the road. He knew Rane from previous council meetings and, on making his important discovery, at once recognized the Brenmarcher, somewhat disfigured though the poor man was by then.

His report caused dismay among all at the council meeting and for several reasons. Rane had been well-liked and respected, and his loss was a personal one to the many who had valued him as a friend. Beyond that, the Brenmarch was an area of great concern. It had experienced much hardship, both of natural and of human cause, and had been in a state of near-turmoil for a number of years. Only Rane's leadership – a fine blend of firmness, compassion, and good sense – lent any semblance of stability to the region. Without him, chaos threatened. Rane's death, therefore, no matter what the cause, was a serious blow, but if in fact, as several voices asserted, it was the result of some Tork-based conspiracy, then the security of the council and of the whole land might be in greater peril than previously believed.

Then, around midday, yet another report made the rounds of the encampment: "Riders coming!"

"We're going through *there*?" Beth asked dubiously. It was less than an hour since she and Aynyxia had left Marcus, and a light rain had begun to fall. Directly ahead stood a sheer mountain of rock with a vertical crack not much wider than Beth herself. "So," she continued, gazing at the entrance to the pass, "it looks" – *what? too small? too dangerous? too ridiculously closed in for anyone who enjoys breathing?* – "a little difficult."

"Yep. Little dangerous, too," Aynyxia agreed matter-of-factly. "Important thing in the pass is, keep moving . . . and keep quiet."

Why? Beth wondered, alarmed. Who might hear them? "If someone's trying to find us," she asked nervously, but following her guide all the same, "they might guess we'd come this way, right? They might be hiding in there, waiting for us?"

"Nope," Aynyxia dismissed the idea. "Nobody hides there; got to keep moving in the pass," she repeated. "Out the other side is where they'd be waiting, if they had a mind to."

"Oh . . . well," Beth mumbled, "*that'll* be all right then!"

"Hmmm?"

"Nothing."

"In we go then," Aynyxia said cheerfully, actions suiting her words.

"Sure," Beth replied weakly, following. "In we go."

"Riders coming!" The words were repeated throughout the encampment.

"It is Rowan," one of the better-informed council members told her companion as they made their way toward the meeting place. "Therin and Blom rode out to meet him when the watchers reported his approach."

Soon after, Rowan DeMeulyn himself approached the hastily-reassembled council to make his report. It was clear by his gait that he had been wounded and many marveled that he had been able to return to them so quickly in such a state, particularly since he had arrived on the back of Blom's horse and his own animal was nowhere to be seen. But, of course, he had been chosen for the mission because of his remarkable resourcefulness, determination, and valor.

For generations and generations again the DeMeulyn family had answered any call to service for the defense or glory of Gwilldonum. Rowan had not hesitated, therefore, when three leading members of the Council of Ten approached him privately one night about a secret undertaking of great import – escorts were being specially chosen to travel to the three known sanctuaries of Gwilldonum, for it had been prophesied by the mysterious and revered Silent Ones that a champion from afar, as in stories of old, would soon come, and such champions were said to arrive by way of the sanctuaries. No company of guards would be sent for protection, for agents of the Torks could be anywhere and would not fail to report such a thing. There would be a chosen few along the paths who knew something of the nature of the mission and would keep a quiet watch, but the escorts were to travel alone. Discretion was crucial, and even the remainder of the council had not at that time been apprised of the plan, though it soon would be.

All council members and their closest attendants would be sworn to secrecy, of course, but oaths had been broken before.

Rowan's task had been the most dangerous. The sanctuary of the Meadowlands, where the walkabout Aynyxiacichorium had gone, lay hidden in a fairly close and safe region of Gwilldonum. The southwestern sanctuary was in distant untamed territory where savage beasts posed the greatest threat and where enemy spies would hesitate to enter. But the northwestern sanctuary, where Rowan had gone, was in an altogether perilous location. Close by in one direction were the neighboring Ferinians, who had already revealed themselves as friends to Myrmidon Tork, and in another direction was the Brenmarch, where, it was believed, there was not a hectare of land without a spy hidden somewhere about; if that were not enough, the sanctuary itself lay at the very border of Gwilldonum, close to the Western Waste, beyond which lay the lands of the accursed Torks themselves.

Trouble had indeed befallen Rowan, but on his return he did not immediately tell the council members how he had been wounded or what had become of his prized steed; those stories would wait until they could be shared at leisure, over a pint of southern ale perhaps, in the light of a blazing fire. What the council most desired to know, it knew at once: he had returned alone.

"I reached the sanctuary by the appointed day," he told them, "but the time came when I knew it was right to return." He did not explain *how* he knew. In truth, the disembodied voice of one of the mysterious Silent Ones had come to him (he heard nothing aloud, but the voice in his head was strong and clear) and it instructed him to return . . . but one spoke little of such sacred things, so it was enough to say that he knew the time was right.

Though he could not serve Gwilldonum as he had hoped, Rowan did bring the council news of import. "The Ferinians have thrown in their lot with the Torks," he announced. Although his own eyes did not turn toward the Ferinian ambassador Gaarius as he said this, many others' did.

"We have heard this already," Harac responded, a little puzzled. "Gaarius has these many days been urging the council to surrender Gwilldonum's throne to Myrmidon Tork, an idea fully endorsed by his native land, as he tirelessly assures us. But surely you knew their position before you left us?"

"I did. But there is more to it now, or at the least more to it than we have been told heretofore." Now his gaze did fall on Gaarius. "Not only has Ferinia offered its support in any bid the cursed Tork might make for the throne of Gwilldonum, it has also entered into a firm alliance with him not conditioned by any decisions made by this council."

This pronouncement was followed by a silent moment, but soon a commotion grew, and while some voices asked what Rowan could mean by this, others understood the situation at once. Two of the voices carried strongly over the others: "Their alliance is with *us!*" cried one while the second shouted with vehemence, "You mean to say that they have bound themselves to take the part of the Torks, even *against* Gwilldonum? Even in warfare, though they are under treaty with *us? Treachery!*"

When the various competing voices finally quieted, Gaarius' high, nervous one could at last be singled out. "There is some mistake, I am certain. Truth, there were a *few* in the Ferinian senate who favored an alliance with the Torks over a continued alliance with Gwilldonum, but they were in the minority, I assure you. Ferinia and Gwilldonum will never forsake one another, I am certain! Rowan has brought us back some morsel of gossip, that is all. It must be so." He held his hands together, though whether the action was meant to demonstrate some sort of plea or merely to keep his hands from trembling was not clear.

"I heard it from the mouth of trustworthy friends —" began Rowan.

"Trustworthy, no doubt, but mistaken nonetheless."

" —friends who bear the name of Riddian."

This seemed to settle the matter for all but Gaarius, and even he did not know how to respond. The name of Riddian was known throughout the Southlands. Though no longer the powerful family it had once been (the best of the Riddian warriors had always been at the forefront of great battles, and many had come to the aid of Gwilldonum and been lost in the Invasion), it was yet the leading family of Ferinia in honor and fame.

"The entire household of Serrilla Riddian, daughter of Serril the Elder, down to the last serving maid and stablehand, has left behind whatever carriages and carts cannot carry and are removing to the Northern Mountains where they have kin. They will not stay to defend their home under the leadership of an outsider tyrant should war break out with Gwilldonum, as they foresee; nor will they take our part and fight against their own homeland. Rather, they choose to leave Ferinia while they may still do so unopposed."

"Unopposed?" Gaarius repeated, his voice quavering. "What can you mean? Unopposed by the Torks?"

"*Not by the Torks*!" Rowan answered loudly and in unconcealed contempt. "By their own people! By *your* people! Do you not hear what I say? Do you truly not know the situation in your homeland? Ferinia's alliance with Gwilldonum is no more! They are one with the Torks!"

Silence overtook the assembly.

Once inside the Kritt Pass, Beth felt some relief. The passageway widened immediately, though she could see a narrowing ahead. From an opening above, a dull light filtered in – for the time being, at least. "I have a tinder box," she remembered, hoping to be useful. She'd gotten it from the Gribbs, of course, and Gerta had shown her how to use it to start a fire. "Should I light . . . something?" She should have looked around outside, she supposed, for something that would work as a torch, but she hadn't thought of it. There was nothing promising in here.

It didn't matter, apparently, because Aynyxia quickly responded, "No. No fire. Draws kritts. Makes 'em crazy."

Beth didn't know what kritts were, but she certainly didn't want to make them crazy. Crazy kritts didn't seem like a good idea, no matter what! Looking around warily, she asked, "Are there *many* things that live in here?"

"Almost nothing" was the answer. "Just kritts and the cave plants they live off, mostly. They prefer flesh, o' course, when it wanders in."

Oh, lovely! Maybe, Beth told herself, *I should just stop asking questions!*

Entering the narrower, darker section of the passage, Aynyxia said, "Stay close, and—"

"—keep moving," Beth finished with her.

"Yep. And don't sleep."

At least, that's what the words sounded like to Beth. Don't sleep? *As if I'd curl up for a nap in a place like this!*

Streaks of light soon became meager and occasional. Beth stepped carefully and, after an unpleasant encounter with a rock ledge at forehead height, kept her hands stretched in front of her.

"Kritts make you sleep, you know." Aynyxia's voice echoed eerily back at one point. "Little cowards, every one. 'Fraid to come near most of the time, unless you're asleep."

Well, that was a relief. It's not like they were going to have to spend the night here or anything. Were they? It hadn't occurred to Beth to ask how long it would take to get out the other side of the pass; now, she wasn't sure she wanted to know.

Except for warnings like, "Watch your head," or "Step up," they didn't speak again until Aynyxia stopped short and Beth asked, "What's that smell?"

"Something dead" was the answer. Aynyxia kicked at it, whatever it was, and they kept going. From that point, Beth – who wasn't normally claustrophobic – felt an increasing, nervous longing to be in open space. One part of her brain told her that they might have been in the passage for only fifteen or maybe twenty minutes, but its disturbed neighboring part suggested that it had been a week or two and that it would probably be that long again before they were out.

Following mechanically after a while, she began to picture what it would be like when they came out on the other side of the pass. If she could focus on that, maybe she wouldn't keep imagining what kritts looked like or what the "something dead" had been. It soon occurred to her that she'd been coughing frequently. Must be the air in here, but outside it would be fresh and pleasant. . . . *Just focus on that.*

Unnoticed, her pace slowed as she imagined what it would be like when they stepped out of the pass. She pictured a lovely meadow full of colorful flowers. The rain would have stopped and the sun would shine brightly. A rainbow would be nice, she added. And a pretty brook (babbling, just as brooks ought to). Suddenly, Beth was certain that the scene was real, not imagined. They were out of the pass, and it was beautiful here, and the babbling of the brook made her feel so peaceful that she thought she would simply curl up and take a nap.

"Don't!" cried a sharp voice. "Don't sleep!"

"What?" Beth didn't know who had spoken and wasn't even sure whether it was her own voice that answered.

"Don't breathe!" she heard.

Don't breathe? Who would say such a stupid thing? she wondered with a sleepy smile. She started to yawn, but suddenly something covered her mouth and nose, smothering her. She couldn't breathe. She couldn't— Then, just as suddenly, the thing was gone and she gasped and opened her eyes, astonished that she was still in the pass and that she'd only been dreaming.

". . . smell they give off," came Aynyxia's voice, close by. "Puts you to sleep. Then they eat off you. . . . Don't breathe," she advised again, as if that were a simple thing.

Beth held her breath and stood up (she found she'd been kneeling), promptly bumping her head. Scurrying noises surrounded her and she thought something (or a few somethings) had fallen from her clothing. "Kritt bugs," said Aynyxia, taking Beth's hand to lead her away.

Beth covered her mouth with a corner of her jacket and breathed into it, hoping that would be good enough. Not breathing at all seemed impractical. After a few minutes, she let her jacket fall back in place and judged that the air around her was normal again. She sighed her relief.

Soon Beth glimpsed a stream of light ahead and Aynyxia said they were nearly out, but almost instantly she added, "Tricky part here . . . . Watch it." Beth thought she could do very well without any tricky parts, but there was enough light now for her to see a dozen feet ahead. Nothing ominous met her eye. Smooth rock formed an inclining pathway and glistened with moisture, but Beth supposed she could manage a few slippery rocks.

And she nearly did.

Practically crawling, gripping what she could, she was almost at the top of the rocky incline when she misstepped and her left foot slid into the shadows – straight into a nest of kritts. Her stomach hit the rock surface and her face came close to doing the same, leaving her so low that when the kritts scattered from their nest, she ended up eye-to-eye with one, a shaft of light hitting its face perfectly.

Big, bulgy eyes stared at her, and two antennae wiggled in her direction. The creature had as many legs as any insect, but it was the size of a small rat! That's as far as her observations got. She whacked the thing and sent it flying.

"Ah – ah – ah!" Beth gasped. Kritts were crawling up her leg. It didn't hurt – they hadn't bitten yet – but it was *so* creepy! "*Eeeww!*" Beth squealed, scrunching up her face and pulling away from the nest. By the time she had dragged her leg up into a shaft of light, Aynyxia was swatting away the kritts, though the passage was too narrow for her to reach as far as Beth's jeans. Beth hit at the creatures too, using her sleeved arm instead of her bare hand (striking Aynyxia by mistake in the process), and did her best not to look too closely at the icky little things. It was a most unpleasant business, but soon the last of the kritts scurried back into the darkness.

"Told you," said Aynyxia, actually sounding pleased. "Little cowards."

First tree rats, now these disgusting bug-rats! Beth was more anxious than ever to get out. With every remaining movement forward she was braced for a kritt to fall into her hair or run up her pant leg. Then, Aynyxia whispered, "Wait!" and they both stopped short. Alert, Beth, by now able to stand nearly straight up, saw the fuller light ahead and felt the fresher air and knew they were almost out . . . but she also heard voices – disagreeable ones – coming from somewhere out in that well-lit fresh air.

Aynyxia took a few steps forward and around a curve in the rock wall, flattening herself against it as she went. She returned quickly, whispering, "Back." Beth felt a clutching in her chest at the thought of going back through the passage, but she started to move at once. After only a half dozen paces, however, Aynyxia stopped her, saying, "Up." Beth hadn't noticed before, but a foot or so above her head was a large opening carved into the rock wall. Aynyxia scrambled up to it in a way that Beth found impossible to imitate. With her guide's help, though, she managed the climb and immediately found herself entering a short rock tunnel. Following Aynyxia, she crawled through it to a ledge from which the two of them could peek out into the gloriously wide-open (kritt-free!) space and listen to the voices below. Lying flat on their stomachs and hidden by a curtain of foliage, they had only glimpses of the two speakers (mostly they saw the tops of their wide hats moving about), but the conversation was clear enough.

"You just listens to what I says!" came one voice.

"And why shoulds I?" responded the second petulantly. "Who made you chief? That's what I wants to know!"

"Well, then, you gots a dozen of them Wastelanders and them's friends staked out right down by that bridge. Why don't you takes up your questionings with them?"

That convinced the second speaker, who hesitated only briefly before saying, "Awright, then, awright. But I still don't sees why I shouldn't gits to stay here. It be's my turn! You coulda sent that fool-headed oaf Mohrn down to the bridge instead of me – *if* you could finds where he's gots hisself off to!" he added sulkily, moving away nonetheless.

The first speaker remained and Beth wondered how she and Aynyxia could possibly get past him unseen. The second speaker, still walking, yelled back. "But, Harl, if you finds that walkingabout thing coming out of that pass, I wants my fair share of the reward!"

"Shuts your mouth!" was the answer he got. "You wants the world to hear? . . . You idiotic!"

Beth's heart sank. *That walkingabout thing!* Aynyxia had called herself a walkabout. Were these guys after *them* – Aynyxia and her? The second speaker was disappearing from view, presumably moving toward the bridge where others were staked out and waiting too. Probably it was the same bridge she and Aynyxia were supposed to cross. Maybe they could just sneak off in the opposite direction, though, and find some other way through. Except that the first guy was still here, directly below them, presumably guarding the exit from the pass.

But . . . he *wasn't* still guarding the exit. And he wasn't heading in the direction of the bridge either. As soon as his friend was fully out of sight, the one called Harl crept from his post and began to scurry down a hillside into a clump of trees below.

Aynyxia had remained silent, but now shook her green head regretfully. "Haven't done well by you. Shortcut won't work. Can't use the bridge. Have to go by Greenwood after all."

Not wanting to make her feel worse, Beth tried to sound casual as she asked, "So, we'll have to go back through the pass again?" *Please say no, please say no, please say no.*

"No," Aynyxia responded obligingly. "Greenwood's that way!" She jerked her head left. The bridge, the Wastelanders, and "them's friends" were, it seemed, all to the right. So . . . going left sounded good . . . enough.

Beth wanted to say something encouraging, but didn't know what that would be. Instead, she asked whether they'd lose much time. Aynyxia seemed to be shrugging in response, though it was hard to tell because she was already making her way out of their hiding place, climbing down the short distance to the ground below. Beth followed, but couldn't help asking, "Is it safe?"

It seemed safe enough, for the moment. No one came running out at them, though Aynyxia drew her knife just in case. Beth supposed she should have done the same, though she wondered if she could actually bring herself to use a weapon on another person anyway.

There *was* no other person, however. They had *that* much luck, at least! But someone could show up at any moment, so she expected Aynyxia to start moving as quickly as possible in the "Greenwood" direction. Beth planned to be right behind her; she might even pass her up, just to be on the safe side.

But Aynyxia *wasn't* hurrying in that direction. Or any direction. She stood thoughtfully, then said, "It's not right." She stayed like that for nearly a minute, then, yielding to the force of her instincts, she began to move – not toward Greenwood, but toward the clump of trees where the "Harl" guy had disappeared.

"But—" The word died on Beth's lips. *Not that way,* she thought. *Not straight into trouble,* because she knew that whatever lay hidden in those trees, it was bound to add up to trouble. The Greenwood plan sounded like a much better idea to her, but she could see there was no use saying so. Clearly, Aynyxia was determined – determined to discover what Harl was up to down there in that clump of trees.

Straight into trouble, Beth thought again.

But she followed.

CHAPTER FIVE – Mistaken Identity

Though the council meeting had adjourned, somber activity continued all about the encampment at Arystar's Green. Meals and serious thoughts were shared, traitors and oath-breakers denounced, plans (some secret, some open) formed and reformed.

On the outskirts of the camp, Lady Gweynleyn was deep in private conversation with Therin Mandek when she suddenly stopped speaking and closed her eyes.

"What is it? Are you unwell?" her companion asked quickly, though even as he finished the words, he realized that whatever sensation had overtaken her was not merely physical in origin.

In answer, she shook her head almost imperceptibly, concentrating on a different communication. When she opened her eyes, she stated merely, "A Silent One is near." He understood. Inclining his head to her, he kissed her hand and wordlessly took leave.

"Mariza!" she called before turning purposefully toward the deeper woods. Her attendant, never far, followed at once.

Aynyxia and Beth lay flat on the ground at the edge of an overhang, positioned to watch and listen while remaining (as they hoped) unseen and unheard. In a clearing below, they observed two repulsive-looking characters arguing. Beth recognized Harl by his clothing; the other, she soon gathered, was Mohrn, the "fool-headed oaf" she'd heard mentioned earlier.

The creatures stood upright and were shaped more or less like stocky humans, but their skin was of a dark purple-gray and something bestial characterized their noses and mouths – *and* their expressions. Their faces in general looked as if someone had tried to flatten them with irons, with isolated spots resisting and bulging out. When, a little while later, Beth got a better look at the hands of one of them, she saw tufts of fur on the back and long nails protruding from slender fingers. As the two stamped about in their heavy boots, a tawny weasel rested close by, unconcerned, a proprietary collar around its neck.

Centered between Harl and Mohrn was a long-leafed plant that seemed too brightly green to belong among the browns and darker greens that surrounded it. Then the plant moved, extending upwards, and Beth saw that it had a face. She hadn't guessed that it was a plant-person, a walkabout like Aynyxia; it wasn't dressed, and until it lifted its head it had looked all huddled in on itself, limbs and leaves blended together. At a sneering look from Harl, it huddled down again at once, and Beth realized it was cowering in fear. When Mohrn grabbed a stemlike arm and the poor creature shuddered in response, Beth was sure it was being held against its will. She turned reflexively toward Aynyxia, who was studying the scene intently and straining to hear the words carrying up from below.

"'Course I ain't told him that we gots this one! Thinks I wants him gittin' in on our gold? But we don't even knows yet if it be's the *right* one!" That was Harl speaking.

"It be's one of them walkin' plant monsterostities, ain't it?" responded Mohrn, holding up the thin, leafy arm. "Must be's the one they wants. We're gittin' that reward, Harl!"

They think it's Aynyxia, Beth realized. *The poor thing!*

"You idiotic! It's all alone, I keeps tellin' you. And asides, it's too young and we don't even knows if it be's a girl plant."

"You's a girl, ain't you?" Mohrn asked the plant, slapping it against the head. It – or she – nodded pitifully. "See, Harl? I done told you. And how do you knows it be's young? You don't knows 'bout walkin' plants. You ain't never seed one 'til now."

"Oh, and you knows all 'bout 'em, I s'ppose? Idiotic!" repeated Harl. "I'm gittin' might sick of tellin' you, Mohrn, that it likely ain't the right one 'cause it were walkin' round here all by its little self."

"You don't knows that!" Mohrn countered stubbornly. "They said to watch the crack in the cliff and we did. She were lurkin' around there might suspistitiouslike. T'other one must still be's inside. You just goes in and gits him and we gots our fortunes made."

63

"You go gits him yourself, if you're so sure! . . . They say there be's flesh-eatin' monsters in that pass and I prefers to keep my skin on me, thanks you very much! . . . Asides," he countered, resuming his earlier position, "I still says it mights not be the one we wants. But it could tell us plenty, I wagers. Can't you, girlie-girl, if that's what you be? We'll git some informalation out of you, we will!" The two creatures laughed odiously and even at a distance Beth could see the plant-girl tremble.

It was enough for Aynyxia. Laying her green hand on Beth's arm, she whispered, "Wait," then immediately reconsidered, scrunching up her face as she tried to work it out quickly enough. "No, you go," she decided. "To Greenwood." She gestured behind them.

Beth thought she must not have understood correctly. *Go? She can't mean—*

"Not far. Straight to the meadow," Aynyxia motioned again, whispering, "then the road that crosses the meadow." She seemed to be working hard to get out all the words she needed. "Only road there; goes straight to Greenwood. Find Rendel Singer," she told Beth finally, starting to scoot backwards and away. "If you can't, then get to Mirella of Saar – on the Dayrn." By now she was up in a crouching position, far enough back to be out of view of those below. "Won't find her on your own." As Aynyxia moved away, Beth wasn't sure she heard the last whispered words, but they sounded like, "Woodlanders will help."

It was by far the longest speech Beth had heard her make, but it just wasn't enough! "What-? How-?" No use. Aynyxia was already too far for whispers, and Beth dared not call out. What was she supposed to do *now*?

Thoughts rushed through Beth's mind. Did Aynyxia really expect her to go on alone? That was crazy! How could she find this Greenwood place on her own? Why couldn't she just wait for her companion to do whatever she was going to do? Unless . . . If Aynyxia tried to rescue the plant-girl but got herself into trouble instead, then of course she'd want Beth safely out of the way first. And even if she *was* successful, she might need to run away fast and Beth would probably slow her down. *Definitely* slow her down. But if Beth could get a headstart to Greenwood. . . . That was it. She probably wouldn't need to go far on her own. Aynyxia would catch up with her. She'd only given her those names of people to look for just in case.

But what *were* those names? Singer — that was easy to remember. Randall Singer, she thought it was. What about the other name, though? She'd been too much taken by surprise to really register it. Miranda? No. And what would it matter anyway if she couldn't find the second person without wood people helping her, and she didn't even know what *those* were, let alone what "on the dare" meant!

Beth, who'd lost sight of Aynyxia, now found her again. What was she up to? She was standing there in the open, in plain sight. *They'd* see her, for sure. What—?

Aynyxia inhaled and exhaled deeply, then yelled across the short distance, "Ai! Selyorum!" The captive plant-girl immediately found the origin of the voice; Harl and his friend were a bit slower. "Been lookin' all over," Aynyxia continued, exasperation sounding in her voice. "Get home! Stop pestering these fellows. . . . Beg pardon!" she said genially to the two cretins. "Little one been an annoyance? Trailing after our cousin, she was. On important business, *that* one is!" She spoke proudly and then confidentially. "Can't tell you what. Very secret! . . . And not *your* affair!" she told the plant-girl sternly. "You go on home!"

The poor plant-girl, who had simply found herself in the wrong place at the wrong time (and who in fact went by the name of Selyorum), now saw her chance and profited from the distraction by disappearing into the woods in a green streak. One of her captors (the stupider one) made as if to follow, but then seemed torn, half-turning one way, then back the other. It seemed that little plant-thing hadn't been the one they wanted after all. The weasel jumped up on all fours, ready to chase at his master's word; when no command came, it settled down to rest again.

Harl gave his companion a slap, motioning to Aynyxia and saying in a voice too low for Beth to hear, "*This* one be's worth hanging on to. Forgits the other!"

"Just let her go!" Aynyxia told them cheerfully, referring to Selyorum. "Just go, go, go!" she repeated, waving her arms for emphasis, but this time she looked in the direction of Beth, who knew the words were intended for her.

What was she to do? Obviously, Aynyxia wanted her to leave, but how could she? It certainly *looked* like her new friend

65

was in trouble, with those two creeps already advancing on her as she began to back away from them while still trying to seem friendly and casual. But how could she, Beth, help anyway? She had her bow, but didn't know if she could use it. *And what if she hit Aynyxia by mistake?* Or even if she could hit one of those creatures, what if the other attacked Aynyxia before Beth could do anything else? They were so close now. How could her friend possibly get away? But she seemed to be able to take care of herself. Maybe she *could* get away all right, if she didn't have to worry about Beth being near enough to get caught too. Maybe she'd be running already if she weren't afraid of leading them toward Beth. The two creatures were looking for a walkabout *and her companion.* Maybe by staying behind, Beth was making things *worse.* So . . . she should go?

"Tells us 'bout this cousin of yours!" Harl had just said. Maybe Aynyxia could talk her way out of it, Beth hoped.

"Always going, that one is! Go, go, *go!*" Aynyxia's gestures were wild, but Beth could not mistake the meaning in them. *Go, she wants me to go, and she's probably better off without me here.* So, unsure as she was, Beth went, heading in the direction Aynyxia had indicated earlier, all the while thinking furiously but unproductively. Getting to this Greenwood couldn't be *too* hard, she told herself, or Aynyxia wouldn't have thought she could make it on her own. And it wasn't far, she'd said (but who knew what "far" might mean!), and she'd find help there. *There was help and it wasn't far.* Then she should go get it! Or . . . maybe she should stop and wait to see if Aynyxia would be coming right behind her. And then if she didn't come, Beth should . . . either go forward or go back. Or wait longer.

What was she to do?

Head to Greenwood, she kept supposing as her feet carried her forward, and hope she'd recognize it when she found it. From the lookout in the cliff, she'd seen woods in nearly every direction. What she *hadn't* seen since she'd come to this place was a single road sign! Uncertain of her direction, she stopped in her tracks and groaned aloud, then started when she heard a sound.

"Friend?"

She didn't see anyone at first.

"Friend?" a hesitant voice repeated, and that time Beth was able to pick out a green face mixed in among wild bushes. For the slightest instant, Beth thought it was Aynyxia and that her dilemma was over, but she quickly realized her mistake. It was the young plant-girl.

"Yes, I'm a friend," Beth tried to reassure her. As the girl emerged from the bushes, she shook her head and looked frustrated.

"Ayn-iksi-a-ci-kor-i-um friend?" she tried again.

"Ayn- Oh, yes. I'm Aynyxia's friend. Aynyxiacichorium's friend." That was it, apparently, because the plant girl smiled.

"Thanks her," said the girl, satisfied, turning and starting to slip back through the bushes.

"No, wait," called Beth. "Can you help me?" The girl turned back with a puzzled look. "Greenwood," said Beth. "Can you tell me where Greenwood is?"

"Greenwood, yes. There way." She pointed through the trees in the same direction Beth had been headed. "Woodlanders. Good helps." Now it was her turn to smile reassuringly. Once she had, she darted away before Beth could finish repeating, "No, wait!" (Apparently those root-feet could move quickly when they wanted!) Beth wasn't sure what the girl had meant by "good helps" but she hoped it meant that the woodlanders – not the wood *people*, as she'd been thinking – would give her the help she so clearly needed.

"All right, all right," she told herself softly. "I'm going to Greenwood and someone there will help me. Or probably Aynyxia will catch up with me first anyway," she revised hopefully, "especially if she can run away fast like that other plant-girl." She moved more quickly now and kept her eyes looking directly ahead to keep her on a straight course, but she was still plagued by doubt. *What* had Aynyxia been thinking, sending her off on her own this way? But Aynyxia believed she was someone else – someone who, apparently, thought nothing of finding her way through strange woods alone.

"This is crazy!" she muttered a few minutes later. "What am I doing here? This is *so* far beyond me!" Although she had no watch and couldn't guess how long it had been since she'd left Aynyxia behind, she decided to give herself only ten more minutes to find someone, hopefully a good-helps woodlander, before she'd turn back. Probably. Just ten minutes. Or so.

As it happened, it only took her six.

When Gweynleyn reached the hooded and cloaked figure of the Silent One, the two of them exchanged the traditional greetings but then came quickly to the reason for which he had summoned her.

"Your champion comes."

"Yes. I received an angeli from the walkabout, Aynyxiacichorium. This is good news . . . yet you seem troubled. You bring dire tidings?"

"I see them in grave danger – the walkabout and the Prophesied One."

"Now?"

"Soon."

Mariza stood nearby, but she heard nothing of this conversation. All these years by her lady's side, but she still could not hear the thoughts of the Silent Ones. It was not the way of her kind. Once, though . . . *once* she wondered if she *had* heard, but it must have been mere imagination. Not that she indulged much in imagination. That was not the way of her kind either.

But Lady Gweynleyn could hear the Silent Ones. Their thoughts could enter into her mind and she could hear them there as clearly as if they had been spoken aloud. It had long been so.

"What must I do, O Wise One?" Gweynleyn was asking, though her lips were still.

"They need aid. It will be too much for them alone."

"Whom shall I send?"

"Look closely."

Gweynleyn closed her eyes and tried to see into the other's mind. "I know this place," she said as an image came into view.

"And the visage?"

"I see it."

"And you can do this thing? You can reach him? I know you are weary, my daughter, my sister."

"I am," she conceded, "but I will do this thing . . . at once," she added aloud, opening her eyes.

Though she'd been hoping to see someone, Beth panicked as soon as she did. How could she know who he was (if it *was* a "he")?

A lone traveler approached. Though not far ahead, he hadn't yet seen her, she thought, for he was in an open space ("That must be the meadow I was supposed to look for and there's the road") and she was close in among the trees. At once, she darted to the left, aiming for a safe spot that could hide her while she got a better look.

Unfortunately, she picked the wrong direction for darting, particularly since the shaded ground was still slippery from the recent rain. A patch of thin branches matted with soggy leaves gave way under her feet and Beth found herself tumbling into an earthen pit, three or four feet deep. An animal trap, she realized in a frustrating moment, and she was the one caught.

She straightened up, wiping her hands off on her jeans and groaning once before remembering to be quiet. She froze and listened intently. Though her eyelevel was above ground, she couldn't see the stranger from where she was. He'd been headed straight in her direction, but perhaps he was following a path that would curve away; there was certainly no clear path close by Beth. And yet, she could hear him. Getting closer.

She felt very uneasy about calling to him, but she supposed she needed to take a chance. She was looking for help, after all, and it would be a bit difficult to find any if she hid every time she saw someone! There hadn't *seemed* to be anything sinister about him. Still . . . he could be entirely the wrong person to trust. *If* he was truly leaving the meadow and coming her way, as he must be if she could now hear him so clearly, she would duck down until he had gone past, then quietly peek out and at least get a sense of what sort of creature he was. Then she'd decide.

It wasn't a bad plan, but it didn't quite work out. Beth did duck down, but the footsteps headed straight toward her, not past her. When she knew the stranger was standing above, presumably looking down at her, she anxiously turned her own face up to see what she could find in his.

Therin Mandek, seeking Gweynleyn, came across a girl whom he recognized as her newest and youngest attendant, though he could not place the name.

"Where is your mistress?" he asked abruptly, startling the girl and causing her to drop the basket she carried and scatter its contents. "Do you know?"

69

"Oh! No, m'lord. I do not, m'lord!" Even under the best of circumstances, the girl found Therin Mandek intimidating. Now, she twitched nervously, unsure whether she should bend down to gather up her things or remain standing to show her respect. He resolved her dilemma by bending himself to pick up the items, so she hurried to do the same, practically grabbing some of them out of his hands.

"You do not know at all?" he asked. The girl regarded him blankly. "She is not, though . . . in her tent?" he prompted.

"Oh, no, m'lord." She showed her surprise. "I would not think so. It has not been so very long since she rode off, so I do not think—"

"*Rode off? She rode off? Why did you not say as much when I asked where she was?*" he yelled. When he saw that the girl looked positively terrified, he regretted his booming voice. She was not one of his soldiers, after all, and Gweynleyn always treated her attendants with courtesy.

"But, m-m'lord," she stammered when she was able, "I do *not* know where she is, m'lord. I would have told you straightaway had I known—"

"All right, all right. Peace. You do not know where she is. You do not know where she rode?" She shook her head vigorously. "So, tell me," he tried to speak patiently, "do you know with *whom* she rode?"

"Oh, yes, m'lord," she was extraordinarily pleased to say. "With Mariza and with the Eyndeli. . . . I mean, with her atten-"

"Yes, yes. I know both Mariza and the Eyndeli." Three of Gweynleyn's attendants – two sisters and their cousin – were of the renowned Eyndeli family and acted as her perpetual guard. Arena, Celiess, and Daneea Eyndeli were numbered among the best archers in the land. In addition, Therin had never known Daneea to meet her match in swordplay – unless it had been in him, of course.

He considered, then asked Imre, "Were you aware that your mistress had a visitor earlier?"

"The Silent One?" the girl whispered reverently. "Yes, m'lord."

"And was it soon after this that the lady rode off?"

"Yes, m'lord. I believe she did so at once." She had relaxed a little – a very little – now that he was asking questions she could answer.

"Very well . . . *Imre*," he added, suddenly remembering her name, for in that instant she bore a striking resemblance to the bird for which she had been named. Imre was pleased, nearly overwhelmed, that the captain of the guard knew her name.

He began to walk away, then returned and whispered to her in a confidential manner, "I am truly not so frightening a person as I seem, you know. But pray tell no one else. It is a great secret." Then, he actually winked at her!

She flushed and began to sputter, "Yes, m'lord. I mean, no, m'lo-. I mean . . . As you wish!" She bowed her head and scrunched her face in embarrassment where he could not see it.

Walking away, he smiled . . . until he returned to wondering about Gweynleyn.

Two miles away, in a chamber at the Stronghold of Arystar, Gweynleyn reclined but was not yet asleep. "You have accomplished all that you hoped, m'lady?" Mariza asked softly, laying a soft blanket over her mistress.

"I credit that I have."

"Then you must rest." Mariza extinguished a lamp as she spoke.

"Yes," said her ladyship faintly before she drifted away, more peaceful than she had been for some time. The champion had come to Gwilldonum. She was in need, but help was on its way. Gweynleyn trusted the prophecy. All would be right.

"May I help you, then?"

Anyone who cannot understand (and, if necessary, excuse) Beth's reaction to that question and its speaker, has no doubt never slid into a muddy pit after traveling alone and frantically through the woods only to look up into kind eyes and a delightful smile. For an instant, Beth forgot entirely about trying to decide whether this was the wrong kind of person to trust and thought instead only of the dirt-leaf-and-twig decor her hair had so recently adopted. She must look awful! And muddy.

Tentatively, as if it were a question, she gave a weak, "Yes?"

He reached out a hand. Taking it, Beth somewhat ungracefully made her way out of the pit as the stranger used his second hand to help pull her up. She still had her pack and her bow, but a few of her arrows had spilled out of the quiver, and the stranger retrieved them for her, dropping into the pit and climbing back out again as easily as if there had been stairs for that very purpose. Once he had done so, he asked, "You travel alone?"

There was something not entirely casual about the question, and Beth was on her guard again. "Oh, no!" she answered emphatically. He seemed harmless enough, but how could she be sure? Better safe than sorry, and all that. Better not to admit she was alone. "My friends are behind. *Several* of them. Really a lot, actually, and they're not far back there. I just ran ahead because I . . . because I'm anxious to get to Greenwood. . . . I can't wait!" she added for good measure, but it occurred to her at once that she wasn't a very convincing liar.

"You know Greenwood, then?"

"Yes. I mean, no . . . except that I've heard about it."

"You have friends there perhaps?"

"Yes," she said before she could stop herself. *Stupid! That was stupid!*

"*Several* of them, perhaps. 'Really a lot'?" He said the last words carefully, as if unaccustomed to that phrasing. He was quoting her, of course, and she felt herself blush. She really was an *awful* liar, as he had obviously recognized.

"No," she answered in a quiet voice, embarrassed.

He understood and, regarding her kindly, leaned forward to say in a confidential way, though there was no one to overhear, "But it is wise to be prudent, is it not? If you were, let us say, alone here, then to admit that fact might incur unnecessary risk. We are, after all, entirely strangers." Straightening up again, he spoke in a louder voice, "Let us begin to rectify that situation. I am Rendel . . . of Greenwood."

CHAPTER SIX – To the Rescue

"Oh! You're *Randall*! Randall *Singer*? From Greenwood?" Relief filled Beth's voice.

The stranger's mouth twitched and his green eyes . . . twinkled. They actually twinkled, as if specks of glitter danced in them. Unless Beth was imagining it.

"I am oft called by that name," he confirmed. "*Ren*del Singer. And yes, I am a woodlander of Greenwood." A wide, engaging smile brightened his already pleasant face. He was quite attractive, as Beth couldn't help noticing.

He wore a soft brown hat, from the edges of which escaped curls of cinnamon hair. His clothes (which perfectly suited, to Beth's thinking, the name "woodlander") were simple, except for a great number of objects hanging from the sides of his wide leather belt. Most of the objects were either pouches (distinguishable from one another only by their sizes and various earthen shades) or small reed pipes of varying types. A short knife mixed in with the other items (a fact which Beth didn't notice right away), but the woodlander carried no large weapon (a fact she did determine at once). He was certainly taller than Beth, but not so very tall. She couldn't be sure of his age, but guessed him to be a few years older than herself. He had the confident look of a young man on his own, but his fair skin looked soft and smooth in a youthful way. His most striking feature, however, was the glittering effect that had overtaken his sea-green eyes.

So fascinated was Beth by those eyes, which soon returned to their normal state, that she almost missed the gentle correction of his name. "Oh!" she repeated. "*Rendel*. I'm sorry. She told me it all so qui— *Oh!*" she exclaimed yet again, but this time with urgency. "We've got to hurry. She must be in trouble. Aynyxia, I mean. She told me—"

"Aynyxiacichorium? Then, you are—" He was quite serious now, the urgency of his tone matching that of hers. "Where is she? What has passed?"

"Well, there were these two—"

"My apologies, but perhaps you ought to explain as we go. You were not hurt by your fall?"

"No," answered Beth, already turning away from him and trying to determine the direction from which she'd come, "if you don't count being really embarrassed." She'd spoken the last words softly, with her back to Rendel, but he'd heard her all the same and smiled again.

"You came by way of the Kritt Pass?" he asked as she hesitated to move forward.

"Yes, that's where I left her, right near the—"

"I know the way." He began to move at once, and she nearly had to run to keep up. She explained in bits (because of needing to catch her breath frequently) about Selyorum and Harl and Mohrn. When she got to the part of the story where she'd decided to leave Aynyxia, she guiltily wondered again whether she should have stayed. It felt so much as if she'd run out on a friend who wouldn't have run out on her. But now, at least, she'd found someone who could do some good – fight those guys, or something . . . although, now that she thought of it, she wasn't sure Rendel was big and strong enough to take on those other two, especially without any decent weapon. Still, he'd know better than she would what to do!

If they weren't too late! So much time had passed!

In reality, however, not as much time had passed as Beth thought. Mere moments had seemed many times longer to her, especially when she'd been moving away from Aynyxia. Now, she was amazed at how quickly they reached the spot where she'd spoken to Selyorum, and it wasn't many minutes after that that she and Rendel found themselves settling into the very spot where she and Aynyxia had first spied the captive plant-girl. This time, though, it was Aynyxia who was held captive, as they saw at once.

Her green hands were tied together in front of her, and a second rope bound her at the waist to the large oak at her back. Harl had learned from his mistake with the first walkabout; he had no intention of letting this one get away too. She might be the one

74

they wanted, or she might just know something about the whole business. Either way, he was determined to get some gold!

"You stays here and keeps an eye on her, Mohrn," he growled at his companion, "or say good-bye to your hide, 'cause I'll be takin' it off you if this one gits away!"

"I knows, I knows. I ain't lettin' her git away! And that last one, that were just as much your fault as it were mine! . . . And asides, you're the one who said it weren't likenly the right one!"

"Shut your trap! And if'n I brings the cap'n back here, you better not be no idiotic and go talkin' 'bout t'other one! . . . 'Cause then *he'd* be wantin' your hide too!" With that, he left.

Once Harl was out of view, Mohrn turned to Aynyxia. "You'll tell us what you knows. Because'n if you don't—"

He fingered one of the leaves protruding from her sleeve and then yanked it hard, separating it from her arm. Aynyxia's face scrunched up as she let out an anguished cry.

Beth gasped, but Rendel put his hand on her shoulder and whispered close to her ear, "Be assured, she scarcely feels it. She wisely feigns distress, for if they believe that tearing her leaves pains her so, they have no cause to attack her in some other way." Then, suddenly, he said, "Come."

Under cover of the creature's taunting, Rendel and Beth made their way to a different vantage point, though Beth saw no particular advantage in the change – they weren't any closer, didn't have a better view (it was slightly worse), and didn't have any clearer path for charging ahead in some sort of attack, if that was the plan. She didn't understand until some time later that Rendel was positioning himself with respect to the sheer cliff through which cut the Kritt Pass. His choice was not a matter of proximity or of viewpoint, but of acoustics.

Rendel cupped his hands around his mouth as if to call out, and Beth's throat tightened. She hoped he knew what he was doing! But the voice she heard in the next instant was not the one she'd expected and it did not sound from beside her. Harl was returning! Either that, or he hadn't gotten far in the first place. In any event, he seemed to be having some sort of trouble, for she heard him calling to his companion from the distance with an urgent, somewhat muffled voice. "Mohrn, over here! Gits over here!"

This circumstance seemed to cause Rendel to change his mind, for his hands slipped away from his mouth as he watched carefully Mohrn's response. Mohrn, not a quick thinker, hesitated visibly, taking only two steps before stopping in his tracks. He was accustomed to responding quickly to summonses from Harl, but he shouldn't leave the walkingabout thing alone!

As Rendel's hands returned to his mouth, Beth still didn't realize what he was doing. It wasn't until she heard Harl's voice a second time, telling his friend to hurry and calling him an "idiotic," that she understood. Rendel was disguising and throwing his voice.

Beth was amazed. She'd seen a ventriloquist once before, but it had been nothing like this (the guy wasn't all that good). This time, she'd been *sure* the voice had originated beyond the far side of the clearing. And it had certainly sounded like a muffled version of Harl's gruff tones! And he'd even called Mohrn an "idiotic" – but maybe that's what everyone said here. Beth stared in wonder at Rendel's profile as he kept his eyes fixed on Mohrn, then she turned when she heard the creature's command, "You! Keeps an eye on this here plant thing 'til I gits back!" But who was it he meant? Was there a third captor, hidden from view? Her eyes searched.

She saw in a moment that it was to the pet weasel that Mohrn had barked his orders. The animal had been resting out of view, and Beth had forgotten its existence. But it was easily visible now, scurrying around in front of Aynyxia in a manner that reminded Beth of Cicero – her yippy little dog at home. But her pet was a friendly creature, and the weasel looked like a fiercer watchdog than Cicero could even dream of. It snarled and glared and snapped, daring Aynyxia to make a move. Leaving his prisoner under the weasel's watchful eye, Mohrn hurried away in the direction from which Harl's voice seemed to have called.

"Come!" Rendel's voice was urgent, but his steps were cautious, his gaze fixed on the weasel. Keeping his eyes ahead, he fingered the reed pipes at his side, withdrew one from the bunch, and brought it to his lips. Softly, he began to blow into it, and his breath transformed into soothing, gentle notes that escaped into the crisp air.

The weasel, which had turned at Beth's first noisy step, now began to move slowly in their direction . . . but soon, it stopped; then it lay down; then, incredibly, it settled its head as if to rest, closing its eyes. It was the music, of course. Rendel was lulling it to sleep.

All the while, the woodlander advanced. Without interrupting the tune, he motioned to Beth to move ahead, down the slope into the clearing toward Aynyxia. Beth crept carefully past the weasel, drawing her dagger as noiselessly as she could manage, and then set about trying to cut her friend free. The coarse rope was harder to split than she'd expected, but she managed it at last. An instant later, Aynyxia had gathered up her things (Harl and Mohrn had emptied her pack onto the ground but had not yet come to terms as to which of them would keep what), and she and Beth were moving stealthily past the weasel. More slowly, Rendel followed them away, still blowing gently into the little pipe.

When they had nearly reached the top of the slope, Beth lost her balance. She caught herself, but her hat fell from her head and slid down straight toward the sleeping weasel – and woke it! It was up on all fours at once.

"Go!" said Rendel, and she and Aynyxia went, quickly, while he began his music again. Aynyxia led, though Beth was already beginning to recognize the way toward Greenwood.

Beth matched her guide's pace (or perhaps it was the other way around), but the running was leaving her short of breath. When they'd gotten nearly as far as the meadow, close by the pit into which Beth had fallen, Aynyxia stopped, turning to look back; Beth did too and saw that Rendel was speeding toward them. "Mohrn comes this way," he said even before reaching them. When he was beside Beth, he stopped for an instant, judging whether they had time to move ahead to and then across the open stretch (where they'd be in plain view) before Mohrn caught up with them.

Rendel, though he had sprinted toward the others, did not seem at all winded. Beth, however, was breathing hard and her forehead and cheeks were flushed. It was clear to her new companion that she could not cross the meadow quickly enough to escape being seen. "This way." Putting his hand on Beth's back, he guided her toward a thick patch where they might be able to hide themselves. Aynyxia followed immediately behind.

With no time to spare, they concealed themselves as well as they could before spying Mohrn in pursuit. He moved more quickly than Beth would have guessed likely, given his bulky form, and was soon close enough for Beth to recognize her own crumpled hat clutched in one furry hand; his other hand held a jagged knife that made her spine shiver. When he paused to look around, his pet weasel darted about in front of him with malicious anticipation.

"Awright, awright. Where be's they?" Grunting repeatedly, Mohrn seemed to Beth (who had a better view of him than previously) even more animal-like than before. Ugly tufts of hair sprouted from his brow, and his teeth and jaw looked utterly inhuman.

Mohrn reached down and held the hat out to the weasel, which began to sniff it energetically. Once again, Rendel put cupped hands to his lips, but Beth wondered if he could do much good. Even if Mohrn fell for the trick again, the weasel wasn't likely to. Its nose would be its guide. The animal was already at work, sniffing them out, turning in their direction. It wouldn't take long. Seconds, maybe.

This time, however, when Rendel threw his voice, it was a snarling wildcat he imitated. The weasel perked up, his head jerking about, the remainder of his body tense. Rendel snarled again, louder. The little animal sniffed. Nothing. But the sound was one it knew and feared. It cowered, then abruptly turned and fled in the direction from which it had come.

"Wh-, how-, *Ai!*" Mohrn sputtered, ending in an offended yell. "Gits back here!"

So much for the weasel! It was gone from sight. Mohrn, though unnerved by the threat of a wildcat, remained, clutching the knife tighter. Tentatively, he moved forward, narrowing the gap between himself and the three who hid from him. That he hadn't already spotted them, Beth could scarcely believe. All he had to do was to turn a little. And he *was* turning . . .

"*AaaeeeeaaeeeaaYAHYAHYAH!*"

Beth started and caught her breath in a loud gasp, though the sound of the sudden shriek covered her. Rendel pressed her arm to reassure her, but his puzzled face was turned upwards, his eyes scanning the tree branches above. Beth knew that the alarming sound had not come from him this time.

Then a second cry came – a ghoulish, tortured wail – louder and nearer this time. Beth felt herself quiver, but she tried to stay calm and was reassured by the fact that she sensed no fear on

78

Rendel's part. Mohrn, however, could not manage as well. The region was foreign to him, and for all he knew some flesh-eating fiend had escaped the Kritt Pass. He saw no creature, but that fact frightened him even more, wondering if it was a thing that *couldn't* be seen. The cry came again, this time from above and descending fast. . . but still no creature could be seen.

That third blood-curdling screech sent Mohrn racing away from the place, barely remembering why he'd been there in the first place and caring even less.

As soon as she dared, Beth whispered shakily, "What *is* it?"

Rendel, whose face was turned up and away from hers, did not answer at once; when Beth realized that he was beginning to tremble, she supposed that he must be afraid after all. A delayed reaction, maybe. When he turned toward her, though, she saw this his eyes were glittery again and that he'd been shaking from rippling, silent laughter. "A southern shrieker," he answered at last with false gravity, "a fierce creature that gobbles its victims whole – small insects, for the most part. Anything as intimidating as, let us say, an earthworm would be too much for it. . . . A shrieker is a very small bird," he explained, finally laughing aloud and making his way out of the thicket, followed by the other two. "There is not the least harm in it. The poor creature can barely defend itself against any other, unless by its cry it can scare off some ignorant thing. They are rarely in these parts." He moved about as he spoke, looking from various angles into the branches above, though it hardly seemed to Beth, anxious about Mohrn's possible return, to be the best time for birdwatching. "It must have become lost, for this is not a suitable place for it to make its home; it is not a very clever bird, I fear."

"Uhm," Beth divided her glances between Aynyxia and Rendel, "shouldn't we be getting ou—"

"Ah!" Rendel interrupted her. He had spotted the elusive bird and began at once to coax it toward him. It came readily enough and perched on the side of his hand.

"Oh! What a pretty little thing!" Beth exclaimed, her anxiety to be gone stifled for the instant. The creature was striking both in its deep green color and, despite the magnitude of its voice, in its small size. When it shrieked, its look was less elegant, for its neck ballooned in an unattractive way; at the moment, though, the huddled figure was quite appealing.

79

"Yes, it is lovely," Rendel answered, "and *now* we may go on our way." He smiled at her, eyes still glittering.

He carried the bird with him as they walked, shielding it close to his chest. When they reached the open stretch, he lifted the little creature to his lips, made some sort of sound to it, then released it, tossing it into the air in a southerly direction. For a few seconds, they watched it go; then Rendel said, "Let us cross the meadow quickly, if we can, before we are spotted."

They did move quickly – Rendel as nimbly as if his feet didn't touch the ground, Aynyxia in a typically awkward-looking yet efficient manner; and Beth, to her own way of thinking, not at all gracefully; she couldn't manage to run without her pack and quiver thumping against her inelegantly. Her legs were still too sore from the previous day to make running easy in any event, and, to make things worse, a light rain began to fall almost at once.

When the three companions reached the shelter and relative safety of the woody area on the far side of the meadow, Beth caught her breath (the others didn't seem to need to) while Rendel greeted Aynyxia. "Aynyxiacichorium, my friend." He took both her hands in his, then pulled her forward, kissing her affectionately on each cheek.

"Good to see you," Aynyxia answered with perhaps a bit of embarrassment. "Thanks for the help."

"I am delighted to have been of assistance, of course. And I would be equally delighted to hear from both of you of the adventures you have shared. But perhaps we should continue on our way at once. We go to Greenwood?"

"Yep," Aynyxia answered, dispiritedly, beginning to walk. "Made a mistake coming by the Kritt Pass."

"Perhaps. But you could not have known how it would be. You have lost little time in any event. And you are the wiser for your misfortune, for you have learned, from what I gather, that the enemy is aware of your mission." Aynyxia nodded. "Aware even that it was a walkabout who was commissioned," he added thoughtfully. Again, she nodded. "This is disquieting indeed."

With a change of tone, he said after a pause, "You will be our guests at Greenwood tonight, I trust. And in the morning, we will travel northward, I assume, since the way east seems perilous . . . if I may be allowed to accompany you, that is. I know you were to travel alone, but the situation is somewhat altered, now that your purpose is discovered."

Aynyxia was speaking very little, Beth realized as they walked on, and apparently didn't mind that Rendel seemed to be taking the lead. She wondered if that was because he somehow outranked her or simply because she had such an unassuming personality.

Soon, Rendel was addressing Beth. "May I now have the privilege of knowing your name, or do you prefer to keep it a secret?" She thought at first he was being sarcastic (that's what she got for spending so much time with Luke!) but then realized he was serious.

"Oh, no. It's all right. . . . I mean, I *guess* it is." She glanced questioningly at Aynyxia, who shrugged. "I'm Elizabeth DeVere, but most people call me Beth." Feeling that she ought to have more to say, she added, "I come from a place called Fairspring Township."

"Elizabeth?" Rendel repeated with some surprise in his face. "This was the name of my grandmother and my grandmother's grandmother. I have always thought it a charming name, though I have not known its provenance. It is from *your* world, then?"

Beth was too surprised to answer, and Rendel misunderstood her reaction.

"My apologies. I have misspoken, it seems. I assumed that you came from . . ." His voice trailed off in a questioning way.

"Oh, no!" Beth said quickly. "I mean, yes, I do. It's just that . . . You don't think that's . . . *odd*? That I come from another world?"

"Truth, it is odd! *Wondrously* odd! Indeed, I should be delighted to understand more of how this can be possible."

"Yeah, I wouldn't mind understanding that myself!" Beth agreed with an attempt at a laugh. Further conversation along these lines was interrupted when a sweep of somewhat heavier rain broke through the treetops and several particularly thick drops assaulted Beth's wide eyes.

"You have no hat," Rendel said. "Please, take mine." Before she could object, he settled it onto her head and it began to shelter her from the falling water. Glistening raindrops scattered themselves among his cinnamon curls instead.

81

They moved more quickly then and talked less.

By the time the three reached Greenwood, evening had not yet fallen, but Beth felt as if it had been a day or two at least since she'd left the Gribbs' comfortable home. So much had happened! And she was so very tired! And wet. And pretty cold. And thirsty. And she might be hungry too, but she was too tired and wet and cold and thirsty to be sure.

At least it wasn't raining anymore. Or, if it was, the huge trees of Greenwood were so thick at the top that they adequately sheltered the woodlander community that lived in and among them.

Greenwood was, just as it sounded, a forested area, and in its center lay the woodlander village. Beth would have found her first view of the village altogether entrancing if she hadn't begun to shiver by then. Quaint cottage-type homes fit perfectly into the natural setting, some built right around the trunks of tall trees, some constructed up among the branches, rope ladders hanging down from their charming front doors. The woodlanders themselves (in dress resembling Rendel's, except that some of the women wore skirts) were all busy, some chatting together while engaged in food preparations, a few sitting together and sewing, others involved in a woodworking project together. A steady stream of contented voices flowed through the area. Several of the woodlanders had acknowledged their approach with smiles or waves, though none had come forward to greet them.

The great number of people surprised Beth at first, then she checked herself and realized there were probably not more than twenty-five or thirty in view (though she guessed that there were others close by). It only seemed like such a great number because it was the first time since she'd come to this world that she'd been in the presence of more than three or four other people at the same time. She'd seen hardly anyone for the last twenty-four hours, and here, at last, was a whole little community. A very pleasant one, it seemed.

When they had nearly reached the large clearing that seemed to be the center of the village, Rendel stopped his companions for a moment while he went forward to address a young boy tending a campfire. Shortly, he returned to Aynyxia and Beth, while the boy went off in the opposite direction.

82

"Come," Rendel said, leading them to the fire. "Warm yourselves." Soon the boy returned, bringing them three full mugs, then left again. Thirsty as she was, Beth could not be excited by the contents of her mug – thick black liquid that reminded her strongly of tar (though thankfully without the corresponding smell). In a brave effort to be polite, she told herself that it was just a really, really dark chocolate and took a sip. Surprisingly, she liked the drink, and it began to warm her just as quickly as the fire was doing. Soon, she returned Rendel's hat to him and took off her jacket.

When they were all feeling more comfortable, Aynyxia said suddenly, "It's time. Time for questions." Then, jerking her head in Rendel's direction, she added with a very labored wink at Beth, "A storyteller, he is. Can tell you all about it." She walked away to get more of the thick, black drink and did not return immediately, for as soon as she left them more than one woodlander friend came forward to greet her and chat.

Once she was out of earshot, Rendel, smiling knowingly, asked Beth, "She has told you little of why you were called?"

"Practically *nothing!*" Beth answered with feeling.

He smiled more broadly and his eyes twinkled again. "Speech does not come easily to Aynyxiacichorium," he explained in a gentle voice. "She is a walkabout, and it is not their way."

"Oh!" Beth's face registered her surprise as she took this in.

"She speaks with more skill than any walking plant I have known, but when the subject of her speech is of a complex nature or of great import – and this subject is both – the task strains her. There is too great a range of thoughts for her to order into words at once."

"Do you mean," Beth asked slowly, "that plants don't usually talk in . . . this language" – she had almost said "English," then wondered if that would be the right word, then made a mental note to think later about why they *were* speaking English, her own language, no matter what it was called here — "or do you mean that they don't talk at all?"

"By nature, the plants of our land speak no language that is expressed in words, as you and I would know them. But most of them – most of the *minded* plants, that is – can understand spoken language, and any of the ones that wish to move about have learned to speak words as well. And Aynyxiacichorium takes great delight in moving about, as you may have discovered."

This conversation interested Beth considerably. She supposed that "minded" plants were intelligent beings and that there must be an ordinary sort too. Oh, she hoped so! She was sure she had absentmindedly broken off twigs or leaves since she'd been here and trampled on growing vines; and she didn't even want to think about the berries she had picked and eaten!

Rendel himself had a great curiosity about the plants of Beth's country, and an even greater curiosity about her country in general, but he had a task to accomplish and such pleasantries needed to wait. "Will you tell me what you know already of our present state and of the reason you were called?" he asked. It took Beth only a few sentences to summarize all the pertinent facts she had learned. When she had done so, Rendel told her, "Then I shall explain the rest now." He spoke quietly after that, leaning in close to her, and though Aynyxia rejoined them a few minutes later, Beth noticed that no woodlander approached the whole of the time that Rendel spoke.

CHAPTER SEVEN – Rendel of Greenwood Explains

Rendel began his tale in the eleventh year of the reign of King DarQuinn the Good, also known as DarQuinn Mandek, "mandek" being a name of honor accorded to great warriors and defenders of their homeland. In that year, an invasion was begun by Karstidon Tork, king of the land beyond the Waste. Karstidon's followers had been raiding the Southlands for some time by then.

"Do you know what I intend by 'the Southlands'?" Rendel interrupted his narrative. When Beth shook her head, he explained. "The country in which we find ourselves is Gwilldonum, as you have learned. It is by far the largest country of the Southlands, but for generations and generations again the lord of Gwilldonum has also been overlord of a number of smaller surrounding lands and has been in close alliance with the few other lands of the south that have retained sovereignty. DarQuinn was both King of Gwilldonum and High King of the Southlands."

Rendel resumed his story.

More and more, the raids were by soldiers rather than civilians and what had already been suspected for some time became clear – that the orders for these outrages originated with Karstidon Tork himself. He had long claimed that the raids were carried out by renegades and were in general spontaneous acts; in any event, he had insisted, they had never been part of a royal campaign. In the beginning of the eleventh year of DarQuinn, however, all pretense dissipated. Destruction in the Brenmarch, a subject land that lay between Gwilldonum and the Wasteland, was followed shortly by an invasion of Gwilldonum itself. War had begun.

The Southlanders responded with vigor and valor, and it was not many months before complete victory seemed within reach. It came as a cutting surprise, therefore, when DarQuinn the Good, in the twelfth year of his reign, fell in the Slaughter of Wicent Pratum. It was certain that treachery lay behind the defeat, though no traitor was ever unmasked.

As soon as the king fell and in the heat of battle, Risardas Mandek, Captain of the Guard (who must already have suspected that his own fate would be no different from his lord's), dispatched two quick-thinking and quick-moving brothers by the name of Reston. The younger, Edwyn Reston, made straightway to Dunryelle, the ancestral home of the late queen, DarQuinn's wife. There the king's daughter, Arandella, accompanied by only a small company of personal attendants, advisors, and guards, had gone into seclusion both for mourning and to await her time of delivery, for she had been with child at the time of her own husband's death at the Battle of Greyvic, just as the tide of the war turned.

Edwyn's brother, Alwyn Reston, sped east to intercept Therin, son of Risardas Mandek, with the order that he and his company make all haste to Dunryelle for the protection of the princess, soon to be queen. Risardas had surmised that the enemy would seek her out at once, and he feared that her whereabouts might already have been made known to them through whatever villainy had betrayed the king. In both these matters, he was correct.

At Dunryelle, Edwyn found Arandella and imparted the news of her father's death and, by consequence, her own accession to the throne. Several years earlier, when the princess had attained the age of all rights, King DarQuinn had anointed her as his chosen successor; upon his death, therefore, all that remained was for her to accept rule and renew her vows. This she did at once and in the presence of Edwyn, through whom these events were later made known.

Sir Simon of Norwood, a wise and valued advisor to the royal family for many years, was present at Dunryelle. He had known the princess her entire life; once the trouble with the Torks began, he never left her company. Indeed, when in time the enemy reached Arandella's residence, Sir Simon died fighting by her side.

Rendel paused for a moment. The fire crackled and all other noises seemed muted and distant until he spoke again, continuing the account.

Sir Simon was a leading member of the Council of Ten and had, in such extraordinary circumstances, full authority to act on its behalf, offering the kingdom to Arandella and receiving her vows of fidelity. Rhysmenn of Eleyn Gryf, who also served as advisor to Arandella, was present as well. All was done in great haste, but the ceremonies were correct. Arandella was rightfully queen. Hers was to be the shortest of reigns, however. A large enemy company had already been sighted and escape seemed improbable.

The new queen ordered Edwyn away at once in search of aid. Her own company in flight would be easy prey for the enemy, but Edwyn traveling alone could outmaneuver them; besides, the Restons are said to make their horses fly, they run them so well and so fast. Edwyn resisted. Knowing that there were few horses left at Dunryelle (and none to match his own), he pled with Arandella to take his steed herself and be away on her own if not in company, but she replied that her first act as queen would not be one of flight. There was no time for further discussion. She ordered him to go and he did, "though I believe," Rendel added, "that he does regret it to this day."

"Was she preg- . . . I mean, was she still with child then, or did she already have her baby?" Beth asked. "Either way, that would have made it hard for her to get away very fast."

"Truth, but I do not believe she would have abandoned her household and her companions in any event. And yes," Rendel glanced at Aynyxia, "the child had been born."

"What about the baby? What happened to it?" Beth asked after a pause, hoping the answer wouldn't be too sad.

Again Rendel looked to Aynyxia, who remained silent. "The first assistance Edwyn Reston came upon was his own brother, who, by good fortune, had quickly located young Therin and his company and had joined them as with great speed they made for Dunryelle. It was an excellent company, by all accounts, and cannot be faulted. They arrived in time to intercept the enemy's party before it could withdraw, but, alas, not in time to save the new queen's life. Her body still lay warm where she had fallen, close by her advisors'. But the queen's child was nowhere found – neither living nor dead.

"Few survived the attack on Dunryelle," Rendel told her solemnly, "and of those, none could give news of the child, not even to say whether Arandella had borne a son or a daughter. Even Edwyn Reston, due to the confusion of the time he had spent with the new queen and the heavy news he had brought her, had not had occasion to see the child or receive news of it. Moreover, there had been no customary celebration at the birth both because the princess awaited the return of her father, which she had had reason to expect would occur shortly, and because she was still a widow in mourning and had not thought it seemly. Of the queen's closest advisors and those attendants who were allowed in the private chambers during those days, there were no survivors, save possibly one whose whereabouts have never since been discovered . . . but it is not believed," Rendel added quickly, anticipating the question Beth was considering, "that she took the infant with her. Nor is it believed that any from among the enemy was able to escape with it.

"At first, nothing was known of the child's whereabouts or whether the queen had performed the ceremonies of anointing on the infant, though it seemed unlikely when so little time was left to her. (In our land, when the *princeps* – our traditional title for our ruler – has chosen an eventual successor, the ceremonies of anointing fix the choice so that the path to succession will be clear. When there has been no anointing, the Council of Ten deliberates and seeks what guidance there may be from the Silent Ones and then itself chooses the new *princeps* – always of the same family, but not always the first child of the last *princeps*, as is the custom in some of the lands of the north.) As I have said, at first nothing was generally known of the child's fate, but once peace was fully restored, the Council of Ten sent word throughout the Southlands that the child had in fact been anointed but had been sent to a place of security to be raised until the age of all rights.

"Some met this news with great joy, and I believe that much ale was drunk to the health of the child and the future of our land. But others wondered, especially as time passed, why the child should not be returned to be raised at the Stronghold of Arystar and to sit alongside a regent, if in fact our land had returned to the peaceful stability that the council claimed for it. Through many regions, discussions of these matters took place over the drinking of many more pints of ale. Soon, the grumblings increased as it became clear that not all members of the council were privy to the whereabouts of the Anointed. In certain corners, this fact caused resentment and offense and the drinking of even more ale, for there are those in our land who consider that such drink will bring great clarity to complex situations."

Beth looked up when she registered what Rendel had just said. He was smiling at her. "And now that we speak of drink, will you have something more? And I see that food is laid out." He

88

nodded toward the center of the woodlander village. "Do you wish to take supper now? We can resume our discussion afterwards."

"Oh, yes, please!" She was suddenly ravenous, barely having eaten since she'd left the Gribbs' that morning.

He rose and motioned for her to accompany him. Aynyxia rose too, but said she'd walk down to the stream for a soak. Rendel led Beth in the opposite direction, toward a long table set out with many types of food. Still more food was being brought, mostly by woodlanders who stole glances at Beth and then looked away quickly, though in a shy rather than in an unfriendly way. The table had been empty when Beth and Aynyxia first arrived with Rendel, but now there seemed to be enough on it to feed the whole community. No one was eating yet, but after Rendel handed Beth a plate and took one for himself, others began to follow suit.

When her plate was entirely full, Beth followed Rendel and took a seat beside him on a wooden bench. "I regret," he apologized after a few bites, "that we cannot offer a proper feast to honor you, but our time is not our own and we have much to discuss."

"It seems like a feast to me!"

"A guest of one is a guest of all, so we share our meal together tonight, but a proper feast is an elaborate affair and requires much time for preparation and much time for enjoyment. We did not know this morning that we would have you as a guest this evening," he said, smiling at her, and once again his glittering eyes fascinated her. She stared for a moment until she realized she was doing so.

"Do they all know why I'm here?" she whispered to Rendel a little later.

"No, none. Only I," he answered. "But the others understand that we have matters of import to discuss privately."

Beth supposed that that explained why no one came near to greet her, though they all smiled in a friendly enough way when they caught her eye, but as soon as Rendel introduced her to one and then another of the woodlanders, several others began to come over to make her acquaintance as well. Eventually, a few children came to chat with her too, some rather timidly. She felt like a celebrity.

After a while, it occurred to her that the children seemed small for their age, and some of them might even be her own age, though they were several inches shorter. She had judged one woodlander girl, who was about her height, to be not much older than herself, maybe thirteen or fourteen – but then the girl had introduced her husband (her "mate," she'd said, which sounded so odd). Beth wondered if woodlanders got married at a young age or if they were all a lot older than they looked. Maybe they were even a hundred years old or something; how would she know? She wondered about Rendel, who looked like he could be a teenager or a young man . . . but maybe he was someone's father; or grandfather, even! Too strange!

But Beth liked these people and their woodland home. It seemed so peaceful here – really, *really*, peaceful, though she couldn't quite say why. She supposed it had to do with the forest animals that wandered freely about, so clearly unafraid.

She'd been lost in thought for a few minutes when she realized that Rendel had offered her more food.

"Oh. No. Thank you." And then she added for good measure, "Thank you very much; it was very nice."

Rendel smiled, saying, "Then perhaps we should move apart and continue our discussion." Just then, a woodlander came forward and silently took their plates from them, and another appeared with a pitcher to refill their mugs.

When Rendel and Beth had settled back in the spot they'd earlier occupied (Aynyxia was nowhere to be seen), Beth said, "I think it's really interesting, everything you've been telling me, and I do really want to know what happens next, but I still haven't got a clue what any of it has to do with me."

"Of course," said Rendel. "Aynyxia told you that I am a storyteller, and perhaps I am too much of one. Let me see if I can more quickly bring us to the part you will play in the story."

"Oh," said Beth, afraid she had offended him, "I didn't mean . . . I mean, it was a very *good* story. Well, no, not *good*, it was sad and everything, but—"

He understood and stopped her with a smile and a gentle touch on her knee. "You are right to bring me to the point. Our time is short enough and there are still plans to be made for the morrow.

"Let me tell you, *briefly*, what our situation in Gwilldonum is now. The invader Karstidon Tork met his death shortly after the events I have described and was succeeded by his much younger

90

brother, Myrmidon. Myrmidon is of a different sort from his brother, but no more worthy of trust or friendship, in my view. Still, he exceeds his brother in both cunning and charm and is slowly gaining support in the Southlands."

"Really? Even though his brother was the enemy and everything?"

"As I say, he is cunning in all things and artful in his efforts to charm. He denounces his brother and offers apologies, claiming that if he himself had not been of such a tender age at the time he might even have risen up against Karstidon. Moreover, times have been difficult in the Southlands these many years. In a number of regions, the forces of nature have been harsh and crops have been poor; strange diseases have stricken animals. Many say that these things will not be set to right until a *princeps* takes the throne at Arystar. There is also the matter of goblins—"

"*Goblins?*" repeated Beth, surprised and a bit unnerved, but then she added, "Oh! Or . . . are goblins *nice* here?"

"*Nice?*" It was Rendel's turn to be surprised. "Not at all! Are they nice in your world?"

"No! Well, I mean, actually, we don't have any. Well, just in stories . . . but they're not *nice* stories."

"Nor are our stories of goblins nice!" Rendel responded with feeling. "We have no such creatures in Gwilldonum itself, but there have been recent reports of them in outlying regions and even rumors of planned incursions from the north, where the goblin population is significant. The Southlanders fear the goblins even more than they do the Torks, and there are those who so desperately desire a *princeps* to lead them that they would see even a Tork on the throne, if they credited his abilities as a warrior-king."

"But I thought the king or queen would have to be from the same family as DarQuinn and Arandella."

"Truth," answered Rendel, "but the Torks *are* of the same line, though the connection is now a distant one. Myrmidon is a descendant of Kerridon, called Torquis (from whom the Torks derive their name), elder brother of Krispin the Swift, an ancestor of King DarQuinn. After instigating a rebellion against his brother's rule, Kerridon was expelled from Gwilldonum and sent with his company to the lands beyond the Waste, where his family has ruled since. This was generations ago, but the Torks have never lost the desire to reclaim Gwilldonum for themselves, as they believe it should have once been ruled by Kerridon. For some time now, Myrmidon has been campaigning – peacefully so far, as near as can be proved – for his acceptance as king in the absence of any other claim on the throne.

"In addition to all these things, there is now a growing belief in my country that the rightful heir is dead, or perhaps was never born in the first place, for the child would have reached the traditional age of all rights by now – or so it is said, though the exact date of the child's birth cannot be established, and the ways of the past are often misunderstood in any event – but no child has yet been brought forward. Never in memory has the Council of Ten ruled for so long without a *princeps*. In light of these circumstances, Myrmidon petitioned the council to allow him to put forth his case formally at the Festival of Errastisye not many days hence. I fear that his support has grown to the point that the council will not dare refuse him, particularly since his greatest support comes from Ferinia, a neighboring country close to Greyvic, the city where the festival will take place. Therin Mandek (the same Therin I mentioned earlier but who is now Captain of the Council Guard) awaits the order (or perhaps he has by now received it) to give safe passage to Myrmidon and his company, escorting them from Ferinia to Greyvic on the first day of the festival – the day after the morrow. The festival lasts nine days. On the eighth day, Myrmidon would be allowed to present his case formally to the whole assembly – unless by that time the council can bring forward the Anointed or argue convincingly that it will do so shortly.

"For all these reasons, the need to find the rightful heir is an urgent one. Tanek the Wise, the Silent One—" Rendel stopped. "Do you know of the Silent Ones?"

"No." She'd heard him use the name earlier but hadn't known what he'd meant by it.

He smiled. "To explain the mysteries of the Silent Ones would make this account a longer one by far, and the hour grows late. Do you know the word 'prophet'?" he tried.

"Yes."

"Then we shall say for now only that the Silent Ones are prophets and that Tanek has given a prophecy to certain members of the council that a champion would come from a distant land to bring the Anointed forward. The details of the matter have been kept as secret as possible, for even the council members' own attendants cannot be assumed above suspicion in these days. Escorts were sent to the three known sanctuaries, the most sacred places in the Southlands, to await and receive the champion." Rendel paused, watching her carefully. "It was Aynyxiacichorium who went to the sanctuary of the central lands . . . and she found *you* there, Beth." He paused again, then spoke softly. "*You* are the champion who is to return the Anointed to us and bring all things to right."

Beth couldn't say anything. Instead, she repeated Rendel's words in her head to be sure she wasn't mistaken. *She* was their champion. She was their *champion?* She was supposed to bring them this child she'd never heard of before now?

It's a mistake, she wanted to say. *I'm very sorry, but I stumbled in here by mistake and if you can just point me back to Indiana. . . .* But it was no use; her mouth wasn't cooperating and the words didn't come.

Rendel seemed to understand her dilemma and gave her time to consider what he had said. Then something beyond her caught his eye, and he looked up to see Aynyxia approaching. To Beth, he said, "Do not be distressed by this. I know it is a burden, and I see that you are weary. Allow me to make arrangements for the night so that you may rest. Aynyxiacichorium and I will see to plans and preparations for the morrow, if you are willing to leave those matters to us, and we can discuss all these things again in the morning. For now, I leave you with your friend." After briefly laying his hand on her shoulder, he rose and left, just as Aynyxia joined her.

This is all wrong. I shouldn't be here. Far from the peace she'd felt at suppertime, she now experienced a fast-growing, overpowering panic, like thunder rolling over plains.

"It's a mistake!" she could finally say aloud. "I'm not the one you want!" she told Aynyxia, fixing her with an intense expression. "I tried to tell you at the beginning, remember? I tried to say I wasn't the one."

"No, you're the one," said Aynyxia with an easy confidence.

"But I'm *not!*" she answered desperately. "*I* can't do what you want! I wouldn't even know how to begin!"

Aynyxia puzzled seriously over this for a good ten seconds before cheerfully answering, "Well, then, you *will* . . . when it's time."

"It's no use," Beth thought, "she doesn't get it." They sat there a while, silent, until Rendel returned and offered to take Beth to where she could rest for the night. She was more composed by then but followed wordlessly.

They were stopped on the way by a group of woodlanders. "Rendel," one asked a little shyly, "we wondered if your friend would join us for a nightdance?" She turned to Beth with an inviting, expectant face, then added, "And Aynyxiacichorium too, of course." She beamed, and her eyes were glittery, like Rendel's. The others of the group smiled their encouragement.

The woodlanders all seemed very nice, and Beth didn't want to disappoint them, but she really didn't feel up to it, and—

"I think my friend may need to rest," Rendel answered, looking at Beth hesitantly as if to be sure of what she wanted. What she most wanted was to get away from everyone as quickly as possible before she burst from confusion. Or collapsed from exhaustion. One of the two. It was pretty much a toss-up.

What in the world was she doing here?

"Please dance with us," said a woodland child, coming forward from behind her father. "If you do, we'll all be allowed to stay up until the moons cross." Three other woodland children confirmed this with vigorous nodding of heads. They were very cute, all of them. And everyone had been kind. Beth didn't want to hurt their feelings or be rude or anything, but . . .

"Well, I'm pretty tired," she began. Seeing their disappointment, though, she finished by saying, "but I'm sure I'd enjoy *watching* you dance for a little while." This brought pleased responses from adults and children alike.

Now fortunately for Beth, a woodlander dance is a marvelous thing to see, and in this case it was even marvelous enough to distract her from her most serious thoughts. As she listened to the music – flute music, mostly, which she loved – she found that the melody washed over her like a cool stream, carrying away her heavier thoughts. And the dancing was pretty and joyful, and everyone joined in, including Aynyxia. Though she wouldn't have believed it a little while earlier, Beth even let herself be pulled in by the second round and then by the third surprised

94

herself by laughing along with the others as she made missteps and wrong turns. At least she had a sense of the rhythm, though, which Aynyxia apparently did not. Aynyxia turned every which way whenever she felt like it, her thin limbs twitching about in irregular patterns, and everyone else merely continued the dance around her. Beth steered clear of her, however, because having her plant friend dance by messed her up more than anything.

She'd meant to make her excuses and go to bed after a short time, but she danced right up until the end ("when the moons crossed") and then suddenly felt too exhausted even to stand.

As everyone else made their ways to their homes for the night, Rendel showed her to the place she could sleep. A large canvas was draped to form a makeshift tent with one large side left open. At some other time, Beth might have been disappointed to miss the opportunity to sleep in one of the cute treehouses, but at the moment the only thing that mattered was the inviting bed in front of her. Rendel said good-night almost at once but left her in the care of Ellena (the woodlander who had first invited her to dance), who inquired if there was anything she needed. When everything was settled, Beth stretched out on her little bed and wished she didn't have to get back up for a few days. She'd decided not to let herself get into a panic over the champion thing – which meant not thinking about it at all. It could wait until morning and no doubt everything would be clearer after a good night's sleep. At least, that's what her mother would say. Luckily, she didn't go too far in thinking about her mother, interrupted in her thoughts when she heard Rendel's voice again.

"Beth." He was coming back toward her, a figure following behind. "You have a visitor." Before she could even guess who it might be, Rendel stepped aside and Beth saw a familiar face.

"Mr. Gribb!" she exclaimed with pleasure, rising at once. "What are you doing here? Did you know I'd be here too?"

With a cunning smile, he answered, "Aye, that I did. Knew you'd changed your course. I have my ways, I do. Not much coming or going in the southern parts gets by Gert and me. Ask the young woodlander here." He nodded in the direction of Rendel, who smiled, agreed that Marcus "had his ways," and then left them to visit privately.

"Well, how has your charming self been getting along?" Marcus asked at once, but before Beth could answer, he seemed to change his mind, waving his hands in the air as if to erase the question, and saying, "No, no. I'm not here for a chat, I'm not. I've got a special reason for finding you, as you'll have already guessed." Beth hadn't guessed, and couldn't think what the reason might be. "Let's both sit down, let's do, and take care of our business at once, for I see you're ready for sleep and well in need, I'm sure."

Beth sat down, but she couldn't imagine what business they might have. She waited patiently for him to explain.

Then she waited some more.

For three minutes at least Marcus Gribb said nothing, though once or twice he made a noise that sounded like, "Hrrmm," and more often than that he seemed about to speak but didn't. Finally, he reached into his jacket, pulled out something that had been concealed there, and set it on the ground before Beth.

It was a weapon. A knife in its sheath, it seemed.

"There. There it is," Marcus said. And then, as if to himself, "Sure enough." His odd little thumbs twitched. Though he sighed deeply and seemed sad for a moment, his manner changed quickly when he began to speak again.

"Gert fair took my head off when she found I was holding this back. I knew myself I should be giving it to you, I did, but – well, I'll be honest. I knew I could get a might good price for it one day, if I just held it 'til the right customer came along. And, then, too . . ." He gazed at the weapon for a moment until he remembered himself. "I guess I've always had half a mind to keep it myself. Not to use it, I don't expect, just to keep it . . . secret-like.

"Course I thought about it while you were with us last night, I did, and again this morning, but I couldn't bring myself to hand it over, I'm ashamed to confess. But the more I thought about it, the more certain I was that it was yours by right." He paused while the fingers of his left hand ran through his hair, stopped to twist the ends absently, then fell to his lap again. "I've got this notion in my head that it's because I'd one day meet you that it came into my hands in the first place. . . . A good story, that is," he told her, remembering, "maybe I'll tell you one day. . . .

"Anyway, after I'd left you and got back home, I couldn't help but go bring it out from the place I'd hidden it away; and there was I behind one of the storing huts just turning it about in my hands, I was, and staring at it, and so lost in my own thinking that I never did hear Gert coming 'til she was right upon me. 'What've you got there, Marcus Gribb?' she says in that knowing way of hers. 'Nothing,' says I, trying to hide it away fast. Well, you must know she'd never let that go, she wouldn't. Kept on 'til she had the whole story from me – what it was, what it could do, how it had come to me. I'd never told her, you see, though there aren't many secrets I keep from my Gert." He laughed. "Couldn't keep many if I wanted to, but I don't want to." He looked at the weapon, then at Beth. "But I kept this secret, I did. And you'd do well to keep it too. I've got a notion the magic is stronger that way, but don't ask me what got that notion in my head."

Magic? Beth didn't know what to make of the speech, from beginning to end. She was intrigued and touched, but mostly confused.

"I wouldn't let the secret on to anyone, I wouldn't, even those you trust the most, until you have no choice."

"But what *is* the secret, Mr. Gribb?" Beth asked.

He sighed again, staring at the weapon. Maybe he was making sure of his decision, maybe he was already regretting it, maybe he was simply finding a bittersweet pleasure in the sight of the thing one last time while it was still his own.

"Draw it from its sheath," Gribb told her, looking up, resolved.

Beth lifted the weapon solemnly with two hands, then with her right one pulled the hilt away from the sheath. The dagger that emerged was etched with faint symbols. She supposed that Gribb expected her to understand it, but she couldn't.

"What does it mean?" she asked.

"The writing?" He shrugged. "Couldn't begin to tell you, I couldn't. It's no language I've ever seen."

"I don't understand. Is the secret—"

"Put it back in the sheath," he interrupted, too excited now to hear her out.

She did, then passed it to him when he reached forward.

When he stood up, Beth did too. When he looked all about to see if anyone else was in view, so did Beth. When he drew the weapon, Beth did nothing but stare in amazement, her mouth open.

"But . . . how . . ." She was at a loss. Gribb remained silent, enjoying the moment, until Beth could finally say, "It's amazing!"

"Truth, it is!" With pride, he displayed the weapon – no dagger this time, but a full-length sword, perfect in aspect, unmarked by time or use, and shining as brightly as the day it had been forged, generations ago.

It's beautiful! But it must be four times as long as the sheath, Beth realized, looking it over closely. "And it's magic," she added aloud. "Really magic!"

"Aye. Magic."

After admiring it for a moment longer, Marcus returned the sword to its sheath and handed it to Beth.

"You're giving this to me? It's wonderful, but you should keep it. I don't even know how to make it work. It was just a little dagger when I pulled it out."

For a moment, Marcus seemed tempted to accept it back from her, but then said hurriedly, "No, no, no. It's for you. I'm sure, I am. And you can bring forth the sword." He looked around him again as he said, "Pull it out three times. On the third, it will be a sword."

"But—"

"Just do it. You'll see."

So she did. She pulled out a dagger once, then twice. On the third try, she pulled out the long, gleaming sword. She was pleased, but said, "I don't understand. *You* didn't pull it out three times."

"Truth," he answered with a chuckle. "And neither will you after this. It will be a sword any time you expect it to be. I added in that bit about three times myself," he chuckled again, "to make it easier for you to believe. Seems more magic, don't you think? But now that you know you *can* do it, you *will* do it. Try again."

Still perplexed, she returned the sword to its sheath, and started to pull it out again, stopping when she saw the dull, gray end of the dagger emerging.

"No," said Gribb. "You must *expect* it. That's the only secret."

Beth wasn't sure she really wanted to try again, for fear that she wouldn't succeed, but she closed her eyes, took a deep breath, and pictured herself holding the beautiful, shining sword in front of her. As she pulled on the hilt, she opened her eyes in a squint.

It was working!

She pulled out the sword, and Marcus beamed like a proud teacher whose student has done well.

"Now remember what I said," he warned, "keep it secret. Hide it away and tell no one you have it unless you must. There's no one I know more trustworthy than your woodlander friend, but I wouldn't tell even him, I wouldn't. No one but Gert and you and my humble self know you'll be carrying this, and that's for the best. Can't tell you why I think that, but I do. I feel it inside." He slapped his chest to emphasize the point.

After showing her how to carry the weapon close to her person in a concealed but not too uncomfortable fashion, he began to take his leave.

"Already?" she asked, disappointed. "Will I see you in the morning?"

"No, you won't. You're rightly tired, I see that, and ready for bed. You get yourself to sleep for you've got your trials ahead, I daresay. I'll have a few winks myself, but I won't be napping long. I don't mind night travel, and I'll be up and gone before it's light. Gert will be waiting, you know." He added secretively, "I'll be taking her back some jackberry jam. She surely does love it, and nobody makes jam like a woodlander!"

With that he left her, and Beth felt alone and a little sad. But mostly tired.

She hid away the magic dagger under her pillow and settled down to sleep. "What a strange day it's been," she thought. "And so *long*!" She remembered then, with surprise, that her whole adventure in Gwilldonum had only begun the day before. But she didn't want to think about everything that had happened since then. Or think about anything at all, for that matter. She was exhausted, and what she wanted most in that moment was a good, long sleep.

As so often happens in adventures, though, she didn't get it.

CHAPTER EIGHT – Night Flight

Beth was only dreaming. Otherwise, the idea of sitting down to dinner with oversized villainous rats in pastel frocks would have been far more unsettling. As it was, her only response to the scene was to ask politely for more potatoes. If that wasn't strange enough, the scene changed suddenly, the frilled feasting replaced by an irregular line of chickens crossing a road in single file while a voice called to them to wake up.

"Awake!" the female voice repeated with insistence, but it resounded differently this time. "We must leave at once. We must cross the road before dawn, I tell you!" Her voice was impatient, for her own young ones could awaken, alert, in an instant.

Beth took longer. Gradually, she registered the words and then, as she remembered where she was, their meaning. Lastly, her eyes focused on the speaker, whose face was quite close to her own, and the resulting jolt of surprise finished the job of awakening her. The face, barely more than a foot from hers, had an eerie look in the flickering yellow light of a crude lantern.

Beth did not recognize this person and did not believe her to be a woodlander. For one thing, even crouched down as she was, she gave the impression of being significantly taller than Rendel Singer and the others Beth had met. For another, though there had been some variation in the coloring of the woodlanders, none had had the ebony skin or the jet black hair of this woman. But the most striking difference was in her distinctive yellow-green eyes. There was something startling about them even apart from their color, but Beth had no opportunity then to identify what it was.

"At last!" The woman practically growled her relief, leaning back from Beth, who was then able to sit upright. "Be quick! We've little time. We must away!"

"I . . . . Uhm, I don't—" What could she say? *I don't know what you're talking about? I don't know* you? *And even if I did, I'm not sure I'd want to go anywhere with you?*

"It is all right, Beth," a familiar voice assured her.

Looking beyond the stranger, Beth saw Rendel advancing. The light was insufficient for her to make out at once Aynyxia's form, beyond him, but she did see two woodlanders in disheveled nightclothes emerging from the darkness, one bearing a cloth and a large metal bowl, the other a plate and mug.

On seeing these last two arrivals, the stranger grunted disapprovingly. "We must away!" she repeated, but this time she directed her words to Rendel.

"A moment," said Rendel. "She needs a moment."

Answering with a look but no words, the stranger moved away from them and was absorbed into the darkness, leaving the lantern on the ground beside Beth. Near it, the two woodlanders set down the items they'd been carrying then also retreated. Rendel followed, though he first said to Beth, "It is true. We ought hurry. I will explain as we travel."

Aynyxia came forward then. "Eat," she said, sitting down companionably, not sounding in the least rushed.

The mug contained the thick, hot drink Beth had tried the night before. The plate bore only a chunk of bread covered with something she couldn't identify, but she was hungry enough and had already learned to eat when she could, so she took it willingly. The large bowl, she discovered, contained warm water and she used it and the accompanying cloth to wash up.

Beth felt heavy-headed with fatigue but nonetheless managed to do quickly the few things that needed to be done before departure. She was so tired that she nearly forgot to retrieve the magic sword from under her pillow, but she remembered in time and discreetly hid it under her clothes as Gribb had advised her to do.

Taking the lantern with them, she and Aynyxia soon joined the others at the edge of the woodlander village, beyond the long table, now bare, where supper had been laid out the night before. Although the stranger did not say, "At last!", the thought was clearly in her mind. All she did say before turning to lead them away was, "No light." Rendel took the lantern from Aynyxia and extinguished its flame.

101

Beth's eyes could not adjust quickly to the darkness and at first she could only hear but not see the others. She felt a hand gently take hers as Rendel's voice said, "It will be easier soon. The moons are bright tonight, but we are too hidden from them at the moment." To the newcomer (who had moved so quickly that she was already many yards ahead) he called quietly, "Sharana, she is human and has not night eyes. She will need time." A low grunt was the only response.

This whole adventure thing was certainly taking on a different flavor, Beth thought as she stumbled along, following Rendel's lead in the dark. She'd assumed she'd be traveling today only with him and with Aynyxia, both of whom she'd come to like very much, though she'd only just met them. And, of course, she'd thought they'd be leaving after a good night's sleep, not while it was still dark out! This new person . . . well, maybe she wasn't *un*friendly, exactly, but she certainly wasn't friendly either. She was too . . . *brisk*. Wanted to get things done without wasting time being nice along the way. Or maybe she *was* unfriendly. Rude, even. Beth supposed the woman had reasons for acting the way she did; still . . . it's not like Beth had asked for any of this. But if she *was* there to help them, at least this *Sharana* could act a little grateful. At least until it turned out that she couldn't really help after all, she corrected herself, remembering that there wasn't really anything to be grateful for.

Beth determined to keep up as well as she could, despite her lack of "night eyes." And what did Rendel mean about her being human? Wasn't *he*? She supposed not, though he seemed awfully close. Aynyxia wasn't, of course, but what about the stranger? She appeared human. She looked like someone Beth could have met back home. Except for the unusual eyes.

As her own eyes began to adjust, Beth moved with a little more assurance; when, after a few minutes more, the moonlight reached them more fully through the thinning trees, Rendel dropped her hand and everyone's pace picked up. They moved through the woods single-file, mostly, and almost silently. At least, the others were almost silent; Beth felt as if her own movements were crashingly loud by comparison.

For some time, there was almost no talking among them, but when they finally did slow down a bit, Rendel came alongside Beth, near enough to converse with her quietly. "Our guide is

Sharana Tey," he informed her. "I will introduce you properly when we have reached our destination, but she was the second of the three escorts chosen by the council. She was returning from the sanctuary of the southwest when she received word that you were traveling with Aynyxiacichorium. She—"

"Received word? How?"

"She did not say. She explains no more than necessary." After a pause, he added, "I trust you will not take offense at her manner. It is her way to concentrate as fully as she is able on whatever task she undertakes. She means you no discourtesy by the curtness of her speech. . . . In any event, I surmise that it was through one of Lady Gweynleyn's angeli that she learned you were traveling with Aynyxia. . . . Have I told you? Lady Gweynleyn is the leading member of the Council of Ten. The angeli are her messenger birds."

"I think Aynyxia had one," Beth volunteered, remembering the conversation she had overheard at the Gribbs'. "But if that's right, the message she sent back was a strange one – something like, 'Nothing to report'."

"An arranged deception, I suspect, in case of interception."

"Yep," confirmed Aynyxia, ahead of them, though Beth had not known she was listening.

"In any event, Sharana arrived in the night with news that the Great Road, which is just ahead of us now, will be heavily traveled tomorrow by a large company of Brenmarchers, now camped a short distance west of here. There are many Wastelanders among them," he added heavily. "She thought it prudent that we cross the road before light dawns. . . . I know this is difficult for you, Beth. Your journey thus far has been greatly taxing, I fear. But we will rest soon. Not far beyond the Great Road we will come to—"

"*Hush!*" They were all quiet at once. Beth could make out the form of Sharana Tey, who had been quite a bit ahead the moment before, returning to them rapidly, though her feet made virtually no sound crossing the forest floor. "Someone ahead," she informed them in a guttural whisper. "Wait." She turned and was gone again into the darkness.

Rendel motioned for Aynyxia and Beth to follow him to a better-hidden spot, out of the moons' beams, where they could kneel behind a thickening of plants. Beth sat all the way down, her legs folded under her, because she didn't think she could hold a crouching position very long and was afraid of making noise at the wrong moment if she fell over or something. Since they were completely out of the moonlight, she thought they must be well out of sight – until she realized that the "someone ahead" could very well have night vision like the others. Perhaps everyone here would see each other better than she could see anyone. *What in the world makes them think* I *can help them with* anything? Beth asked herself again. She immediately suppressed the thought as well as she could. There was nothing she could do about that right now anyway!

Instead, she began to think about comments that Aynyxia and Rendel had made about the possibility of spies being anywhere or of even people connected to the council being suspect. So what about this Sharana person? What was she doing right now, and how could they know she hadn't led them into some sort of trap? *How* had she known that Beth was in Greenwood? It hadn't originally been part of the plan to pass through there. But maybe Beth was only asking herself these things because she didn't like being woken up in the middle of the night by someone who didn't explain herself and wouldn't smile.

She wanted to ask Rendel about Sharana but hesitated, unsure whether it was all right for her to talk. She couldn't see or hear anyone else around; still . . .

"Something troubles you?" Rendel had leaned in close to whisper.

"You trust her?"

"Sharana?" He sounded surprised. "Yes!" Then, sensing Beth needed more to reassure her, he leaned even closer, barely breathing his words. "You may trust her, also. With a deep passion does her kind despise and fear the Torks; not one would betray us. And above the rest, Sharana has proved her loyalty."

Beth wanted to ask what "her kind" was but she knew it wasn't the time. She also wished she could be sure she hadn't offended Rendel. Perhaps he and Sharana were great friends and he felt Beth had insulted her by questioning her loyalty.

Even at home, it was easy for Beth to feel unsure of herself in new situations. Here, she was *way* out of her depth! There were so many things she didn't know or understand. But her instincts told her to trust Rendel and Aynyxia. She'd just have to follow their lead for now.

She closed her eyes and tried not to think too much.

Unlikely as it may seem under the circumstances, Beth had actually begun to fall asleep when something roused her. She sensed at once that Rendel and Aynyxia, though they said nothing and she could not see their faces, were tense, alert. She did her best to freeze, especially when she realized that someone was approaching.

It was only Sharana.

"Now is the time," her throaty voice told them. "The road has been watched, but the worthless guard sleeps." She spit on the ground to show her contempt. "Come, he is toward evesun, we will move toward mornsun." (Beth did not understand these terms at the time but learned later that some creatures of Gwilldonum used "mornsun" to mean "east" and "evesun" to mean "west.")

Then Sharana added, "Daggers drawn."

In response, Aynyxia drew her dagger (Beth caught the glint of it) and kept it close, but Rendel made no similar move, as far as Beth could tell. She wondered about that; perhaps he thought their guide was being overcautious. After an instant, she wondered whether she had been expected to pull out a weapon herself. She didn't particularly want to. Then she wondered about something else – Sharana herself had drawn no dagger. Although it hadn't occurred to Beth before, she now realized that Sharana carried nothing. No weapon (not visible, at least), no pack or satchel, nothing at all. Not even a hat or jacket were part of her simple dark outfit. It was strange.

They had already begun to move as Beth made these observations, and it took almost no time before they reached the Great Road; Beth supposed that this was the same road she and Aynyxia had originally hoped to join farther along, before they'd run into those thug-types by the Kritt Pass. It was a wider road than any she'd seen so far (not that she'd seen many here). The moonlight brightened the stretch of road that went off to the left, so the small party edged silently along to the right until there was a place to cross under cover of full shadows.

This was a danger spot. Even in the dark, they'd be vulnerable in the middle of the wide road . . . and someone had been on guard nearby. Watching for them? The guard was sleeping now, Sharana had said, but he could always wake up. And there could be others.

They waited, motionless, alert. The others tensed as they strained to hear, so Beth also tried hard to discover any unusual sound. She couldn't at first (but how could she be sure what was normal and what wasn't?), then registered a low, rhythmic sound from beyond where they'd first reached the road. She could barely hear it, but it sounded sort of like . . . snoring.

After a moment, Sharana moved forward, crossing the road alone before signaling (with a single click of her tongue) to the others to join her. As they did, a tingling sensation passed over Beth and her heart beat fast. But the crossing was uneventful and the party quickly disappeared into the woods on the far side.

Once they were well beyond the road with no sign of having been discovered, a certain amount of tension melted away from the travelers. They soon began to speak freely among themselves.

"What was it you found, Sharana?" asked Rendel concerning the time she had left the other three behind.

"Two haggitts, lying in wait near the road."

"Bandits?" Aynyxia suggested, in a voice that came across as oddly hopeful.

"I do not credit it. They sought particular prey. . . . I watched and waited to glean any news of worth before seeking an opportunity to strike. Soon, one of them left . . . to report to his captain, he said. I thought to dispose of the remaining one as soon as he was alone, but the sluggard abandoned his vigil almost at once. I left him snoring among the creybushes." The last sound came out like a hiss of disgust. "Better to leave him alive than to draw attention," she concluded, though without sounding entirely convinced.

"And *did* you glean news of worth before the first haggitt left?" Rendel inquired.

"They were keeping watch for a walkabout and her companion." This statement, though flatly delivered and not especially surprising after the events of the previous day, engendered a melancholy silence. Forewarned might mean forearmed, but it was a blow to have proof that the enemy was nearby and on the lookout for them.

"Did they have any other task?" Rendel asked with one particular thought in mind.

Sharana understood. "They were watching for another prey as well, but it does not signify," she answered, quickening her step. "They could never have found me."

"That's right!" thought Beth as she forced herself to keep following. "There were three escorts. Anybody who's after us is just *guessing* that Aynyxia is the right one. It could've been Sharana or it could've been— it could *be* the third escort." Maybe the *real* champion was at the third sanctuary and it was just a fluke that she'd shown up at one too. This line of thought should have had a much greater impact on Beth than it actually did, but she was simply too tired to think about it for even a minute longer.

Soon the trees grew thicker again, but the sky that Beth glimpsed between them began to lighten. Morning was breaking through. This did nothing to drive away Beth's fatigue, however; the rush of adrenaline that had come when they sneaked across the road had helped, but exhaustion returned with full force as the journey continued and the conversation waned.

When Beth stumbled and realized that her eyes had just closed, she made herself talk to keep from falling asleep. "What are haggitts?" she asked Rendel drowsily.

"They are known mostly in the western parts." *His* voice didn't sound tired. "Their business here is generally as mercenaries. You know this word? It means they lend their allegiance for silver."

Beth tried to nod, but that seemed to set off a little roller coaster inside her head, so she stopped. "I meant, what kind of *creatures* are haggitts?" She made herself ask, though she wasn't sure she wanted to know. Even in her sleepy state, they sounded creepy.

Rendel understood and said lightly, "Quite dull ones, by all accounts. I have known field mice to exhibit more cleverness than an average haggitt is reported to possess."

After only a brief pause, Beth said sleepily, "You know that's not what I meant. You just don't want me to be afraid. Which means you think I *would* be afraid if . . . ." Her voice trailed off and she never did realize that she hadn't finished the statement.

After it was clear she was done speaking, Rendel said, "Such slow-witted creatures are nothing for *us* to fear. We are

107

much too clever, you and I, to worry about such things as haggitts, for—"

It's not that Beth didn't hear the rest of his answer – she did, more or less – it's just that she forgot each word of it about three and a half seconds after hearing it. She hoped they hadn't been discussing anything important. When she tried to shake her head awake and open her eyes really, really wide, she realized that Rendel was talking to someone else.

"We are sufficiently away from the road," he was saying, "do you not think?"

"Perhaps. But we will not stop here." Then, looking back at a rather dazed Beth, Sharana asked, "Can she not move faster?"

"She is young," Rendel said in a tender but firm tone, "and in need of rest."

"She will rest at the lair" was the answer. "You know it is not far. We are not safe here."

The lair? Too tired to question and not wanting to seem unable to keep up, Beth put all her energy into pushing forward and none into observing her surroundings or talking with anyone or wondering what might be ahead. She could barely hold her eyes open, but her feet kept moving. Later, she had a vague recollection of the moment when Aynyxia had taken her bow and quiver from her and Rendel had taken her pack, but, strangely, she had no memory of having taking anyone's arm. And yet she must have done so, because she saw, a minute or an hour later, hooked inside Rendel's elbow, her very own hand. Her immediate thought was to withdraw it, but her brain must never have passed that message on, because Beth noticed a little while later that her hand was still there.

She was *very* tired.

Fortunately, they really did not have far left to go (Beth's ideas about "far" having adjusted themselves admirably over the previous couple of days). They reached the lair, and it seemed to be exactly that – an animal habitat.

Sharana led Aynyxia and Beth into some sort of cave, and then she and Rendel disappeared. The ground, when Beth nearly collapsed onto it, was hard and smelled strongly of animal, but these things did nothing to prevent her falling into a deep sleep.

Just before she did so, she had some confused thoughts that, untangled, would have been along these lines: "This must be

108

the home of some wild beasts. Probably a bunch of them, and they'll all be angry when they get back and find me here. . . . I'd better take a nap."

"This road's been crossed in the night." The speaker, a haggitt named Tred, was studying faint markings where Beth and the others had stolen across the Great Road in the early morning hour. Both Rendel and Sharana had been light on their feet, but Beth and Aynyxia had left a trail clear enough to catch an experienced tracker's eye.

"No, not last night, it wasn't. I been watching." Then the second haggitt, who answered to the ill-fitting name of Grin, corrected and contradicted himself in one stroke: "Not that a body could expect any other body to see half a thing from where I was waiting . . . where *you* told me to wait, *if* you will recall the matter rightly!" Grin liked to cover all his bases when there was a question of blame.

"Watching, were you? With your eyes opened or shut?" Tred knew his companion well.

"I was watching, I tell you! I earn my pay. Ask anyone. Those tracks are old and could might be any creature's at all."

"They're fresh. . . . And though there's something in this I can't make out, I'd wager all my pay and yours too that these marks right here belong to a cursed-unnatural walkabout. A walkabout traveling in this region at night?"

That got Grin's attention and his tone changed at once. "Look here, let's just think a bit." Grin always found that activity a bit tasking, but this particular time he worked fairly quickly. "Let's, say we don't go telling the cap'n. . . . We can take care of this ourselves, can't we? Track 'em down and bring 'em back? If we miss 'em somehow, or if it turns out these aren't the ones we're after, the cap'n never needs to know we let 'em get by us in the first place" – Tred scowled at the use of *us* – "but if it's the right ones and we get 'em, the reward's all ours. No splitting it with the rest of the company and the cap'n won't care about nothing that happened in the night if we bring him what he wants before day's out." Studying the tracks, he said, "Could be more than just the two of 'em. Maybe three, I'd say, but no more. We'll need Fret and those beasts of his, but we don't need nobody else. Just the three of us on the three of them. We can do it and the reward's ours!" Under other

109

circumstances, the odds would not have seemed particularly good to Grin, who was remarkably cowardly for his mercenary line of work, but the assistance of his colleague Fret's fierce hunting animals would sufficiently boost what passed for his courage.

No one had ever accused Grin of possessing even an average wit, much less a remarkable one, and yet there were times when he showed a natural cunning well-suited to the situation before him. "We'll let the others start passing by first, see" — he referred to the company of Brenmarchers and Wastelanders already on the way — "then you, me, and Fret will drop off to the side and then out of sight once there's a break in the passing. Then off we go into these here woods. But we got to get rid of all this." He began to rub out the telltale tracks with his foot, then marked where they had left the road by stamping his great black boot on the spot and then breaking a fresh branch to throw on top of it. "We'll give the animals a good sniff right here, then pull 'em aside as if they're starting to wander a little and dragging us off with 'em."

"And why do we need to let Fret in on it?" asked his companion, whose brain had begun to work quickly at the mention of the reward. "I can get a couple of those devil beasts away from him for a few hours; I'll spin him a yarn and he'll be none the wiser. Then just you and me can do the job."

"That's it!" approved Grin. Looking north into the Lower Caverna woods, he added, "And as for *them* . . . Traveling by foot at night . . . they'll need their breaks. Even with a little delay, I 'll wager a week's pay we'll catch up to 'em and still get back to the cap'n before the sun's down. Mark my words!"

Beth easily could have slept twice as long, but she gratefully settled for the couple of hours she was given. When Aynyxia's cheerful voice woke her, her first thoughts were about how much better she felt than when she'd arrived; her second ones questioned her surroundings.

Alert and sitting upright, she looked around. Clearly, she was in an animal's den. She vaguely remembered having registered as much the night before. Or rather, earlier that day. "Where are we?"

"Sharana's home," Aynyxia answered. "Come see."

110

Beth stood up (at least, as far up as she could) and ducked her head to follow her friend out of the den, which had been formed in the large recess of a rocky wall.

Once outside, she did not see Sharana but immediately noticed Rendel sitting by a moribund fire, where he kept warm two tin mugs of water. To these, he was adding a dark powder from a small pouch.

"Good day, Beth," he said in a friendly way, swishing together the powder and water and offering her a mug.

It was a cool, pleasant morning – much nicer than the previous one, which seemed so long ago now. The storm that had threatened yesterday had never appeared and the light rain that had rolled over them in short spurts left behind an invigorating crispness. Beth took a deep breath before sipping the warming drink Rendel had passed her.

Aynyxia walked a little bit away from them, her attention caught by something in the bushes. She stretched out one of her stem-like arms and held it still until a small blue and white bird alighted on it; then she drew the bird toward her and stroked its feathers with a graceful gentleness Beth hadn't seen in her before.

Once again, a fascination with this strange world overtook Beth. There was so much she'd like to know, so much to experience and explore. . . . She wouldn't have believed it the night before, but she felt quite ready, and perhaps even anxious, to set off on their journey again. She still had to stop herself, though, from thinking too much about what would happen at the journey's end. What would be expected of her? Was there really any chance that she could give these people what they wanted? . . . And whether she could or not, would they be able to send her back home? If they'd brought her here, they could send her back, right? But Beth was sure that if she considered these questions in any depth, she'd start to panic.

So she didn't consider them . . . as far as she could help it.

"Good morning," Beth answered Rendel a little belatedly, smiling happily. "Thank you. This is good." She took another long drink before asking where Sharana was.

"Visiting with her young." There shouldn't have been anything surprising about this answer, given that Aynyxia had already said this was Sharana's home, but there was something odd

111

about the way Rendel spoke. Beth looked at him in a questioning way, which made him grin widely. And his eyes glittered.

He took a couple of good gulps from his mug, then set it down. He rose and said, "It is time for proper introductions. Will you come with me?" Instead of waiting for an answer, he took her hand in a quite natural way as he began to walk.

The familiarity of the gesture had an unexpected result: Beth missed her mother. She wanted to touch her hand, her face. Joy DeVere had been intentionally and fairly successfully banished from her daughter's conscious mind for close to forty-eight hours and her sudden reappearance there was unsettling. *Don't think about her. Just don't!* There was no point in missing her mother, Beth told herself matter-of-factly, because there was nothing she could do about it anyway. Not yet.

All in good time, she could almost hear her mother say. *All in good time.*

Fortunately, a distraction awaited Beth not many yards away, where she came to a sudden stop. Looking down a grassy incline before her, she saw two small cats and two larger black ones – some sort of panthers, by the look of them – who had been playfully wrestling but were now still, returning her stare.

Her grip must have tightened on Rendel's hand, for he looked at her and said at once, "I am sorry, Beth. I did not mean to frighten you. It is only Sharana and her family."

"No, it's all right. I—" And then, as his words sunk in and to be sure she'd understood him, Beth gave a second look around. Seeing no one else, she whispered, "So . . . what you're saying is . . . Sharana is one of those cats?" That *seemed* to be what he was saying, but she didn't want to look like an idiot or anything. A person as a cat. Well, why not? Aynyxia was a plant, after all.

"Yes," Rendel answered her. "Come." She accompanied him down the slope into the beginnings of a small, pretty meadow. "You know Sharana Tey," he said, indicating the nearer of the large cats, "and this is her mate, Restann Feyn." He indicated the other. To the cats he said, "And this is Elizabeth DeVere, known to us as Beth, of Fair Spring Town Ship from a land beyond."

"Hello," Beth said. Neither cat responded. At least, there was no response that she could recognize, though each met her gaze. She understood then the strangeness in Sharana's eyes that she'd been too tired to think through earlier. They were a cat's eyes

112

– and the only thing about Sharana that was the same in either form she took.

"And these," Rendel continued, kneeling down and beginning to stroke and scratch the smaller cats that had run forward to the visitors, "are Rassann and Rashara." This time Beth said nothing, but after a brief hesitation she squatted down to pet the two kittens. Immediately, the adult cat called Restann tensed, but after an imperceptible (to Beth) signal from Sharana, who did not object, he relaxed somewhat.

"They're so cute," Beth said, as she scratched one of the soft little animals under its jawline. There was no further conversation (if one discounts what Beth said to the kittens) until a few minutes later when Rendel said to the adult cats, "We will leave you for a while." When he stood up, Beth did too, but when one of the kittens rubbed against her leg, she bent back down to pet it again.

"Good-bye," she told it, when she was ready to follow Rendel away.

"I *am* sorry, Beth," her companion said at once, though she didn't immediately understand why. "I had thought to surprise you with the unusual nature of the Caverna cats, but it was ill-considered. I am too ignorant of your world to assume what surprises will be welcome ones. I did not mean to frighten you."

"No, it's all right, really. It was definitely a surprise, but an interesting one. *Very* interesting. And I *am* –" she searched for the right word— "interested," she finished feebly, then hurried on to make up for it. "So, Sharana can change into a cat whenever she wants, is that it? Can all of them?" She tried to picture the kittens as young children.

By this point, they had returned to their starting point, where they had left their mugs. As they continued the conversation, Rendel prepared a simple meal and Aynyxia joined them while they sat and ate and talked.

"Sharana does not 'change into a cat'. It is more fitting to say that she *is* a cat, whose gift it is to be able to take on human form at will. She never ceases to be a cat. As to the others of her kind, it is only given to the females to change. The kitten Rashara will be able to, though she has not learned to yet."

"There's nothing like that in our world," Beth said, biting into a juicy yellow fruit. When she had swallowed, she asked, "Are there others that can change like that?"

"Into human form, do you mean? It is said that there were quite a few, long ago, but I know of none in our land, save the Caverna cats and the white wolves of the north – the wolves of Lupriark." He looked to Aynyxia. "Do you know of others?"

"No, not now," she answered, her mouth half full of some dirty, gritty substance Rendel had given her. She seemed to enjoy it, but there was just no way Beth would have put any of it in her own mouth!

The three continued to talk for several more minutes. When they had finished eating, Beth said with feeling, "Your world is so different than mine!"

With an equal depth of feeling, Rendel said, leaning toward her, "I should very much like to hear –" He stopped because Sharana, once again in human form, arrived. She was dressed in the same plain black outfit as before. Beth was curious about how that part of the changing took place (the being dressed part) but wondered if it was something she shouldn't ask.

Businesslike as usual, Sharana announced, "It is time."

"It's time," said Grin to Tred, watching the backs of the mixed company of travelers moving down the road ahead of them – Wastelanders and Brenmarchers, mostly, heading for Greyvic. Some of the latter were innocents, on their way to the festival merely to hawk their wares and see the sights. As to the former, their motives were much different. They were supporters of the Torks and hoped that the festival of Greyvic would mark a great change for Gwilldonum. . . a land they had long held in contempt.

"They're so slow! . . . We'll catch back up with 'em afore they even notice us being gone." He spoke with more confidence than he felt. Waiting for the large company of travelers to get on its way had caused more of a delay than either Grin or Tred had anticipated. Maybe they'd let their prey get too much of a head start. Nevertheless, Grin said aloud, "We're all right. It's too late to tell the cap'n now anyway, but we'll get the ones we're looking for . . . and then I'll slit one throat, you slit another, and we'll toss for the third." He seemed to have forgotten the possibility that the party might not even be the one they wanted in the first place.

114

"We get a bigger reward if we bring the right one back alive."

"Aye," Grin answered uncertainly, "but that'd be a might more dangerous. I say we take care of all three and be done with it."

"There may have been a fourth," said Tred, leaving aside the question of slit throats for the moment.

"I only seen three," countered Grin, who was no expert tracker, "because there *was* only three. Maybe even just the two. And anyways, we got these four little beasties," he went on, indicating the animals they held on leashes, "and they could take on two apiece with their eyes closed and all their little feets tied together, so why should we care if there's four, or even five." Then, to show off his mathematical abilities, he added proudly, "Or more'n six. Two apiece for each critter would be more'n *six*."

"Are we going to stay here jabbering for the rest of the day? Give 'em the scent and let's get moving." Even Tred, whose standards were quite low, sometimes grew tired of Grin's stupidity.

CHAPTER NINE – Pursuit

When they were about to set out, Rendel pulled a spare hat from his knapsack to replace the one Beth had lost the day before. "I packed this for you last night. You ought wear it, now that it is day." Settling it onto her head, she realized that it was nearly identical to his.

She smiled at him broadly before beginning to follow behind Aynyxia, asking over her shoulder as she went ahead, "Do I look like a woodlander now?"

"No, you do *not*," he laughed, coming alongside.

"Oh. . . . Well, from a distance, then." Of course, her jeans were machine-stitched, but you had to be close up to notice and her too-long Gwilldonian jacket covered a good bit of them anyway. Her boots (obtained from the Gribbs) wouldn't give her away as an outsider. Her hair was certainly not curly like Rendel's, but she had noticed more than one woodlander girl whose hair was straighter, like hers.

"From a distance, perhaps," he conceded, "though your bow betrays you, if nothing else."

"My bow?" she answered, surprised. "Woodlanders don't use bows?"

"No" was his first answer, but then he amended it. "I suppose it depends on what you signify by 'use'. I have a childhood friend (who is also by good fortune a cousin of mine), and I confess that the two of us have found a good deal of pleasure in cultivating the archer's skill." Speaking as if of a great secret, he added, "We even compete between ourselves from time to time. . . . But we are oddities among our kind in that respect. And in other respects, perhaps." He grinned at Beth widely and his eyes twinkled.

"But woodlanders don't usually use bows and arrows for hunting? Or for fighting?"

116

"No, not for those things. Not ever."

After a moment, Beth said, "I suppose you use traps, then?" She thought of the trap into which she'd tumbled on her way to Greenwood.

"Traps? For animals? No, there is seldom cause. In general, they come to us of their accord when there is need."

She was about to say that she was talking about trapping animals for food, when she realized that she had seen no meats set out on the long table the night before you.

"Do woodlanders eat meat?" she asked thoughtfully.

"No."

"And . . . you don't use bows and arrows to fight? You don't ever use them as weapons?"

"No. We have no weapons."

"You're carrying a knife," she pointed out.

"There are other uses for a knife besides as a weapon. We do not fight."

"At all? Ever?" But it seemed such a dangerous sort of a world to live in.

"It is not our way."

Beth was quiet and Rendel did not interrupt her thoughts.

Eventually, she fell into conversation with Aynyxia, and he with Sharana, but after a while, they ended up side by side again and Beth asked, "Are you worried about Greenwood? It seems like there's a lot of trouble around. And that group of Wastelanders and whatever – the ones we've been trying to avoid – wouldn't they be passing close by Greenwood by now? They're going down that road, right?" She'd been thinking about the fact that woodlanders didn't fight and that had led her to consider the Amish that lived not far from her home. She'd heard stories about people picking on them or hurting them for fun, because they knew that Amish people wouldn't fight back. "Will your friends be OK?"

Her concern touched Rendel, but he said confidently, "Greenwood is well protected."

Beth wondered how well protected Greenwood could be, if woodlanders never fought. "Are there sentries or something?"

"We do sometimes learn through the behavior of wood creatures when there are visitors to our home . . . . But perhaps that is not the sort of sentry you envisioned." He smiled.

117

"No," Beth answered, thoughtful. "Do the animals protect you?"

"At times, I suppose. And we them. We understand each other's ways and live together quite harmoniously."

"All right," she said, after a pause. "I give up. If woodlanders don't fight and the animals aren't much help, then how *are* you protected?"

Rendel laughed. "In a variety of ways. Our greatest gift, I credit, is to understand the ways of creatures around us, and that makes peaceful relations easier to achieve. But also, we have learned, through many generations, ways that might calm an anxious or angry spirit."

"Like when you played your flute to make that weasel go to sleep."

"Precisely. There is a magic in music, and though we may never learn to master it, we have at least learned to wield it to good effect on many an occasion. . . . And then, too, we have another gift." He smiled and Beth waited. "We run fast. In fact, we run away, we climb, we swim, and we hide exceedingly well."

"But . . . you seem very brave to me," she told him a little shyly.

"Thank you," he answered seriously. "I hope that I am. But do you not agree that there are times when it is prudent to flee danger – at great speed, if necessary?"

"Yes, I do. Of course."

"So we flee (rather well, as I have said) when it seems prudent . . . and we face danger as squarely as we are able when that seems to us the better course. . . . But you had in mind, I credit, a greater sort of conflict. You wish to know, perhaps," he suggested gravely, "what we will do if war breaks out with the Torks, as it may?"

"Yes."

He considered. "In the past – and I trust that it yet holds true – Gwilldonians of surrounding regions have stood together as our physical protectors – not only because of whatever goodness and honor is in them, but because they value and respect our ways and because . . . we and they are all parts of a whole. Each of us would become something different, something less, without the other." He stopped speaking and Beth could tell he was searching

118

for a better way to explain. She thought she understood, though, and said as much.

After a moment or two, Rendel continued, "Greenwood is also protected in other ways. Our ancestors provided for us well."

Beth found the comment intriguing, but Rendel seemed disinclined to continue, and the conversation was interrupted in any event because the party had reached a shallow but swiftly-flowing stream.

"We will stop here," Sharana announced, "briefly."

They filled their water containers and Aynyxia began to soak.

Beth realized then that she had to go to the bathroom – or "to the woods," as the case happened to be. (That was something they didn't always tell you in stories – even in the greatest adventures, sometimes you've just got to go!) When she returned a few minutes later, Sharana was nowhere to be seen. Beth assumed that she had slipped away for reasons similar to her own, but after Rendel offered her a biscuit and some fruit, he told her, "Sharana has gone in search of a meal."

It crossed her mind fleetingly to wonder why Sharana wasn't eating with them, but she immediately realized that biscuits might not appeal much to a cat. No doubt she had gone off to find something more to her liking, something . . . alive! And raw! *Ick!*

Beth's reaction apparently showed on her face, because Rendel said, "This is distasteful to you?"

"Well . . . yes, I guess. Is it to you? I mean, *you* don't catch living things and eat them." Not that Beth objected to eating meat; she especially liked chicken (though the DeVeres never ate ones they had raised themselves). Still . . .

Rendel shrugged. "It is her way. It must be thus or she could not survive."

Beth understood that, but nonetheless found the image of Sharana ripping into some little animal to be unappetizing – not so unappetizing that she refused the biscuit and fruit, however. She never knew these days what or when her next meal would be.

While eating, she sat leaning against a tree, though she was afraid that after sitting down she wouldn't want to get up again. She understood that the break was to be a very short one because they were nearing the river docks where they hoped to meet up with Mirella of Saar (whose name Aynyxia had first told her yesterday . . . or forever ago . . . whichever).

Rendel moved to sit near Aynyxia, who was soaking in the stream, but he turned toward Beth and addressed her. "You asked before if I worry about Greenwood," he began. "I do. The Torks would bring despair to all Gwilldonum, but there are some ways of life that might not survive their rule at all, even if it is a short reign (and I dare not fathom a long one!). Myrmidon Tork would despise the ways of my kind, and I cannot be confident that we could long withstand his wrath, once he credits himself secure on the throne. That is one reason, Beth, why it is so important that you complete your task here."

Food stuck in her throat for a second, but once she'd swallowed it, she asked desperately, "But what if I can't? What if I can't help at all?" Out of the corner of her eye, Beth noticed that Sharana, in human form, had silently rejoined them. She didn't want to talk about this in front of the cat-woman, but her anxiety prevailed. "Really, Rendel, I don't even know what I'm supposed to do!"

It was Aynyxia who answered. She had her eyes closed and her head was leaned back, her face caught by a ray of sunlight that pierced its way through the trees. "Told you," she said in her simple way, "you *will* know, when it's time."

"This is wisdom," Rendel agreed. "I confess, Beth, that I had expected some sort of warrior to appear as champion." These words seemed to confirm what Beth had told herself repeatedly – this whole thing was a mistake! Even Rendel, who'd been so kind and supportive, must have been disappointed when he'd realized who she was. She felt embarrassed by the fact, as if that had been her fault, but Rendel was continuing. "It was ill-considered of me. Even in these days, when our numbers are lessened and our strength is not what it was, we yet have great warriors left to us in Gwilldonum. You bring us something other than a soldier's hand. I cannot tell what it is, but be assured that you need not seek it. It is in you already. Let your mind be at peace on this."

Beth knew that Sharana had been following the conversation. She glanced at the dark face and expected to find something like disdain there. But what she saw seemed to be thoughtfulness.

Beth was right in supposing that the cat too had expected a great warrior and had not seen why her time and efforts should be given to an unremarkable child. But though Sharana was proud, even vain, she was yet capable of admitting error. To herself, at least. Rendel's words had given her pause to reconsider.

Still, there was nothing new in her tone when she announced yet again, "It is time," and they recommenced the journey.

That leg of the trip was not long. The stream by which they had stopped was a tributary of the Lower Dayrn River, where they were headed. Beth knew by now that they hoped to voyage upstream with Mirella on some sort of cargo vessel – not a large one, she gathered – and to lose themselves among the many travelers on their way to the Festival of Errastisye in Greyvic. Their own party would leave the river well before Greyvic and would journey a short way east to Arystar's Green.

When they had traveled for only twenty minutes or so after their break, Sharana indicated that the others should wait while she went ahead to the docks. If all there was as it should be, she hoped to return for them within the hour.

"So, we must be really close," Beth thought with relief, "if she can get there, check on things, and get back so quickly. Although I suppose she can travel a lot faster when she's a cat . . . and without someone like me to slow her down." A boat ride would be very nice after so much walking! Of course, if they were going upstream on a small boat, she would probably have to take a turn at rowing or something. That could be tough. Oh, well! At least she'd be able to take off her boots and rest her tired legs and sore feet.

She wondered how Sharana had made the arrangements for their boat trip in such a short time, but then remembered that the cat had been an escort too – she must have had others watching for her along the way just as the Gribbs and Rendel had been watching for Aynyxia. This Mirella of Saar must be one of them and Sharana must have planned to travel by river if she ended up being the one to find the champion.

As Beth, Aynyxia, and Rendel set down their things and did their best to get comfortable, Beth looked around. The landscape had changed. They were in an area of greatly uneven terrain webbed with creeks and gullies and the jagged lines of earth that cut down to meet them. The trees had shortened and thinned out, affording enough sunlight to nurture a diversity of shrubs. Thickets and dark brambles were all about, but so were colorful flowers. ("Weeds, I suppose," thought Beth, "but such pretty ones.")

It was a pleasant enough spot to wait and rest a bit. They had seen no sign of danger since crossing the Great Road in the early hours of the morning. They had scarcely seen any creatures at all, except the wildlife. "So we can just relax for a while," thought Beth gratefully.

"Got it!" said Grin triumphantly, and he actually did grin for a change. "Look at 'em!" He pointed to the animals that he and Tred had successfully separated from Fret. "The scent must best be a strong one!" The ugly beasts snorted and growled and strained their leashes. "We'll have 'em now! You take any other ones you want," he told Tred, "but the walkabout's mine. Think its blood will come out green?" His wide grin revealed missing and half-rotted teeth. To the anxious beasts attempting to drag him forward he said, "All right, now, you know what to do," and he released them.

"Do you eat meat?" Beth asked Aynyxia, curiously. They'd been waiting for some time and hoped to see Sharana any minute. The quiet, so welcome at first, had begun to weigh on Beth, so she'd decided to break it by raising the next topic that crossed her mind.

"Meat? Well, guess I do. Flies have meat. And I like some other little things too, but it's flies I like best if I'm eating something alive. Don't do it around your kind, though." *Good*, thought Beth, almost sorry she'd asked. It was not an appealing image.

"And you?" Rendel inquired.

She might have felt awkward admitting to him that she did, if he hadn't accepted Sharana's habits so easily. As it was, she said simply, "Yes. But not much red meat." This puzzled both her listeners, who wondered about the variety of colors from which Beth could choose. "I mean, I like chicken best." This puzzled them further, and Rendel surprised Beth by asking what chicken was.

"Ch'kn, ch'kn," Aynyxia repeated; then she laug' distinctive, inhaling laugh and concluded, "Funny word. C

Beth laughed too, then explained. "Chickens are mean, birds; poultry, that is; they don't fly. Well, not really, have wings and feathers. They can sort of—" She used her hands to show an unsuccessful attempt at flight. "We have some at home, but we don't eat them. Not our own, I mean, but we eat their eggs."

"Ah, feathered and egg-laying," Rendel said, "but not birds of flight. . . . Or rather, birds of little flight?" He imitated Beth's gestures of a moment before but managed to look more dignified than she had. "It may be that we know the same creature under a different name. Perhaps," he added, "if you come to us again, you might bring one. You breed them?"

Taken aback by this casual reference to coming again, as if they were neighbors who might drop in on one another at will, she didn't answer at first. Then, before she could, something happened.

In the briefest instant, the atmosphere changed dramatically. Rendel straightened, alert, holding his hand up as if to keep the other two silent. Aynyxia, who had also come to attention, watched him closely.

The woodlander strained as if to hear a distant sound or isolate a particular smell. Then he had it. "*Devil boar!*" Immediately he and Aynyxia grabbed their things. "More than one. Come!" As he spoke and rose, he pulled Beth, somewhat roughly, up with him. She had already started to snatch at her things as soon as the other two had, and now she began to run when they did. In the hurry, she left her cup behind and a length of rope fell out of her open pack, but she knew better than to stop for either. She didn't even take the time, at first, to sling her quiver across her back properly and she held her bow awkwardly in her hand, but she couldn't run well that way since she kept bumping or catching at things as she went. When she stopped to reposition them and catch her breath, it took her only seven seconds before she was off and running again.

There was no clear path, and the three friends rushed ahead any way they could in the general direction that Sharana had gone. At first, the noise of their own movements kept Beth from hearing any sounds of pursuit from behind. Then she did hear, but she didn't look back and only hoped that devil boar were more boar than devil. That would be bad enough!

123

She ran as hard as she could, but she knew she was keeping the others back. She sensed that the pursuers were gaining on them. Then Rendel yelled "Go!" and motioned her off in one direction while he veered in another. She turned to look after him, but Aynyxia grabbed at her and said, "Here," pulling her arm and then pushing their way through an opening in a massive thicket. They made it through to the other side, though in the process a pair of thorns scratched marks onto Beth's left hand and ripped at the sleeve of her jacket.

When Aynyxia paused to look around, Beth turned back too and, through the branches of the thicket, caught sight of Rendel. He was now standing still, face toward the pursuers. Hands lifted to his mouth, he was making some sort of animal call.

Aynyxia moved in close beside Beth and they both saw two of the animals that had been chasing them appear. They seemed small for boar, but growled as fiercely as big, angry bears. And they were running. As their distance from her shortened, Beth could see that the animals' teeth were bared and ready for attack, even as they raced.

Rendel remained still. Why didn't he run? They were almost on him.

Then he did run. Very fast, as he'd said he could. The two beasts, soon followed by a third, went after him and directly away from Beth and Aynyxia. Then a stocky two-legged creature came along, moving quickly despite his size and calling gruffly after the devil boar, "Not him, not him, you blasted things!" Was *that* a haggitt? Beth's view was brief and obstructed, but she saw that, although it roughly resembled a human, its face looked half animal – not so different from a boar's, in fact, if you shrunk its teeth and flattened its snout. Though its body was more like a human's, the creature reminded her of those she'd seen outside the Kritt Pass.

Despite concern for Rendel, Beth felt some of the tension escape her body as the haggitt (for such it was) turned its back on her, rushing after the three beasts, trying to call them back. Supposing that she and Aynyxia were safe for the moment and trusting that Rendel could in fact run, climb, and hide as well as he'd said he could, she had time for one sigh of relief before Aynyxia turned her sideways and, pointing, whispered softly, "Straight that way. Run to the docks. Don't look back."

Run away alone? *Again?*

Before she could ask if they shouldn't just wait where they were for Sharana, not to mention Rendel, Beth heard unwelcome sounds and looked back through the thicket. There was a fourth devil boar, more diligent and less easily distracted than the other three, slowly making its way forward. Low grunts punctuated snuffling noises as it picked out its trail. Worse, though, were the sounds of a gruff voice and heavy, booted feet coming up behind it. Another haggitt. She could see it and in a minute it was bound to see her too: the boar was nosing its way in her direction.

"Run straight. Don't look back," repeated Aynyxia, so close that her breath tickled Beth's ear. "Go!"

No debates this time. Beth did go – quietly at first, so that she wouldn't rustle the branches of the thicket; then she ran, forward and uphill. She hadn't gone far when, alarmed by what she heard behind her, she darted behind a wide tree and did look back.

She saw the lone boar charging at Aynyxia; it was *her* scent it had been following and when the wind changed it had caught a strong whiff and made for the walkabout in a rush.

Aynyxia had hoped to lead it away from Beth's path, but she'd barely moved when the boar raced through the thicket where she and Beth had hidden. She was turning to face it, dagger drawn, when it lunged powerfully, nearly leaping from the ground and taking her a full second before she was ready. She was on the ground at once, struggling with the snarling beast atop her. The haggitt was trying to cut his way through the thicket by then (he was much larger than Aynyxia and Beth), egging the animal on as he made his way. "That's right! Rip her up! But leave that little green neck for me!"

At that point, several things happened in quick succession. Aynyxia's dagger found its mark and the devil boar squealed in pain. She stabbed anew and the creature twisted in a frenzy before running off erratically, trailing blood behind and making horrible noises. The haggitt swore in anger and surprise and ran at Aynyxia, still laid flat on the ground, but a familiar sound stopped him and he turned toward it.

Beth, for her part, had not remained hidden and motionless. On seeing her friend knocked down, her first impulse was to rush back toward her. Her second was better.

When Rendel had first sensed the approaching devil boar and the three companions had begun to run, Beth had for an instant considered – as her bow and quiver bumped against this tree or that – simply dropping them, so that she could move faster unencumbered, but she realized almost simultaneously that the time for using her weapon might be almost on her, and from that moment she had tried to steel herself for it. When the boar jumped on Aynyxia, Beth wanted to run toward her, but she didn't. She knew she couldn't shoot at the beast for fear of hitting Aynyxia instead, but she knew also that the haggitt would be close behind. In a single sweeping movement, she had her arrow out and on the string.

Could she shoot it, though? She'd never aimed at any live target before, let alone a humanlike one. Then she saw the dagger in his hand and the delight in his face: he expected to enjoy hurting Aynyxia.

She let the arrow fly.

Her hands weren't steady enough: the arrow went amiss. All she'd done was to draw her target's attention. But Beth DeVere was her mother's daughter, and by the time the haggitt's eyes fixed on her, she had a second arrow ready. He saw it, but not in time.

It was a hit. She couldn't tell exactly where or how serious, but the creature stumbled and fell into a spiky bush, crying out as he did. Beth dropped her bow and both hands flew to her mouth as her stomach lurched. She thought she would be sick.

Quickly, she recovered (enough) and started to make for Aynyxia. Surely the haggitt's cry, if not the boar's squeal before it, would bring the others back! Besides, her arrow would likely only delay the haggitt, not stop him entirely, but she couldn't bear to follow it up with another.

As soon as she began to move, however, Aynyxia yelled urgently, "*NO! Run!* Not me they want!" Beth turned to look beyond the thicket. Something was coming. From her raised viewpoint on the hillside, she could see a boar returning. Probably the others – and the second haggitt – would be close behind.

Think fast!

Aynyxia had pulled herself to a sitting position and braced her upper body against a tree. She clutched her dagger in front of her, but clearly the boar had wounded her. She wouldn't be able to put up much of a defense against three more of them at once. She wouldn't want Beth to come back for her, but Beth couldn't leave her to the mercy of those animals even if Aynyxia *was* willing to make that sacrifice for her.

Suddenly she knew what to do, turning and sprinting to the crest of the little hill. Just as the boar was nearing the thicket, she turned back. Out of the corner of her eye, she saw something else moving too – probably the other haggitt trying to catch up, but she didn't bother to make sure. She whistled. At least, she tried. Her mouth was dry and she didn't think much noise had come out.

Still, she caught the boar's attention; it changed directions, determinedly targeting Beth.

She took off. *Run,* she told herself, *run!* She realized too late that her bow was still behind her, lying where she'd dropped it. She hadn't meant to leave it, but at least she could run faster. *Run fast, just keep running! That's all that matters.* She still had her dagger (*run!*), plus the gift from Gribb (*faster!*) – the sword . . . *if* she could make the magic work.

She didn't look back. She tried to steer in the direction Aynyxia had indicated, clinging to the belief that the docks weren't far. There *had* to be someone there who could stop a wild boar! If only she could run fast enough. If only she could keep on course. *Just make it to the docks.*

Moving in a straight line was impossible. Beth wound her way through brambles and ditches, aware she was being pursued but still not looking back. (*Run!*) When she came to a shallow creek, she tried wading upstream, hoping to throw the boar off her scent, but that slowed her too much (slowed her enough that she noticed the pounding in her chest) and she knew almost at once that it was a waste of effort anyway – the boar's grunts were closing in. As she stepped out on the far side of the creek, she finally did look back, just long enough to glance the beast cresting the small rise of bank behind her. She stumbled up the bank on her own side, hoping against hope that the boar was afraid of water, too afraid to cross. Not that she was going to wait around to find out! She stumbled a second time at the top of the bank, then recovered and caught her breath.

Something was different. She inhaled again, more deeply. The air held the smell of a river. She knew it. She didn't know *how* she could be so sure, but she *was* sure. The docks were near. She thought she even heard voices in the distance, though she couldn't pin down the direction. Time to move. *Run to the docks. Run to the river. Almost there.*

The boar, scarcely slowed by the creek itself, had more trouble than Beth making its way up the neighboring bank. The delay bought her an extra minute or so, but it wasn't enough. The boar was running hard and made up the time quickly. Beth knew the moment to turn and face her pursuer was almost on her.

When she reached a deep ditch that cut long in front of her, she knew there was no time to go around it before the boar could reach her. She hesitated to go straight down into the ditch, particularly since the remains of an old fence separated her from it. (The fence was too low and too decrepit to provide any real barrier, but its incongruency in that otherwise-untamed wood struck her as some sort of warning.) Besides, she was simply too tired to keep running. She did the only other thing she could. She turned to face the beast. She caught her breath while standing her ground and waiting for it.

Watching it run toward her, she knew what she had to do. There was no choice, really. She had no bow and didn't want to take a chance with the short dagger, which wouldn't be useful until the boar was practically on top of her. It was all or nothing now. She knew those teeth would rip right into her if she didn't defend herself.

She fumbled for the hilt of Gribb's magic sword, wondered if she could withdraw the weapon in time, saw the boar's black eyes, felt suddenly weak, and pulled hard just as the thought that "this will never work" shot through her mind.

She pulled out the *dagger*, not the sword. Her heart sank.

Still . . . it was pointy! It would pierce the boar's hide if she could force herself to strike hard enough at just the right moment, but her failure with the weapon increased her panic. She reflexively backed away from the charging animal and tripped over the low fence. She dropped her dagger to free her hand to catch herself, but she couldn't keep from tumbling down into the ditch. Her fall was cushioned by a great tangle of thick vines waiting for her at the bottom. Immediately she tried to pull herself up and scramble to the opposite slope, which was not as steep as the one down which she had fallen, but as soon as she tried to get up, something grabbed at her right hand (she gave a little scream) and then at her legs and soon she'd been pulled all the way flat to the ground again. What—?

The vines! The vines were moving, all on their own! They were trying to hold her down. And doing a pretty good job of it! She'd have to cut herself free.

Her dagger! After she'd let if fall from her hand, it had slid down partway after her. She could see it, but it was well out of reach. The "regular" dagger was still at her side and she tried to get to it, but the vines cruelly worked against her, as if they understood her intent. She struggled for a moment, unsuccessfully, before it occurred to her to look for the devil boar.

There it was, above her, watching and pacing, but not following. Soon, it turned and disappeared from view. She hoped, with no real confidence, that it had given up on her.

But it hadn't.

It was searching for a better way down to her and soon found it. Now it was winding its way unhurried, understanding that its prey could not run.

Beth strained her neck, holding her head as far up as she could, both to keep it free of the vines, if possible, and to keep her eyes on the boar. She didn't look up to the spot from which she'd fallen, but she could hear someone approaching from that direction. She wished she could believe it was Aynyxia or Rendel or Sharana or even some stranger coming to help, but she just couldn't (and she was about to be proved right).

Her eyes stayed focused on the boar. This was it. With a burst of energy, her whole body struggled hard to free itself, but to no avail. She couldn't get loose. The beast was approaching, salivating, baring its teeth, gurgling in triumphant anticipation.

There seemed no hope.

CHAPTER TEN – A Friend in Need

The White Queen from inside Alice's renowned looking glass may have found little difficulty in believing six impossible things before breakfast, but for Beth, believing two before supper was quite enough.

First, *impossibly,* the boar fell.

Beth knew that before she took in the cause. Then, an instant after realizing that a black arrow had mortally wounded the now-squealing-and-convulsing animal, she heard the most impossible words: "Nailed it!" followed by an uncharacteristically weak, "Whoo-hoo!"

But it couldn't be.

It sounded like him, but not exactly like him. And it couldn't be.

Yet there he was.

Unless she was imagining things.

But she was looking right at him: Luke McKinnon, her very best friend in the world (in both worlds!), looking down at her from the very spot where she'd tripped and fallen.

He was breathing heavily, as if he'd been running hard (which he had) and didn't want to take another step (which he wasn't anxious to do). With effort, he smiled down at her, but at the same time his eyes darted about, alert for signs of danger . . . and he already had, Beth noticed, a second arrow on his string.

He found nothing new to alarm him, but he sent his second arrow flying anyway; he thought he might hurry the boar out of its misery that way. He'd never shot a living thing before.

That done, he blocked the animal from his mind and turned to Beth. Beginning to catch his breath, he smiled a bit more naturally and began to move carefully down the slope toward her, half climbing, half sliding. As he got close, he panted, "So, hey . . .

Beth . . . how you doin'? . . . Wouldn't be anything, I don't know, *new* going on in your life . . . would there?"

How could he do it? How could he possibly joke at a time like this? But when the initial shock of seeing him had passed, Beth realized that Luke was actually quite upset. His voice was shaky, his grip on his bow was fierce, though he seemed unaware of the fact, and his eyes were full of worry as they moved back and forth between her and their surroundings. Before he came within reach of the tangled vines, he stopped and said breathily, "So, like, I'm here to rescue you and all that. You need anything?"

"Think you could cut me out of this stuff?" she asked gratefully. "And . . . I'm kind of glad to see you."

"*Kind of?*" He laughed weakly. "*Kind of?* Well, aren't you the funny one under pressure!" While saying this, he wasn't looking directly at Beth. He was trying to figure out how to cut the vines nearest to her without getting himself caught too. "I take it this is a kind of girl-eating plant or something," he said, while setting his bow, quiver, and pack on the ground and looking around for something better suited to his task.

He found a long, sturdy branch and stuck it down hard into a web of vines close to Beth. Then he braced himself with one foot on a large rock, using the branch for support while he leaned forward as far as he could to cut Beth's legs free. As he did, he muttered, "Glad to see you, too . . . but let's not get all weepy about it or anything." He added the last comment after noticing in surprise that his own eyes had gotten moist.

"If you could get my hand free, I could start cutting too," Beth suggested.

"Give me a minute. I'm doing the best I can here," Luke answered, trying to keep his balance while grasping the heavy branch with a single hand.

"It's just, there might be oth- *Look out!*" she cried suddenly; she tried to point behind him, but her arm couldn't move that far.

Pushing back, he spun around and let go of the branch, which struck Beth's right arm and just missed hitting her head as well. When Luke saw the haggitt approaching from above, he scrambled for his bow and arrow.

Tred, for he it was, jumped behind a tree, knowing that at a distance his dagger, no matter how sharp, was no match for a well-

131

placed arrow – and he'd already glimpsed what had happened to the boar.

Tred was clever, as his kind go, and guessed quickly that the boy hadn't been with the party that had left tracks on the Great Road during the night, so it was probably the *girl* that everyone wanted. She was the one that would fetch him that reward, dead or alive . . . and there she was practically tied up like a little package for him. What he had to do was keep that boy from freeing her.

He grabbed a fist-sized rock and threw it at Luke. Then he threw another. Luke dodged them both, though the second one brushed his arm. He didn't realize that the rocks were not particularly intended to hit him; they were intended to move him away from Beth, which is just what the third rock did when Luke lurched sideways toward the shelter of a thick bramble.

Now, a few rocks in rapid succession would take care of the girl, Tred judged. Only her legs had been freed and she was struggling to keep them so. Her upper body and her fragile little head would be easy targets. He grabbed the heaviest rock within reach and, targeting Beth's face, began to pull it back to put his full force into the throw . . . but he never let it fly. He was arrested mid-motion by ferocious snarling that grew louder even in the instant it took him to identify its source.

Luke heard it too. Some angry wild beast rushing toward them from the far side of the ditch. He turned just in time to see a black wildcat leaping in his direction.

Everything happened fast. Luke had nearly readied his arrow for the haggitt, but by the time he could aim at the cat instead, he hesitated to shoot. The animal itself seemed to have targeted the haggitt, a fact that Tred realized a good two seconds before Luke; he'd already begun to flee, though without much hope. With a swiftness Luke found incredible, the cat had run down into the ditch, leapt clear over the tangle of vines and then disappeared up the other side again. Tred's headstart wouldn't save him.

Returning to Beth at once, Luke told her, "Well, that was lucky, at least, but let's get out of here before that big cat comes back our way or before anybody else tries to kill you!" As he spoke, he cut at the vines so furiously that Beth was a little worried he'd get her by mistake.

"OK," she answered nervously, all the while trying to pull away from the vines. "But that wasn't luck. I mean, it was, but not *just* luck. The cat, I mean. She's with us." He stopped and stared but only for a second – questions would have to wait.

He'd just gotten Beth free and pulled her away from the mutilated vines when they both heard voices. They froze, except to look at one another and exchange worried glances.

Then, wonderfully, Beth smiled and let out a loud sigh of relief. She'd recognized one of the voices and now it was calling her name.

"Down here!" she called back, almost crying from happiness. "Aynyxia, we're here!"

In just a moment, she saw *two* familiar faces looking down at them. "*Mr. Gribb!*" Beth exclaimed before turning speechless. This was too much!

"Aye," he answered, beaming. "Marcus Gribb, at your service. Brought you your friend, I did," he added, indicating Luke. Turning then to Aynyxia, who had one arm supported by a sling hastily crafted out of Gribb's jacket, he said, "You make your way 'round to the other side. I'll go down to the young ones."

Descending into the ditch in a wobbly fashion (but still somehow more gracefully than either Beth or Luke had done), Marcus was with them at once. When he stopped to pick up the weapon she'd dropped earlier, Beth dropped her eyes in embarrassment. He had entrusted her with his secret treasure, and not only had she been unable to wield its power, but she had let it slip right out of her possession. She picked up her pack where it had landed. Then Mr. Gribb was beside her.

"I believe this is yours," he said, handing over her bow; she hadn't realized he'd been carrying it. "And also this," he said in a quieter voice, covertly returning the magic weapon.

She took them both, but couldn't say anything, not even to thank him.

Fortunately, he spoke immediately. "Up we go, and on to the river, as I understand it." Though Beth's head was whirling with questions, she said nothing, preferring to put her energy into getting away from that place. She avoided looking at the boar, which had by then taken its last breath.

They climbed out of the ditch as quickly as they could. When they reached the top, Aynyxia joined them. The first boar had scratched her up and left a bad gash in her arm, but she was otherwise unharmed and greeted Beth with her typical, cheerful expression. Beth smiled back, then immediately said, "Oh!" because Sharana, now in human form, was approaching.

"The woodlander?" she asked as soon as she was near enough.

"Tried to draw off the haggitts and devil boar," Aynyxia answered. "Mornsun," she added with a jerk of the head meant to show the general direction.

Luke didn't know what thaggitts and mornsun meant ("devil boar" pretty much spoke for itself), but it all seemed clear enough to Beth, who said anxiously to Sharana, "You didn't see him?" and then to no one in particular, "Do you think he'll meet us at the docks?"

"No doubt," Gribb said in answer to the latter question, though his answer would have been the same no matter how many doubts he'd had. "Best to go on in any event."

"We are agreed," Sharana announced without waiting to be sure her statement was true. With barely a glance at Luke, she uttered a predictable, "We must hurry," and set off toward the north. Aynyxia followed at once, but Beth turned to look back first, hoping for a glimpse of Rendel coming toward them. Gribb watched her. When he caught her eye, he wordlessly jerked his head forward and he, Beth and Luke all began to move quickly after the others.

Beth could still barely believe that Luke was right there with her. Most of what she wanted to say to him would have to wait for a calmer (and more private) moment, but she couldn't resist whispering to him as soon as she had the chance, "*That's* the cat we saw before. Her name's Sharana."

Luke turned a "You're kidding!" face toward her and then said, "Just what have you gotten yourself into, Ms. Elizabeth DeVere?" But clearly, he was impressed! After a pause, he added, looking ahead at Aynyxia and Marcus, who had caught up to her, "You know, Gribb and I are practically best buddies now, but what is that thing next to him? Looks like it ought to be planted somewhere in your back field."

"Quiet!" said Beth, though he'd already been speaking quietly. "She's a friend of mine."

"Curiouser and curiouser," he muttered, making his eyes wide and shaking his head. He still hadn't quite calmed down and returned to his normal self . . . but he was getting there.

A minute later, he leaned in and said quietly, "So I get it that we're all going to a river and there are docks there. But the important thing is, do *you* know how to get us home from there? 'Cause I sure don't. It's one little part of this whole search-and-rescue thing I haven't quite got worked out."

"Oh, we can't go back," Beth answered.

"*Can't go back?* . . . She never told me-"

Just as Luke said, "She never told me," Beth said, "I mean not *yet*," so that while Luke repeated, "Not *yet?*" Beth was saying, "She? She who?"

They were interrupted then. Voices sounded from nearby and Sharana motioned her companions to take cover. They did and waited silently until a small party of travelers had passed safely beyond. There seemed nothing sinister in it, though, and Beth and her oddly-assorted escort were soon out and walking again.

This time, Luke ended up beside Sharana and soon attempted to engage her in conversation on a point that intrigued him. "So, Beth says you're a cat," he began. "*That* must be pretty weird." Under any other circumstances, Beth would have been dying to hear how the proud and reserved Sharana responded, but as it was she felt an urgent need to speak to Marcus while she could do so unheard.

"I'm so sorry, Mr. Gribb," she said quickly, sure that he would know what she had in mind.

"I saw what you did to that haggitt that was after your friend," he answered unexpectedly. "Didn't you tell me back at the cottage that you'd never shot a living thing before?" She nodded. "Well, that explains it. It's a might distressing thing – no shame in that! Can't be expected to have all your wits about you at such a time, you can't, and maybe not for a good while after. . . . You're still not quite yourself, I'd wager," he added, looking her over.

"But it came out as a *dagger*," she whispered sadly.

"Aye. But the next time you won't let your fear get in the way of your believing, you won't." That was all he intended to say on the matter, and if he had any misgivings about having returned the remarkable magic sword to her, no one ever knew it.

It was a fortunate thing for Beth and the others (though not so fortunate for the two haggitts involved) that Grin had suggested such a renegade approach when Tred first detected walkabout tracks on the Great Road. If the two had instead reported (as they were being paid to do) such an interesting finding to Captain Starkr of the Tork army, things might have turned out much differently. Starkr, who was traveling with the Brenmarcher and Wastelander company in the guise of a merchant, had an excellent grasp of Gwilldonian geography despite this being his first expedition into that country. Had he been informed that the party he sought had crossed the Great Road at night and was apparently headed north into the Lower Caverna Woods, the captain would have guessed at once that its destination was the Dayrn River and would have taken appropriate steps to have his quarry intercepted there.

As it was, he had not particularly expected the walkabout and her companion to cross his path at all; no doubt they were farther east . . . *if* in fact the walkabout creature had actually found the companion she had sought. When he had set out the haggitt guards along the Great Road the previous night, it had been as a precautionary measure only. The ambitious but practical captain had already resigned himself to the idea that some other company would seize the glory of capturing or killing the accursed champion of Gwilldonum, if such a one existed.

But there would be other chances for glory. Soon. War was brewing; he was sure of it. As a seasoned soldier, he could sense when a battle was nearing. And at this moment, he could practically smell it in the air.

"Who remains?" Lady Gweynleyn asked her attendant.

"Nearly all, though not for much longer, it seems," Mariza answered. "Only Cassian and his company have already departed for Greyvic" – she did not include Therin Mandek and his troops, for Gweynleyn had seen them off personally some hours before – "but most of the others break camp as we speak. With respect to Daasa, I cannot say. I have not yet seen her this day." (Being a faun, Daasa had passed her nights in the shelter of deeper forest, where she was most comfortable, rather than under cover of a tent on the Green.)

It was not long before the question of Daasa was settled. She appeared shortly before Gweynleyn and, as was her way, came at once to the point. "I wish to be gone to Greyvic, my lady, to keep my eyes on the Torks. I trust none of them and this Myrmidon least of all. However, if you command me to stay with you and await this champion, I will." Personally, she had little hope for a champion from afar but also saw little need for one: she was prepared to fight the Torks single-handedly, if necessary. Still, she knew how to take orders as well as to give them.

"It is not mine to command you, Daasa, as you know." This point had come up between them a number of times in the years of the council's rule.

"If you *request* it, then," the faun amended.

"Thank you, but I do not. And you are correct: the Torks are not to be trusted and must be guarded with a steadfast eye. I should be glad to know you in Greyvic and am half decided to go there myself."

The last statement surprised Daasa, but she said nothing, merely inclined her head, took a few steps backward, and then returned to her company to make as quick a departure as possible.

One after another, council members came and announced their departure. The lady herself had let it be known that her own company would depart as well, leaving only two or three attendants behind to await the remaining escorts, should they return.

This turnabout surprised many, but disturbed few; in fact, it relieved some council members of the misgivings they had felt concerning their own decisions to leave. All the members felt the urgency of the situation in Greyvic pressing upon them and found the passive state of waiting a difficult one to bear. That Gweynleyn should feel the same, however, was unexpected.

One council member's attendant, nonetheless, found the lady's decision simple enough to explain. "Come to her senses, that's all. Let these prophecies work *themselves* out, I say. Better for us to be in Greyvic, daggers drawn. . . . War's brewing and the lady knows it as well as the rest of us."

Like Captain Starkr, he could practically smell a battle in the air.

Through a large, rustic window in a one-room cabin, Beth peered down at the Dayrn River and the lively activity that spread along it. This view of Gwilldonian life differed from any she'd had so far – so many different types of people (if it was right to call them all "people") and so many different things going on at once. Both sides of the waterway boasted several small docks, but the hustle and bustle and the wider variety of persons were all along the opposite bank, which, Gribb informed Beth, had a quaint little trading town just beyond it. She should visit there someday, he suggested, if ever she got the chance.

Sharana had led the party straight to the cabin and there introduced them (briskly and without flourish, as was her way) to Mirella of Saar, a tall, angular woman with sun-darkened skin and a strong grip. Mirella greeted them in a businesslike but cordial way and invited them to make use of the supplies set out for them; then she left, promising as quick a return as she could manage.

In addition to supplies for their journey, Mirella provided fresh bread and warm vegetable stew for anyone who wanted it. The meal was simple but welcome, and all that kept Beth from enjoying it thoroughly was Aynyxia's freshly-bandaged arm (which bothered Beth more than it did her friend) and the fact that Rendel wasn't there to join them. Gribb tried again to reassure her, pointing out that the woodlander knew where they were headed and was probably just taking a little extra time to make sure he wasn't followed.

Time was still a pressing factor, and there was little opportunity for relaxed conversation among the travelers. Nonetheless, Beth's curiosity was satisfied on a couple of important points while they ate.

"How in the world did the two of you meet up?" she asked Luke and Gribb as soon as she had the chance.

The latter answered. "I was just getting close to home, I was, coming back from Greenwood, and what should I see but my Gert in a pony-cart with this lad right there with her. On their way to find you, they were, and Gert thought the woodlanders could advise her."

Beth looked at Luke questioningly, but he only said, between mouthfuls, "Long story." Since in general Luke had no objections to telling long stories (even when short ones would do), she supposed this was a story he didn't want to tell to the whole group. Either that, or he was really hungry . . . which was also a good possibility.

"And how did you find us in the woods?" Beth asked Gribb.

"Well," he answered, more loudly than necessary, "you had a cat with you, didn't you? And I hope I know how to track a *cat* in the woods!"

Sharana, clearly irritated by the remark, glared at him briefly before turning away. If she'd been in feline form, she'd have hissed.

"Besides," Gribb confided to Beth in a low voice that only she and Luke could hear, "when I got back to Greenwood, Ellena told me, she did, that she'd overheard Rendel talking to Sharana Tey in the night. 'Heading to the Lower Dayrn,' she said. 'Meeting someone at the docks,' she said. Bound to cut across that last stretch of wood eventually, weren't you?" Beth started to laugh, but Gribb hushed her. "Our secret," he said, tapping his nose, and she smiled and nodded. After a pause, he added, "Takes herself a bit too seriouslike, that Sharana does . . . . A good one, though."

When they had finished eating, Sharana said, "By good fortune, the day turns cold." Beth didn't see why this should be considered a good thing until hooded cloaks were passed around. The chill in the air, she realized, would give them sufficient reason to keep their hoods up without drawing undue attention. Beth's cloak was a comfortable brown one that fit her perfectly. Aynyxia chose a gray one that was too long for her, and Beth hoped she wouldn't end up tripping on it, awkward as she could be.

Once they had restocked their packs with the rations left for them, there seemed nothing left to do. When everything was ready but no one made a move to go, Luke said, "So, what now?"

"We wait," Sharana answered. "Mirella will come for us when it is time."

"But what about Rendel?" Beth asked with concern. "We'll need to wait for him." She was suddenly overcome by a wave of alarm on his behalf coupled with guilt that she'd sat calmly (more or less) enjoying her meal while not knowing his fate. Everyone else seemed confident that he could keep himself safe, but they couldn't *know* that he was all right, could they? What if . . . . "You didn't see any sign of him when you chased that haggitt?" Beth asked Sharana directly. "And there was more than one devil boar. Did you see any of the others?"

"I dealt with the haggitt and saw one boar, but it ran from me, of course, and I did not trouble to pursue it. I did not see the woodlander, and there was no time to search. *Nor is there now*," she added with emphasis. "We must—"

"The woodlander?" Beth interrupted. "The *woodlander?* He has a name, you know." She spoke quietly but with intensity. "And he's your friend. Rendel is your friend and he plays with your children. Maybe he's in danger. What do you mean 'there's no time'?" She glared at Sharana, waiting for a response. Luke, for his part, was amazed. This didn't seem like Beth at all.

"I mean that if he is not here when the boat is ready, *we will go without him*," Sharana answered firmly.

Go without him? Beth wasn't sure she wanted to. She turned to Luke, who gave her his best don't-look-at-me-I-just-got-here expression.

"*We must!*" There was a near growl in Sharana's voice. Then, yielding only a little, she sighed her frustration and said gruffly to Aynyxia and Gribb, "Explain to her."

Gribb spoke up at once. "Don't you worry, child. Our Rendel knows how to take care of himself in the woods, he does. None better. But I'll go back and find him, I will. I'll find him, dead or alive!" He seemed unaware of the widening of Beth's eyes and sharp intake of her breath at his last three words. "So, you go on with the others when it's time, just as he'd want."

Beth was grateful to Marcus, though only partly relieved. "And what about you?" she asked. "There are at least two devil boar out there, and there might have been more coming!" Then she added for good measure, "And who knows what other trouble there could be!"

"I've got my little ways of dealing with troubles, I do," he answered cryptically, tapping twice the side of his plump nose. "And besides, it's not me they're hunting, is it?"

She understood but pointed out, "But it's not just Aynyxia and me they want; they chased Rendel, after all." She was worried that Gribb wasn't taking the matter seriously enough. He wasn't all that much bigger than a boar, and she thought it quite unlikely that he was faster than one.

"Truth, but I expect that's because he wanted them to. Drew them off of a purpose, as I understand it. Woodlanders have got their ways with animals, they have. But I've got my own little ways, as I've been telling you. Don't you worry about me." He reached his hand to her shoulder and regarded her fondly for a moment. "You're a good child, you are." He sniffed loudly.

"Think I ought to go with you?" Luke offered Gribb, but he threw a pleading look in Beth's direction.

"No!" answered four voices at once, three of them strongly and Aynyxia's rather casually.

"Well, OK!" Luke answered, greatly relieved. "If you all say so. I'll try to hold myself back."

"On your way then, if you're going," Sharana told Gribb impatiently. Gathering up his things, including the new cloak (which he didn't need but which he judged would fetch a good price when he was done with it), Gribb gave Sharana a sour smile and Beth a friendly one. He nodded to Aynyxia and shook Luke's hand. Then he was gone.

"He'll be all right," Aynyxia told Beth with characteristic optimism. "They both will."

Beth had her doubts.

CHAPTER ELEVEN – On the Dayrn River

Standing on the bank, Beth looked out over the Lower Dayrn River, thinking. Or maybe trying not to think, trying only to absorb the scene around her – the sights, the sounds, the smells. She was still on the less active side of the river but now had a closer view of the far side. An arched footbridge, not far from her, connected the two riverbanks; beyond it on both sides were lines of docks. No large boats must travel that river, she decided, since they would never fit under the bridge. It wasn't an especially wide river in any event, at least not at this point. Aynyxia, in her own clipped way, had explained that the Dayrn was a major river, but by the time it reached this region it had divided into three parts - the Upper, the Lower, and the Central. The Lower Dayrn, as the section in front of them was known, was the narrowest but the most frequently traveled because it was so calm and had been tamed by a system of river locks. Luke, interested in all things technological, questioned her animatedly about this, but she was unable to explain in the detail he wanted. He kept trying nonetheless and Beth's attention wandered away.

Mirella had returned to the cabin almost immediately after Gribb left it. She'd led them down near the water, pointed out from a distance the flatboat they'd be taking, and shown them where to wait. She'd left them again but had assured them that it shouldn't be long before they were on their way.

Hoods up, they were trying now to make themselves as inconspicuous as possible – run-of-the-mill passengers on their way to Greyvic for the great festival. Sharana was silent, but the other three talked softly amongst themselves; they stopped, though, when anyone was near enough to hear. It was easy enough to pretend that their own attention was claimed by this passing boat or that unusual company, making lulls in conversation understandable.

142

Beth's emotions shifted around unevenly. She was so glad to have Luke with her and so curious to hear how he'd gotten there. She was anxious for Rendel's safety but fascinated by the scene around her and excited by the prospect of the river trip. Every time she looked at Sharana, she felt annoyed, but when she looked at Luke's grinning face and bright eyes gleaming from under his hood, she was happy and comforted.

"Can't wait to hear your 'long story'," she'd said to him as soon as Mirella had left them.

"Yeah, and I'm thinking you've got one or two little tidbits to share with me as well," he answered. "Can't believe you got us into all this!" he added with a mix of mock reproof and genuine admiration. "Weird creatures and all this top secret stuff! . . . So, who's after us, anyway?"

She hushed him then, because a small group of 'weird creatures' was about to pass by; as it turned out, though, they were too interested in their own affairs to give anyone else much notice.

By the time it was safe to talk again, Beth's gaze had fallen on Sharana, who stood a little apart from the other three. "Does she even care what might have happened to him?" Beth silently asked herself, irritated.

Her thoughts must have been written on her face, because Luke asked, "Just who is this Rendel guy you're so worried about?" and Aynyxia said quietly to Beth, "She's his friend, too. Needs to get you to Arystar, though. Rendel'd want it. But she's worried, you know." The last words surprised her.

Beth didn't like to admit it, but Aynyxia might be right. What mattered most to Sharana – getting Beth to Arystar – mattered to Rendel too. She remembered what he'd said: the Torks would bring despair to all Gwilldonum, and so she must complete her task. Of *course* Sharana would think that completing the "task," whatever it was, was the most important thing. But maybe she was also more worried about Rendel than she'd let on. Maybe. The feline eyes kept returning to the woods. Was she watching for new pursuers or for Rendel's safe arrival?

As Beth thought through these things, Luke watched her, stunned. He didn't repeat his earlier question, though she had made no answer. He wondered if she'd even heard him. After the plant-thing had spoken, Beth had stared at the cat-woman for a minute, then turned to look out over the river, lost in thought. She seemed

143

so far away. And different, though he couldn't have said how. It had only been a day. Or was it two? Anyway, it just hadn't been that long, and yet Beth was . . . Well, he didn't know what she was, but he just didn't get what was going on here. If only they could sit down somewhere, just the two of them and no strangers, and talk about stuff!

Maybe they'd get a chance on the boat. He'd heard Beth ask that boat person, Mirella or whatever-her-name-was, how long the river trip would take, and it would be a couple of hours, apparently. . . . Funny, Beth speaking up to strangers the way she'd been doing – especially that Sharana, who would never be voted Miss Congeniality! Beth was usually so quiet around strangers. Not shy, exactly, but pretty reserved. She watched people for a while when she was getting to know them. Stayed in the background. *That's* the Beth he knew.

He asked himself again what had been happening with her. He'd already noticed scratches on her hands and rips in her jacket, and he'd caught sight of an ugly bruise right where her neck sloped into her shoulder. And she seemed really tired. And older.

That was it. That was the difference. She seemed older. Not physically (or maybe it *was* physical, too), but in the way she acted. And something was really bothering her. A best friend knew these things. Then, finally sensing that Luke was staring at her, Beth turned to him and flashed a smile, and she didn't seem different at all.

"Listen, Beth, I just gotta ask—" But he didn't ask, because Mirella returned.

She began speaking to them before she had even reached them and didn't seem to mind if anyone overheard. "You may come now. We are ready for your journey and I trust it will be a pleasant one. The clearest skies we could hope for, though you'll find the air cold on the river, especially after the sun sets. You'll be glad for those cloaks," she added approvingly. The monologue was smooth and cheerful, like a salesperson's . . . which, Beth supposed, is what she hoped to appear. A cargo boathandler, making a little money on the side by ferrying travelers to the festival.

Mirella's boat was tied up at the third dock on the far side of the river, so she led them at once to the footbridge. As they began to cross, Beth noticed two people who seemed to be lurking around Mirella's boat. By the time her party had crossed the bridge and turned toward the flatboat, one of the two boarded it. Mirella also noticed and stopped short.

"What is it?" Sharana asked at once.

"Dock officials," Mirella answered in a cautious voice. "Supporters of the Torks, rumor says, but probably only here to inspect the cargo – there is a new tax levy just in time for the festival. Still, best be wary." She motioned to them to stay behind and she went forward to talk to the officials, her cheerful countenance once again in place.

"So who are these Torks? Anybody I should know about?"

Luke had whispered, but Sharana heard him, said "Later!" in a stern voice, and gave him a quelling look.

They were, at that point, standing around awkwardly in the middle of a footpath while people passed on each side. Their inactivity amidst so much commotion risked making them conspicuous, so Sharana said, "Move about a bit, but . . . do . . . not . . . *speak!*" She glared at Luke, who had already made quite an impression on her, short though their acquaintance had been.

They were near a produce stand and Sharana began to inspect the fruit, as if considering a purchase before her journey. Aynyxia moved off to the side and pretended to be searching for something in her pack. She kept her head down, so her face was entirely hidden from view. Her hands were covered by gloves, Beth noticed; she must have put them on at the cabin. Her root-feet, though bare, were hidden fairly well by her cloak, and Beth understood now why she had chosen the longest one offered. She supposed, rightly, that Aynyxia didn't want to draw attention to the fact that she was a walkabout. It occurred to Beth then that she hadn't noticed any other walkabout plants near the docks. Looking around now, she couldn't see a single one.

An enticing aroma drew Beth to a stand with several kinds of baked goods laid out. She began to inspect them, but when a vendor noticed her and approached, she smiled and turned away quickly before he could engage her in conversation.

She soon gave up on trying to move about naturally and went to the water's edge, close to where Aynyxia was still rummaging through her pack. She decided that gazing out over the river ought to seem a natural enough thing to do and was safer than milling about. Luke joined her shortly. "Too hard for him to wander around and keep his mouth shut," she thought, smiling.

A wooden railing separated them from the water. Luke and Beth each leaned forward on it, their backs to the various other travelers, and started to make quiet comments to one another. They stopped when a mother brought her child nearby to point something out to him. She caught Beth's eye and smiled, but when she opened her mouth to speak, Beth turned away. Rebuffed, the mother quickly left with her little one.

Soon, Beth was aware of someone else standing beside her, but this time she kept herself from looking, facing toward Luke instead, and waited for the stranger beside her to leave. When he put his hand on her shoulder, a shiver passed through her and she didn't know what to do . . . until he whispered her name.

In a flash, she spun around, causing her hood to slip down off her head, and started to throw her arms around him. "Ren-" She stopped when he gently pushed her back, saying, "Shhh!" but her enthusiastic greeting had clearly pleased Rendel. He smiled affectionately and kissed her forehead before pulling her hood back into place.

"You're all right? You're not hurt?" She spoke urgently, but quietly this time. "Oh, I'm so glad!" He leaned in close and whispered something, making a slight motion toward the opposite bank. Beth looked across the river and up beyond the bank. There, nearly hidden among the trees, was Marcus Gribb. Beth wisely refrained from waving, but she thought Marcus must have seen her looking because immediately ·afterwards the small figure disappeared from view.

Luke, observing, was astonished by the easy affection between Beth and this stranger. *Just what's going on here?. . . And I don't ever kiss her head, and I'm her best friend!*

Then, unexpectedly, Aynyxia came close and said to Beth in a serious tone, "I should leave you now."

"*What? Leave?*" Completely taken by surprise, Beth responded in a louder voice than she'd intended. Her elation at seeing Rendel was replaced by a sickening feeling in her stomach. "You don't mean— You can't— *You're* the one who was supposed to take me. *Please* come with me!" she implored. The despair in her voice surprised even her. She and Aynyxia had become friends, of course, but . . . it was more than that.

146

Aynyxia was the one who had been meant to find her, the one who *had* found her, on that first day, there by the water . . . the one who'd been her connection between this world and her own. And that was it, really. Beth was gladder than she could say that Luke was with her now, but all the same, losing Aynyxia would be like breaking the thread back to her real life. At least, that's how it felt.

For his part, Luke was bewildered. What exactly had happened between Beth and this green person with leaves popping out all over? Hadn't they only just met? And who *was* this Rendel guy anyway? Did he save her life or something? How could they be so . . . *however-they-were* after knowing each other for no time at all?

Meanwhile, Aynyxia seemed uncertain what to say, but Sharana (who had silently reappeared and wanted to end the conversation as quickly as possible) said, "She is right. They know a walkabout is with us. We will be safer without her. In any event, she is wounded." The sling Gribb had quickly fashioned in the forest had been replaced in the cabin by a more efficient and less conspicuous one. Beth had helped to bandage the wound, which hadn't seemed deep, but still . . . she hadn't seen Aynyxia use that arm in any significant way since the attack; even throwing the cloak over her shoulders had been a little tricky.

"The injury does not seem serious enough to hold her back," said Rendel calmly. "I carry an herb that will ease the pain, but walkabouts heal with remarkable speed. You know this. By the morrow, she will scarce pay it heed, if I know my friend."

"They know she is with us," Sharana repeated impatiently, looking around covertly as she spoke. "It will be better without her."

Beth felt the urge to yell at her but instead turned to Rendel. "*Please!*"

After only a slight hesitation, he stated simply, "Aynyxia will remain with our company."

Sharana made a sound of disapproval but resigned herself at once. "Very well." Looking away from them, she caught sight of Mirella approaching and said, "It is time."

Mirella had satisfied the dock officials, who had moved on to the next vessel, and she wanted to get her flatboat boarded and on its way before they found a reason to return. Quickly, she led the others to it and indicated where they could seat themselves. It seemed to Beth like little more than a large raft, really, and the accommodations were far from luxurious. Given the choice of sitting on top of one of the cargo boxes or down on the wooden planks that made up the floor of the vessel, she chose the lower position, where she was less noticeable from the dockside and where she had a crate to lean up against. Luke quickly settled in next to her and began to speak at once, quietly but urgently.

"Beth. I've got, like, a thousand and three questions for you and this might not be the best time for them, but I've got to ask you one thing right now. OK, two, actually. . . . Well, there'll probably be more, but first . . . have you been here before?"

Not quite recovered from the elation of seeing Rendel, the panic of thinking Aynyxia might leave, and her irritation with Sharana, Beth didn't immediately grasp what Luke had in mind. For a variety of reasons, she was feeling quite nervy inside and began to answer in a distracted way, "Here? Do you mean *right* here, or do you mean—"

"I mean here in this *world*," he whispered. "You know, this world that isn't *our* world?"

The intensity in his voice helped her focus. "No, of course not."

"OK. And have you been here for a really long time or just since yesterday?"

"Not yesterday, but not long either. A couple of days, I guess. And how did you get—"

"No," he interrupted, "we'll get to me next." He spoke more slowly now. "You go first, because I've got a feeling you've got a whole lot more answers than I do. . . . And besides, maybe after I hear your story, mine won't seem so hard to swallow. I'm still not sure I didn't dream part of it. Who knows? I could be dreaming right now – *that* would explain a lot!"

They were interrupted briefly then, but as soon as Mirella had pushed the boat away from the dock and, using a long pole that reached the riverbed, gotten it into the middle of the river, the two friends finally got the chance for the long talk they'd wanted. Beth recounted how she had watched for water to return to the well, how she had touched it and found herself in this world where Aynyxia was waiting, apparently for her. She gave a short version of the adventures that followed and of her introductions to the

148

woodlanders and Sharana (but she couldn't speak entirely freely, suspecting that everyone on board could overhear). Briefly, she filled Luke in on the Torks and the missing heir, feeling awkward that she should be the one explaining a situation that everyone else there knew better than she did. She wasn't sure how much to say in front of Mirella, but twice when she hesitated, Rendel seemed to indicate by a nod that it was all right to go on. It didn't occur to her to keep any of those details from Luke, except that she was vague in discussing her own role. She never mentioned the words *escorts*, *sanctuaries*, or, especially, *champion*; she said only that she had been brought to help somehow and that Aynyxia had been waiting to take her back to the Council of Ten at the place called Arystar's Green. There, presumably, she would learn what she was supposed to do. Thinking wishfully, she spoke of her own part as if it were of little consequence. After all, how much of this could really depend on her?

"Everything depends on this champion." Weariness marked Lady Gweynleyn's voice.

"Truth," responded Mariza evenly.

There were so few noises around them now after days of commotion. "The others have all gone?" the lady inquired.

"So I believe," confirmed her attendant.

They sat quietly for a long while – Gweynleyn lost deep in her thoughts, Mariza waiting patiently.

Then the lady repeated, "Everything depends on this champion."

"OK. Your turn," Beth told Luke. "And I don't think you have to worry that anything you say will sound unbelievable to me."

"Yeah, I guess not." But he still seemed reluctant. "OK, well – I waited for you by the well; I guess that's the first thing." He was speaking more quietly than Beth had, less comfortable with the idea of the others listening in.

"But that can't be the first thing. What made you go to the well?" Beth asked. Then, in a bit of a panic, she added, "How long have I been missing? Was everyone looking for me?" She'd been hoping, when she'd let herself think about it at all, that it would be like in the stories, where no time passed when someone left our world and then came back again.

"No, it's all right; it wasn't like that," Luke reassured her. "I *saw* you go. You disappeared! It was the freakiest thing that's ever happened to me. . . . Well, up to that point, at least," he amended. "It's kind of a toss-up now."

"But—why—?"

"Your mom called my house. So I guess *that* was the first thing. She got kind of spooked about leaving you, like maybe something wasn't quite right. Must've been a 'mom' kind of a thing, because she sure called that one!" He stopped then, since the mention of Beth's mother seemed to upset her; her face looked strained, like maybe she was trying not to cry. But when, after a pause, she said, "And?", he went on.

"She wanted me to come over but not go out of my way to let on that she'd asked me to. You know, just to hang with you for a while. So I said OK. And as soon as I hung up, I started thinking about how weird you'd been acting for the last week and I guess I got a little spooked too, so I took my bike instead of walking and when I was almost to your house, I could see you going out the back way and I knew where you'd be headed. I tried to call you, but that stupid little dog of yours was yipping like a maniac and the wind was sort of loud, so you must not've heard.

"Anyway, I dropped the bike and tried to catch up with you. I don't know why I didn't try calling you again when I got close, but I was starting to get kind of creeped out and I wanted to find out what was going on. All week I'd been feeling like there was something you wanted to tell me but wouldn't. So I figured I'd just watch and see what you did. And then . . . *man*, it was weird! One minute you're there and the next . . ." His voice got even quieter with the amazement of it all. "I thought I was really losing it! I saw it myself, but I couldn't believe it."

When he didn't continue, Beth prompted him. "What did you do then?"

"I didn't know *what* to do! Call the police and say my friend just got swallowed up by an empty well? And it *was* empty; I checked. No water, no you, no nothing. My parents would be less than zero help, of course, but I knew your mom was at that co-op meeting and I figured I should call and tell her what happened even though she'd probably think I'd turned nutcase on her and she'd

150

never let me within ten feet of you again. But I didn't go call. . . .
I'm not sure why, but I guess it was mostly because I thought . . .
well . . . I thought maybe you wouldn't want me to. . . . OK, so the
thing is that I kept thinking about the time when you were talking
about the well and magic. And then, too, right before you
disappeared, I was sure you said something, so I thought . . . well, I
wondered if . . . if maybe it wasn't some sort of spell. And you'd
made yourself disappear. And so . . . By the way, what did you
say?"

Beth thought about it, then smiled and said, "I think I
must've said, 'I knew it'."

"Huh. Well, that's kind of boring, but what I thought at the
time was that it was some cool spell or something and maybe you
knew what you were doing and if I just waited you'd bring yourself
back." He seemed a little embarrassed at his line of thinking even
though, in retrospect, it wasn't such an unreasonable one. "So,
basically, I spent maybe half an hour telling myself to go call your
mom and then not doing it. I kept pacing around, then I'd sit and
stare at the well, then I'd pace around some more, all the time
hoping you'd just pop back up, until finally I made up my mind
that I had to tell your mom *something,* and then . . . I saw it. The
water in the well. Just like you must've seen a few days ago (or
whenever that was). I just kept staring at it, so it wouldn't
disappear if I looked away.

"It was pretty dark out and hard to see anything, but the
water reflected little bits of light, and then . . . it actually got
bright, so I thought maybe you were coming back, but . . ." This
was the part he found hardest to explain, though he wasn't sure
why. "It wasn't you." He'd forgotten for the last minute or two that
he was trying to keep the others from overhearing and his voice
had grown louder, but he suddenly got quiet again so that even
Beth could barely hear. "There was this face in the water. A
woman's face." The most beautiful, most enchanting, most
knowing face he'd ever seen . . . but he didn't say that. "And she
tried to talk to me. Her lips moved, but I couldn't hear anything.
She seemed to want me to answer, but I couldn't make out what
she was saying. She tried a few more times, and then – this is
weird – her lips stopped moving, but that time I *did* hear her. But I
didn't. I mean, I knew the words she was saying – at least, I

151

thought I did – but they weren't coming in through my ears. It's like they were going straight to my mind."

"You seek to aid your friend?" the woman asked.

Luke couldn't believe it. It couldn't be real. All the same, he mouthed a silent "yes." She must have understood, because she reached out her hand invitingly. "Then, come. The door is yet open."

Seeing his hesitation, she'd seemed uncertain as well but repeated, "Come," and then added anxiously, "The door may close." Her face became less clear and the light that had brightened the well began to fade.

The urgency moved him and, without knowing at all what he was getting himself into, he stretched his hand to the water and touched the spot where he could still make out the shape of her hand.

"And then," he told Beth, "I must've transported to the same place you did, only I didn't have my own personal tour guide waiting. . . . But *she* was still there. The woman in the water. Her face was still watching me from that little pool, but it was clear again. In fact, clearer than before. And she said to me (or *thought* to me, I guess), 'Follow my messenger.' Well, fine, but I didn't *see* any messenger. And then she closed her eyes and looked really tired like she was going to faint and then she disappeared.

"So here I was, in this little garden place (that was so quiet it was spooky!) and there's no messenger and no magic face talking to me and no you. I tried to explore a little, but whichever way I went, I ended up back at the pool of water. It was like I was in a big garden room, but there were no walls anywhere and all paths led to the middle. So I sat down and waited and tried to figure out if I should be really ticked off at you or – well, you know, worried about you or something. And I kept trying to picture the woman's face again, but it started to seem so dreamlike that I couldn't be sure I hadn't imagined it. And yet there I was. Somewhere else. Somewhere that definitely wasn't part of your back field at home. So it had to be real or I'd gone a little crazy." It had been so different from anything he'd known (except in books), so hard to believe, so magical, that he'd thought it would be hard to tell even Beth about it. But it turned out to be not so hard after all. Still, he didn't tell her that he'd kept seeing that woman's face in his mind, kept feeling like he wanted to find her – almost as much as he wanted to find Beth.

"Anyway, somewhere along the line, I fell asleep," he continued, "and when I woke up there was this yellow bird – really sort of golden – about three inches from my face and I could tell it wanted me to follow it. Shades of Narnia, you know?" he added, referring to the robin the Pevensie children had followed in the first book. "It went out the same kind of opening you did (I swear it wasn't there before) and I didn't follow at first, but it kept going in and out until I did, just as the hole was starting to close up.

"I didn't know if I was being incredibly brave and adventuresome or just pretty stupid, but I followed it a long time until I couldn't have found my way back if I'd had to. At first, I tried to keep my eye on the position of the sun, but it was so overcast that I couldn't very well . . . and soon it didn't matter because I was in this foresty area that was pretty dark, and halfway through there I realized I had *no* idea which way I was headed . . . . I could always make out the golden bird, though. It seemed like I'd been following it forever – and I hadn't even run into a single person! – and it was getting dark and I was about to give up and just sit right down until somebody found me" – he didn't mention that he'd been hovering somewhere around the verge of tears; no need for Beth to know *that* bit of trivia – "and then up comes Mrs. Gribb, driving a cart pulled by a really funny-looking pony or something. Even in the dark – oh, and by the way, have you noticed they've got *two* moons here? Well, I guess you must've – oh, yeah, you can sort of see them now. Anyway, even in the moonlight, she looked pretty weird to me (though not compared to what I've seen since!) and I wasn't sure what to make of her. But I was ready for any kind of company at all by then and she seemed friendly enough and even kind of worried when she said, 'You're the one, aren't you?' Well, I couldn't really know the answer to that, could I? So I just said, 'I'm looking for my friend Beth', and she said, 'Then you're the one.'

"And, to make a long story short, I joined her in the cart and I got to ride a part of the way that you had to walk (but I think you took a more direct route than we could) and I spent the night at the Gribbs' place and then you know the rest. We left as soon as it was light in the morning and I caught up with you eventually.

153

Well, I guess we could've made it a little bit earlier, but Mrs. G fed me and gave me clothes and a bunch of other stuff. Anyway, when we were finally on our way, Gribb was just coming back from seeing you. So we all went to Greenwood together in the cart, but Mrs. Gribb took it home again, because Gribb said we'd be cutting through the woods after that and the cart wouldn't go. . . . And I guess that's pretty much it."

He paused and caught his breath before adding, "I really liked the Gribbs. I think the Mrs. wanted to adopt me or something." He remembered, without relaying the incident to Beth, how Gert had pulled his face down close to hers when she'd left him. She'd planted a big, wet kiss on his cheek . . . and he hadn't minded at all.

"Wow," said Beth. "I couldn't believe it when I saw you." Day had turned to dusk, and they sat in the dimness and the silence for a moment before Beth added, "I'm really glad you're here. I hope . . . I hope you don't mind or anything."

"Mind? *Mind?* Are you *kidding?*" His smile and his eyes were wide. "No, I don't mind. Not one little bit. In fact, Beth, I'd have to say that this is . . . *awesome!* Totally, incredibly (and I mean that literally) awesome!"

Then Luke McKinnon stretched out his arms and legs and leaned back, side by side with his best friend, and enjoyed the rhythmic movements of the riverboat and the dancing of the moons' light on the water.

CHAPTER TWELVE – Arystar's Green

A good bit of the boat ride was done in the gray of evening, but the moons were bright and Mirella knew the river and the locks perfectly. As she punted along, she hummed softly. Though simple and repetitive, the tunes drew Beth in and she wished she knew the words.

After a while, Rendel took out a flute and played a few notes to match one of the tunes. Mirella, unaware until then that she'd been humming, smiled. Then she sang a couple of lines in a voice that was low but rich and with an accent (sort of like a Scottish one, only not quite) that Beth hadn't heard in her speech.

> *Hey, tarry now by me, by me,*
> *Tarry, tarry now by me.*
> *My hand is warm*
>   *and my heart is yours,*
> *Tarry, tarry now by me.*

By the second line, Rendel's flute accompanied her, continuing as she sang the verses, which began slowly with low notes but gradually increased in tempo and pitch so that the final stanza had an almost desperate urgency to it. It amazed Beth that Rendel's crude flute could play so many perfect notes in such quick succession.

> *You wake in the morn*
>   *when the whitebirds near,*
> *Hey, tarry now by me.*
> *They sing you a song that I canna' hear,*
> *Tarry, tarry now by me.*
>
> *The wind blows kell*
>   *and it carries you along,*

155

Hey, tarry now by me.
It whisp'rs you a tune
          and you follow its song,
Tarry, tarry now by me.

Hey, tarry now by me, by me,
Tarry, tarry now by me.
My hand is warm
          and my heart is yours,
Tarry, tarry now by me.

I see in your eyes,
          you'll be leavin' me again,
Hey, tarry now by me.
You say you'll return
          but you canna' say when,
Tarry, tarry now by me.

Our time passed here,
          must it be so cort?
Hey, tarry now by me.
Another day mair canna' mult import,
Tarry, tarry now by me.

Hey, tarry now by me, by me,
Tarry, tarry now by me.
My hand is warm
          and my heart is yours,
Tarry, tarry now by me.

The road calls your name
          and you canna' let it be,
But the world that I see is enough for me.
I know every path, every stream,
          every fen,
But the world beyond is beyond my ken.
The road rises up where I canna' see.
The life that I have,
          will you have it with me?
Will you tarry, tarry now by me?

Hey, tarry now by me, by me,
Tarry, tarry now by me.
My hand is warm
and my heart is yours,
Tarry, tarry now by me.
Will you tarry, tarry now by me?
Tarry, tarry now by me.

Beth loved the song, though the words were bittersweet.
When it ended, there was silence for a moment, then Mirella began
to hum the refrain again. The moonlight reflected off her face and
Beth could see that she was looking expectantly at Rendel. In
answer, he smiled, eyes glittering even in the dim light, and sang
the chorus back to her, though his words were of a different
language.

Hy felli on fairhr may, fairhr may,
Felli felli on fairhr may.
Minh ayr bruil fiynh á minh kieyrh estinh,
Felli felli on fairhr may.

He sang it a second time and then a third, but with each
repetition the notes rose higher and the melody grew fluid as the
master singer played about with the tune. Beth had found Mirella's
voice warm and rich, but it seemed almost ordinary in comparison
to Rendel's. As his voice danced lightly over the notes, she
remembered that he was called Rendel Singer.

There were more songs after that. Most of them were
happy, sometimes nonsensical, folk songs with repetitive choruses,
and Beth was able to join in on parts; others were slow and sad,
and one melancholy ballad actually brought tears to her eyes,
though no one but Rendel knew it. When all the music except
Mirella's humming had faded away, Beth leaned her head back,
eyes closed, and listened to the sounds of the night. There were
bird calls and crickets and the rhythmic lapping of water against
the riverbank. She drifted into a light sleep and dreamed that she
was just where she was, sleeping on a flatboat on the river, only
the sun shone warm on her and it was flowing music, not the skill
of a boathandler, that carried the vessel gently along.

Luke, who'd been awake longer than Beth, slept as well. Sharana had been able to nap even during the singing, though she could always rouse quickly when there was reason. Aynyxia stretched out flat on her stomach and her long arms allowed her fingers to trail in the water. Rendel stayed awake and kept Mirella company, though mostly in silence, sometimes taking over as boathandler so that she could rest.

"Will you rest now, milady?"

"Yes, Mariza, I will, after I enjoy the serenity of the night but a few minutes longer."

"Do you desire anything?"

Yes. Yes, I desire to see our champion safely arrived and in our midst. I desire to see the Torks leave us, never to return. I desire to see the Anointed sitting on the throne of Gwilldonum and ruling with wisdom and justice. I desire to see the creases of worry gone from Therin's brow. . . . And I desire this blackness that creeps about me and presses on me like the heaviest of weights to vanish forever.

Aloud, Lady Gweynleyn said, "No. Thank you." Mariza withdrew.

When Gweynleyn was about to retire as well, she stopped at the sound of someone's approach. "Harac!" she exclaimed an instant later. "I knew not that you tarried. Will you not leave for Greyvic until morning?"

"I willn't leave for Greyvic at all, lest you do as well."

The lady smiled and gazed at him for a moment. She knew that he was anxious to be gone. "Thank you, my friend, my brother."

"Has there been more news?"

"No, but we could scarcely expect it." She looked away, across the wide meadow, toward the deep woods, though the night was too heavy for her to see much there. "I trust they draw near and we will have news from their persons ere long." She spoke with more hope than confidence and a great weariness hung on her.

Harac attempted to raise her spirits, expressing more optimism than he felt. "We know that the champion has been met by the walkabout, and no doubt the great cat" – as he referred to Sharana Tey – "received the message to intercept them. I expect they're well enough." For his own part, he would have sent a party

158

out in search of them earlier, while there were still others about who could be sent, but Gweynleyn had not revealed to any council member but himself that Aynyxia's message had been received or that she had subsequently communicated with Sharana. As time grew shorter, Gweynleyn grew more closed – not without cause. The death of Rane, so soon after he had left them and in a spot so near, had been deeply unsettling to Harac as well. Still, to entrust so much to so few. . . .

"Is there none within our council that you trust without reservation?" the dwarf asked Gweynleyn now.

"There is you, Harac. I trust you with all. And there is the captain of our guard; I have long put my confidence in Therin Mandek. But beyond that . . . There are others of the council that I credit with certainty to be loyal to Gwilldonum and to the house of DarQuinn, but we must trust not only to their loyalty but to their discretion."

"Aye," Harac agreed, a little sadly. " Rane was as good a man as any, but could show too little wisdom in the choosing of companions and confidants."

"It is so."

Following his own train of thought, Harac said after a moment, "If— *When* the champion arrives, we will be so few to aid him." Though he himself was reluctant to put much trust in the champion and itched to be at Greyvic, Harac admired Lady Gweynleyn deeply and her great wisdom awed him. He put his trust in her and she had put hers in the champion.

"We can get word to Therin quickly, if need be. But we know, Harac, that small numbers have done great things before this day and will again. Beyond that, I can say no more, except that my confidence is in the champion to make all things right, as the prophecy has said."

"So, OK, say more about this prophecy thing. You kind of skimmed over that part before." Beth had been hoping Luke wouldn't notice.

Their party had left the boat about an hour earlier and Mirella had led them by lantern light to an empty cabin close by the riverside. The cabin was used sometimes by Mirella, sometimes by other boathandlers, but it was apparently free at present.

The place was not many hours' journey from Arystar, but the woods were thick and dark and not without danger, so the decision was made to wait until dawn before setting out. Mirella, who would not be traveling with them on the morrow, volunteered to keep watch through the night so that the others could sleep.

Sharana might not have consented to this delay had the others not agreed that she would go ahead at once to Arystar as messenger. She preferred thick, dark woods to almost any other type of terrain for travel, and the blackness of the night was nothing to her save an advantage. She would travel as a cat, of course, taking on human form only when she approached the Council of Ten at Arystar's Green.

Supplies in the cabin were minimal, but luckily there were three mattresses and twice as many blankets. Since Mirella would be staying awake and Aynyxia preferred sleeping on the ground, Rendel, Beth, and Luke would each have a bed for the night. As those three spread out the thin but adequate mattresses, which had been stacked up to leave as much open space as possible in the little cabin, Luke whispered to Beth, "Don't suppose there are any clean sheets around here, do you? *Who knows* what kind of thing slept here last! I think we should all sit down for a little lesson on good hygiene right about now." Beth knew he had a point, but after the hard ground of Sharana's cave and the wooden planks of the boat she was glad enough for the comfort of the mattresses.

It was a little after that, while the two of them were outside filling canteens by lantern light, that Luke asked Beth about the prophecy.

"Oh . . . well . . . ," she began unhelpfully. "The prophecy . . . well, you know."

"No, actually, I don't. Not at all . . . which, incidentally, is why I'm asking."

"Well, like I told you before – the prophecy says someone will come from a faraway place and somehow that's supposed to help them get the right person on the throne. . . . It's not very clear. You know how prophecies can be." She smiled weakly.

Luke set down his canteen and looked at Beth thoughtfully for a moment before saying, "You mean *you're* supposed to get the right person on the throne. *You*, Beth DeVere. They're practically on the brink of war here, as far as I can tell, and you're going to be their hero and save the day, is that it? . . . *Cool!*" He smiled brightly. "So, fill me in. What's your plan and how are you going to fit me into it? I mean, you *have* got some really awesome part for *me*, right? . . . 'Cause I'd do the same for you!"

"I'm still working on the details," Beth answered dispiritedly, turning and taking her canteen back to the cabin.

A little while later, soon before they retired for the night, another incident lowered her spirits even further. After chatting with Mirella for a few minutes outside, she walked back into the cabin where Luke was in conversation with Aynyxia. Beth hadn't heard Luke's comment, but Aynyxia's reply ended with, " —how it got the name Gwilldonum – means Gwilliam's land or something."

"Gift," Beth said automatically.

"What?" Aynyxia looked up.

"Oh!" She hadn't particularly meant for anyone to hear. "Nothing." Three pairs of eyes were looking now and no one resumed the conversation, so Beth explained quickly, "*Donum* means gift, so if you're saying that the *Gwill* part stands for the name Gwilliam, then Gwilldonum must have come from 'Gwilliam's gift' or something like that." Then she added, "I guess," because even as she was speaking she realized that *donum* could mean anything at all in this world and just happened to mean "gift" in an ancient language of her own world. And probably even had other meanings there, now that she thought of it. She suddenly felt flushed and embarrassed and rather stupid and wished she hadn't said anything. "Anyway, just go on. Sorry."

Still no one spoke and Beth didn't understand why Rendel and Aynyxia were looking at her the way they were. She glanced at Luke, who shrugged to show that he didn't see what the big deal was either.

"You know the tongue of the ancients?" Rendel asked then, ending an awkward pause.

"Well, 'course," Aynyxia decided abruptly. "Must know all that sort of thing. That's why she was called."

Her words, though spoken with such assurance and intended as encouragement, caused no small amount of anxiety within Beth. It didn't help at all that Luke jumped in, agreeing. "Yep. Beth knows all kinds of stuff. She's a whiz at Latin – I mean, the tongue of the ancients – and, well, everything. Yessirree," he concluded, grinning broadly and talking in an almost goofy voice, "our little Beth is sharp as the proverbial tack." He expected Beth to look over and glare at him – in a good-natured way, of course – but she didn't. In fact, she didn't look directly at anyone for several minutes.

The conversation died out and it wasn't long before everyone was ready for bed. When Rendel started to talk to Aynyxia about their plan for the morning, Luke took advantage of the semi-private moment to ask Beth, still quiet and distracted, "What's up with you?"

"We're almost there, Luke," she answered softly but passionately. "They're going to expect me to do something, to *find* someone. How can I? . . . And I hardly know any Latin," she added as an afterthought. "And I won't know any of the *other* stuff they think I will."

"Beats me how you're going to pull this off," Luke replied casually. "All I can say is, better you than me." He grinned, hoping she'd at least make a small attempt at a smile; when she didn't, he said, "OK. Never mind. Let's try this instead: 'One thing at a time'. Your mom's always telling us that – or, something kind of like that – and this time I've gotta say she'd be right. Right?"

"Right," Beth agreed hesitantly, and then, more convincingly, "Right. The first thing to do is get to Arystar's Green . . . . We can worry about the *next* thing after that."

Luke had reassured her a little but spoiled it by adding, "Of course, in this case, 'the next thing' is a majorly big deal, with the fate of a whole big old country hanging on it."

That time, Luke did see Beth glare – just before Rendel extinguished the lantern for the night.

The morning passed uneventfully.

The small party (now reduced to four) rose at dawn, breakfasted, and set out at once. For the first short stretch of the journey, there was no clear path, but they knew the direction they wanted and were able to steer a straight course with no significant obstacles to circumvent. When they did reach a road, they traveled parallel to it rather than on it, affording themselves better cover should they need it. Of the several travelers they saw along the way, none caused them any alarm. This seemed a good thing to Luke and Beth, but both Rendel and Aynyxia seemed puzzled and somewhat disturbed. They were not surprised at the lack of festival traffic – Greyvic was to the north and they themselves had now turned east – but why were there no watchers to report their coming, no soldiers to escort them to the council? They were nearing Arystar's Green.

Everyone was relieved when they came upon Sharana, returning toward them, who informed them that they were within half an hour of the Green. They were gladdened by this news but not sure what to make of Sharana's subsequent report that the council had disassembled and that only Harac, Lady Gweynleyn, and a few attendants remained. At the Stronghold of Arystar itself, two miles' distance from Arystar's Green, a minimal company of servants and guards awaited her ladyship's orders, but Lady Gweynleyn had not suggested a meeting at either the stronghold or the green. Rather, she had directed Sharana to a third and unexpected site – the nearby ruined Tower of Sapientia where the lady and her attendants would go to await the arrival of the champion.

As they followed Sharana to the tower, it occurred to Beth that if she were ever going to distrust the cat, this probably ought to be the time. The change of plans brought a sense of uneasiness – though Beth's feelings at present were so complex that no one cause could account for them. And yet, though the plan had been imparted to Sharana alone and involved going to a location that not even Rendel or Aynyxia had anticipated, Beth found that she didn't actually doubt the message. She disliked many of Sharana's ways (though she was becoming accustomed to them), but she no longer distrusted her. Not that she had a lot of experience with that kind of thing, but her gut feeling was that Sharana was on the same side as the rest of them – Rendel, Aynyxia, the Gribbs, Mirella. Now Beth was on that side too, wanting what they wanted, working for what they were working for.

And the time had finally come to discover whether there really was something she could do to help.

Or whether there wasn't.

When, after a short time, they found themselves approaching the designated tower (a medieval-looking ruin that would have commanded all of Beth's attention under different circumstances), a striking woman advanced to them from it, soon followed by two younger women who had been standing guard at the entrance. Those two women were similar enough to be sisters –

163

they had the same brown skin, the same dark hair pulled back from their faces and the same alert black eyes. They carried weapons.

The other woman had such an arresting presence (Luke, gaping, literally stopped in his tracks) that Beth had no doubt of her identity. This had to be the Lady Gweynleyn, of whom Sharana had spoken. Tall and elegant, she wore a silky blue gown encased in a diaphanous outer gown embroidered with silver threads that sparkled like dew in the morning light. Her face, framed by golden brown hair that cascaded toward her waist, was striking in its vitality and intelligence. As the lady neared, arms extended in welcome, Beth also saw kindness in her clear blue eyes.

"I am Gweynleyn," she said warmly to the girl. "Welcome . . . and to you, welcome," she added, turning to Luke with a smile of familiarity. Beth managed a quiet "Hello," but Luke merely stared. "Forgive us that our welcome is meager and hurried, but Sharana informs me that you know our situation and understand it to be urgent and despairing. Will you allow us to dispense with formalities and the customary civilities in the hope that at some later time we will have the leisure for better acquaintance and for according you all the honors and ceremonies to which you are entitled?"

When Beth realized that this was a question she was actually expected to answer, she said, "Yes. Of course."

"Then we will at once to the matter at hand." She turned to the two women who had followed her and motioned them forward, then said to Sharana, "May I ask you to stand guard with my attendants?" Sharana nodded her consent, and the three moved by unspoken agreement toward strategic positions.

"Do you wish us to leave, my lady – Aynyxiacichorium and myself?" Rendel asked.

"No, friend. You are both welcome to stay. You have rendered a great service to Gwilldonum and to all the Southlands. . . . Come," she added to Beth, leading the way back to the tower.

"She's the one," Luke finally managed to whisper. "She's the one I saw in the water."

Just as Gweynleyn was about to enter the tower, she stepped aside and a robed, hooded figure (he reminded Beth of a monk) came forward through its doorway. He held his hands together at his waist and kept his head lowered. Lady Gweynleyn inclined her own head as a sign of respect, and everyone else

164

stopped where they were and waited, leaving an open pathway for him if he wanted it.

Beth was surprised and nervous when the stranger walked directly toward her. When he raised his head to look at her, his eyes fixed on hers and hers on his. She noticed nothing else about him. She realized later that she couldn't have said what color his hair was or if he had a beard or whether he'd smiled at her, but she thought she would know his eyes anywhere.

In a swift movement, without warning, the stranger placed his hand over Beth's face. Luke made as if to go to her, but Rendel stopped him (which irritated Luke, but he held back anyway). Then, almost as quickly, the hooded figure removed his hand and turned back toward the Tower.

When he disappeared within it, Rendel said quietly, "This was a Silent One, Beth. It is a great honor and a gift that he should lay a hand on you in this way."

"Looked kind of creepy to me," said Luke, unimpressed.

"It's all right," said Beth to quiet him. Her voice sounded a little strange to him, but also sort of . . . calm. "Really, it's all right."

As soon as the Silent One had entered the tower, Gweynleyn followed, with Beth, Luke, Aynyxia, and Rendel close behind. The whole lower floor consisted of a single, open, circular room – and it was unoccupied. There was no sign of the Silent One. Directly across the room from Beth, a stairwell twisted upwards, but she didn't see how he could have ascended it and disappeared from view so quickly. No one else commented on his absence, however (though Luke brought it up later, when they were alone), so she said nothing either.

Someone else was in the building, however, and was soon descending the stairs, carrying what looked like a crystal ball. The newcomer was short, stocky, long-haired, bearded, and dressed like a warrior. "Whoa!" came Luke's soft voice from just behind Beth, "He looks like a—" But he stopped himself before saying "dwarf."

"This is Harac," announced Gweynleyn, "of the Council of Ten." To Harac, she said, "This is Beth, who is specially come to us, and her friend, Luke." Beth was surprised for an instant, then remembered that Sharana would have related their names to Gweynleyn and probably to Harac as well. "You know Rendel

165

Singer of Greenwood." Harac nodded. He was already acquainted with Aynyxiacichorium, of course, and had met with her not so many days earlier to discuss the matter now at hand. They acknowledged each other with nods – Harac's was more of a formal bow of the head, Aynyxia's a friendly, jerking movement.

"We will at once to the matter at hand," Gweynleyn said again, and she motioned to them to take seats. Beth moved to one of the chairs that formed a circle against the wall and sat down on it gingerly (because it looked like it belonged in a museum with a Do Not Touch sign strung across it), and Luke took the one nearest her, carelessly pulling it up right next to hers, and settled in comfortably, stretching out his legs in front of him.

The room was sparsely furnished. Lit torches lined the wall, and in the center of the ring of chairs was something that looked to Beth and Luke like a birdbath. It was there that Harac reverently placed the crystal ball. Or whatever it was.

When it was settled in its place and Harac had taken a seat, Gweynleyn walked forward to the ball, touched it gently with her fingertips, and was silent for a moment. Then she addressed her audience in a clear and purposeful voice. "This is the orb of Arandella," she explained. "It is a rare messenger orb and carries forward to us the words of our queen at the hour of her death. It provides the only indications she could give us concerning the Anointed of Gwilldonum, whom we seek with loyalty, fidelity, and vigor." She smiled bittersweetly as she added, "And, in these last days, with some desperation."

Placing both hands flat against the orb, she closed her eyes, and said, "Let us hear the words of Arandella, the words of our queen." Then she took her seat in the circle, but only after a green mist began to swirl within the orb.

CHAPTER THIRTEEN – The Riddle of Arandella

The voice that emanated from the orb and echoed off the tower walls was that of a young woman – young but strong, Beth thought. Listening intently to the words, Beth never allowed her eyes to stray from the twisting green light within the orb, as if by staring hard she might catch sight of the queen as she spoke.

> *I am Arandella, daughter of DarQuinn Mandek of the House of William Princeps, the Aethling, the Law-Giver.*
> *I am Arandella, now Queen of Gwilldonum, High Queen of the Southlands, Protector of the Thessalyn Islands.*
> *I am Arandella, and leave this word for my people, for the Council of Ten, and for the champion who will one day right the wrongs of this hour.*

There was a brief interruption in the speech when only the sound of the queen's breathing could be heard. Then a deeper breath ended in a sigh before the voice, calm but speaking quickly, resumed.

> *The enemy has proved cunning and our end is certain. My guard, though true and valiant in all, is vanquished and help will not reach us in time. We are now but four, to my knowledge, and all barricaded within the highest tower chamber that we might perform one final service for our realm while life we still hold.*
> *I, Arandella, in the presence of my most trusted advisors, Simon of Norwood and Rhysmenn of Eleyn Gryf, and of my most cherished attendant, Kaysa, who is a changeling, and in accordance with the guidance of the Silent One, Tanek the Wise, have performed the most*

exalted ceremonies of anointing. Trusting that we have delivered the Anointed safely from this place to be raised until the age of all rights, we leave this message for the champion who will one day restore rule to the chosen line of the Princeps.

Here, for the first time, the voice slowed. Each word was pronounced carefully, that none should be missed or mistaken.

As the father of the Romani, as the daughter of Cerenthai, so shall the Anointed of this House be saved this day and kept sure until the due time. You, O Champion foretold, bring back the true, the most beloved Anointed to the seat of our ancestors to set right the ways of this realm.

There was silence for an instant and then a faint but urgent voice in the background sounded: *Your Majesty!*

The queen spoke again, softly but firmly. *The end is upon us. May peace return to my people.* They recognized the sound of steel as the queen drew her sword. As the light within the orb began to subside, and the mist to dissipate, the fading voice of the queen uttered a few more words, barely discernible. *Kaysa. Quickly, take—* The light and mist were gone, the silence was final.

No one spoke. Beth heard the crackling, unnoticed until then, of the torch nearest her. Somewhere without, in the distance, whitebirds called.

At last, Harac said, "The bodies of the queen and her highest advisors, Sir Simon of Norwood and Rhysmenn of Eleyn Gryf, were found in the uppermost tower chamber. The attendant, Kaysa, was not there and has not been discovered since by any who have sought her, but she is a changeling and could have made her escape when the others could not. She will not be found now unless she wishes it."

"You think she's alive?" Beth asked. Harac nodded. "But no one can find her?"

"Many have tried. No doubt she is among her own kind. But if the queen swore her to secrecy, she will not break the oath. And her own will keep her hidden if that is her wish." He smiled, but without any joy. "It is no easy thing to track a changeling, as you must know!"

Beth did not know, of course, but was beginning to get the idea.

Luke's thoughts had gone in another direction. "So, why the highest chamber?" he asked. "I mean, it might make sense if you're under siege and trying to buy time" – "buy time" was an expression not common to the Gwilldonians, but his audience grasped the meaning sufficiently well – "but if you want to make an escape, or if the queen was trying to get her baby away to safety, why go up?"

"We believe the queen answered that herself. 'As the father of the Romani, as the daughter of Cerenthai, so shall the Anointed of this House be saved this day'," quoted Harac. "You'll not be familiar with our stories, lad.

"In an ancient legend, the young daughter of King Cerenthai had been out walking with her tutor when she spied her father, newly returned from a long journey, as he rode with companions beyond the far side of an old and decaying bridge that crossed above a deep chasm. A more experienced or a more cautious eye than the child's would have seen that the bridge was no longer safe for crossing – indeed, the king and his company had chosen to pass that way for the express purpose of surveying its state and planning its repair – but the joy of seeing her father filled the girl's vision with his person alone, leaving no room for any immediate peril to find its way into her sight. With abandon did she rush toward the bridge and then onto it before her imprudent tutor perceived the danger and called to her to stop. She paid him no heed, but her father heard at one time the tutor's call and the clattering of the battered bridge and then caught sight of his daughter. Rushing toward her and then throwing himself down from his horse, he hesitated only when he came to the first step of the bridge. His end of the bridge was marked by broken and frayed rope, rotted and missing planks, and he feared that any approach of his would bring the bridge down with his beloved child still upon it. The king yelled to the girl, now almost halfway across, to turn back. Even as he watched, there was a snap of rope caused by his daughter's slight weight; he knew that his own would never be borne. At the same time, his daughter let out a scream as the board beneath her feet lost half its support and others slipped away entirely, crashing hard somewhere below. The girl clutched at one rope beside her and tried to balance her feet on another stretched below it. In the meantime, the useless tutor had finally attempted to

169

follow the girl, but too slowly and with more concern for his own welfare than his charge's. His lukewarm efforts may have done more harm than good, for at his earliest steps, another snap of the rope sounded and he scrambled back to safety. Again, the girl screamed, and this time she fell, still clutching the rope, which now hung down from what remained of the bridge, swinging her to and fro over the chasm. Her hands caught on a knot and she bravely held fast, waiting for the rope to steady. Miraculously, the remnants of the bridge did not crash down upon her or batter her against the side of the cliff. But the child hung there, midair, the broken skeleton of the bridge above her, hard rocks below. Two of the king's companions were already riding hard to another place where they could cross to try to reach her from her own side of the bridge, but the place they sought was far. The remaining two companions made frantic efforts to secure what was left of the bridge so that the smaller of them might attempt to climb across it and reach the girl from above. But the king himself turned toward the Great Cliffs and loudly called out words that no one else among them could understand. When his daughter cried out to him in anguish, he turned toward her and perceived that her grip had loosened. Indeed, she could hold tight no longer, and the king watched his only child slip down the rope towards its end. Then, as her hands left the rope and all hope died inside her father, two mighty gryphons swooped down and one of them caught her up, carrying her to a place of safety. For it was to the gryphons of the Great Cliffs that the king had called.

"Or, so goes the tale," Harac concluded. "It has never been known in our time for a gryphon to be summoned in such a way by a human. Still, it is said that the father of the mother of Arandella once performed, in his youth, a great service for the gryphon clan. So we have supposed that the queen's message means that she, like King Cerenthai, called to the gryphons for aid and that they, to return a favor to her family, flew from the cliffs where they dwell to the highest window of the high tower of Dunryelle and carried her own child out of danger and into a place of safety. 'As the daughter of Cerenthai'."

There was a pause as the newcomers considered all this. It must be as the others had surmised. Arandella had called on the gryphons, because what else could the reference to Cerenthai have meant? But that only explained half of the queen's riddle, and Beth

170

considered the remaining half. "If the Romani are Romans, then the 'father of the Romani' would be Romulus, I guess," she said quietly, looking to Luke, who half-nodded, half-shrugged in response. He knew the name, but Roman history was more Beth's thing than his (except for the military stuff, which he liked and she didn't care about).

Beth stared at the floor, wondering what sort of clue that had been for them. What legends might they have about Romulus? Everything she knew about him could be said in a couple of sentences. Or maybe the father of the Romani was somebody entirely different for them – maybe the founder of their own line of Latin-speaking peoples.

When she realized that no one was talking, she looked up and found every eye fixed on her. What had she said? Only that the father of the Romani must be Romulus, but she must have made some sort of mistake. She supposed that here they considered someone else to be the founder of the Romans. But why were they looking at her that way? Unless she'd offended them.

"I'm sorry. I thought that meant something else," Beth said a little confusedly. "It must be someone from your stories. Please go on." She could hear the nervousness in her voice and she was sure she had turned red, even though the others might not be able to tell in the amber light.

Beth felt she was sinking away inside. They had all expected her to solve some sort of riddle and now she'd made it clear that she couldn't begin to understand it. This was it, then. The moment she'd been dreading. The moment when they knew that she was the wrong person, that she could never be their champion. She only now realized how much she'd been hoping that somehow, miraculously, she'd be able to give them what they needed.

"Who is this Ra-r-ramullis?" Harac asked, stumbling over the name.

"Nothing. I mean, no one. . . . Oh, well, uhm . . ." She wanted to rush through it, but the words wouldn't come fast enough for her. "In our world, the Romani (the Romans, for us) were a great ancient people who started out in a city called Rome. Their legend said their founder was named Romulus, so I thought . . . well . . . But never mind. Would you please explain what that part means – 'the father of the Romani'?"

Gweynleyn, who had been quiet for so long, stifled a laugh of excitement. Her moist eyes shone and glistened in the torchlight as she softly spoke. "We cannot. The stories of the Romani are ancient among the ancient, and this one seems to concern the founding of the Romani of your world, not ours. Arandella was most learned and in her youth studied long among the hermits of Eleyndria Mar. She knew stories that even I, who have lived an age longer than any others of the council, have not heard. 'The father of the Romani' has been a mystery to us these many years."

"But . . . then why would she pick that story? She must have known you wouldn't understand."

"Truth. We would not understand. But neither would the Torks, should the orb fall into their hands. She knew the chance for that was strong, though in the end the orb remained hidden until loyal Gwilldonians drove the invaders from our land. In *your* land, though, such a great one as the founder of the Romani must be known to all." Luke raised his eyebrows at that and turned a look of obvious incredulity in Beth's direction. He did not catch her attention, however; her gaze was fixed on Gweynleyn. The lady came forward and knelt before Beth, taking the young hands between her own. "In time, we learned that before the Anointed's birth Tanek the Wise had foreseen a champion from your land – the land of the first Romani – who would one day come to the aid of Arandella's child in a time of great need; this he promised the princess, though he knew not what the crisis would be nor how soon it would come. He counseled her that, should the crown one day pass to her, she should in turn anoint her child at once. He did not know how soon those events would come to pass; he foresaw only that one day the champion would come to make all things right. *Today* is that day and *you* are that champion, come to remove the veil and reveal all, restoring rightful rule. For ten years and more, others have tried to discover the hiding place of the Anointed, but in the end, the place would only be discovered when the time was right. That time is now."

"Aye. Tell us now," Harac's husky voice joined in as he nearly leapt toward Beth. "Tell us now where to find the Anointed. At once . . . before it is too late for Gwilldonum."

At that moment, miles away in Greyvic, the Tork scholar Eustarius was addressing his lord, Myrmidon. He spoke in a hushed voice, though the two of them were out of doors and no one seemed near enough to overhear. Amid unwelcoming hosts, the rest of the Tork company was still settling into its quarters or tending to its horses, having recently been escorted to the city from Ferinia's border under the ever-watchful eye of the despised Therin Mandek. Myrmidon Tork himself was conscious of being observed from at least three separate vantage points even now. Despite Gwilldonian vigilance, however, his advisor Eustarius (not a military man himself and therefore dismissed too lightly as a subject of interest by Therin's subordinates) had already managed a secret communication of import. "I bring word from our 'friend' concerning the Council of Ten and this supposed champion," he reported, greatly satisfied with his own cunning.

"Let us walk about and I will hear it." Myrmidon listened intently to each word his advisor spoke, though for appearance's sake he walked with as seeming a lack of purpose as a soldier's gait would allow.

"Of the council members previously gathered at Arystar," Eustarius reported, "Harac alone has stayed behind with the lady Gweynleyn. By all appearances, she remains convinced that a champion will yet come and will somehow lead the anointed child to the throne; the rest of the council members are less certain, though they hesitate to speak strongly on this point in her presence. Of the three escorts, only one returned to Arystar and he brought no champion." Eustarius moved on quickly from this point, for it was a failure of the Torks that Rowan had managed to return at all. "A second escort sent word of a similar lack of success. Soon afterward, an angeli – that is, a messenger bird trained by Lady Gweynleyn – arrived. By then, the lady had become very closed and did not make known the message she had received, but we may guess that it came from the walkabout escort . . . . One of the Silent Ones was in the lady's company at about that time." Here Eustarius touched on another delicate point, for the Torks hated passionately the Silent Ones of Gwilldonum, while knowing themselves nearly powerless against them. The most Myrmidon could reasonably hope for in that regard would be to drive them back into their sacred hills, never to be seen by that generation again.

Only the clenching of one fist and the momentary tension in his neck muscles bore witness to the disturbance Myrmidon experienced on hearing this last bit of news. The walkabout was the least experienced of the escorts – the council had been foolish to send it out – and Myrmidon had hoped the offer of a generous reward would lead to its apprehension. "Go on. The rest of the report. How came the council to disband earlier than anticipated?"

"Rane of the Brenmarch left immediately on receiving news from his homeland . . . as we had expected. The brewer Gort and his companions disposed of him along the road; the fools evidently expected the deed to remain hidden, or at least to appear as an accident. But fortune and a modicum of sense on the part of the council members worked against them. Rane's body was discovered at once and foul play suspected from the start. However, this fact may have given an advantage to us in the end, for it disturbed the council greatly. Two members and their parties made immediate plans to leave, expressing fear of similar plots among their own kind; others became increasingly uneasy, speaking urgently of their desire to hurry on to Greyvic to be present on the very day of our arrival."

"But this Harac, of whom we have heard so much, remained behind," Myrmidon said thoughtfully. "And has he a personal entourage with him?"

"No, none. It is his way to travel singly, more often than not."

"And the lady?"

"Half a dozen personal attendants and a groom. None more."

"You are well informed," Myrmidon responded appreciatively and Eustarius bowed his head slightly in gratitude. "So, such is the meager assembly that will greet the champion, should one in fact appear." He was silent for a moment but thinking furiously. When at last he spoke, it was with a certain frustration. "What is in her mind?" he asked rhetorically, Gweynleyn foremost in his thoughts. "Does she secretly know the location of the Anointed or does she not? And if she knows, how can it be that she finds herself, with all the resources of Gwilldonum at her disposal, unable to bring the child forward? Or is it that she has the child hidden somewhere at hand but looks to the champion to rally forces against us and drive us out entirely before she dares to bring a weak and ill-equipped whelp to the throne? She will not find that an easy task! Indeed, I flatter myself

174

that, without first presenting a royal child to the restless mobs, she has not a chance of driving us away! The tide is too much with us now!

"Or," he continued, "are the whereabouts of the child unknown even to Lady Gweynleyn, as our informant believes, and the task of the champion is to go in search? But in that case, what miracle can she expect if she hopes the missing child to be produced before this festival has passed? . . . How can this be?" This was a matter of supreme practical importance to Myrmidon Tork, but it had also become a matter of a more mundane strain of interest as well. Here was a mystery he could not unravel! And Myrmidon Tork did not like mysteries.

After a few moments of consideration, he said, "I should very much have liked an eye kept on Harac and Lady Gweynleyn. Our informant would have done well to stay behind. We could have learned at once the identity and the designs of this champion, should he in fact appear. "

"It could only have been done with great awkwardness, it seems. Lady Gweynleyn made pretense that she would depart for Greyvic along with other council members, leaving only two of her attendants and the groom to give direction should the last escort return, but her plan from the outset was to stay behind at the last moment. Only by a combination of happenstance and subterfuge did our informant learn of this deception and by then any change of plans would have met with suspicion."

"The lady suspects those at the council. Perhaps even the council members themselves?" Myrmidon asked thoughtfully.

"I posed this question as well. 'She suspects all' was the answer I received."

"She is wise in this," Myrmidon responded with some irony and a smirk, "though rather late." An idea struck him. "Is it possible that the lady stayed behind not to await the champion's arrival, but because the champion had already reached Arystar, unbeknownst to the others, and was in hiding nearby?" He spoke more to himself than to Eustarius.

Too many questions! Too many answers unknown!

A curse on this champion that had begun to plague his waking and his sleeping! Who *was* he, whence came he – if indeed he had come – and what powers did he possess? *Was* he there at Arystar already? Had Gweynleyn *encouraged* the departure of all

175

but the one she trusted with surety? "Could it be—?" He considered a possibility which he found unlikely but disturbing. "Could it be that they prepare to ride on us even now, with this great warrior-champion at their lead? . . . Or," he reconsidered, "is it truly *knowledge* he has brought them – knowledge that will somehow free the Anointed to come forward and claim the throne? *But what can he know that the others do not?*"

Tell us now, Harac had said. But how could Beth tell them what she didn't know? How could she tell them where to look in a land she barely knew when they themselves had been trying for years?

"I . . . uhm, well . . ." She looked to Luke in desperation. *Help me!* her eyes pleaded.

What am I supposed to do? his expression did its best to answer back . . . but he was already beginning to think fast.

Beth looked at the expectant eyes around her, especially those of Gweynleyn, who had dropped Beth's hands and fallen back from her a bit but who still gazed at her intently. Beth turned and leaned in close to Luke, whispering, "I just can't do it. And there's so much riding on this!"

"Then . . ." *Focus,* he told himself. *She's smarter than she thinks. She's probably got the key somewhere in her head; she's just panicking.* "Then, pretend there *isn't!*" he whispered back, though he figured the others could probably hear him if they were half-trying. "It's just a game. A role-playing video game and you're going to show me up by solving the riddle before I do. Not that I'm saying you could pull that off in real life, but let's just say you can do it here. All the magical air and stuff. And . . . and here's something you've never heard me say before: Just ignore me for a while." He stood up and made little shooing motions to her with both hands. "Just get up there inside your own little head and ignore everything else."

Luke figured that the best thing he could do for Beth was to stall for time and draw attention away from her so that she could calm down and think everything out. As for himself— *Just jump in,* he thought. *Start talking and make it up as you go.*

"So," he said, beginning to pace about, gracelessly breaking up the circle that had begun to tighten around Beth, "here's what we've got so far. I'll sum up, if I may." (He said the words in the

176

same tone he'd recently used for an oral report on the major developments of the Industrial Revolution in eighteenth-century England. He thought it would be just the right approach.) Taking a deep breath, he quickly selected his next words.

"First we have the queen and those other guys heading up to the uppermost chamber." That seemed like a good enough place to start. As he spoke, he gestured with exaggeration, hoping that the motions would somehow help his overall stalling efforts. At the least, they inspired Harac to move back a good three feet. "The *upper*most chamber – and we all see the significance of *that*, don't we?" As he nodded knowingly, he looked over his audience one by one. "It's the daughter of Cerenthai thing, all right. And, by the way, you don't hear *that* name every day, do you? So, we've got to figure that the whole gryphon angle is the straight stuff (and it makes for a very cool story, I must say!). The gryphon flies the little baby away to a safe place. And just how old is that baby, are we thinking?" Unfortunately, this question led to only the slightest of digressions (the exact date of birth was unknown, though the infant could not have been more than several weeks of age and would be nearing eleven years by now), and Luke was forced to resume his efforts momentarily.

"So anyway, that's point one. Baby, gryphon, fly away. OK. Next. Do we know yet if it's a baby boy or a baby girl? Answer: no, we don't. It's still a major toss-up, because even though the father of the Romani is a male, of course, the daughter of Cerenthai is, well, a girl. So, 'The riddle gives us nothing on that!' is how I'd sum up the whole girl-or-boy thing."

While Beth was trying to collect her thoughts and slow down her heartbeat, she couldn't help looking around to see how the others were reacting to Luke's ramblings. Harac seemed torn between exasperated impatience and a bewildered fascination. Rendel and Aynyxia were simpler in their expressions, his being one of polite attention, hers of pleasant interest. When Beth looked at Gweynleyn, who was nearest her, she thought she detected a strain of amusement in the lady's profile, but just then the lady turned toward her with a look of such anxious concern that Beth's heartbeat sped back up. She could feel drops of sweat at her temples and knew they hadn't been caused by the heat of the torches.

Luke, on his end, wasn't sure if he was impressing his audience with his reasoned approach or making a colossal fool of himself. He was inclined toward the latter view, in which case Beth owed him big time.

"Now, the next question is, what have you done about the whole gryphon end of things? You've been busy following up on all *that*, I hope!" Harac, assisted to a certain degree by Gweynleyn, explained as patiently as he could that a number of brave and loyal persons had risked their safety to approach the gryphons, for the way to their cliff dwellings was a hazardous one, but on their return had had little to show for their troubles. The characteristic response of the gryphons was that they preferred not to involve themselves in human affairs. At best, they answered inquiries with vagaries and enigmas. More typically, they answered not at all. The last and cleverest of the questers had two minor successes; she brought the chief gryphon to these admissions – first, that the family of DarQuinn was deemed honorable and was favored by the gryphons, and, second, that no human had passed more than one night in their cliff dwelling for a generation and a generation again (for some had wondered whether the gryphons themselves were raising the Anointed, unlikely though this seemed). There was nothing more of significance to relate.

Harac hurried through the explanation, anxious to hear from Beth. Luke knew the time had come and hoped Beth was ready.

"Last, we come to the part you've all been waiting for," he was saying, slowing his speech. "The father of the Romani. That would be Romulus, as just about anyone at all would know in our world, for sure. He's the one, all right. Romulus. No doubt about it. But how does that help us?" He glanced back at Beth for the first time since he'd started talking. "Good question. And that's just where our champion comes into it. Be-e-th?" He drew her name out as if it had an extra syllable or two, a rising note in his voice; he sounded hopeful but unsure. "Now you can tell us, nice and slowly, everything you know about Romulus." He leaned in closer and whispered, "It'll be all right." Then he moved away again, taking his seat beside her.

For the last several minutes, Luke had been racking the one available corner of his brain for anything else, besides the founding of Rome, that he could associate with Romulus. He knew that there was another R-name that went with it – Rebus, he thought. Beyond that, he had only a vague association with Star Trek. Beth was bound to come up with more than *that*, at least.

"Well," she began at last, "according to legend, there were two brothers, Romulus and Remus. I think they got in a fight or something and Remus got killed, so it was Romulus who was in charge of the new city, Rome. I don't think there's much more than that. . ."

C'mon, Beth! thought Luke. *All that top-of-the-line stalling I did for you . . . c'mon, you can do it.*

"Except," Beth continued, "there's a story about the brothers as babies."

That's right! Luke knew that story too. Why hadn't he thought of it himself? Because he'd been picturing Romulus as a grown man founding a city, of course, and he'd drawn a total blank. But it would be the baby story that mattered. Only . . . how could that be?

"When they were babies," Beth continued, "they were put or thrown in a river, but I'm not sure if it was to drown them or to save them." Luke was concentrating intensely. *A river . . . doesn't fit with the whole gryphon thing, though. Unless . . .*

"I'm sorry, I'm not sure I'm getting the details right," Beth apologized. "But somehow they were rescued by . . ." She paused for eight seconds that seemed much longer. "Of course!" she whispered.

"*Of course!*" Luke exclaimed loudly, and he actually hit his hand to his forehead. "But . . ." He wasn't sure it was possible. Then he knew that it *must* be possible – he saw it in Beth's face. She'd figured it out.

The others saw it too.

Rendel moved close to her, kneeling, and took her hand. "What is it, Beth?"

"I might be wrong."

"You must tell us nonetheless." It was Lady Gweynleyn's voice, she knew, but it sounded far away.

Intense faces focused firmly on her own, but Beth would not meet anyone's eyes. She concentrated hard, making sure she had it right before she said it out loud.

"Well, blast it all, girl! Come on with it already!" burst out Harac, who was finding the wait intolerable.

"Who rescued Romulus?" asked Gweynleyn in a soft but insistent voice. "Who rescued the father of the Romani?"

"Not 'who' . . . *'what'*," Beth said with relative calm, now confident that, for whatever it was worth, this was the best she could offer. "It was a mother wolf. There's a famous statue of the wolf nursing the babies. She raised them." While the others let this sink in, Beth turned to Luke, who was still missing a piece of the puzzle. "Think of Sharana Tey," is all she said, but it was enough. She turned back to Rendel. "You're the one who told me the other day that you know of only two kinds of animals here that can take human form: the Caverna cats and the white wolves of– I don't remember the name. But is it possible? Could the queen have sent her child to live with wolves? Are the white wolves . . . safe?"

After looking around at one another, each person's gaze eventually fixed on Gweynleyn, the only one present to have known Arandella well. "This is possible," she answered at length. "I would not call the wolves 'safe.' They can be quite fierce and they are greatly distrustful of humans (not without cause, I fear), but they are not disloyal to Gwilldonum. They keep to themselves and may brutally drive trespassers from their territory, but I believe it is a matter of their own defense more than for any other reason. . . . Yes, it is possible," she repeated thoughtfully, trying to weigh the matter as Arandella must have. "They would keep the secret well. And consider, what better hiding place could she have found than the wolven forest of Lupriark? Though it is not so very far, who among us, or among our people, has ventured into it these many years? Scarce any. And," she had remembered something, "I do not recall the cause of it, but I believe the Tork clan has long hated and feared the wolves above any other creature. . . . *As the father of the Romani* . . . Yes," she smiled and a long-absent peacefulness settled into the lines of her face, "I can believe that Arandella sent her child to safety, to live among the wolves until this day."

"Then we are away at once," said Harac decisively, "to the wolven forest. To Lupriark."

PART TWO

CHAPTER FOURTEEN – The New Journey

"Imre is from the northeastern parts, is she not?" Gweynleyn asked concerning her youngest attendant. The lady was seated in the Great Hall of the Stronghold of Arystar, the castle that was presently her primary residence but that would have been instead the chief residence of the *princeps,* if only there had been one.

"She is, Lady," answered Mariza. Knowing what her mistress had in mind, she added, "The home of her family is not far from Lupriark, as I recall, close by Little Down's Keep."

"Bid her join me here, if you will."

"Yes, Lady."

Gweynleyn awaited Imre's arrival silently, not speaking to or even glancing toward the only other occupant of the large room. Beth, resting on a small sofa in a shadowed corner, was glad to be left alone, feeling almost invisible, absently sipping the warm mint cider someone must have handed her.

On the short horseback trip from Arystar's Green earlier that day, she'd ridden double with Luke, who'd been surprised that Beth had shown no interest in being the one to "drive" the horse, as he'd put it. She seemed a little out of it, he'd thought, and must need some recovery time. A few hours later, drinking her warm cider alone in the dark corner, she was still recovering. She'd shown a spark of interest while being invited into a real castle for the first time – but not *that* much interest, all things considered; she'd taken a little of the refreshment offered to her, but *only* a little, though she ought to have been hungry. Luke, by contrast, had sampled every dish but one (a grayish soup that elicited a rather rude whispered remark that only Beth heard). He'd been feeling pretty satisfied with the events of the day so far, but Beth had still been trying to take in everything that had happened . . . and what was about to happen.

The expedition to Lupriark, the wolven forest, was to begin at earliest light on the following morning, and Beth and Luke were to be a part of it. While Beth sat alone in her little corner of the castle's Great Hall, Luke was off somewhere with Harac and Lady Gweynleyn's groom, seeing to the horses, whatever that involved. He'd been surprised that Beth hadn't come along – she loved horses. She was too tired, she'd said, and he'd gone without her.

But it wasn't so much the aching of her muscles that made Beth feel exhausted, as if all energy had been drained from her. Her emotions had been taking too many drastic turns lately. She'd been so tense, so on edge. Then came the relief, the excitement of knowing that she had helped the others after all – but nagging doubt quickly marred the relief. *Had* she done her part right? Had she solved the riddle correctly? She couldn't be sure – and now it seemed that her adventure had only begun. Was there *more* that they would expect of her? Not that she was sorry to be going on with the others in the morning. Luke was certainly excited about it, and she supposed she would be too when it was time. For the moment, though, she was really, really tired. Tired in her body and tired in her mind. She thought she might be in shock, because she shivered sometimes and someone had brought her a blanket.

When preparations for travel had begun all around her, she wanted to do nothing more than stay curled up on the sidelines, picking at her food and mechanically sipping her cider while watching in a distracted way the activity around her. She let her mind wander where it would, and she would have been hardpressed to recount afterwards .what thoughts had occupied her until at last her attention was caught by the arrival of Imre, a slight young girl – around her own age, Beth supposed. She seemed nervous.

Though Imre had been in service to her ladyship for an entire year and had known nothing but kindness from her, the girl still held Gweynleyn in awe and was anxious at having been singled out to come before her in what was so clearly a critical time. "Yes, m'lady?" she asked timidly.

"Your family is from the northeastern parts?"

"Yes, m'lady," the girl answered evenly, though surprised at the question.

"I leave for Greyvic on the morrow," Gweynleyn explained, "but others of our company turn to the east. Toward

Lupriark." Beth heard the intake of breath at the name, and she fixed her attention on Imre, though she could see her only from behind. Gweynleyn said nothing more for a moment, and her servant began to understand.

"Will you have me go with them? Into Lupriark . . . beyond the Dark Rim?" Imre asked after the pause. Though Beth heard a quiver in the voice, she was certain that the girl stood taller and had tilted her head up toward Gweynleyn as she spoke the last words.

"No," the lady answered gently, "not so far as that. But I would have you guide them well on their way, if you will it."

"I will it and more," Imre answered, relieved.

"Very well. Harac will be of the party, and you may look to him for guidance and instruction, as circumstances warrant. Go make what preparations you wish so that you may leave by dawn, and you have my gratitude and favor."

Though she had been dismissed, Imre hesitated. "M'lady?"

"Yes?"

"I would go as far as you would have me."

"I know this." Gweynleyn smiled kindly. "I doubt not your loyalty. But if you take this company as far as the edge of the Dark Rim, you will have served me well. You will have served Gwilldonum well."

The interview was over and Imre went back in the direction from which she had come.

The conversation did not have the effect on Beth that one might have guessed. Clearly, the idea of going into Lupriark had disturbed Imre, so it would not have been surprising if her uneasiness had spread to Beth. But Imre had also been brave – brave and loyal and ready to do her part. She had revealed it only in small ways, but that was enough to stir a kindred sentiment in Beth.

Though still not entirely sure she'd done her part right so far, Beth felt a new seed of excitement growing. She was sure the journey ahead would be filled with challenges, but she hoped to rise to them. And she wouldn't have to be the "champion" any more! She'd just be one more part of the group. Aynyxia, Rendel, and Luke would be with her. Sharana was not going to Lupriark and had already begun her journey home, but Harac would be joining them instead (she thought that would be an improvement, though she wasn't quite sure yet). The five of them (six, including Imre) would travel together and do this thing for Gwilldonum. She was ready. Even a conversation she overheard later that evening didn't dampen her resolve to do something brave and . . . *noble*.

Or maybe it did, but not *so* much.

It happened when Luke was still with the horses and Aynyxia was somewhere soaking. Gweynleyn, Rendel, and Harac were discussing arrangements for the next day, and Beth was near enough to overhear.

"I could send an angeli with you," Gweynleyn was saying uncertainly. She looked to Rendel for an opinion.

"They are of a sensitive nature," he responded. "They would not gladly enter the Dark Rim, I fear, nor is it likely that they could cross the wolven territory in any but a much disturbed state. They have always served you well, but perhaps—"

"It is too much," she agreed before he finished.

"And as for the horses—" he began.

"No, not the horses either. They will speed you on your way, but the wolves certainly would not welcome them! You must enter Lupriark on foot."

"And if what I've heard tell of the Rim is true," Harac joined in darkly, "the horses would do us no good there in any event. Even if there were trails for them to follow, which there are not, the young cubs that make up half our party would probably be thrown and then trampled at the first sign of a ghoul, and our poor horses would run off wild into the darkness and be lost there forever."

"So, you're good with this, right?" a very upbeat Luke McKinnon asked Beth first thing the next morning. If he'd overheard any discussion of ghouls or the Dark Rim, he'd shown no sign of it. Beth wondered if she should tell him, though she knew he wouldn't back out of going even if she did – even if it scared him, which it certainly ought to! She decided against it. For the moment.

"I'm good," she answered with a nearly-natural smile. "But do you think we should talk to someone about how we get home after all this? Rendel and Aynyxia obviously don't know, and I'm not sure Harac would either, but I wondered if—"

"Lady Gweynleyn. My thought exactly." His tone changed as he added, "I'll go find her. I— I kind of wanted to talk to her anyway." He'd had almost no direct conversation with Gweynleyn, but he'd hoped to get a chance before they went their separate ways.

It was only minutes later, in an alcove off the main courtyard, that he found the opportunity. Gweynleyn was alone, seated on a stone bench, and seemed so lost in thought that Luke nearly turned and left her again. Before he could, she looked up.

"You wish to speak to me, Luke?" Her voice was solemn – a little sad, maybe – but inviting.

Yes, he wanted to speak to her. He wanted it very much, but he wasn't sure what it was he wanted to say. Hesitating, he began – rather pathetically, he thought immediately afterwards – by telling her, "You're the one who brought me here." Well, *duh!*

"Yes."

"Uh . . . thanks." Pathetic . . . again!

What was it he really wanted to say? There were things he'd been pretty curious about, of course. How had she found him? How had she known about him in the first place? But more than that . . . what *did* she know about him – about his life, his family . . . . his thoughts? Because he couldn't help feeling that she *had* known his thoughts somehow, that she'd found a way into his mind and understood what she'd discovered there. That was scary . . . but intriguing . . . and . . . and . . . something else. He couldn't put into words how he felt about it.

And there was another thing he wanted to ask: was this calling-someone-from-another-world business just not a big deal to her? Because it kind of was to him, and he'd been wanting to talk about it – talk to *her* about it – partly because *anybody* would find that kind of interesting(!), but partly because there'd been something so personal about it all when it happened. Something intimate. Since seeing her face in the well, he'd felt this totally irrational connection to her. It didn't matter that the connection was probably all in his mind – he *had* to talk to her. But now that he was alone with her, he was tongue-tied and unsure.

"A Silent One came and showed you to me," she explained after a moment, though he'd asked nothing aloud. "He had seen that your friend would soon be in peril, so he showed you to me and showed me the place where you were, and I called to you there and brought you to aid her." Well, that answered some of it. But he still wanted to know— *What*, really?

Who *was* she? She was different from the others here (not to mention anyone else he'd ever met in his own world). She understood things. He could see it in her eyes – he'd seen it from the start, when her face had appeared to him in the well water. She'd understood . . . *him!* It had felt that way, at least. But how could she? Nobody really understood. He supposed he'd imagined that special connection between them.

It occurred to him then that he should have responded, so he answered belatedly, "Yeah, well, thanks again for that. I'd've hated explaining to Beth's mom that some wild, ugly pig ate her. In another world." He smiled and hoped she'd keep the conversation going. When she didn't, he asked, "By the way, was it hard to do – calling me here, I mean?" He thought he might as well get around to asking whether she could also send them back – just to get that little matter out of the way – but her answer distracted him.

"It is a great task and greatly fatiguing, especially so now that I am in a weakened state."

He regarded her in surprise. "You don't look so weak to me!" he blurted out, adding quickly, "Ma'am. I mean, my ladyship. . . or, you know, *your* ladyship." Whatever! "Are you . . . sick?" Maybe she had cancer or some other bad thing people got here.

Smiling bittersweetly, she explained, "When Gwilldonum fares ill, I fare ill as well. My soul is bound to that of my homeland." Even as the words left her mouth, Gweynleyn marveled that she had spoken them aloud. She had long found her connection with the land (a legacy, for better or for worse, from her dear father) to be too great a thing to commit to common speech and, especially in these last years, too great a burden to share – even when it came to Therin, whom she esteemed and cherished. And yet she had shared it with this boy! This boy who was so very different from her . . . and yet *alike*. She had sensed the likeness in him when she had called him through the water.

"Well, then," Luke told her sincerely, "I hope Gwilldonum fares better. . . . We'll do our best to help," he added encouragingly and was immediately certain of sounding like an arrogant idiot. "If we can," he amended, not sure whether the addition was an improvement or the contrary.

Though Lady Gweynleyn didn't immediately speak, Luke sensed she wanted to. He remained quiet for a couple of minutes, but when she seemed to lose herself more and more in her thoughts, he wondered if he should leave.

At last, turned away from him and sounding as if she were speaking as much to herself as to him, she said, "There is a great evil that plots against us."

"You mean this Tork guy?" Luke spoke uncertainly. Gweynleyn's manner made it unclear if he was even still part of the discussion, but she responded readily.

"Myrmidon Tork is baneful enough" – though her answer was soft, a depth of feeling lay behind it – "but I speak of another, for the Torks do not act alone. I speak of one who has true evil in his heart. . . . " She was quiet again, and he wondered again if he should just slip away. He didn't *want* to, but he wondered if he should. "Luke," Gweynleyn said after the pause, this time turning her clear eyes directly toward his and putting one soft hand on his arm, "the course of any evil must always collide with the course of good in the end. And the greater the evil, the greater the good that must rise before it."

She was clearly, earnestly directing the words to him, but Luke couldn't help feeling as if he'd wandered into the middle of someone else's conversation. What great evil did she have in mind, and what did it have to do with him? He was just helping out in rescuing this kid and then he'd be on his way. Luke McKinnon was at a total and unaccustomed loss for words.

For her part, Gweynleyn marveled again that she had shared her own grave concerns with him. She ought not have. He had come upon her at a moment when she was facing her own fears and distress, but she must control such things. This matter did not concern him. It was not his burden to bear. For the present, at least, it was hers alone.

Attempting a smile, she altered her tone to one more usual for her. "But this is not your part, Luke. Nor is it Beth's. Pray do not repeat my words to her or convey the anguish that I know you have seen in me; her burden is sufficient already. If the two of you succeed in returning the Anointed to us, it will be enough. We of Gwilldonum will then stand together with our *princeps* and face what we must in the years ahead. And you will return to your people to stand with them in their own times of need."

189

"Uh, yeah, I guess. Actually, about that—"

"Yes?"

He hesitated, then shook his head. "Never mind." Gweynleyn clearly had problems of her own and she must have been trying to work them through alone in the courtyard before he'd interrupted her there. The conversation had taken a bizarre turn, and now it somehow seemed petty to ask about going home after that heavy "evil colliding with good" stuff. It could wait.

On parting from Gweynleyn, he found Beth again almost at once.

"Did you ask her about us getting home?"

Luke gave her an odd look, and all he said was, "Wasn't the best time. Maybe later."

When they were nearly ready to leave, Gweynleyn and Harac exchanged parting words. Beth, who hadn't had much to do to get ready, was waiting beside her horse and overheard them.

"Instruct her as you will," Gweynleyn was saying concerning Imre, "but remember her youth."

"Aye, I'll treat her exactly as if she were a dwarf-girl," Harac answered. Gweynleyn looked rather alarmed at the prospect until she glimpsed the twitching lips between the dwarf's mustache and his unruly beard. "A jest," he assured her. "No need for worry; she'll fare well with us, nowhere more so."

On a different topic, Gweynleyn asked, "Do you count to approach Greyvic by way of Arystar?"

"The road is a good one, but also one likely to be watched, I credit. But more than that, Lupriark is large, by all accounts, spreading long to the north and to the south. I cannot say from which end we will leave it."

That the road to Lupriark might be a false trail entirely, neither Gweynleyn nor even Harac now considered – partly from hopeful thinking but mostly out of a confidence in their champion, who had made a sound suggestion that no one before her had. Still, there was another concern. Though neither voiced the fear, each realized that the one they sought, even if once at Lupriark, might no longer be there. Perhaps all that awaited them was some further clue to send them flying in yet another direction. A year or even a month earlier, that prospect would not have been as unsettling as it was now. As things stood, only a matter of days remained before a critical point would be reached, and no time could be spared. Travel from Arystar to Lupriark and then from Lupriark to Greyvic would certainly cost every day the travelers had, if not every hour.

"I reckon we're most likely to come to you directly from the east," Harac finished, "on not so smooth a path as the Great Road but hopefully a less expected one."

"There are many open stretches along the Queen's Road, if that is what you have in mind," Gweynleyn answered. "You could be spotted easily, could you not?" She spoke uncertainly, knowing that such things fell more to Harac's realm of expertise than to her own.

"We'll stay close to the cliffside when we can; there are places for concealment. And even if we can be seen, by the same token, we'll be able to see what's coming. . . . And maybe we'll get the woodlander to earn his keep by going ahead as scout," he added with a wry smile.

Gweynleyn understood what lay behind the last remark. Harac found himself uneasily caught between a grudging admiration (learned slowly, over a number of years) for the woodlanders' talents and an incomprehension of their refusal to draw arms. He had known enough of them to accept that it was not a question of courage or cowardice, but for all their worthy ideals, why, he wondered, could they not comprehend that sometimes a sword was the only thing that could stop the wrong from crushing the right? It was clear enough to him, Harac, son of a warrior father and a warrior mother, both of great renown.

The rest of the company had assembled by then, and Gweynleyn announced, "I will arrange for assistance as soon as I reach Greyvic and have consulted with Therin Mandek, though to send out a company for your aid immediately on our arrival would surely raise suspicion. But send it we will; or better, at least two companies traveling on different courses. I will rely on the advice of the Captain of the Guard as to the timing and direction, but I credit that one company will seek you along the road from Arystar, a second along the Queen's Road to the north. You will know them by this: they will carry my colors and the mark of my seal.

"We must exercise the greatest caution and discretion – I on my part, you on yours – for once you are nearing Greyvic with our future *princeps* in your midst, it will not be so much a battle we must prevent as an assassination. One well-shot arrow or well-thrust blade will cripple all Gwilldonum. You must at any cost protect the Anointed until Therin's guard relieves you of the task."

When she had finished, she stepped forward to give a parting word to each (though to Luke she said nothing, merely touching her fingers to his cheeks and smiling) and arrived last at Beth. Placing both hands on Beth's head, she spoke quiet words that even Luke, the next nearest person, could not make out. Then she took the girl's hands in her own and kissed each one. When she stepped away, she said nothing, but it seemed to be the signal to depart.

They were taking five horses, Gweynleyn keeping the remaining animals so that her own party could make good time to Greyvic. Aynyxia, though her arm had been healing with remarkable speed as Rendel had predicted it would, volunteered to take turns riding behind the others since she did not like to "drive horses" (she had picked up the amusing expression from Luke).

"We're off then," said Harac, and everyone began to mount. "To Lupriark!"

"What exactly *is* the Dark Rim?" Beth eventually asked Aynyxia, with whom she rode. After such an exciting start, it had turned out to be a surprisingly ordinary day full of riding and resting and riding and resting. Varied conversation provided the main source of interest. In the present instance, the choice of topic wasn't idly chosen – Beth became anxious whenever she tried to picture the Dark Rim.

"Never been there," the other answered, though Beth suspected she could say more if she wanted.

"It is a forest," answered Rendel, who had overheard, "which marks the northeastern border of Gwilldonum – excepting Lupriark, which lies beyond the Rim. It begins close to the Great Cliffs, which are nearly uncrossable and which separate the Southlands from the lands of the north, and from there runs southeasterly, almost to the sea. Beyond the Rim is the corner of Gwilldonum we seek – the wolven forest; beyond that are the Mountains of the Dwarves, which are generally considered to belong to the Southlands but with which we no longer have much connection; beyond that, the lands are ill-known to us though they enter into stories of old."

192

"So, 'it's a forest' is what you're saying," summed up Luke. "I'd been getting the idea it was something on the 'spooky and sinister' side." Beth had repeated to Luke what she'd heard after all, and they'd both noticed a few new troubling references along the way.

Rendel spoke hesitantly. "There are many stories concerning the perils of the Dark Rim. It is difficult to know which carry truth."

"Well, *that's* pretty enlightening!" Luke's sarcastic remark came out sounding rather rude, and a surprised Beth, who rode just to his left, quietly told him so. He didn't respond to her comment (though she was sure he had heard it), leaving her to puzzle over his attitude.

What he did say, somewhat perversely and to no one in particular, was that he might be looking *forward* to seeing that Dark Rim.

"There will be danger," Rendel warned.

"Maybe I like danger," Luke answered defiantly.

There were other times on that first day out of Arystar that Beth wondered at Luke's behavior. He was usually an easy-going guy – on the surface, at least. Even when she knew something was really bothering him, she'd seen him do a pretty good job of keeping his emotions out of view of other people. But something about Rendel must be bothering him, and it kept creeping up to the surface and escaping in snarky comments. She didn't get what was going on.

At one point, when the party had stopped for a stretch and to refill their canteens from a stream, Luke said to Beth, "So, explain something to me. Harac, who seems obsessed with watching for bandits, though I'm beside myself with happiness to say I've seen nothing of the kind, just said that at least we've got 'five blades' because even Imre can use a knife. But I count six. Something weird about the math in this world?"

"Rendel's a pacifist," she answered simply.

"A what?"

"A pacifist. He doesn't believe in fighting."

"I know what it means, Beth!" Luke snapped.

"Sorry, I just meant—" She didn't get it. Why was he so touchy?

193

"How can you live in a world like this and not fight sometimes?" he asked rhetorically. He didn't sound surprised or curious. He sounded . . . irritated. But why? Beth wondered. She would've said Luke was a pacifist too, more or less.

"He doesn't fight, *all right?*" She was beginning to feel a little touchy herself.

Then later, after they'd chosen a spot to settle for the night, Luke pursued the subject with Rendel, making Beth uncomfortable. He raised the same question he had with her – how did woodlanders manage to survive in this world if they didn't ever fight? Fortunately, he'd adjusted his tone. Maybe this time he *was* more curious than anything.

"We have been well protected within Greenwood since time out of memory," Rendel explained willingly. "In times of peace, we travel the surrounding areas in relative surety, and we do have some peaceful means of protecting ourselves, as I have explained to Beth. In more troubled times, most of my kind do not venture beyond our borders."

"But you're venturing now," Luke pointed out. "These are troubled times, right? It's pretty dangerous for you, right?" Beth wondered what he was getting at; he seemed to be trying to bait Rendel.

Smiling, Rendel quoted Luke. "Maybe I like danger."

"I'm serious."

In a graver voice, Rendel responded. "And this is a serious undertaking. If the Torks come to rule Gwilldonum, it may in time (and perhaps not so very much time) mean the end of my kind."

"Then you'll fight, because it really matters this time."

"I will resist with whatever might and abilities I can summon . . . because it really matters this time."

"Resist. But you don't mean 'fight', do you? You wouldn't take a life?"

"I hope I would not."

"But . . . OK, let's just say, for instance, that Beth was in danger. Would you fight to save her life?" There was an edge to the question, a challenge.

What is he doing? wondered Beth, who was increasingly uncomfortable with the direction of the discussion. Why is he pushing? Luke could be curious about a lot of different things. She'd seen him probe people before about the choices they made or

194

the things they believed. But this was different. And it wasn't that he had a problem with pacifism. For some reason, he had a problem with *Rendel*. It was like they were in some sort of competition – only Rendel probably didn't even know it. Quietly, but with emotion, she said, "Just drop it, Luke."

Rendel, however, answered sincerely, "I do not mind, Beth." To Luke, he said, "If I could save her by giving my life, I believe that I would. In fact," he added, settling his gaze on the subject of their conversation, "I can be *almost* certain that I would. If, though, I knew that I could save her only by taking a life, I cannot be certain what I should do . . . except to search first for another way."

"So you might just let her die? And the same if all your woodlander friends were attacked?" he challenged harshly. "You'd just let these Torks come in and destroy everything you care about?"

"*Stop it!*" Beth ordered in a low voice.

Neither one acted as if he had heard, and Rendel answered, "My people are not unaware of the danger to us. We do not take it lightly. I do not credit that you, despite whatever wisdom and insight you possess, can know the weight now pressing on our spirits." Speaking with a quiet passion, he leaned closer. "But you must try to understand, Luke. It is true that if the Torks were to establish rule, our way of life might well be destroyed in time. But if the hour comes when we take up arms to fight . . . it will be lost to us all at once."

Luke said nothing and the conversation was allowed to die away.

If Beth had cause to wonder about Luke's attitude that day, he felt that he had sufficient reason to wonder about hers as well. He considered the matter as he tried to get comfortable that night, stretched out on the ground that wasn't *quite* as hard as it could've been. (Beth was either already asleep or pretending to be.)

He'd understood quite well about her recent waves of emotion related to being "the champion." Though he'd never had reason to articulate it before, he'd understood for a long time that responsibilities settled heavily on Beth. She was something of a perfectionist (some people said the same about him, but he knew they were wrong about that!), and she worried way too much about getting everything right and not letting anyone down. She really needed to lighten up! So, he got it about that whole part of things.

But when she didn't seem to be worried about the champion business, she seemed really . . . content. Not that there was anything wrong with that, of course. Not at all. It's just that she seemed to be . . . well, almost settling herself into this life. Acting like this was more than just a really, really temporary thing. But that's what it was – temporary. They were just passing through.

But she did seem to fit here, Luke admitted reluctantly. Much more than he did. Apart from the fact that she asked a lot of questions, she didn't seem like an outsider. Like earlier – he and Beth and Imre came back with the horses, which they'd taken downstream to a better place for them to drink, and they walked into some conversation among the other three about tree-rat bites. "Oh, *truth*! They're horrible, aren't they?" Beth had joined right in, taking a seat and starting to peel effortlessly some strange-looking fruit that Aynyxia handed her. (*Truth!* She'd actually said that instead of something simple and normal like "yes.") "The pain is *indescribable*!" she'd said next. And the weird thing was, she'd seemed pretty darned cheerful about that indescribable pain! Luke had asked with incredulity, "You're saying you've been bitten by some sort of vampire rat?" A tree-rat, she'd said. A fanged tree-rat. Yes, she'd been bitten, but only once. "Oh, well," he'd muttered, "if it was only *once* . . . I mean, who hasn't?" But *he* hadn't, of course. . . . And he couldn't get the hang of peeling that stupid fruit either!

Obviously, she was having a good time here and making new friends and all that. Well, of course he was glad for her; he was having a pretty cool time too (though *today* hadn't turned out to be his finest hour!). But there was no point in either one of them getting too attached to these people, because they – the two of them, Luke and Beth – were, as he kept putting it to himself, just passing through.

It's true that they were all very interesting, these characters they'd been meeting here. Especially Gweynleyn, of course; he'd never met anyone like her and probably never would again. But it's not like he thought he'd ever end up being buddies with her or anything. She was interesting, that's all. Fascinating, maybe. As for the rest . . . . Well, now he'd met a dwarf and a woman who was really a cat, so he could check those two things off his bucket list.

196

And he'd met a walking plant, which hadn't even been on his list in the first place.

Luke liked Aynyxia well enough. She was funny and unpretentious and looked at the world in her own little way. She didn't exactly strike him as the brightest cookie in the batch, but he was trying to keep an open mind about that since Beth had assured him that there was more to her than met the eye. "She's really good at a lot of stuff and she's brave and she watched out for me on that first day and saved that other plant-girl," Beth had pointed out. "It's just that she's OK. with letting other people be in charge. She sort of fades into the background in a bigger group." Any group bigger than *two*, apparently. And, also apparently, Beth already understood her new green friend inside and out! Like they'd known each other forever. . . . Still, Plant-Friend was OK.

That Rendel Singer, on the other hand, was a different kettle of fish, as Luke's dad would say (his dad had such a flair for words!). Luke wasn't sure about Rendel at all. He couldn't quite put his finger on it, but something about the guy rubbed him the wrong way. The fact that he was such a know-it-all didn't help. Not that Luke had anything against knowing stuff. Actually, he was a really big fan of knowing things. But still . . . that guy! *Beth*, apparently, could see no wrong in him. Luke wondered, even, if she might be getting a crush on him. As far as Luke knew, Beth didn't get crushes like some girls did . . . but she *was* about to turn thirteen, and you never could tell about girls!

Anyway, she'd looked sort of daydreamy earlier that evening, and Rendel had asked what she was thinking about, and she'd said something about woodlander dances, and then the guy asked if she wanted to try one right then! Luke could've told him what the answer to *that* would be! Beth got all shy and said no thanks and changed the subject pretty fast.

And it was right after that that they'd gotten into that whole stupid "not fighting" discussion. Luke felt pretty bad about that. He wasn't sure where all that had come from – it's not like he was some kind of warmonger or anything! He had nothing against non-violence! He even had a quote by Gandhi hanging on his bedroom wall and everything! So, what had he been doing? He was just so irritated by that guy sometimes. And why did Rendel have to stay so calm and friendly when Luke wasn't exactly being calm and friendly back?

197

Luke knew he'd really ticked Beth off. In fact, she'd told him a couple of times that day that he'd been rude. She'd hardly ever said that to him before, except in a laughing way . . . or when she was right. So, maybe . . . well, he supposed she was right this time too.

"Oh, well," he whispered in a yawn, suddenly realizing how drowsy he'd gotten. Too late to do anything about that now. He'd make it up somehow tomorrow, he told himself, dismissing the matter of today. With a nearly clear conscience, he went to sleep.

CHAPTER FIFTEEN – Little Down's Keep

The morning's ride went smoothly. Still no bandits approached, though Harac was ever-watchful. Travelers passed by occasionally, always in the direction of Greyvic, but no one, not even the dwarf, seemed overly concerned by the fact. Rendel was more reticent than usual, Aynyxia seemed as quietly content as normal, and Imre spoke only when spoken to. Luke made no sarcastic remarks for three hours straight (once, Beth thought he was about to, but a violent cough suddenly overcame him, apparently driving his previous thought from his head); he seemed cheerful and relaxed to everyone but Beth, who thought she detected effort behind the facade.

She forgave him for his aggravating behavior the day before – not that he had asked – and he was quite satisfied with his own efforts to be at peace with the world. By the midday break, when the group had dispersed a little, Beth and Luke were able to sit in a companionable silence with no sign of tension between them while she enjoyed the serenity of the scene, allowing her body to relax and her mind to wander, and he made patterns with the trajectories of small stones he flicked down the grassy slope on which they sat.

All was peaceful until Beth broke the silence by observing in a distracted way, "Have you noticed how when Rendel's amused or especially pleased about something his eyes actually twinkle?"

"Yeah, he's a real charmer," Luke answered after a pause, his attention seemingly elsewhere.

"No, I mean, seriously. There's an actual twinkle there."

"Yep," Luke agreed again, but still as if the matter held no interest and merited no more comment.

"No," Beth repeated, turning toward him to make her point more firmly. "I mean that there are times when his eyes actually, truly twinkle. They *glitter*. Literally."

"Yeah, I get it, Beth!" Luke's tone had changed. "They really, truly, actually, literally twinkle and glitter and gleam. OK? Time to move on?"

Both the words and the tone took her aback. After a moment, she said in a perplexed tone, "You really don't like him." When Luke didn't answer and merely continued to propel stones down the slope, she asked, "But why not, Luke? What's he done wrong? He's only helped us, and . . . and . . . he's kind. In fact, he might be the kindest person I've ever known." Except for her mother, but she didn't say that out loud.

Luke was basically an honest person and knew that what Beth said was true. He had no legitimate complaint against Rendel. Maybe that was part of the problem. A little bit of imperfection might have made the woodlander more acceptable to him, but even as he realized that, he couldn't understand why he should feel that way.

At last, he said, "I never said I didn't like him. He's OK, I guess. . . . And I guess he's even sort of cool in his not-like-me kind of way. Who knows? If things were different, we might even get to be BFFs and all that. . . . *But*," he went on, pursuing the train of thought that had been increasingly disquieting him, "*we don't live here, Beth!* You've started talking like them and acting like them and getting all cozy and everything like this is your new little circle of friends. But this isn't our home and it never will be." He stood up and began to pace unevenly, his tone intensifying as he spoke. "We're just passing through. We don't belong here. They're OK; they're *all OK*," he said, referring to their companions generally, "and I agree that being here is pretty cool. It's *incredibly* cool, in fact. Probably the coolest thing that's ever happened to me in my whole life! . . . But the thing is . . . it's temporary. We don't *belong* here. We have homes, we have our own friends, and we have *families*. Granted, mine's always wandering off into Semi-dysfunctional Land, but still, I'm kind of attached, you know? And what about you? Aren't you even thinking about your mother? You're all she's got and by now she must be—"

"*STOP! Don't! . . . Don't say it!*" He hadn't been looking at her, so intent on expressing his own thoughts that he hadn't detected hers. Now he saw that she was covering her ears and taking short breaths, and, though she faced down, he could see two large tears on her cheeks, and no doubt a whole stream of others would be lining up to follow.

He immediately regretted his words. *Stupid! Stupid, stupid! 'Aren't you even thinking about your mother?' Idiot!!* And now she was crying.

"I can't think about that, all right?" Beth blurted out in a choked-up voice. "What do you want me to do, Luke? I don't know how we can get home and I don't think we can anyway; at least, not until we do what we're supposed to do. . . . And after that . . . After *that*, I'll think about going home. . . . And then there'll be a way to, somehow. Right? . . . There's *got* to be." Then she added in a smaller voice, "I need to pretend that we're just away somewhere in a normal way, and when it's the right time, we'll be able to get home. *Someone* will be able to get us back, right?"

"Sure, sure." He hoped it was true. "Lady Gweynleyn can do it . . . I'm pretty sure. She got me here, she can get me back. Both of us, I mean. Or those Silent Ones. A bit on the weird-and-freaky side, but apparently they know just about everything. . . . You know, kind of like you on your more irritating days." Beth made a sound that could have been half of a laugh, or it could have been a sob. "Anyway, I'm-" He'd been about to say he was sorry, but changed it to, "I was being stupid. Airhead me! . . . You can even quote me on that. . . once. And you're right. There's nothing else we can do now, but eventually it will all work out. Forget I said anything, OK? I guess I'm just, you know, sort of . . ." He didn't finish.

"Scared?" Beth suggested, lifting her head.

"Uh, something in that general neighborhood would be about right, I guess."

"Well," Beth said, recovering somewhat and wiping her cheeks with the back of her hand, "we'd be stupid not to be. We're in some whole other world, and we don't know how to get home. This is a dangerous place, they might even go to war or something, we could *easily* get killed—"

"Whoa! Time for *you* to back up. We're not going down that road. Nobody around here is getting killed and that's final! Out of the question! Subject closed!"

"All right," said Beth. She sniffed but had begun to smile. "And let's not talk too much about home either, OK?"

"Deal. Now go wash your face somewhere. You're a mess!"

This time, Luke was sure that it was a laugh that escaped from Beth as she started to rise. "OK," she answered meekly, but she gave him a pretty decent shove as she passed by.

He was still there a moment later, alone and thinking, when Rendel approached.

"I saw Beth," the woodlander said, concern in his voice. "She seemed distressed. Should I go to her, do you think?"

"Well, that's an interesting question." Luke, sorry to have his train of thought interrupted, especially by Rendel, was not in a particularly helpful mood. "Aren't you supposed to know that sort of thing? Understand all the creatures of your world and all that?"

"Beth is not of my world," the other answered calmly, but his eyes studied Luke. "She is of yours."

"Oh yeah, that's right. That's exactly right." Rendel still looked concerned but smiled in a friendly way, making Luke feel that he himself was behaving badly. Which he was. "Well, anyway," he relented, "I'd leave her alone for a while. She'll be all right." Then he opened and raised his canteen for a drink, signaling that the conversation was over.

"Beth is not . . . your mate?" Rendel asked tentatively.

It was unfortunate for Luke that his first swallow of water was just passing through his mouth and into his throat at that moment. "*Mate?*" He choked out the word, sputtering and spewing droplets. "No! Beth and me? We're just kids! I mean, *she* is. And I'm just . . . *No!* Not at all. None of that mating stuff here. *No way!*"

"I see," said Rendel. "I did not think so." He turned to walk away, but not before Luke caught the look on his face. It was a smiling face, and Luke was sure that the woodlander's eyes were twinkling. Literally.

Beth was quiet when they began to ride again. Luke was pretty sure everything was all right between them . . . but he figured that stupid thing he'd said about her mother was probably still bothering her. They were riding through an open space and there was plenty of room to bring his horse up alongside her, so he did and, hoping to distract her, began a conversation on the first subject that came into his mind.

"You know, they don't really have the 'just being a kid' thing down around here, do they? Think of this kid we're looking

202

for who's supposed to stop his whole country from falling apart before he even turns eleven. 'Age of all rights' at ten? Isn't that it? What ten-year-old has all his rights? . . . Or *ought* to?" demanded the fourteen-year-old. "It's ridiculous! . . . *AND* . . . what's all this mating stuff? Totally inappropriate topic, I've got to say!"

"Who's talking about mating?"

"No one," Luke answered quickly. "No one at all."

"You know, when I was in Greenwood I saw really young-looking woodlanders with mates and children. But then, maybe they weren't as young as they looked."

"Maybe they were, maybe they weren't," Luke answered lightly. "But it's all the same to us, because we're just passing through here, you and I, as I believe I mentioned to you earlier today in my subtle and sensitive way. . . . But moving back to that 'kid' thing – look at what they've expected *you* to do and you're only twelve."

"Thirteen."

"You're twelve," he said, fairly sure of himself.

"Well, I was when we left home, but we've been gone about five days – or, I have, at least. I'm figuring that today's my birthday, and so I'm thirteen now."

"Your birth day?" repeated Rendel, drawing his horse up on the other side of Beth. Aynyxia rode with him; Harac and Imre were ahead. "Today is a special day in your life?"

"Well, a birthday is the anniversary of the day you were born. I was born exactly thirteen years ago today." (Luke made a noise along the lines of "Hmmph!") "Do you celebrate birthdays?" she asked Rendel.

"Woodlanders do celebrate days of birth. Indeed, we celebrate greatly whenever a child is born. But you are now thirteen years of age? This is a special time, that you should have a day of celebration for it? But you are missing it because you have come to us?"

"Oh, it's all right. It's not that special. We actually celebrate birthdays *every* year. Usually with presents and cake . . . and maybe friends come over. But," she glanced at Luke, "we hope we're not missing much at all at home." After all, she and Luke had left home on the same day in their own world but arrived in this one on different days. "We're hoping time won't have passed for us there."

She sounded quite uncertain – it seemed so much more unlikely when she said it aloud – but took heart when Rendel answered unexpectedly, "Ah, yes. I have heard of such things. There are remarkable stories of the champions who come from afar."

"There are?" Luke questioned at once, drawn back into the conversation despite himself.

"Truth, including that they do not age when they are here and that all time stops in their own worlds when they leave it. Not all believe such stories, but I am inclined to do so."

"Well, then, I'm inclined to do so too!" Luke smiled, feeling quite charitable toward Rendel in that moment. "Now *that's* something to celebrate." The last word reminded him of their main subject, and he said, "Sorry, Beth, about you missing your birthday and all, but you'll just have it again when we get home. . . . Another birthday won't count as turning *four*teen, though," he added as an afterthought. There was no way she was catching up with him!

"Imre hasn't said much this whole trip," Beth observed to Luke when they'd stopped some time later to give the horses a rest and a drink.

"Yeah, she's a quiet little thing, isn't she?"

"She seems sort of nervous. Think she's scared of us?'

He looked over at the girl, who seemed to be fidgeting with her pack for no significant purpose. "Not to worry. I'll turn on the old McKinnon charm and she'll loosen right up." He made his way over, took a seat beside her, and leapt immediately into conversation. "So, how are you doing, Imre?"

"I am well, thank you," she answered quietly and properly, barely glancing in his direction before looking away again. Then she added as an afterthought, "And you are well, I hope."

"Right as rain, as the old folks say!" That seemed to cover their first topic. "And so . . ." The McKinnon charm faltered a bit. "Well, how old are you?" Seemed as good a topic as any.

Imre lost some of her timidly, answering a bit defensively, "I am sufficiently old. I have traveled this path many times. I will take you to Little Down's Keep and I would take you even into the Rim and beyond if her ladyship asked it."

"OK, OK." Luke realized that his charm had offended her right out of her reticence. "I was thinking of something more along the lines of a number. I, for instance, have been alive for fourteen and a half years. Got any info like *that* to share?"

"I was eleven years when I began to serve her ladyship and that was one full year ago."

"OK, so I'm going out on a limb here and guessing that you're . . . oh, let's say, twelve."

He gave her a charming smile, and she returned it, saying only, "Yes."

"Well, I've got to say," he went on magnanimously, "that where I come from everyone would be pretty impressed that you could be our guide through the woods at twelve years old. *Pretty impressed!*"

Imre smiled again, pleased and grateful. After a few more minutes of conversation (none of it very deep), she felt bold enough to say, "You are the great champion, are you not?"

The question took Luke by surprise, but then he realized she didn't have any way of knowing otherwise. "Well, I . . . No, actually. I . . ." She thought *he* was the champion. "Well, I wouldn't say I'm *great*, exactly. And as for the champion thing," he leaned in a little and spoke in a secretive way, "let's just say I'm here to help. That's all."

"I understand," Imre answered seriously.

They got along quite well after that. In fact, Imre began at once to appear more comfortable not only with Luke but with the company in general, though she was still a bit afraid of Harac. She enjoyed chatting with Luke most of all, though she regarded him with a certain amount of awe. Not that Luke minded. At all.

"Master Luke?"

"*What?* Oh, right. Got it. But you don't need to call me that, OK?" It was late afternoon and Luke and Imre had been riding side by side for some time without talking. "Makes me feel like I ought to be in a galaxy far, far away." Imre did not understand, of course, and Luke said, "Just call me Luke. None of that 'Master' stuff . . . although," he added on consideration, "it *does* have a pretty solid sound to it . . ."

"*Luke*, the home of my aunt and uncle is in view now. You can see it there, in the valley." She pointed ahead, down the

205

hillside. In the distance beyond it, Luke could see what looked like the edge of a village.

They planned to stay that night in an "outbuilding" (a plain old barn, it sounded like to Luke) on the farm of Imre's aunt and uncle. The farm was not far from Little Down's Keep, a village that had grown up around an ancient keep. ("So," Luke had whispered on discovering this fact, "a keep's an old-fashioned kind of jail, right? So, these villagers are probably all descendants of a bunch of criminals, right?" Beth had shushed him.)

When the time came, Harac accompanied Imre to make necessary explanations to her aunt and uncle while the others waited at a short distance. Imre's family was very proud to have one of its own in service to any council member, let alone to the Lady Gweynleyn, and they readily agreed to all that was asked of them. It was a great honor to them to assist in any business for her ladyship, and the secrecy surrounding the matter at hand only added to their pleasure.

Soon after the arrangements were complete, Harac announced that he and Rendel were going into the small town to see what information they could glean from locals about the Dark Rim and Lupriark. Aynyxia stayed behind (to "babysit," Luke said), and Imre visited with her aunt and uncle, whom Beth and Luke did not see for the entire evening (though a delicious warm meal was sent out to the barn).

"Aren't you getting a little claustrophobic?" Luke asked when he and Beth had finished their dinner, nearly an hour after Harac and Rendel had left. Aynyxia had gone out to soak, though she remained within calling distance. "Not just from being confined in this lovely and oh-so-fragrant *barn*, but . . . No offense to your friends or anything, but theirs are pretty much the only faces we've seen for a while now. I mean, this adventure thing has been getting pretty two-dimensional. We ride, we stop and eat, we ride, we stop and sleep. Now, here we are near an actual town for the first time, and we're stuck inside a barn with the livestock. We don't even get to sit down and have a good ol' chat by the homestead hearth with Auntie Em and Uncle Henry. . . . So, what do you figure they do for fun in this Little Down place? Think they've got arcades or anything?"

"Yeah," said Beth, "I'm pretty sure they do. Probably right next to the multiplex theater."

Luke moved about restlessly and then said, "C'mon. What do you say? Why can't we just slip into town for a bit? The sun's already starting to go down, and we've got cloaks with hoods; probably no one will even see our faces. We can't possibly get lost: we saw the edge of town from the top of the hill on our way in. We just take a little stroll, then head on back."

"Just us? You've got to be kidding! We could get into such trouble. We wouldn't have a clue what we were doing. And what about your 'descendants of criminals' theory? The place could be filled with all kinds of . . . ruffians."

"Ruffians? Now there's a word you don't come across every day. But I know what you're saying and – never fear! – Imre told me all about the place. Seems I was – can you believe it? – mistaken in my initial judgment. Peaceful little haven, filled with sunshine and light, 24/7. . . . Metaphorically speaking, that is, because as I've already pointed out, it's dusk, which is exactly the right time for us to meander about unnoticed without losing our way."

"But . . . you know it would be really bad if we somehow gave away why we're here. This is really important. . . . We'd have to be super careful about not drawing attention to ourselves." Surprised, Luke could tell that Beth was actually considering the possibility. Until that moment, he'd only been half serious himself. If that.

"Of course. I'm with you one hundred percent. We'll just sort of scope out the place. We won't even talk to anybody, if that's what you want. We'll just smile and wave from a distance."

"It's too risky."

"We'll be back in an hour tops. Probably less. We could see the edge of the village when we were on the top of that hill – so, maybe ten or fifteen minutes to get us there, we look around for another twenty or thirty, absolute max, then we head on back. . . . You know, the only place we've seen any real signs of life around here was back at the docks, because I'd call Greenwood just a little bit on the sleepy side of things. Don't you want a peek at a real Gwilldom-i-an-whatever-it's-called village? Just a peek?"

"What will we tell Aynyxia?" Beth couldn't believe she was even considering this, but Luke could see that he'd won her over. She'd never have done anything like this a couple of weeks ago, but she'd become quite the little adventurer!

"Well, she isn't exactly Ms. Worry-about-every-little-thing, is she?" Luke replied. "Much more on the 'hang loose and chill' side, I'd say. We'll just tell her we're taking a short walk. She'll probably figure we're staying here on the farm somewhere, but I bet she wouldn't care anyway."

"'Sunshine and light, 24/7,' I think you said," whispered a nervous Beth, looking uncomfortably about her dismal surroundings. She kept her shoulders scrunched in close, as if in fear of something unpleasant rubbing off on her.

It was half an hour later and night was falling faster than they'd expected. Luke and Beth had had a quick look around the outskirts of Little Down's Keep, decided almost immediately that it wouldn't be as easy as they'd thought to wander unobserved, and had made a couple of spontaneous detours to avoid anyone who showed the slightest sign of interest in them. They'd ended up in a sinister-looking district with more stench and grime than light. Even having two moons somewhere in the distance above wasn't enough to brighten this forsaken corner of town.

"Yeah, I think we stumbled down the one proverbial dark alley in this place," answered Luke, equally apprehensive. "But I don't hear anyone saying we've got to stay here."

"Right! This way, I think." Beth made a turn, pretty sure she could find her way back to the main road; Luke was directly behind her until his cloak caught on a rusty piece of machinery he'd missed in the darkness. Beth didn't notice and kept on walking while Luke tried to wrestle the material free. Just as he decided he'd better go ahead and rip it, he heard a menacing – and apparently drunken – voice ahead.

"What have we here?" it asked. "A little girlie. Lost, are you? Well, I can help with that. Come on in here with my friends and me, and we'll think of something to keep you occupied!" The words were garbled, but the meaning was clear enough.

All Luke could see of the speaker was his hulking silhouette, but a sliver of moonlight illuminated Beth's profile and her fear. Not that he needed moonlight to tell him she was afraid. The guy was bigger than the two of them put together! Luke yanked his cloak free, ripping it.

When the stranger reached out and grabbed Beth by the arm, Luke shot over to them, not sure of what he was about to say even as the words began to tumble out. "Hey! You got her! Don't tell nobody, will you, mister?" *Think, think, think!* "My mean old dad'd kill me if he knew she'd got away from me again!" At least he didn't have to fake being scared and breathless, but he kept talking without giving the stranger any opportunity to break in. "And it ain't her fault." OK, he had an idea. "She cain't help what happened to her in that Dark Rim! That blasted Dark Rim!" he added with sudden inspiration and in fair imitation of Harac. "It just comes on her in the moonlight, sudden-like!" Next to him, Beth's body started to twitch and the stranger dropped her arm abruptly. "And she ain't never killed a *person* anyways, no matter what they say – just little animals and stuff." Suddenly, Luke jumped back, jerking Beth with him, and with wide eyes and a horrified voice he asked the stranger, "She ain't gone and bit *you*, mister . . . did she?" Beth's head lunged forward and she snapped at the man with her teeth; she even made a pathetic attempt at a growl. It was hard to growl well while shaking, but she couldn't stop the shaking – a genuine case of the shivers had overtaken her.

Clearly uncertain what to think, the man bellowed with a slur, "Off with you!" He swayed, but seemed to be trying to back away. "Off with you both! Away with you afore I call the reeve! We'll not have the likes of you—" The effort of this long of a speech apparently overcame him for he turned away and made a retching sound. Luke was pretty sure the man was vomiting into the street, but he didn't stay to check for evidence. He and Beth were gone at once, running until they were out of the town and had the farm in sight ahead.

Once they had slowed to a walk and started catching their breath, Luke relaxed enough to say, "So, what did you think of my improvisational skills back there? It was my own little werewolf-slash-Nightmare-on-Elm-Street variation of the Aladdin thing – you know, where he saves Jasmine in the marketplace?" Luke had never actually seen *Nightmare on Elm Street*, but he figured it was the right genre, at least; he *had* seen Disney's *Aladdin*.

"Yeah, I got that!" Beth tried to catch her breath.

"Did you? Then why didn't you help me out a little more? Maybe froth at the mouth, or something."

"Well, I *was* twitching and crossing my eyes and acting like an idiot, but I've never really gotten the hang of frothing on

209

command! Especially when I'm really scared!" She spoke in a shouting whisper, still shaken and now somewhat annoyed with him for having recovered so quickly when she couldn't.

"No? . . . Huh!" He appeared to be trying to take in the idea. "Anyway, we're home free now."

"Are we?" She stopped short and he tensed at once.

"What?"

"Harac and Rendel." Sure enough, the other two had beaten them back and were standing together in front of the barn, looking in their direction.

"Oh, them." They began to walk again.

"Yes, *them. We* were supposed to get back first, as I recall!"

"Shut it! They'll hear you. Let me do the talking. And you – don't act so guilty!"

Harac had restrained himself as long as he could. "Blast it all! Where have you two been?" He was trying to shout quietly, but he had less success at it than Beth had.

"We took a walk," Luke answered calmly.

"A *walk*? What in the name of—"

"Peace," said Rendel. "Let us go within."

Aynyxia was inside, relieved to have them back, but looking more uncomfortable than Beth had seen her before. They'd put her in a very awkward position, Beth realized guiltily.

As if she didn't feel bad enough already, Beth soon discovered that Rendel and Harac had bought her a "Sailor's Delight" cake to celebrate her birthday – that had, in fact, been a main motive for their going into town. Rendel also gave her a gift – the reed pipe with which he had calmed the weasel. "A memento of our first adventure," he'd said.

Beth was touched and miserable. It didn't help that Luke felt compelled to explain how their walk had been part of a calming exercise to prepare them for the great adventure ahead – a "rite of preparation" from their own world, he'd said. It wouldn't have been so bad, but Beth knew how easily Rendel could sense a lie.

As soon as she and Luke were alone again, Beth raced through a list of the reasons they should have stayed put in the barn. "Beth, I get it," Luke stopped her when he could. "You were right, I was wrong. It was a mistake, OK? A bad, bad mistake. I'm

210

just doing my best to make it *seem* like it wasn't. Help me out a little, will you?"

"Oh!" She sounded deflated. "Well . . . all right. Sure. There's nothing we can do about it now anyway, is there? And, I guess there was no harm done. . . . Right? We got back OK, and it was only that one guy who paid much attention to us, and he did seem awfully drunk, and the most he could say was that he saw a couple of kids who were strangers and who were . . . *strange*."

"Right! Absolutely right. That's exactly the way I see it, too." But it was only a little later that he told her, "Seriously, Beth. . . . Sorry. I almost messed it all up. For everybody."

"I think it's OK, though," Beth answered. "No harm done," she said again.

Both hoping she was right, they soon settled in for the night and tried to sleep.

CHAPTER SIXTEEN – The Dark Rim

The next morning, Harac, Aynyxia, and Imre were in the house, packing up food for the next few days; the other three were waiting in the barn (Luke figured Rendel had decided that he'd better be the one to babysit this time). Soon they caught the sound of voices – strangers' voices – outside. Rendel went to the barn's door and cracked it open. "Imre's uncle has visitors," he announced.

Beth and Luke quickly moved to where they could peek through cracks in the wooden-planked wall and see for themselves what sort of visitors there were; each felt a sickening wave on recognizing one of them as the unpleasant drunk they'd encountered the night before, though he'd apparently sobered up in the meantime. Two other villagers accompanied him, and all three were talking simultaneously and with great animation to Imre's uncle, who stood with them along the edge of the road.

The one they recognized kept motioning, though vaguely, in the direction of the barn. *He couldn't know, he couldn't know,* Luke repeated to himself. *How could he know?*

"Ah, geez, Beth," Luke said at last, his mouth suddenly dry, "maybe we ought to . . ." 'Maybe we ought to tell him' is what he meant to say, but he really didn't want to do it; he didn't want to admit to Rendel of all people that not only had he been incredibly stupid himself but he'd also dragged Beth along with him.

Rendel's gifts of perception were more than sufficient for the situation, however. Observing the looks exchanged between Beth and Luke, he told them gravely, "Wait here," and went to see what he could discover.

Luke said at once, "It was my fault! I don't know what's up, and I don't see how anything really horrible could be happening, but if it is – whatever it is – it's my fault! The whole thing!"

212

"You didn't *make* me go" was all Beth said aloud; *inside*, she put herself through a whole litany of self-accusations.

After that, they watched without speaking as Rendel entered genially into conversation with the small group. Though only minutes, it felt like a very long time before the villagers finally left and Harac came out of the house to talk with Rendel and Imre's uncle. Soon after that, Rendel returned to the barn alone.

"Is it serious?" Beth asked at once, her heart beating fast.

"Very!" Rendel answered, his expression suited to his words. "It seems that one of the villagers had a rather unusual encounter last night and word of it has spread rapidly."

"Oh?" Beth mouthed weakly while Luke licked parched lips.

"Yes. Strange tidings indeed." Rendel looked from one of them to the other, purposefully delaying his next words. "It seems that a demon girl escaped from the Dark Rim, killing wild animals with her bare hands and drinking their warm blood. Her keeper, claiming to be her brother" – unaccountably, he glanced at Luke – "dragged her away before the reeve could be summoned."

Since Rendel waited for one of them to respond, Luke forced himself to speak up. "How about that! . . . Huh! . . . Sure hope *we* don't run into those two!"

"But perhaps we might find that experience of interest," Rendel countered. "Strangely, with the exception of the glowing red eyes and the frothing mouth, the girl apparently bore a striking resemblance to you, Beth."

Beth had an impulse to say "I didn't froth!" but stifled it.

"The villagers wished to warn Imre's family to keep careful watch over their property, especially their animals. I surmise that reports of the girl have spread through the night, new details being added with each repetition. The villagers are determined to keep close together and by no means to be found in the vicinity of the Rim."

That didn't sound so bad. "So," said Luke, in what he intended to be a hearty voice, "what you're saying is that everyone's keeping out of the way right now and leaving the road wide open and clear for us! Well, that's a stroke of luck, isn't it?" he ended hopefully.

"Truth," Rendel answered with a steely gaze, "I credit we have been fortunate indeed."

They gathered their things and left the barn, silent until an embarrassed Beth said, "Rendel. Does Harac know too?"

"Know what?" he asked casually, though he understood her perfectly.

She hoped that meant "no." The fewer people who knew how stupid they'd been, the better. "Thanks."

Rendel smiled and said kindly, "It is easy for me to forget how young you are."

"I'm not *that* young!" Beth returned at once, a bit perversely.

"*Yes, you are!*" Luke countered quickly. "I mean," he amended when Beth shot him a glare, "we both are. Very, very young. And you know how young people are! They'll make their mistakes, truth and for sure. But best just to let those things go, I always say. 'No reason to hold a little youthful error over someone's head' is what I'm thinking." Then, with less certainty, he added, "Hope everybody's with me on that." He spoke softly because by that point they were rejoining the others in front of the house.

The travelers thanked their hosts and started on their way, leaving their horses behind. Little was said about the village visitors and nothing at all about the dubious activities of Luke and Beth the night before. There were a few silences that Beth found awkward, but nothing worse than that until Harac unsuspectingly wondered aloud whether they'd see the demon girl, with or without her keeper. Beth flushed and tensed, then heard Rendel answer, "We very well may." His voice was solemn, but when she dared to meet his eyes, she saw that they glittered.

Imre accompanied them for a short way. Harac gave her parting instructions as they walked. He had already, back at her house, given her sufficient money for care of the horses and for hiring someone to help return the animals to Arystar should he send word that their own party would not be returning by way of Little Down. She had assured him that she could manage all five horses on her own, but he'd insisted on a guard-escort in case of bandits. Soon, when they reached the narrow bridge that crossed the River Gil, it was time for her to say farewell and turn back toward her family's home.

Luke, even more grateful for Imre's unquestioning admiration now that he was feeling rather foolish, hung back with her for a moment and said, "Well, good-bye, then. Thanks for everything. Take care of yourself and all that."

He started to follow the others, but turned back when Imre spoke his name.

"Be wary, be safe," she told him fervently, coming close. He read such concern in her face that he impulsively gave her a hug goodbye and, contrary to his ordinary habits, a kiss on the cheek. He regretted the latter action at once because the look Imre gave him made him wonder if she'd misinterpreted the friendly gesture.

He was sure of it a moment later when he joined up with Beth and she muttered, "I think that means you're practically engaged or something!" She made minimal efforts to keep from giggling.

"Shut up!" responded her best friend quietly, keeping his eyes focused ahead.

At Beth's first view of the thick band of forested area known as the Dark Rim, she felt a clutching in her chest and a strong desire to turn back the way they'd come. The origin of its name was clear enough – a thick cloud of black hung over the forest, though pale blue and white dominated the morning sky in every other direction.

All five travelers stopped to stare, then wordlessly began to move as one toward the dense woods. "We must try not to lose our direction," Rendel warned as they were about to enter the darkened area.

"Now *there's* some good advice!" Luke responded automatically, forgetting earlier resolutions.

Ignoring him, Rendel continued, "The black mists will make it difficult."

Entrance into the Rim was not gradual. The moment of stepping out of the bright meadow and into the dark woods was a distinct one. It was as if for an instant they passed through an invisible wall; the wall itself was uncannily quiet for that instant, but once through it the travelers were startled by an unnerving cacophony that permeated the thick forest. Whistling air coiled around them, its sound punctuated by muffled screeches and what seemed to be bestial laments. They stopped, and even the bravest among them felt an impulse to turn back.

Beth said, "It's cold," and shivered.

"Spooky," observed Luke quietly, speaking of the eerie sounds. "Kind of a ghost-and-goblin effect, wouldn't you say?"

"It's naught but the wind," stated Harac, though no one believed he meant it.

"*Goblins?*" Beth, knowing that there were such things in this world, responded to Luke. "Can there be goblins here?"

"I suppose there may be," Rendel answered, too candidly for her tastes, "though it is said that even goblins will not pass through the Rim willingly."

"Well, thanks for *that* cheery word!" It was Luke speaking, of course; and though he was as nervous as any of them, he added, "If we're going to do this thing . . . let's do it."

They all advanced except for Aynyxia, who was examining one of the trees, perplexed. Rendel noticed and stopped, saying, "These are not walkabouts," but it was more of a question than a statement.

"No," she answered, then added so softly that Beth almost missed it, "But might've been once."

Rendel heard clearly enough and gave Aynyxia a sharp look. "They are not *minded?*" he asked, apparently disturbed by the idea. The only answer she gave was to return his gaze with a more serious expression than Beth had yet seen on her green face.

Though Beth couldn't entirely grasp its significance, the exchange had a chilling effect on her and she shivered again. Noticing, even in the dim light, Luke asked in an offhand way, "You all right?"

Rendel looked to her then too and said, "Beth?"

By that point, Harac, leading the way with the one small lantern they had lit (they were saving the oil of the other), was nearly ten yards beyond the rest of them. Turning back, he called, "Are you coming then, or not? Best to keep together here."

Beth began to move forward, saying as she did, "I'm all right." She looked at no one in particular and, in fact, kept her head down for some time after that, her eyes on the back or feet of whichever companion happened to be in front of her. "I'm all creeped out already," she told herself, "and nothing's even happened yet except for scary noises."

216

After a few minutes, Rendel started to play one of his flutes. The music calmed everyone a little, if only because it helped screen the more distressing sounds that continued around them.

It was dark among the trees, but more light reached them from above than they had expected, so it was not so dark that the travelers couldn't see one another or make out the way ahead of them, despite the dimness of their lantern. The problem was that "ahead of them" looked remarkably similar to "beside them" and "behind them." There was a great and oppressive *same*ness about the Rim. The only things that changed were the mists.

The large black cloud that they had observed on their first sighting of the Rim hung over the whole area like an open umbrella, filtering out most of the sunlight that they knew still shone above it. But down lower, in among the trees, were separate, amorphous mists floating along unmarked pathways that twisted through the forest.

The travelers avoided the mists when they could, waiting for them to pass ahead or going around if the mists had temporarily settled. Occasionally, one would take them by surprise from behind and surround them before they could get away, or two mists would come together to trap them; when that happened, no one – not even those with "night eyes" – could see anyone else, not even Harac with his lantern.

The first time it happened, Luke, Beth, and Harac all tried to break out of the dark, clammy air, but when the blackness lifted, they discovered that each of the others had ended up somewhere different from where they'd expected. After that, they all stood still when a mist overtook them, unpleasant though the experience was. They also made more of an effort to avoid the things altogether, but that meant twisting their path more than they liked and they were afraid of losing their direction. "Although," Luke pointed out at one of those times, "it's not like we even know that going straight ahead is the best plan. Everyone seems to think so, but it's not like anyone's ever mapped out this place, is it?" He had a point. A bit later, he had another. "There are more of them," he observed of the mists. "I mean, not more of them altogether – at least, not as far as those of us with regular, old 'daytime eyes' can see – but more of them close up." He added in an aside to Harac, "It's like we're magnets for those creepy, blasted things!" Luke was developing a fondness for the word "blasted."

"The lad's right," Harac agreed. "There are more of them close up than farther out. Either we're stumbling through a favorite path of theirs, or they're coming to us out of purpose."

"Yeah," Luke continued, "I think that's it. They're clustering around us on purpose, and the clusters are getting bigger."

"Then," said Rendel, "we need a plan before they overwhelm us. When they begin to cluster about us again, let us turn and move quickly a score of paces in this direction," he pointed, "which I judge to be north. Then we will turn back to the east. When they cluster again, we will turn again to the north for another score of paces, and then to the east from there. In this way, we will keep our same general northeasterly direction but without traveling in one straight line."

"North? East?" Luke repeated at once. "You may have noticed that we can't see the sun from here and I'm not finding any moss growing on these trees, so how can you be so sure which way's which?"

"You would advise for on a different course, Luke?" Rendel asked.

He had no other plan to suggest, of course. "All right, all right. We might as well zigzag ourselves all over the place, because we don't know where we're going anywhere. . . . Wolven forest!," he muttered to Beth a moment later. "Maybe we should just start to howl and the wolves could answer us. . . . Oh, man, Beth! Think about that! What if the noises we keep hearing *are* the wolves? What if *this* is the place the kid's been raised all these years? . . . Talk about major therapy bills!"

Beth wasn't in the mood to be amused (and even Luke was too tense to smile), but she was glad to hear him talk in a joking way, if only briefly. His eyes darted about nervously and he seemed very agitated, even more than she was. After a few minutes, she said, "Think you can relax just a little?"

"Are you serious? . . . Like *you're* not all creeped out too?"

"Of course I am. It's just that— *What's that?*"

"What?" He tensed even more.

They'd made one of their turn-to-the-north-turn-back-to-the-east maneuvers and were temporarily in a clear space where they could see reasonably well in the dusky light.

"There!" Luke, and now the others, could make it out too. A black shape, like that of a large beast raising its arms in menace, moved toward them. To Beth and Luke, it looked like the blurred silhouette of a grizzly bear. Some of the eerie noises, which they'd hardly been noticing any more, became more pronounced and seemed to emanate from the beast-shape.

Harac drew his sword, but Rendel said, "Steel will not help you here, friend."

All five travelers backed away, unaware of the thick mists coming up to meet them from behind. In an instant, they were engulfed by darkness. Though they hadn't seen its approach, they each sensed that this was a wider, thicker darkness than any they had yet experienced.

"Luke?"

He heard Beth's shaky voice and answered, "Right here. Grab my hand." She tried but couldn't find it. She had been on the outside of the group.

"Beth?"

It was Aynyxia, apparently moving toward her, but Beth warned her to stay still instead. Rendel agreed. "We should none of us move. Hold your ground."

"What of the beast?" Harac asked.

"Speaking of that," came Luke's shaky voice, "I sure hope you put that sword away, Harac, old buddy. I'm not feeling like being shish kebab for dinner. 'Course if you've got a high-tech light saber tucked away somewhere, I could go for that."

"When will you speak in language I can comprehend?" roared Harac, temporarily distracted from his more pressing problem. The words echoed around them until Beth was no longer sure of the direction from which they'd come. Then, in a very different voice, Harac said, "It's lifting. It's gone from me . . . though I can see none of you."

The others tried to aim for the sound of his voice, but it seemed to move about, and they realized that they were losing themselves in the darkness. No matter which way they looked, they couldn't see even a glimmer from the lantern they knew he was holding.

"We must wait," came Rendel's voice, and Beth had never heard him sound so weary or discouraged. "I, for one, will sit."

He did sit, and so did the others, until at last, one by one, they were freed from the darkness. When they could see one another, they were once again surprised to find that each of the others was not in the place they had expected.

"I vote we leave," said Luke.

"A helpful suggestion indeed," responded Rendel, rising.

"This way, I think," said Rendel a while later, pointing, but there was no great certainty in his voice.

"No, by *here*," countered Harac, indicating a different direction entirely.

"Don't think so," Aynyxia said, but the words were too soft for anyone but Beth to hear.

The black clouds had increased in number and in size, and avoiding them had become near impossible. Rendel's plan of regulated zigzags to keep on course was no longer practical, if it ever had been. As an alternative, he had suggested that they find landmarks ahead (such as a broken tree limb or two limbs that connected in a distinctive way – there was no greater variety than that from which to choose) and relocate them once a cloud had passed over. But that was proving difficult as well. Though all five travelers were in the clear at the moment, dark patches surrounded them – some close by, others farther back; in no direction could they see even six yards ahead.

"It's no use!" Luke exploded in frustration, removing his bow, quiver, and pack and letting them all fall roughly to the ground. "There's no point in going on. We're just running around in circles here. None of us knows where we are!"

He was right, and the others knew it. They were all turned about and there was little hope of finding a way out while the patches of darkness shifted around to confuse them. "And not much hope even after they've lifted," Beth thought. "*If* they lift." Then, without particularly meaning to speak aloud, she added, "Maybe they'll just stay with us wherever we go."

Overhearing, Luke said, "Oh, wouldn't *that* be great! Little black clouds following us around and keeping us lost forever." He didn't take the idea seriously – at least not until after he had voiced it and the words were hanging in the silence that followed. In a more subdued voice, he asked, "These black clouds or mists or whatever you call them – you don't think they're anything *alive*, do you?"

He looked toward Harac, but it was Rendel who answered. "I do not think so."

The answer should have reassured Luke, and probably did, but it annoyed him at the same time. "Well, you don't really know, though, do you? None of us knows. We don't know what this dark stuff is, we don't know if it'll go away, and we for sure don't know which way will get us out of this place!" Maintaining grace under pressure had never been Luke's strongest point.

"Fair enough," said Harac, who perceived a need for his leadership skills, "but we do know this: that we are all weary and that 'running in circles,' as the lad puts it, willn't help that a bit. I say that we stop here for a spell of time and get some rest so that we can push ahead harder later on. If the darkness moves from this place before an hour or two have passed, we'll try our best to do the same. If it lingers, we'll be no worse off than we are now and maybe even better off for the rest."

It was agreed that they would stay where they were for a while, having something to eat from the provisions they'd brought from the farm and taking turns napping while two at a time kept watch. In the end, though, no one was calm enough to sleep.

They were silent for some time, an anxious watchfulness having vanquished any half-hearted attempts at conversation. The dark patches shifted about and at one point a large one descended on them all rapidly and thickly as if daring them to hold their ground, but by then the travelers were feeling somewhat defiant about the bit of territory they had claimed for themselves and waited unflinchingly until the cold, moist darkness moved away again.

The wait seemed long. They could see nothing through the heavy mist, and the eerie background noises to which they had been growing accustomed now seemed magnified in the blackness that hung on them. Beth wished she'd sat closer to someone else – anyone else, even Harac, who intimidated her – so that she could reach over and feel another's presence. She could only remember one time when she'd ever felt so alone. That was when her father had left.

Then she heard music. Rendel's flute music, unmistakably. She couldn't have identified the direction from which it came if she hadn't known Rendel was straight ahead – or perhaps off to the side a bit; the clouds always disoriented her. But it didn't really matter where the music had started, she decided, so long as it could make its way to her.

Finally, mercifully, the cloud departed, leaving the friends in a circle of dim light (Harac had extinguished the lantern light when they decided to rest). Luke was the first to say, "It's moving," and soon after that he added, "How long do you figure we've been in this place anyway?"

"Where's your watch?" Beth asked, suddenly struck by the fact that, though he normally wore one, she hadn't noticed it since they'd been here. She hadn't thought about clocks or watches for days (and there were still a few years to go before teenagers routinely checked the time with cell phones).

"Back at your place. I dropped it by the— You know, at the place. Where I was waiting for you." The well, he meant. He didn't know why he didn't say it.

"Oh."

"A watch is an object? Of what sort?" Rendel asked, curious.

"Oh," said Beth again. "It's like a little cl- . . . a little timepiece. You have timepieces? Do you call them clocks? A watch is one that's small enough for a person to carry or wear on a band around their wrist."

"This is wondrous." He smiled and added, "Mr. Gribb would find such a thing of great interest."

"Mr. Gribb!" Beth also smiled at the thought. "I wish he were here. And Mrs. Gribb, too."

Beth didn't mean the words literally, of course – she could not wish her friends to such a forbidding place – but Aynyxia took them that way and answered, "Gribbs wouldn't like it. . . . Bad thing happened to them once." The others waited, thinking she might explain her comment.

When she didn't, Rendel recommenced his music. He chose a slow, sleepy song – and they all listened without speaking, at last letting their bodies relax, until . . .

222

"Who said that?" Luke had been sitting with his back against a tree, his eyes finally beginning to close of their own accord, when he suddenly lurched forward, alert.

"What?" Beth, who sat nearest, answered, though the others had also turned to look in his direction. When he merely looked puzzled and didn't speak, she said, "You were starting to fall asleep. You must have been dreaming or something."

Leaning his head back against the tree and closing his eyes again, he said, "Guess so." But there was such uncertainty in his voice that Beth kept watching – which is why she saw it when, a moment later, his eyes suddenly opened and his head jerked up as if he'd heard a noise. He looked at Beth.

"Didn't you—" He stopped short and she saw doubt and something else in his face before he turned away, saying, "Never mind." This time he didn't close his eyes. When, after another moment, he turned back in Beth's direction and saw that she was still watching him, he rose and moved away, soon beginning to pace restlessly about, since the mists seemed to be giving them a break – surrounding their haven but not invading it.

Beth watched with concern as Luke became increasingly agitated. Every now and then he'd turn his head suddenly as if trying to locate something in the darkness beyond them, but he didn't speak at all.

"Sit down, lad!" Harac said sharply at length. "You make my nerves crawl with your constant turning this way and that." Beth realized then that Harac *did* look very nervous. Disturbed. Something like Luke.

"*What* did you say?" It was Harac speaking again, though no one knew at first whom he addressed; then the dwarf rose and stared angrily in Luke's direction.

"You mean me?" Luke answered after a slight delay. "I didn't say anything!"

"I heard you!" Harac yelled, but doubt crept into his expression even as the words left his mouth.

"Peace, my friend." Rendel had risen. "The boy said nothing."

Harac looked to the others as if to confirm this. Convinced but confused, he shrugged and moved away, but did not take his seat again.

Relieved, in part because for a moment he had thought Harac might attack him and in part for another reason, Luke said, "You heard it? The voice? A whispering voice?"

The dwarf turned back and regarded him quizzically before answering. "Truth, I heard a voice. That was no whisper, though! More of a shout, I'd call it!"

They both turned to Rendel, who was seated again, but he could only answer, "I heard nothing." They looked to Aynyxia and Beth in turn; each merely shook her head wordlessly.

Harac turned toward the darkness and stood, motionless, his face hidden from view. Disappointment replaced the relief in Luke's expression and he began to pace again. Beth hoped he'd pace in her direction so that she could ask him privately what the whispering voice had said (she sensed that it wasn't something he'd repeat in front of the others, although she thought he might tell *her*), but he didn't approach and seemed even to be making a point of not looking her way. She was sure the voice had begun again, though, because of the anguish in his face.

Minutes passed and no one spoke; at least, no one that Beth could hear. Her ears had become accustomed to the "normal" background noises of the Dark Rim and now fixed only on the irregular sounds of Luke's restless feet until she heard a moan escape from him, followed quickly by another. She was about to go to him when he spun around, covering his ears with his hands and pressing them hard against his head. Then, like rocks shattering a window, words exploded from him, "Shut up! Shut up! It's not true! *Leave me alone!*"

Beth could see now that his face was wet from tears. Saddened, frightened, and stunned by the sight of it, she wanted to go to him, but Harac was faster. Reaching him at once, he touched Luke's shoulder and said with an agitated gruffness, "It's not you, lad. It's not you they mean." Then he yelled into the tree branches above, "Come forth! Come forth that I might see you face to face and show your lies for what they are!" He drew his sword and Beth, who by then was close in front of him, jumped back suddenly; Harac seemed unaware of her.

Beth wanted to comfort Luke, but – and this was most frightening of all – he looked at her without recognition. Then he pulled away and covered his ears again, mumbling what sounded like nonsense, except that once she heard clearly, "They won't, they *won't*!" Harac seemed to want to fight the air and kept yelling things like, "Come out and I'll prove it! You'll see the worth of my mother's son!"

"They're going crazy!" thought Beth. "Something's driving them crazy!" She looked to Rendel, but he seemed lost in thought, eyes unfocused, oblivious. "Rendel! Rendel! You've got to help!" she cried.

Immediately Aynyxia was beside him, kneeling and touching him. He looked at her as if surprised by her presence and said sadly, "I cannot be sure of it." Then he repeated the words with greater insistence.

Aynyxia turned questioningly to Beth, as if Beth might explain what was happening and tell her what to do. "I don't know" was all Beth could answer. "I don't know what to do."

She looked again at Luke, who was now sitting cross-legged on the ground, his elbows on his knees and his hands at his ears, rocking. Harac was still shouting at tree branches, and Rendel's aspect remained dazed until he turned to Aynyxia to say earnestly, "I hope it, but I cannot be sure." Aynyxia touched his face and tried to speak to him, but found the words difficult to choose; he seemed bewildered that she was making the attempt.

Aynyxia and Beth looked to one another. What was happening? Rendel was lost to them – lost in some voice they themselves couldn't hear. Lost like Luke and Harac. One by one . . .

I'll be next! Beth thought suddenly. *But I won't listen! I know the voices aren't real, so I just won't listen! I'll shut them out.* . . . "Don't listen, Aynyxia!" she cried aloud. "Whatever we hear, we won't listen to it!"

But less than a minute remained until she would hear the Voice herself; within minutes of that, she would be lost in it too.

CHAPTER SEVENTEEN – Darker Still

"Beth?" Aynyxia was looking to her for instruction.

"I don't know!" Beth cried in frustration. "I don't know!" Through misty eyes, she looked from one of her friends to another, then breathed softly with despair, "I don't know."

It was in that instant that she heard the Voice.

Don't know! Don't know! it echoed in cold, mocking tones.

It didn't come in a whisper, as Luke's voice had, nor did it shout, like Harac's, but it was powerful and she couldn't ignore it any more than they had. She actually strained to hear it, despite her resolve of a moment before.

What's the matter, Beth dear? Can't you figure it all out?

Beth looked around as if she might find the speaker, then told herself that it was stupid to think she could.

Yes, so stupid, Beth, the Voice agreed with false sympathy.

"You're not making sense," Beth yelled. "I won't listen."

Now, now. The tone was lighter than at first – but not kinder. *No need to worry, dear. They don't see it yet. They all still think you're quite the clever one.* The words were close and low this time, and Beth jerked her head away, afraid the Voice was near enough to touch her, near enough maybe to sneak into her mind and stay there.

We *know, don't we?* the Voice was continuing in a superior way. *But they all think that* they *do. They think they know you. Beth. The smart one. The clever one. Beth will figure it out, they all say; she always does. . . . But you can't be quite that clever, can you? One day they'll see,* the Voice spoke as if offering comfort. *One day they'll know you better. And who will you be then, I wonder? What will be left?* It kept talking and talking – Beth wasn't sure how long it went on – talking about how she wasn't as clever as everyone thought; she'd fooled them all. At the beginning, she'd been able to tell herself every now and then not to

226

listen. But she gave that up soon. She *needed* to hear what the Voice would say next. *Clever, clever Beth,* it was saying soon . . . or maybe it wasn't so soon.

By now, Beth had no awareness of her surroundings. She'd lost track of what she'd been doing before the Voice started. In fact, she couldn't quite remember where she was and how she'd come to be there. And why. Why *had* she come here, to this place that belonged to the Voice? She ought to remember that much, at least, but she couldn't – until the Voice itself gave her a clue.

Quite impressed them with your little riddle, didn't you? You did figure that *one out.* The riddle. That was important! She was sure of it. . . . But why? Concentrate. She tried to remember why the riddle mattered, tried to block out the Voice for just a moment. She could always go right back to it. But she *couldn't* block it. Its next words grabbed her back.

But you haven't always *figured things out, have you? Haven't always seen the clues right in front of you? Don't you remember that day?. . . Your family knows . . .*

From the start, the Voice had frightened Beth. Even when she strained to listen, she was afraid of what she'd hear. These last words, though, brought the rush of much greater emotion, like the crash of a wave after the trickle of a faucet. It was enough to shake her free for an instant. "*YOU DON'T KNOW ABOUT MY FAMILY!*" she shouted aloud, though her mouth was dry, so the words came out stifled and malformed.

"*Beth!*" That was someone else, not the Voice. She saw his face, though she didn't know where it had come from and couldn't take the time to place it now. She had to concentrate on the Voice. Why was it talking about her family? What did it mean?

Oh, but I do, dear! I know quite well. This time the Voice neither echoed around her nor sounded from beside her. It was closer than that.

"Don't talk about my family, don't talk about my family, don't talk about my family," Beth chanted, head down, eyes closed. Her hands pressed on her ears, but someone was trying to pull them away. She resisted, but then her hands moved and she could hear in the distance that other voice (who was it? he sounded familiar) saying, "Listen to my voice, Beth. You can hear me now, can you not?" And she *could* hear him. If he would just talk again . . . But then he let go of her hands and his voice moved away. He was calling to someone else, but she could hear the words clearly enough this time. "Harac, come back! You must stay here! Do not leave!"

Leave. That was it, she thought. It was this place. She had to leave this place. *This* place belonged to the Voice. But she didn't want to listen to it anymore. She'd have to leave fast, before it started again.

Suddenly, Beth began to run, though she scarcely knew her direction.

I'll go with you, said the Voice.

"*No!*" shouted Beth, "I won't let you! I won't listen!" Dreamlike confusion engulfed her. She fumbled ahead. There were trees – why were there so many trees? Sometimes she couldn't see. The mists. She remembered them now.

I'm still with you, Beth. Shall we talk some more?

But already she was breaking free; already the Voice was fading. Soon, it was gone entirely and Beth was free. She had gotten away. She was finally alone.

Alone, she thought again, looking about.

Entirely alone.

How long had it been? Five minutes, maybe. Beth had banished the Voice, it seemed, but now she was *too* alone. She had called out to the others as loudly as she could, then waited, straining to hear. Nothing. At least, nothing from them. The other sounds were back – the groans and shrieks of the grim forest. But nothing from her friends. She had called again, at least twice each minute, and then waited.

She remembered that Rendel had spoken to her, tried to help her; and she thought she could remember seeing, in some distorted way, Aynyxia talking to Luke, trying to calm him. And Harac . . . Harac must have run off. Maybe he was alone too, just like her.

She didn't think she had run very far, but she couldn't be sure. She hadn't been thinking clearly and she couldn't judge how much time had passed.

"*HELP!*" she screamed desperately. "*HELP ME!*" By that time, she wasn't calling anyone in particular. It was a general plea. Not that there was anyone to hear.

She would have liked to call to Lady Gweynleyn or to Marcus Gribb or even to Sharana Tey. If only there were some way! What she wouldn't give to be sitting in the Gribbs' cottage with hot soup and fresh bread in front of her and Gerta's warm hand resting on her arm!

It was no use looking for help from any of them, though.

Or was it? Was she *sure* they couldn't help from far away? Not even Lady Gweynleyn? She must know magic because she'd been the one to bring Luke. On the other hand, she'd known they were coming to the Rim; wouldn't she have already helped them if she could? If she had some way of watching over them, wouldn't she have already heard Beth crying for help?

And if Gweynleyn couldn't help, who could?

But there *had* been someone else she'd met, someone else with special powers and knowledge. That Silent One.

"Weird and freaky," Luke had said, "but those Silent Ones seem to know just about everything." Rendel had called them prophets and said that one had foretold she'd come to Gwilldonum. Maybe that was the same one she'd met, the one who touched her face. Rendel had thought the gesture important. Maybe she could call to that one. Somehow.

"Help! Please help me!" Beth said aloud.

Nothing.

She tried again, concentrating hard and listening harder. That time, something changed in the darkness. Not the trees or the shadows or the horrible noises, but something. She took a moment to place it.

A presence. That's what she felt. Someone was with her. She started to reach for her bow, but she'd left it behind. She did carry her knife, though, and, still hidden, the magic sword.

She drew the knife. "Who's there?"

Silence.

"Are you a friend?" she asked. "Are you . . . a Silent One?"

Then, faintly, she heard a voice. All it said was, "Listen." This voice wasn't like the last one she'd heard, the one from which she'd escaped. It wasn't mocking or cruel. It was kind, and she strained to hear it again. She closed her eyes, because at that moment her desire to hear the new voice was stronger than her need to see what might be coming.

"Listen," the voice said again, and Beth knew. It *was* a Silent One – she was sure of it – but not the one she'd met, because this one had a woman's voice.

All other sounds died instantly, as if giant hands held pillows against her ears. But she could hear the voice of the Silent One in her head. "Your weapon will not serve you here. It is only fear that threatens in this moment. You can face that, can you not, my child?"

Maybe. Maybe she could. Or maybe not.

In any event, she opened her eyes and put away her knife. She looked around for a robed figure, but saw no one. "I was listening," came the voice, "and was told to find you. I listened again and heard your voice." Beth waited, then supposed it was her turn to speak.

"I'm lost," she began. "My friends are somewhere nearby, but they're lost too. We're in the Dark Rim, and we're trying to get to Lupriark."

"To Lupriark? . . . Ah, I wondered." The last words seemed directed more toward herself than toward Beth, but then she said, "With this I can assist you. I know the way you must turn and I am able to see you, for the present. And—" She stopped short, and surprise marked her voice when she began again. "You carry the sword of Rheynnon Gwynfaihr? . . . Draw it."

Sword? The magic sword? How did she know?

"I know the blade of old," the Silent One answered, though Beth had not spoken to her and hadn't even meant to be "thinking" to her.

Beth put her hand on the hilt of the sword and wondered if she'd be able to draw it. "You may draw it as a dagger, if you wish," the voice assured her. "Indeed, that would be a better choice."

Beth did as she was asked, pulling out the dagger and holding it in front of her.

"I will point the way," said the voice.

"But I can't see you."

"I see *you*, and I can touch you as well – though you may not perceive it. It will be enough."

Beth felt the dagger moving in her hand, as if someone had taken hold of it. She allowed herself to be guided into facing a new direction.

230

"Before you is Lupriark. Do not turn aside." The voice began to fade away.

"But I can't go without my friends!" Beth said in a panic, fearing that she might be expected to do so.

"They will find you," said the voice faintly. Before Beth could ask how, she was astonished to see the blade of her dagger begin to glow. Its brilliance made her squint and shield her eyes, so accustomed had she become to the ashen light of the Rim.

At the same time, all the eerie noises that had been mercifully silenced returned. She could hear clearly the shrieks and the howls, the rustling leaves, even her own breathing . . . and, in only a moment, the voices of her friends calling from somewhere behind.

Beth turned her head and called out in response, but she kept her feet firmly planted and her arm braced in place, not wanting to chance losing her direction. Just before the others came into view, the dagger lost its glow and she returned it to its sheath.

Rendel and Luke arrived first, soon followed (from a slightly different direction) by Harac and Aynyxia.

"What made that light?" Luke asked at once.

"I don't know," Beth answered automatically, not ready to talk about what had happened.

Luke knew she wasn't telling the truth, but this time Rendel didn't seem to. Strangely, this made Luke feel not only smug – *that* part wasn't so strange – but also more kindly disposed to the woodlander. He did want Beth to know he was on to her, though, and said, "Yeah, whatever," with a look that added, "I'm not falling for that I-don't-know thing – not one little bit!"

For the present, Luke showed remarkably little curiosity about the light; all he knew or cared about it was that it had helped them get back together, which might in turn help them get away from that place. He knew as much about that stinking Dark Rim as he ever wanted to! For all he cared, Beth could know a thousand of its little mysteries and she was welcome to every one of them. For himself, he just wanted to get out!

"So, we are together again," Rendel said, returning to Beth the weapons and pack she had left behind.

"Aye, but what direction now?" asked Harac, who had no desire to discuss his own ignoble departure from the group.

"This way," said Beth at once, though not wanting to explain how she knew. "Straight this way."

Luke realized then how oddly she was standing. She wasn't turned directly toward them – that was it. She had turned her head, but not her whole body, to face them. "How—"

"I just know," she cut him off quickly.

Luke paused only briefly before saying, "OK. I'm with you." He pointed his arm straight ahead and said in a deep voice, "Lead on, O Captain, my captain." Beth had a sudden flashback to the day when he had last said "Into the Thinking Place" in a similar manner, the day she had first seen the water in the well, the day when her life had changed. He'd sounded young and goofy that time, but now . . . not so much.

Beth looked to Rendel, who nodded agreement, and she began to lead.

They walked briskly, grasping hope now and not wishing to lose it. After about fifteen minutes, as Beth began to doubt that she had kept their path straight enough, Aynyxia said simply, "Light." Beth didn't register at first what she meant by it, but then Rendel agreed that there *was* light ahead. It took the other three only an instant longer to be sure of it as well – a thin ray of sunshine made its way through the trees far ahead. Harac made a triumphant-sounding shout, and Luke yelled, "Yahoo!", but Beth merely smiled widely and exhaled a deep breath.

Their pace quickened. The ray of light was soon joined by another and another. In his excitement, Luke took the lead, nearly running, and it was only a couple of minutes later that he announced, "This is it! We've made it." In an instant, the others saw what he did. The streaks of light had been growing, but now there was a larger, brilliant patch ahead. So brilliant that it could not possibly belong to the Rim.

Their spirits lifted as one . . . but only briefly.

At once, a tremendous cackle erupted from behind them, ending in a long, chilling shriek. "That's the sound of a ghoul!" burst out Harac, who had had the misfortune of encountering such creatures in his younger days and never desired to repeat the experience. "*Run!*"

With no further word, the five travelers took off, aiming toward where the light was greatest, no longer progressing in any orderly fashion, but each making a path wherever it could most hastily be made, weaving this way and that, running when possible, and then, when at last they emerged in a bright, mercifully open space, well and truly beyond the Rim, dropping their packs and collapsing beside them.

They were out!

With a shock, Beth realized that the sun shone directly overhead. How could it only be noon? Or was it the next day already? She didn't think so, but it had seemed so much like night in there . . . so much as if they had touched the deepest moments of night.

They lay there, pulses racing. For several minutes, they did not speak; when at last they did, it was not of ghouls or darkness.

Harac, though the most winded (for his pack outweighed those of the other four together), spoke first. "This is it, then. . . . We have made it through the Rim, and this is Lupriark. . . . The wolven forest." He managed to raise himself and point. "Into those hills we'll go, and we'll surely find the white wolves." Despite the heavy breathing, he spoke with a good bit of confidence – certainly more confidence than his firsthand knowledge warranted, though not more than the circumstances desired. "So, what say you all? Do we tarry here a while or move on straightway?"

"A little bit of tarrying sounds good to me," Luke answered, still panting, "but let's move farther away from *that* place before we do it." He gestured back toward the thick darkness through which they'd passed; he did not turn to face it. He didn't want to talk about the Rim, and he didn't want to look at it.

The rest agreed, so the five of them trudged slowly on for a few minutes, then settled in a comfortable, lightly-wooded spot near a clear stream, intending to have their meal there at once. Luke stretched out "for just a minute or two" and fell asleep. Beth followed his example shortly, and Harac, who smiled in a paternal fashion at the way that the young could move from waking to sleeping in an instant, soon did the same. Aynyxia half-dozed while soaking her root-feet in the stream, and Rendel kept watch, wondering what more this day held for them and whittling a fine piece of wood he'd discovered near at hand.

Waking an hour or so later, Luke, Beth, and Harac found themselves famished. Aynyxia and Rendel were already sharing a light meal and the other three joined in.

233

"I have been considering the Dark Rim," Rendel said pensively when he had finished eating.

"I don't suppose you'd want to keep those thoughts to yourself," Luke responded immediately, though his mouth was not quite empty, "because I've got to say that that place doesn't make my top ten list of preferred topics."

Rendel ignored the comment. "We were all greatly frightened there" —Harac harrumphed, but said nothing — "yet we saw no impending disaster and no creature to menace us."

"I know the sound of a ghoul when I hear it," Harac countered defiantly, "for I've had the misfortune to hear it before today!"

"I know this," Rendel told him, "but *you* know that sounds can be deceptive . . . and they can be imitated."

"Truth," Harac admitted reluctantly. "I'm not fool enough to tell a woodlander that one creature's sounds cannot be imitated by another. . . . But what about that monstrous, black beast?" Harac countered. "It looked menacing enough to me!"

"I saw no beast," said Rendel, "only the *shape* of one."

"It's one and the same," answered Harac, as if Rendel were being purposefully contrary.

"Is it?"

Harac considered, as did the others.

"What was it that frightened us in the Rim?" Rendel continued after a pause. "We heard mysterious and unsettling sounds, but we never saw what created them. We saw the shape of a beast, but what harm did that shape cause us? The mists that covered us confused and delayed us, but this was an unpleasant inconvenience, not a threat to our persons.

"And the voices we each heard" —Rendel had been speaking in a detached way, but his tone now reflected more emotion— "they were the voices of our own fears, were they not?" No one answered aloud, though Beth nodded and Luke moved his head about in an uncertain way that suggested, "Yes, sort of, I suppose that could be right."

Beth's eyes squinted a little as she thought back, and then she said, "Aynyxia, did *you* hear a voice?"

"Nope, never heard any of them."

"Why not?"

When Aynyxia shrugged, Beth looked to Rendel, who in turn questioned his walkabout friend. "Yet you feel fear, do you not? I credit I have sensed it in you at times, though rarely."

"Sure."

"Perhaps, though," he suggested after a moment's thought, "there is no fear that you hold close. Perhaps you have no private, no secret fear."

Aynyxia shrugged again, but the others reflected on their own experiences of the voices and realized what Rendel had in mind.

"The voice I heard," Rendel continued slowly and gravely, "spoke to me not of my *greatest* fear, but of what is perhaps my most *private* one. . . . It is that I will one day abandon the ways of my kind. That I will choose wrongly, through some weakness of character, and forsake what is dear to me and not honor the ways of peace that have been preserved and bequeathed by my ancestors. . . . I speak of this to no one."

Silence followed this confidence. Beth thought maybe the rest of them should talk about the voices they'd heard – it seemed only fair. But Aynyxia hadn't heard one, and it didn't seem likely Harac would admit his fear, though the others all had a fair guess as to what it was – either that he would act cowardly or would be judged cowardly by others. She didn't know how Luke would feel about his voice, but she didn't see any good reason why she shouldn't be able to talk about hers. It wasn't such a big deal, really.

She hadn't thought about it before, but she guessed she *was* sort of afraid of letting people down. They expected her to be a certain way and maybe sometime she wouldn't be. . . . It was something like that the Voice was talking about, though already the details were becoming fuzzy. She knew the Voice had mentioned her family, but now she couldn't remember why. Anyway, the rest of it didn't really matter. It wasn't even really a fear.

"I . . . I—" She couldn't quite bring herself to get started, even though *really* it wasn't a big deal. But maybe it was sort of private. Maybe after she'd had a chance to think about it, to figure it out on her own, maybe then she'd tell someone. Not yet.

Luke, for his part, wasn't even going to try. *Nope, no way* is what he thought. *Much better to change the subject.* "So, back to what you were saying before. 'There's nothing to fear but fear itself' is what you seem to be getting at."

Rendel regarded him for a minute, and then said, "This is wisdom."

Luke nearly answered that it wasn't precisely his *own* bit of wisdom, but settled instead for "Truth! Wisdom it is!" He didn't look at Beth, who would certainly have recognized the quotation.

"But it may be," Rendel continued, "that it does not apply in this case. There may have been very real peril all about us, creatures who wished us ill, perhaps. Invisible creatures, even. In short, we may have had, unawares, the narrowest of escapes from grave misfortune. How can we know for certain?"

"You know, you really ought to learn to quit while you're ahead," Luke told him.

"I am merely curious about it all."

"Well, one day I'll tell you what happens to curious cats in *my* country, but for now – talking about that place back there gets me pretty excited about starting up our trek in the opposite direction. Think maybe we should go now and let this conversation die a sudden death?"

As they prepared to continue their journey, Beth reflected on the way Luke and Rendel had been getting along. On more than one occasion in the last couple of days, Luke had been pretty antagonistic. And of course he hadn't exactly been polite to Rendel today in the Dark Rim, but that was understandable – they'd all been on edge. At other times, under more normal circumstances (not that they'd had too much of "normal" since they'd come here), Luke and Rendel seemed to be play-fighting with words . . . except that sometimes only Luke seemed to be doing the fighting, and it wasn't *entirely* clear that it was just play.

Those interchanges reminded Beth of when she and Luke had first started to get to know each other. Although she'd been inclined to believe that he was basically a kind person, he'd sometimes make snide comments or unfairly pick at things she said. In time, she'd understood that he was angry back then – not at her, but at his parents (and maybe, for good measure, the world in general) – because he'd had to move and leave his old life and friends behind. Not getting along with Beth would help to prove that he'd never find a new friend worth having, not even an acquaintance who could carry on a decent conversation. Luckily, that sort of thing had passed quickly and Beth had not found it difficult to forgive his offences; it hadn't (with a little guidance from her wise mother) taken her long to figure out that he was mad because he was afraid. Afraid of being lonely.

But was he afraid now? And why would he take that out on Rendel?

The going was much easier after their rest and refreshment. A fair amount of it was uphill, but that was such a little trouble after what they'd endured that no one complained. Beth could feel the strain in the back of her legs, but that only led her to marvel at how much her body had agreed to do in these last days. Maybe it was like Narnia, she mused, where the air made you stronger.

The travelers barely talked, putting their energy instead into pushing forward, toward the wolves and away from the haunting specter of the Dark Rim. Despite what Rendel had said and what their own reason might suggest, they each *felt* that they had encountered real danger in the Rim – a danger of being lost with their fears, if nothing else.

When at last they came to the crest of the hill they'd been aiming toward and saw that they would in fact have to go quite a way down before they could go up again, Aynyxia asked, "How'll we find them, then?" just as the others had been wondering the same.

When no one else answered, Harac said, "Always keep heading up for as far as we are able is the plan that I would favor. Wherever you can see past these blasted trees, it looks like the rockier areas are on the higher hills. That's where we'll find the dens, I would wager. And if nothing else, we should have a good view of the forest from there." He looked to the others for agreement. His seemed as good a suggestion as any, so in answer his four companions began the descent, and he himself came along last of all.

Going downhill gave some relief to the travelers' tired bodies but little to their spirits. It somehow made their final destination seem farther than it had been. Aynyxia, always fascinated by new places and apparently boundlessly energetic when she was well-soaked, was the only one whose feet did not shuffle along wearily through the loose pebbles, untamed growth, and countless pine needles that carpeted their path.

The party had just reached a clearing where the bottom of one slope stretched forward to reach a new upward one, and Beth had just remarked to herself that they hadn't seen much wildlife for a while, when Rendel said, "Be still!" and they were.

He'd heard something, and at once they heard it too. Movement ahead of them, fanning out to the sides, and then the first howl and the answering howls – two fairly close and a third in the distance – followed by louder and more rapid movements.

Then they saw them. Beth counted five at once. Six, seven. No, more. There were more coming.

In only a moment, the scene had changed dramatically. A wide semi-circle had formed ahead of their party and around to the sides, and all along it dark eyes glared. Low growls emanated from behind bared teeth and more than one long strand of saliva swayed recklessly as it hung from the corner of a half-open mouth.

"Well," Luke said quietly, "I'd say we found the wolves."

CHAPTER EIGHTEEN – Lupriark

See a big wild animal, stand still. That was the rule, right?

Beth thought she could manage it, if only her heart would stop beating so hard. It might knock her right over if it didn't settle down soon. Or maybe her legs would buckle now of all times.

Flight was out of the question, and the small party of intruders had no wish to attack (though Harac had reflexively drawn his sword when he'd seen the first animal and Aynyxia's hand was close to her knife). It was, after all, the wolves they had hoped to see – though perhaps not quite this many of them and preferably not under these exact circumstances. Still, Arandella had trusted these animals, it seemed, and Gweynleyn seemed to think well enough of them. How bad could they be?

But maybe there were good wolves and . . . well, not-so-good ones, thought Beth.

A few of the animals still moved, slowly but purposefully extending a wide arc into a circle that would surround their enemy; the others had stopped, poised to attack, several yards away. Were they waiting for the circle to be complete? Or waiting for a signal from their leader? Beth was sure she had identified the chief. A light gray wolf with a stripe of darker fur cutting diagonally across his face, he stood about twenty feet away, directly ahead of her, his gaze fixed on her as hers now was on him. When their eyes locked, the rest of her surroundings seemed to fade away for Beth. There was something so strong in those eyes. So powerful. So fierce.

Though it did not move, the wolf now seemed closer to Beth than it had, so focused was she on its face. Whether from admiration or from fear, she couldn't take her eyes from him until Luke's hushed voice beside her broke the spell.

"So, you know, Beth, there's that place in *The Hobbit* where Bilbo says, 'Escaping goblins to be caught by wolves'. I'm kind of thinking that's us right now. You with me on that?" He tried to sound offhand, but his voice was breathier and higher than usual.

His words hardly put Beth at ease, but they did break her concentration on the wolf. She became aware of the others in her party again. Harac was motionless, his sword now lowered but his grip still firm on the hilt. Aynyxia's feet remained fixed, but her posture was relaxed as she looked about her surroundings. Though her manner was casual, Beth suspected that she was taking in any detail that might be of significance for them. Rendel . . .

The lead wolf growled and took a step forward. Several of the others did the same.

"Lower yourselves," said Rendel. He himself was already crouching. Luke and Beth thought they understood. They had studied wolves last year and knew that rank was important in a pack; making yourself lower than the dominant wolf showed your submission to it. Aynyxia knew almost nothing of wolves but went along with the others.

Harac was bewildered and reluctant. He would acknowledge freely that a woodlander like Rendel understood things that he never would, but why in the name of everything above should they make themselves more vulnerable than they already were? Surely the situation called for a show of strength, not weakness! Still . . .

The gray wolf turned toward the dwarf and growled again. Against what he considered his better judgment, Harac went down on his left knee and rested his sword on his raised right one. (Crouching is awkward for armed dwarves and they risk losing their balance, and he would *not* make himself ridiculous either in that position or by sitting flat down on the forest floor. Kneeling was perfectly respectable.)

The growling and advancing stopped, but the wolves remained in offensive positions, ready to spring on command. Then a change came over them. A calmness settled on the clearing. Something must have happened, though Beth couldn't at first guess what.

Nearly all of the wolves relaxed their stances, a few of the younger ones even sitting back on their haunches; bared teeth retreated into calmed mouths. The muscles of the lead wolf, however, remained taut. He held his position firm, though his gaze darted about, taking in the actions of the pack while at the same time watching for movement from his adversaries.

Puzzled, Beth looked toward Rendel and saw that his hands were at his mouth. *Of course. It's one of his flutes.* There must be music in the air, audible to canine ears, if not to hers. She thought that the noises dogs could hear but humans couldn't would always irritate dogs, but whatever the wolves were hearing seemed to calm them. As she listened to the wolves' soft panting, she thought of her dogs at home.

Each side was at a standstill, though it lasted only a moment or two, for soon a new commotion arose. Beth heard and then saw a lone wolf approach from the summit ahead. It ran down swiftly, a light streak against the browns of the forest, coming to a sudden but graceful stop when it reached the side of the wolf chief. It was a beautiful beast, its fur entirely white, its eyes black, shining, and penetrating. The intensity of the eyes reminded Beth of Sharana Tey, and she was sure that this was a wolf-woman.

The next minute proved her right. After surveying the scene before her, the animal transformed. She lowered her head, then raised it again, but as her head lifted, her whole body followed, drawing her entirely upright so that she was supported by two legs. Her forelegs hung in front of her at first, but as she drew them back they changed into long, human arms. The wolven fur disappeared from view, replaced by skin striking in its pallor and by an ivory shift that hung from shoulders to knees; long, straight hair, brilliant in its whiteness, framed the face. And the face . . . In a manner that defied descriptive powers, the fine lines of the wolf reshaped themselves into the equally fine lines of a human face. *It was like some sort of computer animation,* Beth thought later, *only . . . not. Not at all.*

"By all the stars!" Harac's voice whispered in amazement.

"Whoa!" said Luke, "That was awesome!" At least, that's what he thought he said. In fact, only the soft sound of the first word escaped his lips; the others lost themselves along the way.

The woman who stood before them was by all appearances now fully human. Nearly. There was still something wolven about the intense, searching eyes. The face was beautiful in an ancient and noble way, as white, smooth, and perfect as a finished sculpture, but there was a coldness in it and an accusation in her voice when she addressed them. "Why have you come? Why do you disturb the peace of our domain?"

Though Beth wasn't looking directly at Rendel, she sensed that he had turned toward her, no doubt to see if she wanted to answer. She supposed she should but scarcely knew how and was grateful when, rising, he did it himself.

"Worthy lady, we mean no harm. We ourselves seek peace and have come to beg your assistance in our endeavors." He turned to Harac then and though he didn't speak the dwarf must have understood his look. Harac took the sword he still held across his knee and laid it out instead on the floor of pine needles before him. Then, tentatively, he stood back up. Likewise, Aynyxia stood and drew her knife, setting it down in front of her, and Luke, somewhat warily, followed suit with his bow, quiver, and dagger. Beth laid her weapons on the ground as well – except for the gift from Gribb, which remained hidden beneath her clothing.

Only when the last weapon was laid out did the chief wolf relax his stance. Though the intruders were now all standing again, he sat, and Beth felt a sudden sympathy for the animals, who, noble and fierce though they might be, must have known that there was no sure protection against sharp steel.

"Speak," said the wolf-woman. "What assistance could your kind seek of mine?"

"We seek the child of Arandella," Beth found herself reciting, though shakily, "the last queen of Gwilldonum. Lady Gweynleyn, who sends her greetings and good wishes for the welfare of all your pack, believes that the wolves of Lupriark are loyal to Gwilldonum, and we thought that . . . I mean, we have reason to believe that the queen entrusted her child to you and . . . " And what? She forgot how she'd meant to say it! "Please, worthy lady," she repeated Rendel's form of address, "do you know where the queen's child is?"

As the wolf-woman once again surveyed the odd assortment of visitors, Beth decided she ought to introduce them. "This is Harac," she began, indicating the dwarf, "who serves with Lady Gweynleyn on the Council of Ten of Gwilldonum." He probably had some more impressive-sounding title, but it was all she could think of. "And Rendel of Greenwood, and Aynyxiacichorium of the Intybus family of the Nethermarshes. I'm

242

Beth DeVere of Fairspring, in a distant land, but I've come to help, if I can. And this—" How should she introduce Luke?

"I'm Luke," he said cheerfully. "I kind of go along with Beth, Your Worthiness."

Beth gave him a panicked I-can't-believe-you-said-that look and hoped his flippant manner wouldn't offend the wolves. He wisely ignored her and looked humbly at the wolf-woman instead.

The latter simply answered, "I am Crhná, mate of R'khan, who is the First Wolf of Lupriark." Then she did something disconcerting. She walked up to Harac, towering over him at first and then bending down to sniff about his head and shoulders. It was an unpleasant and embarrassing experience for the dwarf, but he did not protest and kept still as well as he could. When she had finished, she did the same thing to Rendel, who seemed neither surprised nor bothered, and then she came to Beth. When the woman's face was so close that the long white hair brushed against her cheek, Beth inhaled a smell that was woodsy, canine and . . . *warm*, if a smell could be described that way. When the woman drew back and met Beth's eyes, she searched them as if it were the girl's soul she hoped to glimpse. Beth found that more disturbing than the sniffing had been and was glad when it was over. Luke was next. ("Too weird!" he whispered to Beth when he had been sufficiently sniffed.) The wolf-woman went last to Aynyxia, whom she sniffed at length, fingered lightly, and studied with a puzzled expression, for she had never encountered a walkabout plant.

Finally, she said with a measure of suspicion (or perhaps it was simple disgust), "You smell of horse, all of you!"

"We have lately ridden," Rendel answered, "but the beasts have not accompanied us into your woods. They are left far behind."

She said nothing for a moment, looking each one over again, then returned to the gray wolf, R'khan, and crouched down to consult with him. At least, Beth supposed that they were consulting though she found the slight sounds they made incomprehensible. In the meantime, the party of visitors exchanged glances; there was nothing more to do but wait.

"Well," thought Luke, "she didn't sic the dogs on us, and she didn't say we were out of luck and that she'd never heard of the kid. So far, so good, I guess. . . . 'Course she also didn't say, 'Step this way, we've been waiting for you'."

The others of his party were having similar thoughts – hopeful, but not without doubt. Yet when Crhná, rising, said, "I will take you to the one you seek," they could hardly believe it. One of them gave a short laugh, and the others expressed their relief with exhalations and open-mouthed smiles.

Crhná turned back at once to the way from which she had come and began to walk briskly. The other wolves moved too, some sprinting ahead, some hanging back close by the visitors.

Harac reached tentatively toward the ground in front of him. As there seemed to be no objection, he retrieved his sword but made sure not to advance until he had returned it to its sheath. The others took back their weapons as well and then hastened to follow the wolf-woman up the slope of the hill.

Beth had to run a little to keep up, but a burst of energy sustained her. Such deep relief flooded her that she wanted to laugh out loud or maybe scream or something! Everything was going to be all right! She *hadn't* led them all on some wild goose chase, as she'd feared. She *had* helped her friends, she *was* the one who was supposed to come. Almost giddy, she hoped she wouldn't embarrass herself with uncontrolled giggling.

She hadn't realized until that moment how much pressure she'd been feeling – pressure to be the champion, to know the answer, to do what none of the others could do, and – though she had in fact made no claim to be someone she wasn't – to keep from being "discovered" as an imposter. In short, to keep from disappointing them all. And now it was over – not the whole adventure, of course. But whatever else happened, she had done her part.

They were nearly at the summit of the first hill when Luke said without preamble, "'Course she could be lying; could be a trap." On the other side of him, Harac made a grunting noise that seemed to indicate agreement.

Many miles west, in a castle chamber in Greyvic, Captain Gydon Tork slapped his gloves down on a small table and spat out the words he'd been holding back in the Great Hall, whence he had just returned with Myrmidon Tork (his second cousin as well as his overlord) and Myrmidon's chief advisor, Eustarius. "They sicken me, all of them, with their forms of courtesy and their pretty ways of speech, when all the while their eyes betray the contempt in which they hold us!"

"Would you expect it to be otherwise?" responded Eustarius in a calm, superior tone.

The captain lanced his own look of contempt in the advisor's direction.

Their lord, unconcerned, settled himself into a comfortable chair and stated merely, "We have nothing to fear from contemptuous eyes."

For a moment, only the sound of Gydon's pacing boots could be heard. Then he muttered, "I do not like this whole affair of the champion."

"Ah, so that is what makes you tremble," Eustarius goaded him.

"*NOTHING MAKES ME TREMBLE!*" roared the captain.

"*Silence!*" commanded Myrmidon. "Will you have the servants in the passageway carry back our conversation to their masters?" Exasperation riding on his words, he continued, "Truth, Gydon, you must learn control. Eustarius tugs at your strings and you dance like a puppet. Control and patience! My late brother Karstidon was lacking in both, and you see what he bought by it."

"But, my lord," answered Gydon earnestly, moving toward Myrmidon. "Why be patient in this matter of the champion? Why have we not struck before now, before he appears, if he will, to rally support? They are all wary of us – it is clear enough – but none have expected a move until after your appeal to the assembly. We could have taken Greyvic while the council was away, while even the Captain of the Guard was away . . . and before this mass of lowlife appeared for their precious festival," he added with distaste. "We have Ferinia with us and the Brenmarch, as well as support in other corners where it is not suspected – support within the council's circle and support within this very house. Nor is it yet suspected how many of our own troops wait north of the river – troops that could have joined us a fortnight ago in taking this city while it was yet vulnerable. With Greyvic secured, we could take the Dayrn Valley with the least effort, and that, with the allies we've already made, would give us the whole of the northwest as well as a long and mighty foothold along the western march. We would advance inward from there. Greyvic could yet be ours . . . at once!" He continued tentatively, knowing that the ground was shaky, "If we send word to the north *now* . . ."

"You have given this matter a great deal of thought," Myrmidon answered. He was not surprised, of course; his captain had urged him in this direction for weeks . . . and Myrmidon himself had given the idea serious consideration. But he had taken care to learn patience. As hoped, he had entered Greyvic as a guest and now he would wait for the assembly.

"Perhaps not enough thought," Eustarius responded concerning Gydon's last proposal. "Take Greyvic now, you say? With the best warriors of the land all about us? And what of Therin Mandek? Will he sit back peaceably and observe as we do this?"

"He will be the first to go," the captain responded with relish, "and I will gladly do the deed myself. He is arrogant enough to roam about unattended half the day. The job will be done in stealth, and before it can be known we will fall on the rest of them. Without him, they will be in disorder. They know not which of their own to trust." Then, smiling darkly, Gydon added, "And they trust those they should not! They know how our support has grown and it cowers them," he concluded. "They have opened their doors to us, and we have come in. They are ours for the taking!"

"Enough. Truth, you would let this tale of a champion goad you into action better delayed. We will wait," his lord declared with finality.

But, truth be told, Myrmidon Tork remained uneasy about the question of a champion. He knew the old stories of champions of strange provenance, arrived at opportune moments to aid Gwilldonum in a dire day and then vanished as suddenly and mysteriously as they had appeared. And were there not great ones among the ancients who were said to be of the same race?

And what of this supposed anointed one? *Had* Karstidon allowed the mother an opportunity to perform the ceremonies for her child and then send it into hiding? He should have seen to her sooner, even before he had DarQuinn in his hand, for she was ill-protected at Dunryelle. One blunder after another and he had lost Gwilldonum . . . . Karstidon had been a fool!

"But *I* am no fool!" reflected his brother. "I am halfway to the throne already. . . . And if . . . *if* there should prove to be a champion after all and *if* there is an anointed child . . . Well, that will be an unwelcome delay, but nothing more! We will be patient, if we must – whether for a week, a month, or a year. We will strike when the time is right. . . and we will strike hard. No brat of ten years will keep the land of my ancestors from my hand for long!"

The five of them waited, as they had been instructed, outside the entrance of a small cave near the edge of a clearing. Nearly all the wolves were gathered on a far side of the clearing, mostly resting, though all watched the visitors with interest.

No longer shaded by the forest trees, Beth could see that it was still afternoon. The days were so full here that she felt it had been months since she'd been at home.

Home. She wondered if she'd be sent back right away, now that her part was done. She found the thought comforting, but also disappointing. At least, though, she'd have to get back to Gweynleyn first, wouldn't she? Perhaps she wouldn't leave *too* soon. A *little* more adventure would be nice. Maybe she'd even get to see the whole thing through to the end.

Of course, it could still end with some sort of battle. And no one ever knew what would happen in a battle. Perhaps it would be better after all if . . .

Crhná came out of the cave, but she had taken the form of a wolf again. She looked over Beth and the others one more time, then left them. Her part was finished.

Following her out of the cave entrance was, as Beth and her company were stunned to see, a full-grown man, entirely human-looking, in dress that must once have been rather splendid. It was not his usual attire, for at Crhná's announcement he had put on the finest things still in his possession.

Behind him came a woman – a wolf-woman, clearly. She had the same white hair and pale skin as Crhná. But there was something so different about her. *It's kindness,* Beth realized. There was kindness and warmth and feeling in the face and especially in the gaze of the dark eyes.

The woman now stood close behind the man, partially hidden by him, her right hand pressed down on his right shoulder, almost gripping it. She intended her smile to be welcoming, but sadness streaked it. Sadness and fear, Beth thought.

"I am Alric," the man said. The words were simple enough, but the voice was deep and authoritative. "You seek the son of Arandella?"

Harac, trying to contain his excitement, answered, "Truth, until this moment we have not known whether it be son or daughter we sought. But if the anointed son of Arandella is in this place, we do seek him."

"And you are—?"

"I am Harac," he answered in a different voice, matching the man's in depth and authority, "son of Aracac the Swift and Harana the Victorious, and I serve the Council of Ten of Gwilldonum and the High Council of the Southlands."

"And how should I know that this is true?"

It was not an unreasonable question, from Beth's point of view, but Harac clearly judged it otherwise. For a moment, he seemed taken aback, flustered even, then color came into his face and she was afraid he would become angry. She wasn't sure why he should, but she supposed it must have been an offense for the man to question the dwarf's heritage or his office.

Rendel intervened with a light tone, a pleasing voice, and the characteristic glimmer in his eyes. "Do we seem to you, then, noble sir, to be of the sort from which the Torks recruit imposters and spies?"

The man studied them with a grave expression, but only for a matter of seconds. Then he burst out in a deep laugh and his expression softened as he smiled. "Truth, you do not," he answered. "A walkabout, a callow youth, a young maid, a woodlander, and," here he half-bowed in Harac's direction, "a noble dwarf. If you are spies for the Torks, then indeed your world has turned about strangely since last I knew it."

The visitors relaxed at that, but Luke mumbled, "I'm not so callow!" adding with less certainty, "I'm pretty sure."

After the rest of the party was introduced, Alric asked, "But have you no sign to show that you come on behalf of Arandella? No letter or seal, no . . . trinket?"

They had nothing of that sort to offer.

After a pause, Luke said, "Well, *we're here*." He refrained from adding "Duh!"

"So you are," answered Alric, studying each of them again. He seemed on the verge of asking another question, maybe many more, but forbore doing so. Instead, he sighed heavily, turned back to the cave, and nodded to someone hidden in its recesses. Beth's heart beat faster as she waited to see what would happen next.

She didn't wait long. Almost at once, a young man advanced into the open air, his golden brown hair catching the sun's light as he did so. Though his clothing had seen a number of years of wear, and not all by the person who wore it now, it had been very fine once and made a striking effect, here in the forest. Indeed, the sight of it left Harac, who took some trouble with his own appearance on formal occasions, feeling rather shabby and in need of a good wash. He bore a sword and its polished hilt gleamed brightly, as did the bits of silver that decorated its sheath.

The young man . . . . No, it was a boy after all, but he held himself tall (as tall as Beth, though he was younger) and he mimicked a man's expression and movements. It was the softness of his smooth face that betrayed his youth, and his voice, when he spoke, was loud and firm but lacking the depth of maturity.

"I am Aron Sterling, son of Arandella of the House of William Princeps, the Aethling, the Law-Giver. I am Aron Sterling, chosen and anointed to be King of Gwilldonum, High King of the Southlands, Protector of the Thessalyn Islands. I am Aron Sterling, and I greet you and ask what business you have with my person."

Beth, who'd had a half-formed notion of rescuing a helpless, grateful orphan, was taken aback by the confident and princely manner of this boy who was even younger than she. She could only stare in awe as he echoed the words of a mother he had never truly known.

Luke considered whispering, "So who do you think taught the kid his stuff?" but one look at Beth's face convinced him she wouldn't hear anyway. ("She might as well just let her mouth hang open and start to drool or something!" he figured.) Besides, Luke, nearly as impressed as Beth, found himself uncharacteristically reluctant to risk being overheard.

When the boy asked what business they had with him, Beth knew how she meant to answer. But Rendel spoke at once. "First, to swear fealty to you, my liege." He went down on one knee and inclined his head. Beside him, Harac did the same and pronounced solemnly, "My hand is yours, my liege." Aynyxia, to the right of Luke, also knelt on one knee (awkwardly), but her face was turned up and she said nothing.

As the young prince observed these actions, Beth detected a flicker of relief in his face, and she thought, "He's just a boy after

249

all," and "He was nervous." The look passed quickly, though, betraying him to no one else.

Aron stepped forward to Rendel, who lifted his hands, palms pressed together, as if in prayer. The boy covered them with his own two hands and said, "The fealty of the woodlanders has been a precious gift to my royal family for generations and generations again. I accept yours gladly and will keep faith with you." Next he stepped toward Harac, who lifted his hands as Rendel had done. Covering them, the boy said, "And I accept with gladness fealty from the noble Harac, son of Aracac the Swift and Harana the Victorious." He repeated flawlessly, as if he had known them of old, the names he had first heard only moments ago while waiting within the cave. "I will keep faith with you."

He walked past Beth and Luke, who were still standing, to Aynyxia. Beth wondered if they should have knelt too, then wondered if it would be strange to do it now, belatedly.

Aron had never met a plant-person before, and when he was able to observe Aynyxia more closely, another flicker in his expression revealed the animated curiosity that inhabits the young. His words and tone, however, did not reflect his great interest. "The walkabouts of the Nethermarshes have been worthy neighbors of my own land for generations and generations again. We trust in a long and rewarding friendship between your kind and mine." Then, for the first time, a trace of doubt entered his voice. "You *are* from the Nethermarshes, are you not?"

Aynyxia nodded, and the prince smiled and moved back to Beth and Luke.

"But you are not" –the hesitation was brief– "my subjects of Gwilldonum?"

"No, my lord." Beth had been rehearsing a few words and hoped they'd come out well. "We come from a far-off place—"

"*Way* far off!" Luke added.

"—but we are friends of Gwilldonum and hope to see you as king. You are badly needed. Right away. That's why we've come." Then Beth went down on her knee and Luke, last of all, did too. ("Well, why not?" he figured. Besides, it always looked so cool in the movies when everyone did that. One guy left standing? Not so cool.)

"Such friendship will I always treasure, on my own behalf and on behalf of my people."

Aron turned and stepped back to his earlier position; as he did, his gaze fell on the man and woman who had been silently watching. The woman's smile quivered, but the man nodded with proud approval. Beth couldn't see the prince's face, but she thought his shoulders relaxed. Rendel and Harac stood up then, and the remaining three followed their example.

"My new friends," Aron said, turning back to them and speaking in a younger and less ceremonious voice than before, "allow me to introduce my guardians. Kr'nara has been my nurse and mother since I was first brought here. Sir Alric is the cousin of my mother Arandella, and-"

"By Korisye's light, I should have known it at once!" Harac broke in loudly, seemingly unaware that he had interrupted his future king. "Sir Alric Sterling! I've heard tell of you, to be certain – of the travels and adventures of your youth and of how at length you simply vanished, though your steed came home of its own accord. Some said you were dead, some that you'd conquered a far-off land to rule on your own; others swore you'd been carried off by the Torks, and still others that you'd left everything behind because you'd lost your heart to some sprite of the woods and—" He stopped suddenly, looking from the man's face to the woman's and back again.

Sir Alric, undisturbed, raised his left hand and with it covered the soft fingers that still pressed down on his right shoulder. "Kr'nara is more precious to me than anything I may have left behind," he said simply. "My life is here now."

Aron was regarding the couple with obvious affection when a stabbing grief caught him unawares. He had long known this time would come. From his youngest days he had known who he was and what his destiny was thought to be. With as much diligence as if they had lived at Arystar itself, Alric had groomed the boy to sit on the throne of Gwilldonum. When his tenth year of living among the wolves was complete, he began to look almost daily for some sign that the time had come for him to return to the seat of his ancestors and take his rightful place there. Though his attachment to his guardians and to the whole wolf pack was great, so was the excitement that welled up in him as he anticipated the new life ahead. The age of all rights was upon him, and he found himself anxious to step forward into his manhood, into his kingship.

Now, though, after so many months – nearly a full year – of watching for it, the moment was here and its bittersweet taste was more than he had imagined. Emotions welled up in him, swirling about and competing for dominance.

When he realized that a silent moment had passed, Aron spoke again to the visitors but kept his eyes on his guardians, trying to quell the turbulence within. "Sir Alric has taught me all that I know of my family and heritage, of the Southlands and our glorious history, of the ways of court, . . . of . . ." He paused, a catch in his throat. Swallowing hard, he continued, but in a slow and increasingly wavering voice, his sentiments evident to all. "Of duty and justice . . . of nobility and kindness . . . and goodness . . ." Emotion halted his speech and with two swift movements he was kneeling before his adoptive parents, head lowered, moist eyes hidden from view. Alric put a hand on the boy's head, and Kr'nara knelt immediately beside him, wrapping her arms about him and pressing her wet cheek hard against his.

The depth of the boy's emotion struck everyone present. Beth felt sudden tears, and she wasn't the only one to do so. Harac looked away and gave the appearance of studying the texture of a nearby aging oak. "By your leave, my liege," came Rendel's gentle voice, "we will wait apart and attend to certain matters of our own. Then, at your pleasure and convenience, we have urgent news of Gwilldonum to impart."

"His Highness will be with you shortly," Sir Alric answered on his ward's behalf.

As they moved away, Beth said softly, "I hadn't thought about what it would be like for him to leave a family behind."

"So why does he have to leave them?" Luke responded quietly but with more feeling than he could have explained. "I mean, why can't they all three come?" The scene between the boy and his guardians had touched something deep in him.

"A wolf won't leave her pack," Harac answered with certainty, "and as for Sir Alric . . ." He shrugged.

"You think so too?" Beth asked Rendel.

He nodded. "It is not in the nature of a she-wolf to be apart from the pack. As for Sir Alric . . . I do not anticipate that he will join us either. But we shall see."

By this point, they were far enough away to afford privacy to the small family. They settled themselves in a sheltered spot high and clear enough to give a grand view to the west, the direction from which they'd come and toward which they hoped soon to return. They stretched and relaxed their bodies, quiet and thoughtful until Harac's voice broke out heartily. "To business, then. Is there a question among us as to whether this is the anointed child of Queen Arandella?"

"Oh, *now*'s a good time to ask," Luke responded before anyone else had a chance, "after you've pledged your hands and fealty and all that!"

Harac, never quite sure what to make of Luke's manner, squinted at him for a moment before answering, "For myself, I am convinced. He is here where we sought him, he is with the queen's cousin, he seems to be of the right age, and he has the look of the family. But are we of one accord?"

The others answered that they were.

"Well, then," he slapped his large hands against his knees and spoke with great optimism, "there's nothing for it but to explain the situation to the boy – Prince Aron, I should say – and be off as soon as we can. The Anointed One will take his seat at Arystar, and all will be right at last!" During the ensuing silence, however, the smile left his lips; then, looking into the far distance beyond the woods, he said more to himself than to anyone else, "But I mightily wish I knew what was happening at Greyvic!"

"I cannot agree with you on this, Gweynleyn." Therin Mandek and Lady Gweynleyn were in the castle of Jeron Rabirius in a private chamber given over for the lady's use while she was in Greyvic. She had dismissed her attendants so that she and Therin could speak freely. "Discretion, of course, but you carry it too far."

"And how should we explain the absence of the Captain of the Guard at a time such as this? It would be known at once, I tell you." They were discussing the matter of intercepting Beth and Harac's party to escort them safely into Greyvic – or rather, the matter of escorting the Anointed, if all had gone well. "And the purpose of such an expedition would surely be discovered. You are carefully watched – far more so than anyone of a lesser rank; you would be pursued. And though I know your skills in combat," she added quickly as Therin was about to speak, "there is risk. Then too, if you should happen to" — she hesitated to say the word — "*fail* in the undertaking, that fact would soon be known as well, and the knowledge among so many would work against us severely. The bordering regions already show little enough confidence in the council."

"I ought be the one!" exclaimed the Captain of the Council Guard, not for the first time. "Or is there another whose abilities you more highly esteem?"

"You know there is not, Therin. But you know also that what I have said is true: you above all others are closely watched. If your direction should be discovered and if Myrmidon's support is as great as we fear, think how many he might send in pursuit! Would you overpower them alone? Or do you mean to take your whole company with you? And if that, you deprive us here of our most dependable defense and leave us desperately vulnerable."

"The Tork would not risk such a pursuit when he claims friendship with Gwilldonum," he responded to her first point.

"Would he not?" she asked with feeling and skepticism. "I fear that if he cannot persuade enough council members to his side he is prepared to essay other means without delay. He has Ferinia with him and the Brenmarch and we know not how many from other regions. We cannot even say with surety how much support he counts here within the walls of Greyvic itself.

"We need you *here*, Therin," she told him wearily. "Will you not send Daasa in your stead? She is as trustworthy as any, after yourself, and the Torks look on her with scorn because she is a faun. They will see no import in her departure, even should they notice it."

"She is loyal enough, and brave," he conceded, "but her pride and her temper have caused us difficulties in the past. She cannot keep them in check."

Gweynleyn answered, smiling, "I credit that the same has been said of you, my friend, on more occasions than one."

He was in no mood for this chiding, gentle though it might be, and responded angrily. "*Do you doubt that I-*"

"Peace, Therin. I did not mean to give offense."

He started to speak but then paced about until he had calmed himself. In a different tone, coming slowly toward the lady, he implored, "Do you not see, my dearest? I failed my queen. I cannot fail her child as well." And this, she knew, was his compelling thought – that ten years past he had not reached Dunryelle in time.

Gweynleyn stroked his hair and kissed his cheek softly before pressing her own against it, but she could not agree with him. "Do you think that it is not my heart's desire to see the Anointed One safely to the throne? Do you not know that I believe you to be the surest guard we could send to the child? But the danger here is great, Therin! I am sure of it. Gwilldonum balances on a precipice. And Arandella herself would tell you that you must not sacrifice the security of all the kingdom for the security of the king."

But what hope have we for the kingdom if the throne itself cannot be secured? Therin thought. He took the palm of Gweynleyn's hand and kissed it. With gravity, he inclined his head and withdrew silently. He knew what he must do.

"Imagine having a wolf for a mother! Too weird! . . . 'Course, I guess the whole curfew thing could have its advantages, though . . ." Luke spoke softly; not so much out of consideration for Rendel, who slept close by, as because he didn't know how much farther his voice might carry in the surrounding quiet.

The meeting with Aron had gone as well as anyone could have hoped, and he had declared himself not only willing but anxious to return with them. After a supper that was satisfying enough, everyone had settled in for the night (though it would be several hours before Aron or his guardians would actually sleep). A wolf-girl had led Aynyxia to a stream where she could sink in her feet for the night, and Harac was sleeping in the cave that had been offered for the visitors' use. Beth, Luke, and Rendel had chosen, despite the chill in the air, a soft spot on the forest floor over the hard dirt of the cave. Besides, Harac snored. Loudly.

Beth and Luke could hear him from where they were, but it wasn't that that kept them awake. Though they had been curled up under their heavy cloaks for some time already, they were too excited to sleep and instead talked quietly together. Not surprisingly, they wondered between themselves about the life Aron had led. When Luke concluded that being raised by a wolf-woman was "too weird," Beth answered pragmatically, "But not weird to him, if that's all he's ever known. And look at us. We've only known the wolves a few hours and we're already having a sleepover with them! We're surrounded by a pack of wild animals and I think I'll probably feel safer spending the night here than I would in any other place we've been so far. You know, it's not the same here as in our world—"

"You think?"

Ignoring him, Beth finished her thought. "Some of the animals here aren't so different from us."

"Speak for yourself! Did you see what the wolves did to all those poor little forest animals after the hunt tonight? There's a major *ick* factor there! You don't see *me* ripping apart Thumper with my teeth because I need a little bedtime snack."

"*Luke*," she said in her best patient-mother imitation, "you know what I mean."

He waited ten seconds before admitting, "Yeah, I know. . . . Still . . ."

"Yeah, I know," she agreed.

"And then there's that whole thing of Sir Alric whoever-he-is falling for a wolf and deciding to live the rest of his life in a cave with her. . ."

"No, don't! First of all, I think we can figure she was a woman when he fell in love with her, and there's nothing weird about that, and then it just kind of *happened* that she was a wolf too. And for all we know she stays a woman all the time now and the three of them make a nice, happy almost-normal little family (except that we've come along to break it up); and besides, it's the nicest real-life fairytale I've ever heard, so just don't! Don't wreck it up by saying it's all 'too weird!'."

She said the last words in a self-conscious way, wondering if Luke would make fun of her sentimentality, but he only said, "Real life, huh? So *that's* what we're doing here? Living real life?"

They were both quiet for a while, but pursuing fairly similar trains of thought.

Beth said at last, "You know, it doesn't seem surprising to people here (well, to the ones who know, at least) that we've come from another world or dimension or something. Unusual, maybe, but not unbelievable. How often do you think it happens? I mean, there must have been ancient Romans who made the trip in one direction at least, don't you figure? Because of the Latin words and the Romulus thing and all that. And a bunch of English-speakers somewhere along the way – there had to be. And who knows what other languages we'd come across if we kept looking around."

"Yeah, I've been wondering about that stuff too!" said Luke, his voice rising a little in excitement. "And how about this? Do you think it's only from our world that visitors drop in from time to time, or from some other world too? Or *worlds*? Normally, I'd say that idea's kind of whacked, but here *we* are in a different world, so how do we know? And *another* thing," he went on before Beth could answer the first thing, "do you think we'd necessarily know about it if someone had been here and then come back to our world? Even someone we knew? If they told, they'd probably get carted off somewhere. So they'd probably just keep it to themselves, wouldn't they? Are *we* going to tell anyone? I don't think I will. We'll just slide back into our regular lives, right? Unless of course a lot of time has passed when we get back, and there's some big old police hunt going on for us and we're in the newspa-"

"Stop! We agreed!"

"Yeah, got it. Forget that part anyway 'cause it's just not happening. But back to the whole thing about other worlds. . ."

Long into the night, the two discussed such questions of interest, talking in the same carefree way that they so often had back home, talking in the way that had made them friends in the first place. To Luke, Beth seemed her old self again, more relaxed than he'd yet seen her here. At last, when the conversation had petered out and they were both on the edge of drifting off, he roused himself enough to say, "You did it, Beth."

"You too," she answered sleepily. "We all did it."

"No. You know what I mean. *You did it!*"

And so she had.

But as destiny would have it, what might be her most challenging task, her most harrowing adventure still lay several days ahead.

CHAPTER NINETEEN – New Acquaintance

The next morning, Beth and Luke were able to sleep as late as they wanted. Harac, who had not been on the road as long as the others, was up at the earliest light and Rendel rose an hour or so after that. Aynyxia, still soaking in the stream, drifted in and out of sleep until two playful wolf-girls joined her; they had been sent by curious siblings and cousins to learn more about the strange plant-person and report back.

The youngest two travelers, entirely unaccustomed to the sort of life they'd recently been leading, slept soundly through the morning, barely stirring until the sun was high in the sky. "This adventure stuff can sort of wear you out," said Luke, stretching, when he realized how late it was. Beth, awake but making no attempt to move, mumbled agreement. Then they both drifted away again for a good twenty minutes.

In the meantime, Aron, with the help of his adoptive parents, did everything necessary to prepare for his departure. He helped gather food, and he formally asked R'khan, the First Wolf, permission to leave the pack; he filled his satchel, and he wrestled with his wolf cousins; he sharpened his dagger, and he sat quietly by Kr'nara, listening to all the bits of advice and assurance she had given him many times already.

When Beth and Luke finally got up, there was little for them to do. Departure was imminent. Beth wished they could have stayed longer to get to know the wolves and understand their way of life. When she said as much to Luke, Aron overheard and suggested, "Perhaps when I am well-established on the throne you can return with me for a long visit." ("Like *that's* going to happen!" Luke whispered when the prince was out of earshot, but Beth merely looked thoughtful and said nothing.)

Within the hour, a well-rested, well-fed, fairly well-stocked band of seven left the dwelling of the white wolves, heading west.

Rendel had been right about Sir Alric. He would not accompany them much beyond the wolves' territory (he had long ago vowed never to return to his old life and it was in exchange for that vow that the pack had accepted him as one of its own), but he would start them on their way and had proposed a quicker route out of Lupriark than the one they had taken in. It would lead them just north of the Dark Rim's border with an easier path to Greyvic than if they returned by way of Little Down's Keep. Food and fresh water along the way would be plentiful enough. It was with great spirits that the original party of five received this news, though one matter of concern remained.

"We have horses at Little Down," Rendel said. "Would it not be worth the time of retrieving them so that we can travel more quickly afterwards?"

"And go back through that Rim thing when we don't have to?" Luke asked uncomfortably. "We could get lost in there for weeks. Let's just go with the shortcut."

"Even by the shortest possible route, the journey to Greyvic by foot will be a long and tiring one," countered Rendel, "especially for any members of our company unaccustomed to such travel." Although he looked at no one in particular, Beth supposed he counted her as one of those. It had not escaped anyone's notice how exhausted she and Luke had been. "In any event, there is little time left to us. We would not get to the festival before the Tork is to address the assembly."

"There is another possibility," suggested Alric. "If you follow the route I propose, you will come near to Treyllavic before nightfall; though I have not passed that way in such a long while, I credit you will yet be able to hire horses there."

"Treyllavic? Aye, we will," confirmed Harac, "and I know the place we can do it. . . . Unless all the horses have already been hired by travelers to Greyvic."

"Then a farmer's cart, perhaps, at a generous price," suggested Rendel.

"Aye, that we can certainly do, but our time is so short. A horse for each of us would be best."

"And we have the means?" Rendel asked.

"Aye," said Harac for the third time; he carried more than enough silver to hire six horses.

"Then it is settled," said Alric.

The first leg of the journey was fast and smooth. The travelers went uphill only rarely and in short stretches. Even the weather was kind to them – just cool enough to keep them from being overheated by their exercise. Anxious though they were about the state of affairs in Greyvic, they did not particularly hurry in that first stretch, knowing that this would be Aron's last time with Alric for a long while and understanding that the parting would come soon enough. They talked as they walked, at first all in a group, discussing the Council of Ten and the Torks and the reception the prince was likely to meet (they were not all of one accord on the latter topic), and then they drifted into twos and threes and discussed other matters of interest to them.

Sir Alric, though famed for wide travels before settling at Lupriark, had never been to the Nethermarshes, so he soon found his way to Aynyxia's side. His questions for her were many, and no detail of marsh life was too small to hold his interest. Luke walked beside them and joined in with inquiries and remarks of his own.

Behind them, Rendel and Beth were similarly engaged in conversation, questioning one another and exchanging stories about their respective worlds. They laughed often, though Luke generally missed the comments that led them to do so.

Harac and Aron came along last, discussing matters of politics and reviewing the important names the prince would need to know. Then, after a lull of several minutes, the dwarf said rather suddenly, "Sir Alric will have told you of Rhysmenn of Eleyn Gryf." The prince affirmed it. "He was an elf, you must know. There is no elf left in Gwilldonum itself, save possibly the descendants of Ereydenn, who may yet inhabit Col Portarum. It was a great honor to your family for an elf to serve as advisor to your mother and to your mother's father. . . ." His voice trailed away and only after a long pause did he continue. "When the war began, Rhysmenn gave his oath to King DarQuinn that he would not leave the princess's side until peace had returned. He kept that oath, and he and Sir Simon of Norwood died together with her, swords drawn, all three." Aron was moved by this detail, previously unknown to him, and found a bittersweet gratification in it, though he was unsure why the dwarf had imparted it.

They walked on silently, and Aron believed the conversation at an end until Harac said, quietly but with a certain gruffness, "He was my great friend."

"This," thought Aron, "is what he wished me to know—that ones dear to us were lost together." He considered a moment how to respond; after the pause, he said, "Then I should find honor in calling you friend as well." The answer pleased the dwarf, who smiled his satisfaction.

Harac realized that he liked this boy. If he hadn't, he would have nonetheless resolved to serve and defend him as the Anointed of Gwilldonum, but as it was, he most keenly desired an opportunity to prove his fidelity. No doubt, the dwarf reflected grimly a moment later, such an opportunity lay ahead.

At length, the travelers stopped for rest and a light meal. When conversation lulled, Harac, who knew something of the geography of the region they were approaching, remarked on a distant noise and asked if it were the sound of the Gillen Falls.

"Truth, it is," answered Alric, watching the dwarf expectantly.

"But will we be crossing the Gil so close to the falls?" He had not been able to guess where the shortcut would take them. He had led the original party to Little Down in the first place largely because the Gil River could be crossed there: it was calmer and had been bridged. Crossing near Little Down had meant passing through the Dark Rim, but he hadn't known a way to do so farther upstream (and hadn't known if an upstream crossing would take them close enough to Lupriark in any event – the wolves' territory was not well known to outsiders). "Will we cross over the river above the falls or below?" Either possibility seemed problematic.

"Neither," their guide answered cryptically, exchanging knowing smiles with his ward. Though his response provoked, as he had intended, many questions, he gave no further answer except to say, "You shall see."

When they were once again on their feet and on their way, Alric said, "There are things I will tell you now, for conversation will soon be more difficult." Indeed, though they had not gone far from their resting place, the noise of the falls had already increased noticeably. "What I will show you is a secret of the wolves', and I will trust you to keep it." He smiled at Harac. "We will not cross *over* the Gil, but *under* it. There is a passage, well-hidden but quite safe. I have reason to credit it has been protected by charm since time out of memory, though I may be wrong in this. It is quite dark within, but the wolves have night eyes, and I have come to know the way well. You will prefer to carry light. I see you carry a lantern" – the other one (the one with the oil they'd been saving!) had gotten left behind in the Dark Rim somehow – "and no doubt you have a tinder box among you?" Aynyxia, who saw quite well in the dark and never minded being cold or wet, had little use for tinder boxes, but Harac and Rendel each had one and even Beth had acquired one at the Gribbs'. Luke merely answered, "Must've left mine in my other pants. Go figure!"

It was not long afterwards that the crashing falls began to roar in their ears and conversation ceased. Soon they could also see the Gil – a hard-rushing river both above and below the falls – and it was no wonder to any that Harac had marveled at the idea of crossing it in this region.

At a closer view of the Gillen Falls, Beth stopped short. "Wow!" she breathed, though no one heard. She wondered if the scene before her were the most beautiful she'd ever seen.

She stood near the top of the falls. The curtain of water that cascaded to the pool below sparkled in the sunlight, but not in any ordinary way. The sparkles were bright and of many colors – ruby, emerald, gold, and silver, among others. Luke said later (when his voice could actually be heard) that he supposed the reason for the strange coloring was that the rocks beneath contained some sort of unusual mineral, particles of which kept getting picked up by the water. Beth preferred to think the cause was something magical.

Motioning to the party to follow, Alric walked a short distance north of the falls. The area was rocky, but some plant life managed to survive in patches even among the boulders. Alric approached such a patch, then pulled apart thick vines to reveal a passage behind. It didn't look like much to the others, but Alric gestured to indicate that they would be crawling through the narrow opening.

It was not an appealing prospect. No one liked the idea of crawling through on either their bellies or their hands and knees all the way to the other side of the river! A wolf might not mind this passage, but the rest of them were a bit taller than wolves, and it seemed unlikely that they'd be able to stand straight up inside.

Alric went first, followed by Rendel, who had, unnoticed by Beth, found dry branches of a slow-burning plant and expertly fashioned a torch while she'd been admiring the falls, though he did not light it until he had gone through the opening in the rock. Once he was through, however, a flickering yellowed light made its way back out to the others. Harac went next, though he had to take off his pack to get his rounded figure through the opening. Aynyxia pushed the pack to him from behind, then followed. Luke motioned to Beth to go next.

She hesitated. She didn't like the idea of crawling through such a small space without even being able to ask what was on the other side, but it wasn't *that* that bothered her most. It was the vines more than anything. They too much resembled the ones that had caught and held her when the devil boar pursued her. It gave her a horrible feeling to see them surrounding the tunnel entrance. In her mind, she could see them grabbing at her as she passed through and then holding her back so that she couldn't reach the others.

Luke touched her arm, looking at her questioningly, but even if she'd known what to say to him, he wouldn't have been able to hear over the noise of the falls. She took a breath and crouched low, then passed through her bow and quiver to Aynyxia. She and her pack were small enough to go through together.

Luke followed, saying to himself, "Good thing I'm not claustrophobic or anything. Nope, not me. I'm practically enamored of tiny little spaces with thousands of pounds of water rushing over my head and a handful of burning dead stuff to light the way ahead and a lantern that will probably run out of oil before we're halfway to the other side."

Aron entered last.

Fortunately, the opening led to a much larger tunnel than its first-time visitors had hoped for. Everyone, except for Alric, who had to stoop a little, was able to stand up straight almost at once. Alric and Rendel went ahead, while Harac, carrying the lantern, brought up the rear.

The light was dim, but there was enough of it to dance eerie shadows across the tunnel walls as the travelers moved along. Beth, who had visited a number of caves in southern Indiana and Kentucky, expected the walls to be wet and slimy, but wherever she reached her hand to touch them, the cold, smooth rock was perfectly dry. The roar of the rushing water was muted in the tunnel, but no one attempted conversation. There was no real need for it; besides, this wasn't the sort of place, Beth felt, where insignificant chatter belonged. Charmed, Alric had suggested.

When they came out the other end of the tunnel, most of the travelers squinted into the light of the late afternoon sun. When her eyes adjusted, Beth looked ahead at a pleasant sight.

They were still at the top of the falls, of course, and to their left and behind them, a cliff dropped off toward the pool into which the constantly-rushing water crashed. To the right, the terrain was rough and rocky for a while, but there was a thick wood some way beyond; further still, great white cliffs towered along the horizon. But it was the scene directly ahead that held Beth's gaze. A grassy hill rolled softly out before them until it leveled into a wide, pretty meadow, sprinkled with swaying flowers in lively colors.

"It's lovely," she said, her words drowned out.

After a moment, Beth noticed that Rendel, close by her, was staring not at the scenery but at Sir Alric and Aron. The older man rested his hand on his ward's shoulder and together they looked north toward the wooded area. Beth's own gaze went from Rendel to the other two to the wood and back to Rendel again. When the woodlander perceived this, he came near to answer the question in her mind. He spoke close to her ear but not loudly, and the words were barely discernible over the sounds of the fall. "That way lies Dunryelle," he said, and she understood – Aron looked toward the place his mother had lived and died.

Soon, Alric motioned them all ahead. When they reached the bottom of the hill, they could at last hear each other again without shouting. A little farther still, and they were able to speak in normal voices. It was then that Alric announced he would take his leave of them.

The sad parting between Aron and Sir Alric took place with as much privacy as the others could offer. From a distance, Beth watched the two embrace and speak and embrace again, and then Alric closed something into Aron's hand; it must have been a sort of chain or necklace, because it looked like Aron slipped it over his head. Beth looked away. She couldn't hear any of their words. Not that she wanted to. That would make her too sad, she was sure.

"We knew this day would come," Alric was saying, "my own true son," he added, using words he had avoided so many times in the boy's life. "But as I have told you often, in times of peace a king has great liberty to travel his lands as he wishes. You must return often to Lupriark, you know, to ensure that your subjects there have not become too unruly. You may even need to dwell among us for a number of days to be certain of it." Aron returned his smile, but weakly. "And now there remains one thing alone." Alric knelt down. Aron, not understanding, attempted to follow, but his guardian stayed him with a gesture, saying, "Allow me this: to swear fealty to you, my liege, anointed to be King of Gwilldonum and High King of the Southlands. My hand is yours."

Seeing Alric kneeling before him marked for Aron better than anything else could the ending of his old life and the beginning of his new. "Your fealty is a most precious gift," the prince answered in a wavering voice. "I accept it gladly . . . and I . . . I will keep faith with you forever."

Sir Alric rose and pulled the boy close, each of them shedding tears freely.

When Aron rejoined the others, he indicated with a nod that he was ready to continue the journey. His eyes were red and moist, and he said nothing; the party traveled silently for some time. Only once did the young prince look back.

They learned, as they traveled together, some of the pieces that formed the puzzle of Aron's life. The evening before, Alric had confirmed what the others had come to believe: a gryphon had carried the infant to Lupriark. Alric had shown them an old bit of parchment that had accompanied the boy. "This is my son, Aron, whom I have anointed," the note read. "At the age of all rights, he will be sent for from afar. Until that day, keep, protect, and love him." The words were hurriedly written, but Alric recognized his cousin's hand; besides, she had included a token which he knew to be hers.

Now, walking together, they learned from Aron himself what his life with the wolves had been like and what training he had received from his mother's cousin for the life he would one day lead. At one point, Rendel commented, "It seems, Your Highness, that Sir Alric has kept you somewhat current of the affairs of our land, though when I spoke with him earlier he gave me to understand that he does not leave Lupriark to visit his homeland."

"Truth," answered Aron, "he does not return to Gwilldonum, but the eastern march of our woods is not far from a dwarvish trading camp, and my cousin has made mult expeditions there. I myself began to accompany him from a young age. Many sorts, not only dwarves, engage in commerce at the camp – mostly from the northern lands, but Gwilldonians and other Southlanders also come, mostly by way of the seaport. News is exchanged there as often as silver; and the worse the news, the more detailed and oft-repeated it is!" This answer satisfied Rendel (though he later mentioned casually to the prince that the word *mult* instead of *many* had fallen into disuse in elegant society), but Harac was drawn by the talk of the dwarvish camp. His questions were many and he engaged Aron in long conversation.

At a later time, when Aron had fallen in step with Beth, she had a question of her own. "Sir Alric told us about how you arrived at Lupriark. . . . But how did she know? Arandella, I mean. Your mother. How did she know where he was? I thought he was supposed to have disappeared."

Aron smiled. "The two were not only cousins, but great friends in their youth. She was his confidante, the only one of their relations who knew his whereabouts, and she kept his secret. She even connived to visit him once in Lupriark itself, without the knowledge of her family. In her eighteenth year, she went with a small party to Little Down's Keep; then, accompanied solely by a trusted attendant, she slipped away into the woods. She wished to satisfy herself that her beloved cousin fared well and was content in his new life."

"She went through the Dark Rim?" Beth asked.

The question seemed to unsettle Aron, who knew much of the Rim. "She did. I do not know how the crossing was for her, but I have been given to understand that her attendant, Kaysa, had certain gifts which would have served them well."

Kaysa. Beth remembered the name, of course, but wondered if she should say anything. At length, she began hesitantly, "I've heard of Kaysa. Did . . . did you know that she was with Arandella – Queen Arandella, I mean – on the last day? On the day she sent you away?" She couldn't say "On the day your mother died."

266

"I did not."

Aron was quiet after that.

The farther into Gwilldonum he went, the more real his mother became to Aron. After some time, as he walked beside Harac, he asked, "By what name is my mother known? Her father, I know, has come to be known as 'the Good'."

"Your mother was queen for such a short time, Sire," Harac answered a little uncomfortably, "that she continues to be known by most as Princess Arandella." Hesitantly, he added, "She has sometimes been called Arandella the Misfortunate."

There was silence between them for a moment. Then Aron said, quietly but firmly, "I shall never call her by that name."

Beth overheard the exchange and started another line of conversation at once, addressing Rendel, by whose side she was then walking. "You said that Gwilldonum had been having such a hard time. Bad weather and bad crops and everything. But we've seen so many places, like that meadow back there, that seem so . . . *healthy* and alive." In response, Rendel described the variety of regions in his land (Beth had seen only a small sampling, he said, and was now crossing Gwilldonum at its narrowest edge – the country widened greatly to the south), as well as the variety of fortunes they had known in recent years. Harac entered into the conversation as well, as did Aynyxia, though only slightly. Luke asked questions on occasion, but Aron kept silent and thoughtful throughout.

At length, the discussion came around to the subject of the goblins to the north and then inevitably to the urgency of presenting Aron as heir to the throne. After that topic was replaced by others, Aron made a point of walking close to Beth and said to her – in a younger and more awed voice than she had yet heard from him – "It is you, then, who was sent for me? A champion, the walkabout called you. She recounted to me how you were attacked by devil boar, which I have seen and know to be fierce creatures, and by monsters known as fanged tree-rats, and how you rescued her from miscreants by cunning and bravery, and later led all your friends from the Dark Rim, a place the horrors of which I know too well." It was amazing to Beth that he had been able to learn so much from the reticent Aynyxia in a single conversation. "All this," Aron concluded, "that you could come for me."

"Well, we *all* came for you," Beth told him. "And it was really Rendel who rescued Aynyxia, and Luke rescued me. Everybody did different things. I . . . I just had the idea about where to look for you." After a minute, she added, "There were others who looked for you before, you know. A lot of others, I think."

He nodded with understanding. "But the time was not right then. I comprehend it. All has happened as it should, in due course." And as they walked on, in that late afternoon, a peacefulness settled between them.

After a while, when the party had stopped for its supper, Harac said to the young prince, "We mean you all respect, my liege, but it may be wiser if for a time we dispense with the forms of address that are your due, for we do not wish to give away our business by a slip of speech, should we meet some stranger on the way. The casual conversation of friends and equals, even while in private, may serve our purposes better for the present."

"Of course," agreed the prince, who himself was beginning to tire of selecting words so carefully. "I shall take it as no offence if you address me as an equal for the present time."

"Right! I'm all for casual conversation," agreed Luke, adding, "And we ought to call him by a different name. I like the sound of 'Jack', myself."

"*Jack!*" repeated Harac, incensed. "Like the berry? You would give him a comical name?"

"No," said Beth, quickly. "It's just a regular name where we come from. It's a nickname for 'John'."

"Nick name? John?" Harac considered it and then seemed appeased. "John. Truth, I have heard this name and I credit it to be a noble one."

"Then we scratch it from the list," countered Luke. "We're going for 'un-noble' here (though not to say *ig*noble, I'm sure!). How about 'Harry'?"

"Also noble," said Beth, before Harac, who knew many of the old stories and who imagined that his own name derived from the same root, could say something similar.

"Oh, yeah," said Luke. "Harry, Henry. Got it. . . . All right, then, 'Bob' it is, and that's my last offer."

"'Bob'?" Harac repeated. "This is a name? I have never heard it in our land. His Highness has the look of a Gwilldonian all about him. How should he have such a name as this 'Bob'?'

Fortunately, a minor distraction occurred at that point and, once it had passed, the journey was resumed but the previous topic of conversation was not.

Within the hour, the group had split up. Partly because it would draw less attention, and partly to conserve the energy of the younger travelers, only Rendel and Harac went into Treyllavic to see about hiring horses and, if they could do so discreetly, to arrange for a message to be sent to Imre at Little Down.

Before they left, Rendel did something that all but Aynyxia found odd – he took a small amount of fine green powder from one of the several pouches hanging from his belt and sprinkled it around the edges of the area where the others would wait and where the whole party would camp that night. When Luke asked if this dusting were some sort of housekeeping ritual in reverse, Rendel explained that the powder might be useful if any wild beasts felt inclined to approach in their absence, because its aroma might have a calming effect. When Luke questioned his use of the word "might" and asked whether the green stuff came with a "money-back guarantee," Rendel (who had been deciphering Luke's speech rather well up to that point) simply gave him an odd look and continued what he was doing.

While Rendel and Harac went off in search of horses to hire or purchase, Beth, Luke, Aynyxia, and Aron stayed behind at the encampment. It was a sheltered spot on high ground from which they could observe nearly any approach from the south, the direction of Treyllavic and other settled areas. Just behind them, to the north, was a rough, rarely-traveled stretch over which loomed the great cliffs.

Beth had been curious to see what a "regular" Gwilldonian city looked like – she understood Treyllavic to be nearly three times the size of Little Down's Keep – but didn't really mind staying behind with the others. Her energy had begun to run low and the sensation that she would soon need as much of it as she could muster crept about her. Besides, the narrow escape she and Luke had experienced at Little Down was still fresh in her mind. When Rendel, just before leaving for Treyllavic, had said, "And I suppose that you all will be staying here until we return?", Harac and Aron had seemed a bit puzzled, but Luke and Beth knew just what he meant. Luke seemed about to respond in some sarcastic way until his good friend gave him a marginally discreet flick of her hand on the back of his head.

To pass the couple of hours that they expected the others to be gone, Luke and Aron had an archery contest, but Beth refrained, not feeling the least competitive at the moment. She chose instead to sit by Aynyxia, who was keeping watch. Soon she stretched out on the ground; soon after that she dozed.

She awoke when the boys rejoined them. Luke was asking Aron if he could borrow his sword for a moment to see what one felt like. Aron was quite surprised that Luke had never handled one before ("Well, not *this* kind anyway," Luke had said, "not something *real*") and quite pleased to be able to give his new friend pointers. When he'd become accustomed to the feel of the weapon, Luke regretted that Harac wasn't there to give him some real practice, because the dwarf carried a very fine sword. Beth, of course, had a sword close at hand, but she hadn't yet told even Luke about it. She hesitated now, thinking that it might be a good thing for her to try it out, but in the end she decided against it. Instead, she settled for a turn getting the feel of Aron's sword and decided that Luke's idea about practicing with Harac's was a good one.

After that, Luke suggested they find some sort of game to play, but it took them a while to settle on something. Hide-and-seek hardly seemed prudent, under the circumstances, and they couldn't think of any interesting type of guessing game that was likely to work well with players from different worlds. For lack of anything better (and "just to get us in a game mood"), Luke taught Aynyxia and Aron how to play Rock, Paper, Scissors. Aynyxia seemed quite taken by the game and would have played it for much longer than anyone else would have liked, but fortunately for the others it occurred to Aron that he knew a simple game that could be played with only rocks and sticks. That activity, in turn, inspired Luke and Beth to explain how the game of checkers works. Neither of the other two had played it before, though seeing the "checkerboard" (made up of lines in the dirt) prompted Aron to mention that he was familiar with chess, which he had played often with Alric, and that perhaps he *had* heard the name "checkers" before after all.

The games kept them occupied right up until the time Aynyxia, looking to the south, announced, "Riders." The other three were alert at once. Though hoping, of course, that it would prove to be their friends returning, they were aware of other possibilities. Distance and the dusky light kept them guessing for a bit, and then all at once Aynyxia said, "Yep!" while Luke said, "They're back!" and the other two relaxed their tense poses.

Harac and Rendel had fared much better than they had feared, though not quite as well as they had hoped. They returned with five horses, rather than the six they had sought. Beth volunteered to ride double; Rendel said at once that she could ride with him, to which Luke responded, "Well, who's surprised at that? Can we have a show of hands?" But he'd only been mumbling, and not everyone caught the words.

Harac, Rendel, and Aynyxia divided the night watches among themselves. Aron and Beth each volunteered to take a turn, but Luke, stretching, said, "Not me. I'm headed to bed." Rather than remind the prince, who had been stifling yawns for a good half hour, of his tender age, Rendel said tactfully, "Allow us this service, my liege;" and to Beth he said, "There will be time enough for you to do your part."

Rendel took the first watch. Aynyxia went to soak, but returned within the hour for security's sake. Harac went to sleep almost at once, startling Aron (who had made a bed nearby) with his first loud snore. Their other companions, however, were merely thankful that the dwarf was quieter tonight than he had been on previous occasions.

Beth and Luke, who had risen so late that morning, talked softly together for a long while until all the others except Rendel, still keeping watch, were asleep. In due course, the conversation took a serious turn.

"Luke? If we die in this world . . . "

"Thought we weren't going to talk about that."

"I know, but . . . . Just this once, maybe."

She was serious. No idle curiosity here! Luke sighed and thought and said at last, "I don't know, Beth. You're the one who always has ideas about souls and the big scheme of things and all that. It'd be nice to think that if we died here, we'd just magically pop back into our own world alive and well. But, I don't know . . . probably we'd just be dead everywhere. And then . . . " His voice trailed away, and the ensuing silence was not a particularly peaceful one. Eventually, he asked, "In the end, what does it really matter? Knowing ahead of time, I mean. Whichever way it works, we're still going to do what we have to do, right? And we're still going to try to stay alive. We don't have a lot of choices here."

Beth answered tentatively. "Except . . . well, nobody seems too sure how things will go when we get to Greyvic – it could all work out all right or there could be some kind of big fight or something – so . . . we *could* ask them to leave us behind in some safe little corner and go on without us. We could just wait it out until everything gets resolved."

"'A safe little corner'? And where exactly would *that* be? But anyway, maybe it *can't* be resolved without us. Especially you, I guess. And besides, I don't think we'd do that even if we could."

"No," she agreed.

That time the silence lasted for several minutes, and Luke's thoughts began to drift away until he heard Beth whisper his name in a quavering voice. And then, "What if one of us dies and the other doesn't?" She sounded so young then, like when he'd first met her and thought she was such a little kid.

"Let it go, Beth," he said, and his voice was very gentle.

In the tiniest of whispers, she said, "OK."

Though he couldn't hear it, he thought she was probably crying.

After a while, they both slept.

The next morning, while Aynyxia was soaking and Harac and Aron were tending to the horses, Beth sat by a small fire, finishing her breakfast pensively. Luke was a little way apart when Rendel came to sit by her.

"We are a diverse and interesting company, would you not say?" he observed after a moment. "But each with a part to play, whatever the outcome." He looked at her then, with kindness and sympathy in his face, and she was sure that he had overheard her conversation with Luke the night before. "And even in the safest corner of your world or of mine, Beth, we cannot truly know what life holds for us."

"I know," said Beth.

CHAPTER TWENTY – Mistakes and Misfortune

On the morning that Beth and Luke slept in at Lupriark, Therin Mandek requested that the faun Daasa of the Westmarch accompany three of his soldiers as they set out along the Queen's Road in search of the champion's company. They would carry one of Gweynleyn's angeli birds – the one known to Aynyxia and therefore most likely to aid them in locating the walkabout – as well as the lady's colors and the mark of her seal. Another company of four would search the road to Arystar, and of course several units already patrolled the areas between Greyvic and the northern borders, though Harac would not bring the party by that route unless unforeseen trouble drove him to it. Lady Gweynleyn and the council member Jeron Rabirius, to whom Therin reported the arrangements, approved, the lady being particularly relieved by her belief that Therin was now resigned to staying in Greyvic and keeping close watch on Myrmidon Tork.

The captain had another plan, however, though its details were not yet set. Before he could attend to them, he would find his undercaptain, Rostik, to discuss the security of Greyvic and the borderland, for he could not be unaware of his duty in that matter. Then, he would be free to seek out another – someone whom he hoped would be of great use in carrying out his plan.

"Daasa." It was Voss, one of the three soldiers assigned to her, who addressed the faun. With him was Pyrr Tullius, the second soldier, and between them, looking unnaturally green, was the third, a Meadowlander named Mar. Behind them, for some reason, came a fourth.

"I am ill," said Mar with difficulty, though the effort could have been spared her, for the fact was evident without announcement. She stumbled away from them as quickly as she was able so that she would not be sick in front of them.

The soldier who had been standing behind her stepped forward. "I am Crinna Tanner, and I am to take the place of Mar on this expedition." Daasa did not respond at once, except to look him over carefully. He carried himself well enough and was of an age to have some experience behind him. She did not recognize his face, but there was nothing surprising in that for she had not often, of late, been in the company of Therin's troops. She had no particular reason not to accept the substitution, but stated nonetheless, "The Captain must make any change in our plan."

"He has done so," said Crinna. "The choice was his."

"It is so," agreed Voss.

Daasa hesitated, but, anxious to be on her way, decided that Crinna Tanner's knowledge of their mission and Voss's confirmation that the captain had approved the substitution were sufficient.

That was her mistake.

She did not like Voss – he was overly ambitious, she judged, and too self-serving for her tastes – but the captain had selected him. In fact, Therin's assessment was similar to her own, but he was more tolerant of the faults, believing that he recognized something of his own younger self in the soldier, and chose to entrust him with this mission of supreme importance.

That was Therin's mistake. Both he and Daasa would regret their choices before another twenty-four hours had passed.

"Edwyn? Edwyn Reston?" He thought he had found the face he sought, just before it turned away into the crowd.

"Therin!" Indeed, it was his old friend turning back to him. "Or, ought I to say Therin *Mandek*, as I hear these days?" He smiled, clasping the other by his shoulders.

At the time of the Invasion, they had been of an age, nearing twenty years, and their paths had crossed often. They had enjoyed one another's company immensely, but when peace was reestablished, Edwyn had returned to his family home and to the training of their famed horses, and the two friends had seen little of one another since.

After they had passed a few minutes in pleasantries, Therin said carefully and in a lowered voice, "What think you of this proposal the Tork is expected to make? There is talk of nothing else. An idea worthy of consideration, would you not judge?"

The easy manner of the other changed abruptly. Warily, he regarded Therin. "I am much surprised to hear you say it. For myself," he looked his former friend directly in the eyes, "I would sooner hang for cutting the Tork's throat than see him one day on the throne of this land."

Slowly, Therin's tight mouth spread into a satisfied smile. Leaning in close, he spoke conspiratorially, "I am glad of it. Come with me, if you will."

To any observer, the departure of those two from the Great Hall was a casual one, with no especial purpose or import.

"We have little time," Edwyn told Therin several hours later, moving and speaking quickly. Their plan had been laid. It was time to execute it.

"Trouble?" Therin followed his friend to the far side of the Greyvic castle's stable.

"I am watched by the captain of the Torks and must return at once, but have no fear, my Nightbird will serve you well." Already he was securing the tackle on the strongest and fastest of the renowned Reston horses. Nightbird was a beautiful animal, a pure white (except for the silvery strands in her mane), perfectly groomed. But her beauty was not the thing Edwyn valued most in her. "She will fly for you, my old friend, none will catch her."

When she was ready, Edwyn drew near to the horse's head to whisper. It would be too much to say that the animal nodded in response afterwards, but a toss of the head and the slightest of whinnies seemed to satisfy her master that she understood. "She is yours," Edwyn said to Therin, handing over the reins. "May you find what you seek and return in safety and health."

There were three exits from the large stable, and the two men led Nightbird to the one they judged most discreet. In a moment, Therin was away, alone and on his mission to find the Anointed. Edwyn looked out into the night from the stable door, watching for any sign of someone attempting to follow his friend; then, as he turned back to return to the Great Hall, he saw in the shadows a stable girl who had been watching him with interest. Edwyn held his finger to his lips to indicate that this was a matter of secrecy and then winked and tossed her a coin. The stable girl, who held all the Restons in awe, promised her silence with a shy smile and a nod.

Returning to the Hall, Edwyn Reston was surprised to be cornered at once by Lady Gweynleyn, whom he knew by sight and reputation rather than by personal acquaintance. As soon as she could do so without being overheard, she demanded with a piercing look and near-menacing voice, "What has become of Therin Mandek?"

"I could not say," answered his friend . . . but the lady suspected that he could.

The next morning, both Luke and Daasa, not many hours' ride apart by then, had misfortunate encounters. Luke's was of a minor nature and nearly all its consequences were of short duration – the only long-term result, in fact, turned out to be a favorable one, and after some time passed, he even saw humor in the incident. Daasa's encounter, by stark contrast, was harrowing, its consequences fatal.

Rising early, Luke and Rendel, at the latter's suggestion, took a short hike in the direction of the cliffs to gather berries of a particularly succulent type. When they reached the bushes they sought, Luke picked one of the large berries (which resembled fat, red grapes as much as anything else) and bit into it.

"Mmm. Not bad. These are really juicy."

"They are quite good," Rendel agreed. "Beth will especially enjoy them, I know, because—"

"Well, you just know a little bit about everybody and everything, don't you?" The words didn't come out sounding exactly the way Luke had intended. They were supposed to sound as if he didn't really mean them. Even though he did. He'd actually been feeling quite friendly toward Rendel since their day together had begun (in other words, for about twenty-five minutes), volunteering to go with him and then complimenting his little fruit and everything. *So, why did the guy have to spoil it all by acting like he knew everything? Even about* Beth, *whom he'd known for about a minute and a half!*

Luke's words silenced Rendel, but only briefly. When Luke had trouble breaking off one of the larger bunches of berries, Rendel demonstrated how it could best be done, though there was a wariness in his voice and he offered no more detail than was necessary. Then, he added somewhat mechanically, "And choose from the bunches that are farthest out on the bush, not only

276

because they are ripest and easiest to pick, but also because— *No, not that one!*"

Luke had spotted an especially large, well-formed bunch right in the middle of the bush and, despite having heard Rendel's instruction to pick the ones farthest out, looked as if he might reach for it.

"No, this is a good one. I can get it," he said confidently and plunged in his hand.

"*No!*" said Rendel, grabbing back the offending hand, which Luke then jerked away with an angry look.

"Let go!" Luke exclaimed, just before Rendel shouted, "Do not touch it!" with such urgency that Luke would have complied that time if he'd heard the words a second earlier. But it was too late. He'd already plunged his right hand deep into the bush.

Immediately, he withdrew it.

"*Ow!* . . . *ow, ow, ow!*" His hand, now covered with small black dots, stung tremendously. He shook it vigorously, but to no effect. He was in pain and the dots, whatever they were, clung to his skin.

With one hand, Rendel grabbed Luke's forearm and with the other he began to pick off the black bugs (for such they were) and toss them back into the bush. Soon, the last one was gone but the stinging sensation remained. Reluctant as Luke was to ask for help under such unflattering circumstances, his hand was suffering more than his pride, so he uttered in a high voice, "Uhm . . . it still hurts."

"They've left stingers," the woodlander answered in a pained voice. Luke saw the faint lines of the stingers then and tried unsuccessfully to pull one out. "Not that way," Rendel said. "Watch." Gingerly, he extracted one, then another. It was difficult because Rendel's own right hand had been stung while he was picking the bugs off Luke.

"What *are* those things?" Luke asked as Rendel continued to work at the stingers.

"Creyfilla. They make the juices that are absorbed into the bush and infuse the berries, giving them their distinctive tastes. The creyfilla always nest in the very center of the bush, and there grow the largest berries. Quite attractive berries, yet hazardous. . . . But perhaps you would prefer that I answer, 'I do not know'."

277

"Sarcasm doesn't become you," answered Luke primly as the pain began to abate. Then he watched as Rendel sat down to attend to his own hand. Luke sat down too. "Anyway . . . thanks," he said, but not especially graciously, considering the circumstances.

"Not at all!" Rendel responded, with only a little more grace.

Watching Rendel pick out the tiny stingers one by one, Luke was sure he ought to say something. Something nice.

"So-o-o-o . . ." he began, but his voice trailed away.

"So," Rendel repeated without inflection.

After a pause, Luke began again, speaking quickly. "All right. *So*, I'm sorry about your hand hurting – I know it was my fault – and I'm kind of thinking that maybe I might've been a little, well, you know . . . for lack of a better word, let's say . . . *foolish*."

"Truth," agreed Rendel simply, but his voice rose when he added, "*And perhaps not here alone!*" Luke couldn't possibly have missed the aggravation behind the words, but it didn't disturb him. On the contrary, Rendel's loss of composure put him more at ease.

"OK. Go on, why don't you? Don't feel like you need to spare my feelings or anything." The words themselves were not particularly friendly, but the tone was more relaxed than it had been.

"You have rejected, for no reason of worth, a friendship offered. Is there not foolishness in this?" There was no point in Luke's pretending he didn't know what Rendel meant, so he merely shrugged. After a pause, the woodlander continued in a calmer voice. "You have said clearly that Beth is not your mate, but I see that she is your great friend. And I have seen, in part at least, why that should be. Is it a wonder to you that I also should like and admire her? But, Luke . . . I do like you as well. And *perhaps* I may not be so *very* far from admiring you. We shall see in time. But in the meanwhile, may we not all three be friends together?"

Luke sat quietly, considering. *Well, all right,* he thought, still not looking at Rendel, *he's not such a bad guy and I haven't exactly thrown out the welcome mat. But this has* nothing *to do with Beth. He's* totally *wrong about that because I'm* not *jealous! She's my best friend and has been for forever – like, a year at least! And it's not like I'm afraid of* that *changing – just because she's making new friends, and just because she fits in like she was*

278

born here, and just because, despite everything bad that happens, she seems so happy here, like she totally belongs. It's not like she'd ever stay here with them or anything!! So, it's not like I'm afraid of any of that stuff. . . . Not really. . . . But I suppose . . .

Well, *of course* she could have all the new friends she wanted! Dozens of them, even! Whole armies of them!

As long as he didn't get left behind.

Then, without warning, the haunting voice from the Rim echoed in his head. Not that the voice had talked about Beth; his private fear didn't have to do with losing his friend. It was worse than that. He knew it was worse even though he barely remembered the thing that had started it all. Someone had left him behind once. A long time ago, when he was little. He couldn't even remember the circumstances, but he knew it made him feel sick inside even to try. It had been so terrible and he couldn't stand the idea of feeling that way again. He shook himself and willed the odious memory away, forcing himself to concentrate instead on the situation at hand.

Though puzzled, Rendel remained silent while some disturbing sensation seemed to overtake Luke and then pass off again. In a few moments, it was as if nothing had happened. Luke now seemed to be considering, calmly, until at last he said, "OK," and offered his hand (the left one, of course).

It was an odd gesture for Luke to make. Handshaking was hardly in vogue among the fourteen-year-olds of his world, but he figured Rendel would probably know what he meant by it. Rendel seemed to. He smiled, took the hand, shook it, and repeated, "OK." Then he rose, and Luke followed suit.

"So, I don't suppose we need to mention this whole unfortunate berries-creyfilla-stingers-in-our-hands incident to any of the others, do we?" Luke inquired in a breezy way.

"At present, I can think of no reason to do so," Rendel answered. "But perhaps, with time," he added after a pause, smiling, "one will occur to me."

"Yeah! Very funny!"

When they rejoined the others, Beth commented on how long they'd taken and asked if anything had happened. "Nothing special," Luke muttered. But Rendel, passing close by him, whispered, "Once again, you and I disagree."

279

Daasa's first inkling that something was amiss came when she heard the sound of riders from behind. Voss, who was bringing up the rear, should have alerted her.

"Make ready," she commanded her unit, turning her horse to face squarely the approaching pair. "Daggers drawn." (By that expression, she referred to weapons in general, not daggers in particular. She herself put an arrow to the string, while the other three drew their swords.)

"I recognize the one that is nearer," Voss said shortly, relaxing his stance as he watched the oncoming riders. "We are of the same company and I know that he has the confidence of Therin Mandek. Perhaps he brings us word."

As the distance between the two parties shortened, however, Pyrr Tullius (Ferinian by birth but Gwilldonian by inclination) drew his horse nearer to Daasa's and, his back to the others, said, "*I* recognize the second rider, and he merits neither the captain's confidence nor our own. Something is amiss."

Everything happened quickly then.

Crinna Tanner, who had joined the company only after Mar's sudden "illness," struck at Pyrr. By a soldier's instinct, Pyrr perceived the movement soon enough to turn and attempt to block it, but not soon enough for much success. The sword missed his heart but came near enough to inflict a mortal wound. Pyrr fell toward the ground. By the time he reached it, Daasa's arrow had already pierced his attacker square in the chest from a close range. Crinna summoned enough strength to thrust his sword at Daasa, but she dodged it. Dizzy from his wound, Crinna slid from his saddle and fell into the dirt near Pyrr, whose agitated and riderless horse finished with his hooves the job Daasa had begun with her arrow.

Daasa was skilled and swift, but she was outnumbered, for the new riders arrived nearly instantaneously and joined Voss in attacking her. In general, three against one would not seem daunting odds to Daasa (and besides, even if they overcame her, by such things was glory won!). Still, even in the face of sudden danger, she was keenly aware that a vital mission now rested on her shoulders alone. The completion of that mission, and not her own glory and satisfaction, must be her goal.

She had a fast horse. Though it countered her nature, she considered the possibility of outrunning them and returning to

Greyvic. Surely they would pursue her. Or perhaps she could lead them to where Therin's second company of guards patrolled the road to Arystar. . . . Unless that guard had been overtaken as well. Quickly these thoughts ran through her mind while she began to fend off her attackers. Then, when she saw her chance, she urged horse away. None of the enemy carried arrows, she had noticed, only swords. In an instant, she was out of arm's reach.

To her peril, she did not know that Voss possessed exceptional skill in knife-throwing. He could hit even a moving target when it was as close as Daasa still was. In a flash, the weapon flew from his hand. It gave him great pleasure to throw the knife. He didn't like fauns, and this one was no better than the rest! Running at the first opportunity to save her own skin!

The blow hit Daasa square in the back and pierced her, for she wore no armor. Swaying, she tried to continue on, but her enemy approached fast, forcing her horse close to the edge of a rocky ravine. When the horse stumbled at the same moment that a sword swung toward her, Daasa fell – and she fell far. She tumbled right over the edge and down into the ravine.

Voss dismounted and approached the spot from which she'd dropped, so that he could survey from above the damage he'd done. His companions, meanwhile, tried to secure Daasa's horse, but it had recovered its footing uninjured and was too swift for them and disappeared into the woods. "Well, it's not headed back to Greyvic, at least," said one of the men. "Probably headed home, to the Westmarch. . . . Let it go!" he added, as if they had any choice in the matter.

Voss did not bother to climb down for a closer look at the faun's body. He could see her still form and extended limbs and guessed that her tumbling had pushed the knife even further into her. It had been a well-placed throw with great strength behind it and he was quite proud of his effort. "Straight through to her heart!" he pronounced loudly. "Dead just like the other one." He jerked his head in the direction of Pyrr Tullius, then remounted.

But Pyrr Tullius was not dead, though he soon would be. Unnoticed until it was too late, he gathered the last of his energy to perform a final service for his adoptive country. He could not lift a weapon, but he could lift his unwounded arm and stretch it toward the reed cage that had fallen close by him, for it was he who had been responsible for Gweynleyn's angeli. He *would* release the bird

– either to spare its life or to keep it from aiding these traitors by bearing a false message on their behalf.

He extended his fingers as far as he could, trying to reach the latch of the cage. He nearly had it. There! He'd managed it. The bird was free and took flight at once, knowing instinctively that it must. Perhaps it would return to her ladyship, thought Pyrr, and she would know thereby that mischief had been done. Before he could consider that the bird might instead continue in the opposite direction and point the traitors toward the champion, his eyes closed and he thought no more.

"So," Luke said, looking at the wide plain stretching ahead of them. "We're going straight that way, right?"

"We are," answered Rendel, riding alongside him at an easy pace.

"And I don't really see any trouble anywhere out there just waiting for us or anything, and there's really no place close by to hide."

"Truth," Rendel agreed simply, though curious about his friend's intentions.

"And this is a pretty decent horse I'm riding here."

"It is an excellent animal," Rendel confirmed. "We were fortunate to secure it."

"Well, then." And with that, Luke shot away, galloping, his voice trailing behind in a loud and long, "Wa-a-a-h-o-o-o-o!"

Rendel laughed at the sight, shaking his head, then took off his hat and handed it back to Aynyxia, who rode with him. "Hold on, my friend," he told her. Turning to Beth, he said in a calm but amused voice, "Wahoo." He too began to gallop, Aynyxia grabbing him tightly at once.

"What's gotten into them?" Harac, riding up from behind, demanded of Beth. Aron, just beyond them, looked delighted.

Soon afterwards, they stopped by a stream to give themselves and their horses a well-deserved break. The travelers had been making excellent time and wanted to continue doing so, but most of them were hungry and all were glad for a stretch.

Almost at once, after they had dismounted, Aynyxia pointed and exclaimed, "Look!" A small, lone bird stood out against the blue of the clear sky ahead. It seemed to spot them just

282

about the time they spotted it, and it turned its course slightly to make directly for them with speed and apparent intention.

"It is an angeli," said Rendel as it approached.

"Sent to us by her ladyship, no doubt," added Harac with some excitement.

"So, what exactly—" Luke began, but before he could finish, the bird was already on them. Or on Harac, to be exact – fluttering about his head and shoulders and the coarse hairs of his full russet beard. It tried to light on him but he would not keep still for it, though the bird did not abandon its efforts and merely renewed them as often and as diligently as necessary.

"She seems to fancy your hair for a nest, friend!" Rendel told Harac with a laugh. "Stand still a bit and I credit she will settle into it nicely."

"Get it off me and stop your laughing, you blasted woodman!" Harac answered. His eyes were swiveling this way and that, trying to follow the course of the bird, still fluttering about, and he was making odd movements with his arms and hands because he wanted to swat it away but dared not; he did not doubt that it was one of Gweynleyn's message carriers. All in all, he presented a rather comical sight. Aron and Beth exchanged distinctly amused looks, and Luke laughed right out loud before trying to cover the fact with an extraordinary coughing fit. Aynyxia, who seemed to be curious about every new thing she saw, merely watched the scene with interest.

"All right," said Rendel calmly at last. "Come here, little one, come here. Peace. You have found friends." With gentle words and cooing, he coaxed the angeli toward himself and it ended by perching on his left forearm. "How distressed you are!" he told it as it fidgeted. "What trouble have you seen?" When the bird was calm enough for him to do so, he lifted it close to his face for examination, lightly stroking its feathers all the while. "I credit I have seen this one before," he said after a moment.

"Looks like the one I had with me," Aynyxia observed.

"Then we shall suppose it is you she was seeking," Rendel answered. "The message she carries seems a thick one." Already, he was attempting to detach a small packet from the bird, but the task was too difficult to do with a single hand, the bird still fretting as it was. "Will you take her?" he asked Beth, passing the bird over before Beth could answer.

"Oh. Well, sure, if she'll come to me."

Once the bird was settled on Beth's arm, it was an easy thing for Rendel to remove the packet, which turned out to be a thin piece of vellum, folded several times over.

"Shall I read it?" Rendel asked. Harac, who might have felt that this was his place, could read reasonably well but did so aloud only with some embarrassment. Aynyxia had trouble distinguishing certain letters from others and could only recognize a handful of written words. For his part, the nearer they drew to Greyvic, the more Aron began to feel that the time for all responsibilities to fall on his shoulders was coming soon enough. He was content to let the others of the party take the lead for a while longer.

"Yes, do," the prince answered.

Everyone gathered around while Rendel unfolded the vellum, but when he had done so, they saw that it was blank.

Harac spoke first. "What can this mean?"

"Don't suppose it's one of those lemon-juice-invisible-ink things?" Luke suggested.

"I do not comprehend you," Rendel answered frankly, and Harac's expression made it clear that he didn't either.

"OK, then I'm going to guess it isn't that," Luke concluded easily.

It was at that moment that a strange feeling crept over Beth. Though neither she nor her friends moved, she felt a distance grow between them. She couldn't at first name the sensation that overtook her, but she began to recognize it. She'd felt something like it at home, before she'd seen the water in the well. It was the feeling that someone was trying to reach her. At home, she'd experienced a beckoning sensation. This time was different. This time felt more like . . . a *warning*. But she couldn't make the warning out – there were too many noises in her head. The voices of her friends continued around her, but she closed her eyes and did her best to block them out, missing most of what was said next.

"So, what's the point of folding up paper into a tiny little packet to send to someone if you're not even going to put a message on it?" Luke asked, moving subtly away from the lemon juice issue and not even stopping to think whether the answer to his question was obvious.

"So we'll have something to write on to send a message back," answered the practical Harac at once.

"And we'll know how to fold it right for the bird to carry it," Aynyxia volunteered.

"Is that how it was when you carried the angeli for her ladyship?" Rendel asked. "Was the vellum already folded and attached, waiting for you to add your message and reattach it?"

"Yes."

"Lady Gweynleyn must have sent the bird to us from Greyvic," Harac said, "so we could get a message back to let her know how things fare for us."

"It may be so," Rendel responded thoughtfully, "but the lady promised a company of soldiers along the Queen's Road. It would seem more reasonable to send the angeli with them so that the bird would not have so long a flight and so great an area to search in a short time." Something seemed to be worrying him.

"What?" Aynyxia inquired simply.

"The creature," Rendel answered, stroking its feathers, "does not seem weary so much as agitated. I credit it has seen trouble and not long ago."

"Perhaps there was an accident on the road," Aron suggested, but he saw at once from the others' expressions that they were considering something more sinister.

"Well," Luke tried, though he also understood what was in everyone else's minds, "it *could* have been an accident. And our little birdie friend somehow got loose and took advantage of the fact to take off for a little birdie holiday."

"Her ladyship's angeli are extraordinarily well trained," was Rendel's only response.

"I don't think we can trust them," Beth said a little too loudly, suddenly rejoining the conversation.

"The angeli?" Rendel answered in surprise.

"The guards. The soldiers. The ones being sent for us. . . . I don't think we can trust them."

CHAPTER TWENTY-ONE – Making Plans

"OK, so we need a plan that we can live with whether the guards turn out to be the good guys or the bad guys," Luke summed up a little later as the six travelers sat together in a circle.

Beth had been adamant that any company of guards they encountered could not be trusted. She couldn't explain why she was so certain, but she *was* certain. At least . . . she was certain at first, but after she'd felt compelled to say several times, "It's just a feeling – I can't explain it," she wavered a bit. No voice had come to her, as it had in the Dark Rim. There was no specific warning. Just a feeling. But such a *strong* feeling. (Remembering that a Silent One had put his hand on Beth's face, connecting himself to her in some mysterious way, Rendel wondered if she had received the warning from him – but he did not ask.)

Beth felt it wasn't quite fair to ask the others to depend on a strange sensation they hadn't experienced themselves, but they seemed convince at once. The party as a whole had grown uneasy since the arrival of the angeli and had begun to share a suspicion that something had gone amiss. It seemed prudent to them all to treat any company of soldiers they encountered with caution and reserve; at the same time, it could be costly to avoid such a company and forfeit whatever genuine assistance it might offer. Luke seemed to have taken it upon himself to devise an appropriate plan.

"Wait." He put his hands out in front of him, and closed his eyes. "It's coming to me." The others waited politely until he opened his eyes again. "OK. How's this for a plan? If we run into anybody who seems like maybe they're legit (carrying the right colors and the seal and whatever), but we're just not quite sure, we'll split up. Well, we'll have to split up ahead of time, of course, so they don't *know* we're splitting up; that would defeat the purpose, if you catch my drift. So – let's say that our woodlander buddy stays back with 'Bob' here," he indicated Aron, "to keep him

286

out of trouble, while Harac, Beth and I go ahead with the soldiers or whatever. And Nyxie (you don't mind me calling you that, do you?), you'd better be on our team too, since everyone already seems to know we're traveling with a plant friend. (Your side really needs a little spy refresher course!) Or maybe that's too many," he countered himself. "Somebody else should stay behind. We'll work that out. . . . But here's the really important part. Beth has got to tell them that the kid wasn't at Lupriark—"

"Kid?" Harac interrupted. "Of what kid do you speak?"

He and Luke regarded each other uncomprehendingly. At least, Beth *thought* Luke was uncomprehending . . . but then, he did like to play dumb sometimes!

"*Child*," she explained. "Luke means 'the child.' Not a *goat* kid or anything, if that's what you were thinking."

"Ah!"

"Yeah, OK. Whatever." Luke continued. "So, Beth tells them the *boy* wasn't at Lupriark. Oh, yeah, we're going to have to say right off that we know the k- . . . *child* was a boy so we don't slip up about that later. Anyway, we say he wasn't there but that the wolves knew all about him and had the key to identify him. And as it happens, he's already at this Greyvic place, at the festival . . . only he doesn't even know who he is. That part's really crucial because if it turns out they're the bad guys, they won't want to do us in – well, let's *hope*! – because they need us to get to Greyvic and point out the prince so that they can . . . well, do whatever." He didn't want to be specific about what the "bad guys" might want to do if they got ahold of the prince. "But we'll just—"

"Must we tell them about Lupriark?" Aron interrupted anxiously.

Luke asked for no explanation of his concern, quickly adjusting the plan and speaking in an excited rush. "Right. No Lupriark. In fact, the less info we dish out to these guys (whoever they are), the better." He saw puzzlement on Harac's face and decided to give him a break. "Sorry," he said, slowing down. "I mean, the fewer details we impart to our suspect audience, the more secure our position will be."

"Ah!"

Luke, greatly enjoying himself by this point, said to himself more than to anyone else, "Mysterious is good. We can pull it off." To the others, he added, "Anyway, we go ahead with them, and you" —he turned to Rendel— "follow behind as sneakily as possible. And if you need help, you blow one of those hundred and fifty-seven flute-things you carry around with you – because you do have *one* of them that actually makes a sound that real people hear, right?" Rendel nodded, his mouth twitching its way toward a smile. "And by then, if that happens at all, we'll have a better sense of whether the guard guys are worth taking a chance on, so—"

As was usual when she was surrounded by fast-moving conversation, Aynyxia had been silent for some time. But now she said, "No." The others, surprised, turned to her. Though plants don't blush, Beth suspected that Aynyxia was embarrassed; still, she went on in a quiet but matter-of-fact way. "Beth belongs with the prince," she said simply, "because of the prophecy."

They considered this without speaking until Rendel said, "This is well-spoken, my friend. This is wisdom."

"OK," said Luke slowly, trying to adjust the plan as he spoke, "so, if we need to split up and we need to keep Bob away from the search team, but we also need to keep Beth with him, even though she's the champion everyone wants to find, then . . ."

"Then you must take Beth's place," Rendel finished, addressing Luke.

Luke was silent while his expression changed a number of times. "We-e-ell," he began at last, "here's the thing." He spoke slowly, as if his listeners were not the brightest pupils he'd ever had. "Beth and I" —his index finger pointed alternately to himself and to his friend— "don't really look all that much alike. For one thing – and I'm just using this as the first example that comes to mind – I'm not *a girl!* And I like to think," he added, "that it wouldn't be all that easy for me to pass as one."

"I was imprecise," Rendel answered in a serious tone, any amusement concealed. "You must claim the place of the *champion.* It may not be known that the champion is a girl."

It was true. Even Imre had taken him for the champion. Still, Luke answered, "May not? *May* not? And so, I'm supposed to bet my life on that, I suppose!"

Harac could not keep from speaking up, his tone incredulous. "Would you not forfeit your life for the sake of the future king?"

"Excuse me," Luke answered, "but he's not *my* king (no offense to you, Bob). I'm a democrat. I mean I really like a good 'king' sort of a story and all, but in real life—"

"*Luke!*" Beth interrupted.

"My friend," Rendel attempted, "you have not considered the matter fully. If these soldiers are with us, you have nothing to fear. If they are against us, it is not only the life of His Highness you may save, but Beth's."

"Maybe we need a different plan," Beth suggested quietly. "Maybe we shouldn't split up." *Maybe Luke shouldn't have to risk his life for me.*

Luke understood. "Beth, Beth, Beth," he repeated in a mock scold. "You should know me better than that. I was kidding! Think I'd pass up the chance to be a champion and everything? But, geez, Beth, how many times have I got to save you? I'm going to have to say this is the last time. For at *least* a month."

Harac leaned back, a look of bewilderment on his face. "By the stars, lad, you're a strange one! You speak such taradiddle, but I credit . . . I credit that your heart is right."

"Truth, for sure," Luke answered easily. "Good heart and good at tar-a-a . . . diddl-ing." *Especially when I'm nervous.* "But let's get back to business, because here's the thing: if I'm going to be champion, everyone addresses me as 'O Great One from Beyond' . . . and I'm not backing down on this."

Something about this plan didn't seem right to Beth, though, and she tried to pin it down. "But—" she began hesitantly.

Luke interrupted immediately. "No, I mean it. I'm not backing down."

"Listen!" She spoke with more insistence. "What if they *do* know that the champion is a girl? Gweynleyn knows. She might have told someone. If *I* go with them, they'd probably leave me alone until we get to Greyvic and I can tell them who the prince is. But if it's Luke, they might just . . . kill him, or something."

The thought had occurred to Luke as well; it had also occurred to him – though apparently not to Beth – that even though he himself had said the soldiers would keep the champion alive until the prince could be identified at Greyvic, they might just as easily kill the champion and take a chance that the prince never would be identified – at least not until it was too late. And, of course, killing the champion and leaving him-her alone weren't the

289

only two options: the bad guys might decide to *torture* the champion for information. He didn't think that would happen, not when there'd be a team of them sticking together and a back-up team not so far away, but there was no way he was letting Beth go ahead with the first group without him. "Nope! It's no good, Beth," Luke answered, seemingly unconcerned by the point she was making. "I see what you're up to. . . . You like the sound of it, don't you? 'Great One from Beyond!' Trying to sneak back into the limelight, huh? Sorry, but the job's been filled." He looked her directly in the eye and his resolution was unmistakable.

Softly, she said, "*Luke*," and that single word spoke so much that he flushed and looked away.

"You are right, Beth," Rendel agreed gravely. "There is risk for Luke. But I credit that Aynyxiacichorium is right as well – you belong beside the prince until he is where he belongs and his safety can be vouched for by others. *And* . . . I credit that Luke understands the risk as well as any of us. We must not be so distracted by his amusing ways that we doubt the strength of character that they obscure."

Both Luke and Beth were spared the need to respond, for Harac then voiced his own, encouraging opinion. "I judge that we have little to fear on this point of whether the champion is a lass or a lad. Her ladyship will reveal no more than needs be. She has become quite reticent, even with respect to the council members themselves."

"And her attendants can be trusted, I suppose?" Rendel inquired.

"I credit they can. . . . But it may not signify. Consider. These two," he indicated Luke and Beth, "arrived at the Green together and then at the Stronghold together. The attendants may not themselves know which came as champion, having withdrawn from our presence whenever they were not needed. Mariza, no doubt, is aware, but she is no friend of the Torks – I am sure of it – and she guards her lady's secrets as she would guard her own life. That leaves only Imre who knows, and it is true that she is young and may let the wrong word slip, but she will not yet have left Little Down's Keep. And certainly anyone who has spied us from afar would not be able to discern who the champion is."

"Right. But actually," Luke amended, a little sheepishly, "back to that thing about Imre. As it turns out – luckily for us, I might add — Imre herself may be a little confused on the whole champion question. I'm not sure how it could've happened, but she may have somehow gotten the idea that — well, you know — *I'm* the real one." Beth did him the favor of turning away to conceal her expression. "*And,*" he added, inspired, "I thought it was better protection for Beth if I didn't correct her and if we just didn't get too specific about that whole point. . . . So, anyway," he quickly moved the conversation along, "it looks like I'll be on the go-ahead-with-the-guards team, and Beth and Bob follow discreetly behind. Nyxie's with me, I guess, for reasons already stated." That left Rendel and Harac.

"Your Highness," Harac began, addressing Aron. Luke, who was sitting next to the dwarf, leaned in his direction and whispered from the side of his mouth, "Call him 'Bob'," but Harac merely continued. "I wish nothing more than to offer you my protection, but if the guards are in fact traitorous—"

"You must go with Luke and Aynyxia," Aron said. "It is my wish. For myself, I am well-satisfied with the companions allotted to me." He looked at Beth and then at Rendel, giving a small nod to each.

"So, that's settled. My team goes with the guards, if we ever find any, and Beth's team secretly follows behind until we've got a better handle on the situation. Good enough? Think we could talk about dinner now?" Luke looked around expectantly.

"But," Beth began ("*Again?*" Luke groaned), "even if they don't know who the champion is, they might know something about us. If anyone did spy on us or knows about us leaving Arystar, they'd at least know how many of us there are supposed to be."

"Easy enough," Luke answered. "You, Beth, got lost in the Dark Rim and will probably be wandering around there aimlessly until you're old and gray."

"Not funny!"

"No," said Luke, remembering how it had been for them, "I guess not. OK, then. You fell down a huge waterfall and got carried away, washed out to sea, never to be heard from again . . . *but,*" he amended quickly so that Beth could be satisfied and they could move on to other things (*edible* things), "it was a really gentle waterfall and it didn't hurt a bit and maybe later you landed on some really cool island or something and had a great time there!"

"And I?" Rendel asked. "Was *I* washed out to the cold island along with Beth?"

"That's *cool* island (we're going to have to work on that)," Luke corrected, "but no, not a chance. You got completely devoured by the wolves before we remembered to tell them we were the good guys. Nothing but your cute little woodland hat left behind. Sorry about that! Nearly broke our hearts to stand back and watch it happen!"

"I am certain of it." He spoke dryly and glared at Luke with narrow eyes. Beth, worried that Rendel was finally about to respond to Luke's provoking ways, wanted to say something, but before she could think of what it should be, the other two broke into wide grins, regarding each other knowingly.

They're friends, Beth realized as she watched, and she wondered again what had happened during their berry-picking expedition.

And so the plan was made, though it was modified slightly over mealtime. "Rendel needs to go with Nyxie and me," Luke said without entirely emptying his mouth first. "Harac can stay with the prince."

"I would wish it," Harac answered at once, "but if soldiers are sent out to seek us, they will likely be in units of four at least, and they will certainly be well-armed. Your need may be great. Do not concern yourself with my honor, for His Highness knows that I will still be working to protect him by clearing the way ahead, where the danger is greatest."

Before Luke could finish swallowing and say that Harac's honor wasn't the point he had in mind, Aron spoke up. "Indeed, I do know it. You must not make this change on my account. I am truly content with the two companions allotted to me, for I am aware that woodlanders have their own gifts of protection, though I do not claim to understand them. And I will have Beth," he added simply, with more confidence than Beth thought warranted.

"Yeah, but I still pick Rendel. He's on my team." To Harac, he said, "You're with the prince."

"Think of your *own* need," Harac told Luke, leaning toward him and believing his voice to be sufficiently quiet, for he did not wish to offend Rendel. "You may be glad enough for a *fighting* man to be at your side should there be treachery of any sort."

"No, he's the one." Luke indicated Rendel with a nod. "The Great One has spoken." Then with gusto he attacked the remainder of his dinner.

Luke's tone had been light, but Rendel's was not as he responded softly. "I am honored by my friend."

Luke looked back at him in a thoughtful and quietly pleased way, then answered through a mouthful of half-chewed bread, "Yeah, whatever."

A little later, when no one else could overhear, Beth said, "Luke, are you sure about this? That we should split up?"

"Yeah, pretty sure. Half of us with the prince, half with the guard . . . if there is one. You don't think so?"

"That's not what I meant. I meant the *two* of us, you and me. Are you sure we shouldn't stick together in case . . . I don't know, I mean it just seems like . . . "

She didn't know quite how to say it, but she'd come close enough and Luke answered, "Yeah, I get it." Something could happen to one of them. Something serious. And the other one wouldn't be there to know. And that would make it worse somehow.

Luke exhaled, leaving his lips half-puckered as he stared away from Beth, thoughtful. He wanted to get this right, wanted to think and say the right things. He thought about what it was he and Beth were really doing there. He thought about the people they'd met who were working to put the right person on the throne, about the young Arandella whose last hope was that her child would someday "make all things right" again, about the woodlander ways that wouldn't be safe under the rule of the Torks . . . and mostly he remembered what Gweynleyn had said about great good needing to rise against great evil.

"OK," he said at last, turning to face Beth, "here's the thing. You know I'm not big on making speeches." She must have looked doubtful, because he added, "All right, once in a while, maybe. But . . . well, this is pretty much on the serious side, but it's only you listening, so I don't mind saying it. Here goes . . . " He paused, then began again. "We're in the middle of this really big thing. It's not *our* really big thing; we just stumbled into it. But now that we're here, we've got to . . . We've got to, you know, do the right thing. The really big, really right thing. . . . It's that whole forces-of-evil-winning scenario, if you get what I'm saying." (Beth did get it; they'd first heard the quotation together. "All that is necessary for the forces of evil to win is for enough good men to do nothing." Or in this case, good *kids*.) "So, if we don't do the right thing, we'll be helping the wrong thing, and we'd always . . . you know . . . carry that around with us . . . and everything. So I think we both want to do whatever we have to. We've got to help them, our friends, whatever it takes . . . even if . . . even . . . . Listen, if this does go wrong – if, let's say just for the sake of argument, I end up surrounded by the bad guys and you've got a chance to get the kid where he needs to go – you just do it, OK? Don't look back or anything." Beth was too distressed to speak, so Luke went on quickly. "I'm only saying *if*. What I really think is that the right armed guard is on its way to meet us and we'll all get safely to this Greyvic place and have fun at the festival, just like we're supposed to. After all, this prophecy said you'd be making everything right, and I've got to say – and it's just from my own perspective, but I think I'd have a lot of support in this – things wouldn't really be so 'right' if I ended up dead. Not in this world, not in our world. . . . So, if you have to go on without me, for whatever reason, you just do it, OK? Don't look back. Don't worry about me. . . . I'm a pretty wily guy, you know. And besides, I'll have Plant-Girl and Nature-Boy with me, so what could really go wrong?" As he said the last words, he smiled a goofy sort of smile and bounced his head around, so that Beth smiled despite herself.

Their break had lasted long enough – too long, thought Harac – and it was time to ride again. There was some discussion about what to do with the angeli. It had seemed quite content to stay near them throughout their meal and discussion, and Beth was becoming fond of it. There was talk of keeping it with them as they rode, if it would come along, so that they could use it in any later emergency. But in the end the consensus seemed to be that it should return to Lady Gweynleyn, with or without a message.

"Have we even got anything for writing a message with?" Luke asked. "Because, once again, I seem to have left my ink and quill in my other pants. . . . with my tinder box . . . and all that other useful stuff you people seem to bring everywhere."

"We can use the berries we carry with us for a serviceable ink," Rendel said. "If we wish it to be so, I can write the message."

"Of course, you can," Luke answered cheerfully, "because you just know a little bit about everybody and everything." Under his breath, he added, "Especially berries." Though Rendel feigned exasperation at these words, it was clear to all that some joke lay hidden between the two young men.

"What message could we write, though," asked Harac, dismissing the oddities of youth, "that will do us any good if her ladyship receives it, but no harm if an enemy intercepts it?"

It was Beth who answered. "Write 'Nothing to report'." And so it was done.

Harac and Rendel, who knew the region well enough, agreed between them that it was time for the party to move farther from the cliffs. Greyvic was within a day's ride or so, Harac judged, and it was time to follow more closely the Queen's Road, where any legitimate guard might look for them. The disadvantage of following the road was that the woods that lay just south of it could hide bandits or an enemy lying in wait, but its advantage was that the same woods offered their own party the means for quick concealment. The cliff area was too exposed, but in the woods, the half of the party that was to keep out of sight could covertly travel parallel to the road. They would not be able to move as quickly as those actually on the road, but Luke took it upon himself to guarantee that his own group would not move ahead too fast, with or without accompanying soldiers.

They were getting ready to mount up when Luke spoke privately to Beth. "Looks like we're coming into the home stretch. So-o-o, this might be our last chance. Want to ask them to leave us behind in some safe little corner? . . . Or are you game?"

"I'm game," Beth answered, smiling and confident and ready to tackle whatever was ahead. Probably.

Holding an invisible microphone to his mouth, he said, "Then we're good to go, Houston." Luke turned away then, but not before winking impulsively in Beth's direction.

"I really lucked out," she thought, mounting her horse, "ending up with him as a friend. . . . All of them," she added, looking around at her companions.

They rode off.

CHAPTER TWENTY-TWO – Separate Ways

"So," Beth asked Luke as they rode along together, "are you ever going to tell me what happened when you and Rendel went to pick berries this morning?"

"*Man!* Was that only this morning? Time doesn't exactly fly here, does it? Every day lasts about a week and a half!"

"And that means you're *not* going to tell me, right?"

Luke shrugged. "Well, it's pretty simple, really. First, I was – oh, I don't know – let's just say, an idiot; and then after that . . . I wasn't."

"Oh . . . Well, thanks, because *it's all very clear to me now*," she called to his back as it pulled ahead of her.

During the next hour, Beth's friends moved more solidly to her way of thinking and shared her misgivings more fully. They should be very wary, they agreed, of anyone who approached them, even soldiers carrying Lady Gweynleyn's colors or seal as a sign. *More* than wary . . . and for some reason, they felt this increasingly as the sky began to darken.

"Why don't we just avoid everyone?" suggested Luke at one point. "Even if someone really is trying to help us out, do we even need them? We've done all right on our own so far."

"The dangers will be greater the nearer we come to Greyvic. We know not what awaits us and may find ourselves dependent upon the assistance of others," answered Rendel. "But, Luke . . . in our present plan, the risk is greatest for you; we are not obliged to continue with that plan. You need only say—"

"No, I'm OK." As he had done with Beth, he urged his horse forward in order to avoid further conversation.

Soon after that, it happened. Rendel, who had gone ahead as scout before the full party entered an open stretch, almost immediately spotted soldiers in the distance. He came galloping

296

back, reporting that the approaching company would be in view shortly, but that he believed himself not to have been observed.

As planned, Beth, Harac, and Aron turned their horses immediately and headed toward the cover of the woods, but a moment of panic overtook Beth and she pulled up on the reins and turned her head back. "*Luke?*" They faced each other, and only the slightest pause passed before he answered.

"No, I'm all right. Really. Go on. Go!"

She turned toward Aron, who was already waiting for her among the trees, but as an afterthought she called back shakily, "Good luck!" Luke gave her a "thumbs up" and smiled as brightly as he could manage for as long as she was looking.

More practically, Harac, following Beth and Aron, called back, "Daggers drawn. Nothing suspicious about that. They'd expect you to be on guard." A couple of minutes later, he had dismounted, passed his reins to Aron, and hidden himself nearby, his own weapon at the ready. Beth and Aron, also on foot by then, led the horses farther into the woods. They carried an herb that Rendel had given them to keep the animals calm and quiet at the crucial period. Beth and Aron had been instructed to wait with them there, a safe distance away, but Beth privately hoped to convince her companion to creep back with her toward Harac once the horses were secured and contentedly feeding.

It had been Harac's idea that Luke, Rendel, and Aynyxia not ride out to meet the company but instead dismount and wait to the side of the road at the wood's edge, pretending that they were taking a break for a meal or a stretch. That way, if all went well, the dwarf could be close at hand to see and hear the encounter and make his own judgment about the newcomers. He hoped to recognize one or more of them, for surely Therin would send one of his most trusted officers with the company.

The scene was quickly set; excessive, telltale hoofprints were obliterated, and everyone was in position with little time to spare. Three soldiers – accompanied by a riderless horse — arrived almost at once. By the time Beth had secured the horses and rejoined Harac, the soldiers were already dismounting and introducing themselves. "We come bearing greetings from the lady Gweynleyn," one was saying, "and offer as testimony her colors and the mark of her seal."

It had irritated Harac to see Beth creeping toward him and to observe that the prince was not far behind. He didn't want to risk the noise of sending them back, though, and wasn't sure they'd go in any event. So the three of them hid quietly and listened in as Luke and Rendel told the prepared tale.

The Anointed was at Greyvic, they said; there was no doubt of it. Arandella had had a son and his safety had been assured. Luke, the champion foretold, held the key that would unlock the secret of the child's identity. Neither Rendel nor Aynyxia, Luke made clear, shared in that secret. Even he himself could not fully understand it until he had a chance to see Greyvic in person.

"So, if no one has a better plan," he concluded several minutes later, speaking a trifle loudly and then pausing a bit too long, "I suppose we should continue on toward that fine city now. We should just start moving along right now. If no one has a better plan."

"Yes, O Great One," Aynyxia agreed in a manner that was particularly buoyant, especially for her.

"Well," Rendel added with more equanimity, "our champion has spoken, it seems. Ought we not then turn at once toward Greyvic? I see that you have a horse to spare. This is great fortune indeed, for the three of us have only these two animals between us. For our part, we are ready and more to travel while there remains sufficient light, unless your own party is in need of rest and wishes already to settle for the night."

One soldier answered immediately, as Rendel had hoped, that they had no need of rest and could turn back at once toward the west. Another, however, still seemed to be assessing the party before him. His voice sounded wary, if not outright suspicious, when he asked, "But was there not another of your party?"

There'd been two others, of course – three, if you counted Imre. Were they poorly informed (a good thing) or was this a trick (not so good)? Fortunately, Luke was ready with his response. Judging it wiser to depend on as little fabrication as necessary, he held his hand out as if to signal the conversation to stop, lowering his head and saying sorrowfully, "We must not speak of this. There remain only we three." Rendel followed his lead, inclining his head respectfully, and Aynyxia awkwardly jerked her head down too, then peeked up again.

The soldiers regarded one another questioningly, but did not pursue the matter. *This champion has strange ways about him! But, truth . . . all the tales of champions of old have their oddments to them*, thought Voss, the most suspicious among them. It was he who led the company of guards now that Crinna Tanner was no longer among them. His orders were to dispose of the champion and the Anointed, if they existed, as soon as it could be done – but most especially it was the Anointed whom Myrmidon wished to be rid of. Yet here was the champion, but no Anointed. . . .

Voss knew he could take the boy easily! A walkabout and a woodlander for protection? The idea was almost offensive in its absurdity. But that would leave the Anointed alive in Greyvic. Voss considered himself more likely to earn the Tork's wrath than his praise if he destroyed the only clue they had to the child's identity.

"Toward Greyvic, then," he announced. "Before the light is gone."

Hidden away, Beth unwittingly sighed her relief so loudly that Harac shot her a sharp look.

Voss knew all about knives – the types and materials, the best crafters, the right force to put into a throw for the various weights – but he knew less than he thought about fauns and their anatomy. When he'd said, "Straight to the heart," his ignorance had guided him, for Daasa's skin was thicker than a human's with a protective layer of cartilage that was thicker still, not to mention the fact that her heart was positioned at an inhuman angle. The faun's wound, while serious and painful, would not prove fatal. Her tumble into the ravine had indeed compounded it by jostling the blade, but the more serious effect of the fall was to threaten her with concussion from her first hard blow against the rocks. She lay senseless, face down, for some time after the others had left.

When she first regained consciousness, it was for a brief spell only, and then she slipped away again. When she came to a second time, she forced herself into a sitting position and the movement reminded her that a weapon still protruded from her back. She did not attempt to remove it, for she guessed that the bleeding had stopped and she did not want it to recommence.

She whistled for her horse but felt no surprise when it did not appear. It was yet insufficiently experienced in battle and had

299

been badly frightened by the attackers. She hoped only that the fine animal had escaped them.

The attackers. Voss. Crinna. She should have been wiser, she chastised herself. The fault was her own. She had failed utterly in her mission. How would she face Therin Mandek again? But perhaps she would never have that opportunity. There was such a spinning in her head!

She shook herself, figuratively and physically. What was she thinking? She would not yield. Her legs . . . *they* were not wounded – not much, at least – and they were her great strength, and her arms were merely bruised. Bruises were nothing to her! If only she could think and see clearly enough to make out her direction. She would *run* all the way to Greyvic. She was a faun. She needed no horse to carry her. She needed no rest. She could be there by nightfall.

Or . . . could evening be falling already? Was that the darkness she saw, or was the darkness inside her own head?

How long had she been here? She looked for the sun, but it seemed to be moving about. She squeezed her eyes closed. She *would*! She *would* run to Greyvic. She would run and run until she dropped, and even then she would drag herself along the ground. She must start at once. She rose, faltered and fell, then rose again. Making her way to the top of the ridge, she stumbled repeatedly; once there, however, she pulled herself up tall and paid no heed to the searing pain in her back and the gyration within her skull.

She swayed. She collapsed.

"Drink." The voice came to her from far away. "Drink, Daasa. It is my command!" The final words roused her and she drank, her eyes beginning to focus on the face close to her own. Therin Mandek. He knelt by her, holding the flask to her lips.

Daasa's immediate response was not one of relief or gratitude, but of deep shame. "I have failed you, Captain," she told him, closing her eyes briefly.

"What evil has befallen you? I have seen the body of Pyrr Tullius, though an attempt had been made to hide it." He had seen a second body too – one he did not recognize – and the corpse of a horse apparently wounded in battle and then mercifully given over to quick death.

"Voss," Daasa reported weakly, though the drink Therin had given her was already strengthening her body. If only it could do the same for her spirit.

"Voss! I half guessed it when I came upon this scene. I erred in trusting him. But what of Mar? I saw no sign of her, but I would have sworn—"

"She never left Greyvic. She took ill – poisoned by Voss, I am certain now. He presented me with her substitute, a Crinna Tanner, for whom he vouchedsafe. On your orders, he said." Bitterness streaked her words.

"Mar did not come to me! She did not report any substitution!" He spoke angrily, but Daasa knew where the anger should have been directed.

"No doubt Voss promised to attend to that, for the plot seems to have been well-laid."

"She should not have taken his word!" Therin shouted.

"*I* did." Silence followed Daasa's weak pronouncement. Therin rose and paced about while the faun, with more effort, brought herself to a standing position as well.

"It is I who am to blame, Daasa, not you." Therin's voice was strained, but quieter. "I should not have trusted him as I did. . . . But this is not the moment for reproaches. . . . There is always time enough for that in the end," he added from bitter experience. "We must make a plan. I— I regret it, but . . . if I were to return you to Greyvic at once—"

"Indeed not!" Daasa responded, offended. "We must go east, certainly! Not west! I have lost my horse, but I can run alongside you quite swiftly, I am certain."

Therin, though somewhat awed by the assertion, was not quite as confident. "There is no need for that. You may ride behind me, if you insist on coming. But— You do realize, do you not, that a knife protrudes from your back?"

"I do, sir, and I would humbly ask that you assist me in withdrawing it, if we can find something to prevent the blood from flowing too freely. Not that I care on my own account! No doubt I deserve to have all blood drained from me slowly, but I would not be able to serve you well if—"

"Certainly not! Let us bandage you and be off." Working quickly, Therin removed the weapon and covered the wound, amazed that so little blood seemed to have been lost. But he too was ignorant of faun anatomy.

Both he and Daasa regretted leaving behind the body of the loyal Pyrr Tullius, but the matter of returning it to his family would have to wait for a later time. A more urgent matter beckoned. They did move it to another spot, however, laying it out in a more dignified form.

Then they mounted Nightbird, Daasa riding behind her captain, and headed east.

Luke was on edge from the moment he set off with the soldiers. He distrusted them and not only because he was willing to rely on Beth's instinct (or whatever it was that had come over her). There was something cold and calculating in their manner, though he knew that might just be a reflection of their occupation. He recognized, even, that they might regard any teenaged "champion" with a certain amount of scorn. Still . . . his own instinct warned against them, and he guessed that Aynyxia and Rendel felt the same, though it was some time before he could speak to either privately.

The soldiers were wary too – Luke became convinced of that within the first hour. And then a remark of Aynyxia's noticeably disconcerted them. "Thought there'd be four in your company," she said.

"One fell sick" was the response, but it came neither quickly nor smoothly, and the least experienced soldier shifted uncomfortably.

It occurred to Luke then that Aynyxia's remark hadn't been as casual as it had seemed. She wasn't exactly big on chitchat. She must have had a particular purpose in mind. How about that plant girl! Maybe she had one more taco on her plate than he'd given her credit for!

From that point, Luke tried to think if there might be a question he could ask in an offhand way that would test the soldiers somehow, but he didn't come up with one. He did, however, find an opening for making a point he had been phrasing and rephrasing in his head. When Voss assured Luke of his determination to protect the champion because the Tork leader "would have you killed without hesitation," Luke answered, "Nay, he would not. He is far too cunning a devil for such rash action, as

302

I'm sure you'll agree. If I am cut down, another champion will rise up or the boy will be found in some other way. We both know it's the *boy* the Tork hopes to destroy . . . or he may even want to try to turn him to his own dark side. Who can say? But he for sure and certain won't want *me* to come to any harm until I've done my job in Greyvic." He hoped that would settle *that* matter!

Later, when he finally had the chance to do so unheard, he asked Rendel, "What's your take on these guys?" By that point, the party was settling for the night, the emergence of a thick cloud cover having prevented even the light of two moons from illuminating their path. "Friends or foes?"

"There is deception in them," Rendel told him with a meaningful look.

"That's why we brought you along!" Luke responded. "Nobody knows deception like you! . . . So, what now?"

There was no opportunity for Rendel to answer just then, but later Aynyxia engaged two of the soldiers (the third was nowhere in sight) in a conversation long enough to afford her friends the time to form a plan.

At the same time, another party (not so far away, if only they'd known it) also suffered from the effect of the cloud cover but showed more reluctance to yield to it. In the end, however, even Therin Mandek and Daasa of the Great Wood afforded themselves a few hours of sleep, their scouting efforts sufficiently thwarted by the caprices of nature.

Members of the third party in that otherwise desolate stretch of land were quite satisfied to end their day when they did, the two youngest among them being exhausted and sore. The young prince had never spent so many hours on a horse in one day! He wondered if he would ever learn to do so with ease.

Aron judged himself quite fortunate in his new company of friends, but he had found his first full day away from Lupriark to be a straining one. The tasks at hand, he knew, were nothing to what he might face in Greyvic, but even more than that knowledge, it was the loneliness of being away from the pack that affected him.

While he was in this unsettled state, a small incident occurred which upset him further. Alone with Beth (Harac was scouting about a bit before they finalized their choice of campsite), Aron inadvertently disturbed a restive and previously unnoticed blood-eyed snake. It raised its head and hissed, and the boy found himself paralyzed at the sight of it. Beth wasn't sure how to react – stand still, she thought at first – but the snake seemed about to strike the boy, so she grabbed a long stick and managed to fend off the creature, hooking it and flinging it away from them, stick and all. The deed was done quickly and relatively easily, the creature being nowhere near as large as it appeared to both young people at the crucial moment.

In an instant, Harac returned to them, saying that he had found a better spot for passing the night. "Good!" Aron answered with feeling, his voice shakier than he liked, beginning to move in the dwarf's direction.

"And," Harac added, as if about to tell them of a great treat, "I credit we might even allow ourselves a small fire there without giving anything away. It's a cold night and there are many beasts about. A fire will help with both."

A while later, when they were settling in for sleep, Aron said quietly to Beth, "It was a serpent, was it not? We have none in Lupriark." Once said, it seemed an insufficient excuse for his reaction, so he confessed simply, "I was afraid."

"Of course you were. So was I. . . . Snakes can be pretty dangerous!"

"But your fear did not hold you fast." He seemed quite upset, but there was a rigidity in his face as if he were bracing himself. She knew what he must be thinking: a king shouldn't be afraid. Beth tried to think of the right thing to say. She recognized in him the strange mix of a young man trying to steel himself for what lay ahead, whatever that might be, and an ordinary, scared child. She saw determination, but with twitching around the edges.

"No, it didn't," she agreed slowly, "but I don't think that would've been true when I first got here, which was only" – she tried to calculate quickly how long it had been – "well, however many days ago it was. I've changed. . . . You just weren't ready, that's all. But you will be." She remembered then what Marcus Gribb had said to her when he returned the magic sword she'd let fall, the one that had only been a dagger when she'd pulled it out: "The next time you won't let your fear get in the way of your believing," he'd assured her.

After a moment, Aron asked softly, "You will not tell anyone of the incident, will you?" In the flickering firelight, the look of the young man was gone and the prince appeared exactly his age.

"No, of course not," Beth answered.

Aron rolled over and was soon asleep.

Beth lay awake a while longer. She wondered if they were really safe for the night, then reflected that at least they were safer than Luke and the others. She remained convinced that the guard was a false one. She hoped Harac was right about the fire's smoke not being visible from the distance. She supposed he was; it was a very dark night and they were well-sheltered. In fact, Harac's snores would probably be more likely to draw attention!

But Harac did not snore that night because he did not sleep. He kept watch alone until morning.

Long after he had said goodnight to his friends and (presumably) enemies, Luke was still awake, though barely, when he realized that Rendel was awake as well.

"Can't sleep?" Luke whispered softly. The sound caught the attention of the soldier on watch, so Luke made a yawning-groaning-sleeping noise and shifted his position with exaggerated movement.

A few moments later, when the guard was pacing a little farther off, Rendel answered. "I am keeping watch."

"Don't trust that guy to do it, huh?" his friend responded sleepily and without much thought.

"The object of his vigil differs from the object of mine."

Well, of course. It was over *Luke* that Rendel was keeping watch. "You're not so bad, you know?" said Luke before he drifted off.

A few hours later, Rendel woke Aynyxia, who wordlessly took over the task so that he could get some rest.

The next morning, Rendel calmly announced (as he and Luke had covertly agreed the evening before) that he would return to Greenwood now that his assistance as guide was no longer needed. For good measure, he mentioned casually that he would return his horse to Treyllavic and travel by foot from there. The guards, though taken by surprise, made no great effort to stop him.

They did at first attempt to coax him to Greyvic with talk of the grand attractions of the festival, but Rendel merely responded that he was a simple woodlander who found all the attractions he desired in Greenwood. In the end, they let him go.

Voss could have stopped him easily, of course, and was sorely tempted to do so. But he did not want to show his hand so early without good cause, and, try though he might, he could not see much risk in letting a lone woodlander go in a direction opposite to their own. One less to deal with. Not that there was a one among them that gave him cause to worry!

"Goodbye, O Woodlander Friend," Luke had said formally, stretching out his hand as if expecting Rendel to kiss his ring (if he'd had one).

"Fare you well, O Great Champion," the other had responded dryly, squeezing the hand briefly but making no attempt to kiss it.

Rendel headed due east, as if returning to Treyllavic, before veering southward. He did not look back, sure that he was watched for a while at least. Once under cover of trees, he turned sharply toward the west and moved his horse as quickly as he was able. He soon found the party he sought.

Having watched at a distance his departure from the others, his friends were not surprised by his arrival, but they were full of questions as to the reason behind it. Rendel explained that he, Luke, and Aynyxia were all convinced that the company of soldiers did not merit their confidence. He and Luke had agreed that word needed to be gotten to the prince to move ahead with all haste toward Greyvic and that Rendel's departure was the least likely to be questioned. "Even when safely arrived in Greyvic, however," Rendel warned, "His Highness ought not declare himself until Luke's safety is assured. Once the identity of the Anointed has become known, Luke will be of no further use to those whom we must now regard as his captors. We must be covert in our actions and seek out Therin Mandek at once to liberate Luke and Aynyxiacichorium."

Beth and Aron voiced their agreement, but Harac, who had been keeping watch while listening in on the conversation, had another matter in mind. "Why have they not begun to move? We have waited and watched with constancy to see them emerge from their encampment." A sudden urgency marked his words as he asked, "You do not credit that they have departed by another way, unobserved?"

"No," Rendel answered confidently. "They will surely pass by the stretch you have in view, but I credit that our friend Luke is putting his charms and efforts into delaying the departure for our benefit." He smiled as he said this, exchanging a knowing look with Beth, but his expression changed as he noticed what had previously escaped his attention. "Your company has grown since last we were together!" Beth followed his gaze and saw that he was referring to a fourth horse now tethered with the original three.

"Yes," she told him enthusiastically. "He's beautiful, isn't he? He just wandered in less than an hour ago. We wondered if he'd smelled the other horses. . . . I think he's glad to be here with us."

When it arrived unexpectedly, the chestnut horse had seemed skittish but not unduly afraid of the humans. When Harac had cautiously gathered up its reins and secured it alongside the other animals, it had not resisted and seemed even to be calmed by the action.

"No sign of the rider?" Rendel inquired, approaching the steed with an expression of concern.

"None," Harac answered.

"And you do not recognize the animal . . . nor the tack?"

"N-no." Harac sounded unsure, as if concerned he had missed some clue. "The saddle, though odd in its shape, is finely-made and the horse is strong and well-cared for. A soldier's animal, I credit, but I cannot say whose." He looked again at the saddle. It was beginning to seem familiar, but it was not the sort of thing to which he generally paid much attention.

"What's wrong?" Beth asked Rendel, who had a puzzled, disturbed look.

"I know this saddle," he answered, running his hand over the object in question, but he spoke almost as if to himself. "It is Daasa's – Daasa of the council." Then he brought his fingers toward his face and smelled them. Beth noticed that something had discolored his thumb. Blood, she thought. "This does not bode well," Rendel said. Then, as if remembering Beth, he explained. "You have not met Daasa. She is a faun, and fauns do not ride gladly. They find it unnatural. But Daasa is a proud warrior and has learned that warriors on horseback have advantages over warriors on foot, and so she has learned to ride. This horse has the smell of faun all about it, and I credit that the saddle was specially made to accommodate the form of someone not fully human."

"So, what do you think it means?"

"Nothing of good" was all he said.

Suddenly, Harac ordered, *"Daggers drawn!"* His own sword was already out before Beth even registered the words. Aron drew his weapon as well, a shiver running through him, and Beth nervously put an arrow to her bow. Their eyes and their attention turned in the same direction as Harac's. In an instant, she heard the sounds of approach that had alerted Harac.

Strained and alert, gripping her bow fiercely, she waited.

CHAPTER TWENTY-THREE – Greyvic

Luke stalled for as long as he reasonably could. In a cheerful and unquestioning way, Aynyxia backed him up in everything he said, whether she understood its meaning or not; she knew that he was giving Rendel time to get well away and to seek out the others before their own company departed.

On the previous evening, it had been Luke who halted the journey when it was only dusk, knowing it was darker in the woods and travel would be difficult for his friends. He had solemnly announced that it was time for the "rites of preparation" – customs from his own land that he must observe in order for all things to proceed as they ought. Aynyxia had shown a flicker of interested surprise, but Rendel had smoothly treated the matter as one of routine. The soldiers had seemed a trifle annoyed, but had not themselves been far from suggesting that the party settle for the night and rest the horses.

Since the ploy had worked well enough once, Luke decided to try it again the next day. The "morning rites," he informed the others after breakfast, would take him hardly any time at all.

"It is with the Silent Ones that you communicate?" Despite himself, Voss asked the question with a certain amount of awe; he would have preferred to sound only marginally interested.

Unsure what his answer to this ought to be, Luke smiled and bobbed his head repeatedly as if appreciating the perceptiveness of the soldier; meanwhile, he considered the matter. On the one hand, communication with the Silent Ones would be a pretty decent excuse for delaying their departure, he figured; on the other, what if the soldiers were worried about what the Silent Ones might communicate back? That could push them to some drastic measure they'd otherwise avoid. He was out of his depth here, knowing next to nothing about those revered but somewhat spooky beings.

"A-a-a-h," he answered at last. "The Silent Ones. . . . Your thoughts turn to them, I see." Stepping toward Voss, he leaned in to say confidentially, as of a matter above the heads of those around, "Very admirable, but it is better to speak little of such things, do you not agree?"

"Of course," answered Voss, uncertain.

Luke realized that this was the second time he'd used the let's-not-talk-about-these-things approach. He thought it might wear thin by the third time. "At any rate," he went on quickly, "I must begin the morning rites at once, for I am anxious to get to Greyvic and discover the Anointed One. *That* will be pretty exciting! Truth! *And*," he was inspired to add, "I would be mult glad" – rats! he'd forgotten that Rendel said they didn't use that word so much anymore, though Luke liked the sound of it – "if you were there by my side at that time." *That* ought to be the right approach!

"I should be glad of it myself," Voss answered sincerely, "and then I would most willingly carry the news where it ought to be carried."

"And I'd be glad to have you do it!" Luke answered far less sincerely.

For differing reasons, both the younger man and the older one found their conversation to be satisfactory in the end.

"Who goes there?" Harac shouted threateningly into the thickness of trees beyond them. "Speak, or defend yourselves!"

"Do you not recognize my voice?" came the answer. "For surely *yours* cannot be mistaken!"

Into view, leading his horse after him, came a figure that Beth would have found quite intimidating, even frightening, had Harac not immediately lowered his weapon and shown a deep relief. Toward them advanced a great soldier, she was sure, and behind him came . . . a strange creature with short horns and . . . really? A *faun*?

"Therin! By the stars and the moons, I've never been gladder to see your miserable face!" Harac turned at once to introduce the newcomers. "This is Therin Mandek, Captain of the Council Guard, of whom you have heard much, and this is Daasa of the Great Wood of the Westmarch, a member of the Council of Ten."

For his part, Therin looked past Rendel to Beth, whom he recognized from Gweynleyn's description, and then his face changed as his gaze fell on Aron. "Sire?" he breathed. He did not look to Harac for confirmation; he saw Arandella in this boy. Nonetheless, Harac answered "Aye" as Aron inclined his head in acknowledgement.

With three long strides, Therin approached and dropped to one knee, followed in an instant by Daasa. The subsequent ceremony of swearing fealty helped the prince to compose himself, for the long-memorized words came to him far more easily than original ones would have. He too found the captain of the guard rather intimidating.

When the formalities were complete, Therin asked, "But what of the others of your party? Were they overtaken by the traitors? Have you seen battle? Daasa, that is your steed, is it not?" he asked, noticing that horse. When the faun confirmed it, he asked the others, "How came you by it?"

The last question was answered first and in only a few words. The preceding questions took longer to address, and that task fell primarily to Rendel.

"They believe him to be the champion," the woodlander concluded a little while later, "and if they discover otherwise, or if they in due course learn that the Anointed has declared himself (for we do not know their resources and word may reach them before they enter the city itself), then Luke's life will be forfeit. I am certain of it."

"He sounds a brave lad! No doubt he knew the risk when he took it on," answered the professional soldier in a satisfied way.

"He did take the risk, and gladly," Rendel agreed, "but he did not offer himself as a sacrifice. He knows we will not abandon him."

"Of course we won't!" Beth joined in with vehemence, speaking for the first time since Therin and Daasa's arrival.

Therin considered the matter gravely, assessing one by one the company before him, and then he spoke decisively, primarily addressing Aron. "We will divide into two parties. One will accompany you, Sire, to Greyvic; the other will pursue and attend to these traitors. And free the boy and the walkabout," he added (belatedly, in Beth's view). "I will have a private word with Harac and Daasa, by your leave, and soon we will ride." He strode away.

311

Aron hesitated, unsure of what his own part should be. He did not wish to appear weak, indecisive, or cowardly before any of them. He did not wish to *be* weak, indecisive, or cowardly. He turned to Beth. "I ought not run away," he told her quietly and urgently. "I ought seek the release of our companions and join any battle entailed thereby, ought I not?" Once again, Beth was reminded that for all his rehearsed courtly ways he was just a boy, not even a teenager yet. She understood his feelings. She even shared some. Still . . .

"You've got to get to Greyvic," she told him. "It's your duty. It's why we're all here. Therin doesn't need you for this battle. *He* can take care of Luke and Aynyxia. It's all right. . . . Let your captain do his job."

He nodded in understanding and agreement.

Returning to them shortly, Therin told the prince, "I will see you to Greyvic myself, Your Highness, if you allow it." His words were deferential, though hurried, but his tone suggested that there would be no question as to whether His Highness *would* allow it.

This was not what Beth had expected. She'd assumed that Therin would go after the other soldiers and rescue Luke. He was an experienced fighter. It was what he *ought* to do!

Aron's reaction was apparently the same, for he answered, "I thank you, Captain, but your skills are needed elsewhere. You must see to the safety of our companions."

"Your Highness, it is your own safety that is paramount. Harac and Daasa are worthy and are willing to face the other task on their own. Rest assured, they will plan their attack carefully so that all advantage will be on their side with as little risk as necessary for the boy and the walkabout. But my place is at your side . . . just as it was my place to be at your mother's side. I owe this to your esteemed family. I will not neglect my duty nor my obligation to you." He turned and with a quick stride began to move toward the horses.

Aron looked to Beth, who opened her mouth to speak to Therin but then closed it again, turning to Aron instead. His eyes asked what he ought to do.

"You'll be a king soon," she quietly encouraged him. "And he's your captain."

He understood and braced himself as he called out, "Captain!" When Therin turned, the prince spoke quickly and nervously but with determination. "I thank you for your service to myself, to my mother, and to the father of my mother. You have no outstanding debt to us. However, if such a debt existed, I would by all means consider it quit were you to bring to safety my cherished friends who have risked themselves on my behalf. As for my own safety, I will entrust it to the care of these friends," he indicated Rendel and Beth, "who have traveled with me thus far." When Therin, torn as to his response, stood silent, looking keenly into the prince's eyes, Aron added, "These are my wishes. This is my command. See to Luke and Aynyxia with all speed, for I am loathe to declare myself while doing so increases their peril. Bring them to Greyvic so that I may claim what is mine without knowing their blood to be on my head ere my crown first rests upon it." Boy though he was, raised far from court life, Aron had yet inherited a most royal manner, and it was not lost on his captain.

Still, to entrust the future king to a woodlander and a young girl. It was madness no matter how much they had accomplished among themselves already. "The situation in Greyvic is precarious, I fear. It would be mad— It would be unwise to enter the city openly without my protection."

"Then we shall enter it with stealth," Aron answered with an unflawed show of confidence.

Therin looked around at them all. The fact that Harac had not taken up his own position spoke well for the others. Still, . . . His eyes fell on Beth and wondered greatly that *this* should be their champion. Lastly, he regarded the young prince who had challenged him . . . as it certainly was his right to do. He yielded.

"He'll make a fine king, that one," Harac muttered to Rendel, "*if* you can get him to the throne, that is!"

"As to that," answered the woodlander, "I have a plan."

It was settled at once that Edwyn Reston's mare would be taken by the three who were to speed ahead to Greyvic, but there was a brief delay caused by the question of whether a second and possibly third horse should be taken as well. Nightbird was strong enough to bear the weight of the whole party, if need be, for they were each slight of build, but the three could not ride swiftly in that manner, sandwiched together on her back. They could

313

certainly be spared a horse apiece, Therin said, but none of the other animals would match the speed of Nightbird.

"I thought, though, that I recognized your steed," Rendel said to Daasa as he came alongside the animal in question. "Is he not also a horse of the Restons?"

"He is," Daasa confirmed, "but he was not among their prize animals and he will not keep pace with the other, who is Edwyn Reston's own."

"I credit he will," said Rendel thoughtfully. "By what name do you call him?"

"None," answered Daasa, for it was an oddity (some said a paradox) among the fauns not to treat "unminded" animals in such a way.

"Then I shall call him Sylvan Runner," said Rendel, stroking the animal along the jawline and then making whispering sounds into its ear.

The matter was settled. The woodlander's judgment would be trusted. Daasa's saddle was exchanged for another, and Rendel, Beth, and Aron mounted the two horses. They were to be off at once, for no additional time could be afforded to discussion. The enemy had already broken camp and was entering an open stretch where any approach would be seen from afar and would put the lives of Luke and Aynyxia at risk. Therin, Harac, and Daasa would follow behind and choose well their moment to strike.

"Woodlander," said Therin to Rendel at the last moment, "can you learn these names? They are the ones of my company whom most deeply I trust." Rendel nodded and Therin said the names. After Rendel repeated them back, Therin added, "And most of all, put your confidence in Rostik, who is my undercaptain as well as my cousin and my friend."

With that, they were away.

The ride was incredible!

At first, Beth had been afraid that she wouldn't be able to control such a powerful horse or make it run as fast as they needed, but Rendel had chosen Daasa's horse and Aron had motioned for Beth to mount Nightbird ahead of him. There was no time to argue; they had to distance themselves from the false guard as quickly as possible.

"She will go as you wish," Rendel told Beth, as if having read her thoughts. As soon as they were in a space clear enough to do so, he set off at a gallop and she directed her horse to do the same. Happily, it obeyed. When she urged it to go faster, it obeyed again. Soon, she felt as if she were nearly flying. The wind hit her face so hard that it hurt. But at the same time, it felt . . . *wonderful*! She took the lead within a few minutes and then almost forgot to check to see if Rendel could keep up. When she did take a quick look back, she saw that he had been right – Daasa's horse matched Nightbird pace for pace.

After that, Beth kept her eyes ahead, did not seek signs of a battle in the distance behind her, did not, with the eyes of her mind, try to see Luke's face. She would trust to the skills of the others for his safety.

"Don't look back," he'd said.

Beth would never forget her first view of Greyvic. She had seen nothing like it except in pictures of medieval cities, and those could hardly compare. The riders were still a good distance away from the city but they had an unobstructed view from the sheltered spot where they had finally brought their horses to a stop.

"It is beautiful, is it not?" Rendel directed the question to Beth, but it was Aron who answered.

"Most wondrous! *Magnificent!*" For if it was a captivating sight to Beth, it was many times more so to Aron, who had scarcely even seen pictures of such things. The biggest settlement he had ever encountered was the dwarvish trading camp in the Amber Mountains, and it was of a very different nature.

Greyvic was the largest city in Gwilldonum, and thick walls encompassed the whole of it. Even from a distance, Beth could make out the red and gold flags held up by the easterly wind. Towers rose periodically along the irregularly-shaped wall, and she could see turrets from what must be a castle set well back into the city. Activity surrounded the large main gates of the city, directly opposite her in the distance, and tents and various types of encampments spread out from there toward the west. Visitors for the festival had made themselves temporary homes outside the city walls, for there was no room left within.

"And I am to speak to the assembly there!" Aron suddenly seemed so forlorn to Beth. How strange this must be for him after his isolated life with Sir Alric and the wolves. His guardian had done an amazing job of grooming him for the throne, despite significant obstacles. But was he really ready? He'd never been in a large city before, must never have seen such a mass of people as would be waiting there, no matter how busy the trading camp might have been. And he was not yet even eleven years old.

"Your peoples have awaited you these many years," Rendel quietly assured the prince. "They have coveted your presence among them and will be overcome by the mere sight of you. . . . And you are ready. The time is right."

"And you will be with me? Both of you? You will stay by my side, whatever it is I must do?"

Before Beth could say, "Of course," Rendel answered, "We will do all that we are able for you." Aron did not seem entirely satisfied by the answer, and Rendel added, "My hand is yours, Sire, but times come when a king must stand alone."

Aron nodded, lips tightly pressed together, eyes fixed ahead of him.

"Come!" said Rendel. "We will approach by the main gates, but not directly." He led them off in a gallop toward the west and then turned north again. For some minutes, the city was no longer in view. When next Beth saw it, she did so from the southwest, and a number of large encampments spread out between her and the walls of Greyvic.

"The Newwooders' tents are the red and white ones." Rendel pointed. "There." Some generations before, Beth knew by then, a group of woodlanders had left Greenwood (for reasons unclear to her) and settled in a "New Wood" instead. "I have many friends from among the Newwooders," Rendel had said. "They come unfailingly to Greyvic each year for the festival. They will give us the assistance we need."

As they neared the woodlander encampment, they dismounted. Shortly, Rendel left the other two for a moment, spoke to a little girl playing fetch with a mangy-looking dog, then returned to them with the child, dog bounding behind. "This is Willa," Rendel told his friends. "She will watch the horses for a while." They turned over the reins to the child, who led the horses off, appearing able to handle them well enough.

"Do you know that girl?" Beth asked as she watched Willa go.

"I have only in these last moments made her acquaintance."

"Will the horses be safe here?" asked Aron, who had learned a couple of hard lessons about thievery on his visits to the dwarvish settlement.

"In a woodlander camp with a woodlander child to watch them? Yes, as safe as we ought to hope."

There were campfires about, and people talking and laughing and showing one another the treasures they had acquired at the festival stands. Children happily ran loose, and the scene reminded Beth of what she thought a gypsy camp would be. (Or *ought* to be, at least. She'd heard some sad stories back in her own world.)

She reflected that these woodlanders looked different from the ones in Greenwood. There was more variety among them – of coloring and of height, for instance. And their clothes, Beth realized, also reminded her of gypsies (or whatever it was they liked to be called; she couldn't remember the right word). They looked like Greenwood clothes, but with lots of jewelry and scarves added; several fashion rebels wore unique, colorful hats.

"Rendel!" The excited voice came from somewhere in the middle of the scene and soon a boy (about Luke's age, Beth guessed) followed after it.

"Steffeyn!" Rendel responded in an equally delighted but somewhat quieter voice, clasping the boy by the shoulder. "Greetings, my lad! I am most pleased to see you, but my friends and I have a matter of great urgency – and *secrecy* – to attend to. Is your sister about?"

"She is," the boy responded, green eyes glittering just the way Rendel's sometimes did, "and *she* will be most glad to see *you*!" He spoke in a teasing manner, and Beth wondered what lay behind it.

She thought she could guess.

Rendel said, "Then lead on, but make no effort to draw attention to us."

As it happened, no effort was necessary, for attention came to them all on its own. Every couple of yards, a new voice greeted Rendel by name. Only once, though, did one of the greeters risk delaying the travelers, and at that point Rendel's young friend Steffeyn intervened, "Can't stop to talk now, Tomeyn. Rendel's anxious to see *Sereynel* before he does anything else."

"Oh, of course!" the other laughed, and Beth thought the woodlander woman beyond him was trying to hide a smile. So, was Sereynel his *girlfriend?* she wondered.

The boy led them in among a great number of similar-looking tents all set closely together. When they arrived at the one they wanted (which looked exactly like the ones on either side of it), the boy peeked in and announced, "We have company, sister!" and then motioned for the others to follow.

"Rendel!" The raven-haired young woman threw her arms around Rendel as soon as he entered, and the two exchanged friendly kisses on the cheek. The woman looked as if she might kiss Rendel again – possibly *not* on the cheek – but Steffeyn cleared his throat and she noticed the other two arrivals.

"Oh, I am sorry! Friends of Rendel's, are you? Come in." She warmly touched their arms in welcome, her several bracelets jangling around her wrists. "I am Sereynel, and I suppose you have met my brother Steffeyn."

"Sereynel," Rendel said at once, "my apologies for not introducing my friends to you and also for my abruptness, but we are in great need. Will you help us?"

"Anything," she answered at once.

"Steffeyn, will you wait without? Let no one approach." With a mixture of excitement and disappointment, the boy hastened to comply. To Sereynel, Rendel said, "First, we have two horses being attended by a child named Willa. They are to be returned to Edwyn of the Reston clan. He is here at Greyvic and no doubt often in the stables. Let none overhear your business with him – or send Steffeyn, perhaps – and Edwyn should be warned to speak as little as possible of the matter."

"I know Edwyn Reston by sight. It shall be done. What more?"

"My friends need woodlander clothes. *Traditional* clothes, marking them clearly as having come from Greenwood."

"They are of a size with Steffeyn," she said, considering, "but he possesses only one jacket, and his shoes will not fit the girl." She felt awkward referring to Beth this way, rather than by name. The whole situation was puzzling, but it was not the first time Rendel had entangled himself in mysterious doings. "It can be arranged, though. And what more?"

"The last will be the most difficult. My friends and I must meet with Lady Gweynleyn privately. I would desire, if it can be managed, that she not have even a council member in her presence, and certainly no one suspected of being in sympathy with the Torks. We will not trust even the guards at the gate, though the undercaptain Rostik will assist us if word can reach him discreetly."

Sereynel showed her surprise, then answered, "This *is* most difficult."

"I have the beginnings of a plan," Rendel continued, "though I should value your opinion of it and must ask your help in working it out more completely." Aron and Beth scarcely participated in the discussion that followed. Rendel had a number of questions for Sereynel – how often did Lady Gweynleyn leave the castle? who among their trusted acquaintance would know in which chamber she resided? was Rostik often in her company, and was it easy to find him on his own? what could Sereynel tell him of the movements of the Torks? could it be discovered in what wing of the castle they were staying? was there any meeting or great feast planned that day in the Hall, which all principal parties might be expected to attend? Sereynel answered as well as she could (she was scarcely on intimate terms with Greyvic's gentry, let alone the council members) and, when Rendel explained his plan, offered suggestions of her own. She was friendly with a number of the castle servants and was certain she could get some answers from them without raising suspicions. When she left for that very purpose, Steffeyn rejoined them, and the matter of clothing was attended to. Then Steffeyn left too, promising to attend to the horses as well as seek out some tempting refreshment for his guests.

Rendel suggested that Aron lie down on one of the two bedrolls in the tent and rest while he had the opportunity. Then he released a flap that was tied up along the tent ceiling and it fell like a curtain to partition off a small space including the second bedroll. "And you, Beth," he added, indicating the newly-formed enclosure, "you must be tired." She was, she realized, and when she lay down and closed her eyes, she fell into sleep almost at once.

What seemed like only an instant later (though it was not), she heard voices and moved to where she could see beyond the partition to where Rendel and Sereynel sat together opposite her.

319

Aron was still stretched out on his slight bed, but he was awake and propped up on one elbow. Steffeyn wasn't inside the tent, though he seemed to have delivered on his promise to bring food and drink.

Sereynel, not noticing that Beth had awoken, went on speaking to Rendel. "And will you have time, when your mysterious business is completed, to sit with me beneath the stars and enjoy a loaf of spritebread? I will bake it for you myself." She smiled invitingly, eyes glittering, clearly flirting.

"Well, *this* is embarrassing!" thought Beth. She glanced at Aron, wondering if he felt the same, but the young prince seemed fascinated instead.

A strange thought crossed Beth's mind. Aron had had such an isolated life – what would happen when girls began to flirt with him, as they certainly would? He was really kind of cute, she thought, and soon he'd have the pretty significant bonus of being a king! She doubted that visits to a mountain trading camp had prepared him very well for *that* part of his future.

"Beth?" Rendel had noticed she was awake and had just asked her something. Distracted, she'd missed it. "Are you hungry?" he repeated.

"Oh. Yes. Thank you."

They ate, then she and Aron put on the clothes Steffeyn had found for them. Beth dressed behind the partition and no one saw that she kept her sword from Mr. Gribb with her. All the other weapons, except for Rendel's short utility knife, were to be left in Sereynel's care along with whatever of their own clothing they would not be wearing beneath the woodlander outfits.

While she was dressing, she heard Rendel ask Sereynel if she had been able to locate Rostik. "Oh, did I not tell you? He is leaving the city – has probably already left it – and there seems to be some mystery about it. As it happens, I know a soldier of Rostik's company, who told me that *she* had heard there was some report of goblins, but just as she was saying so, another soldier came along and overheard, telling her not to repeat gossip and assuring me that the undercaptain was leaving on a routine patrol only . . . but he did not speak truly. I am certain of it. Oh, and though you did not inquire about Therin Mandek, it seems that *he* has not been seen of late either."

By the time she had finished speaking, Beth and Aron had finished dressing and came to stand before the genuine woodlanders for inspection. They were even given brief lessons on how to comport themselves in the manner of Greenwooders, as Sereynel called them. "Not so proud in your stance," she told Aron, trying to ease his shoulders forward a bit. Aron had not thought himself to be standing proudly, but it was true that the training Sir Alric provided had included many strictures concerning posture. Aron tried to slouch, but his new tutor said, "Not quite so much like a ragdoll, dear one." His next attempt was better. "Fine, just fine," he was told.

"But you must tilt your head a bit and keep your hat forward," Rendel added. "Your face must be seen as little as possible, especially within the castle, for the resemblance is remarkable."

"Resemblance?" Sereynel repeated, puzzled. "Resemblance to whom?" She looked more closely at the lad's face and slowly her own transformed. Her eyes widened, her lower lip fell away from the upper, and the hint of a tremble ran across her features.

Though she'd actually seen the princess many years before, she was too young to remember from that occasion anything about Arandella's looks beyond her golden hair and elegant dress. But she'd seen a highly realistic marriage portrait of her, and recently too, the image of which had impressed her mind strongly – the image of a joyful young bride who would in such a short time lose her husband, her father, and then her life. And here was Rendel sneaking these two into the castle at a time such as this, and the boy . . . the boy . . . People had been saying . . .

"Oh, my! . . . By the stars, it cannot be! Rendel, it is *not*! . . . But I see by your faces that it is! Oh, my! Forgive me, Your High— Oh, my! *Sir!*" She knelt down at once.

Beth liked Sereynel very much in that moment. Hers was exactly the reaction Aron needed to boost his confidence at such a crucial juncture.

"Oh!" exclaimed the young woman again, her hands flying to her cheeks. "And here was I telling you how to stand properly! Forgive me, sir!"

"No. Please. I am most grateful," Aron assured her. "Secrecy is critical for yet a while longer, and your assistance with our disguises is invaluable."

"Sir!" was all she could say.

A Greyvic guard at the South Gate watched the figures come and go. Woodlanders, Meadowlanders, and even some of those despicable Wastelanders had all made camps outside the walls, then entered and left the city each day for the various activities. Then there were the odd traders who set up here and there on their own, though most stayed in the city itself if they could. The Ferinians – the "regular" type of Ferinians, that is, not the uppity-ups who stayed in inns or were guests at the castle – had their own camp too, but it was on the north side and they used a different gate. Many of these others had become familiar to the guard over the last few days – except for the Wastelanders, who looked too much alike, if you could stand to look at them in the first place. Those woodlanders made themselves pretty similar too, dressing the way they did, though he figured the three coming through now might be new. Woodlanders! Harmless enough. But there were a couple of Wastelanders coming along behind. He'd let *them* know he had his eyes open!

Once past the guard, Rendel said quietly to his companions. "So. We have entered the walls of Greyvic."

"That was easy enough," Beth answered optimistically.

"Truth, it was. But now we must enter the castle."

CHAPTER TWENTY-FOUR – The Home Stretch

Earlier that day, while Beth, Rendel, and Aron made their exhilarating ride to Greyvic, Gweynleyn stood near the southeastern corner of the city ramparts, surveying all within view for anything out of the ordinary. Wind blew her long hair back from her face and tangled it behind her. "They are out there," she said wistfully, picturing Beth and Luke. "A child and a mere youth, and they hold our fate." She expected no response to her words, and Celiess Eyndeli, her only audience, offered none.

Remembering herself, Gweynleyn changed her tone as she said, "I ought not seem to be watching for them, I suppose . . . at least not in too hopeful a manner. No doubt I am observed from one hidden corner or another. Tell me, Celiess, is there despair enough in my countenance and demeanor?" In fact, the lady did not feel desperate, and her lips curled into the beginning of a smile. The angeli had already returned to her, and she had taken its message of "nothing to report" as a most hopeful and heartening sign.

"Walk with me," she said to her companion now, and the two of them moved along the ramparts toward the west, passing a watchguard as they went. Before long, they had reached the southwest corner, from which they spied down upon the Newwooder encampment and a lively circle dance in progress there. After a few moments, Gweynleyn observed, "They seem quite free of care, do they not?"

"They *seem* so, yes, my lady."

Gweynleyn noticed the slight emphasis and studied her attendant's face for a moment. "Yes. Yes, I take your meaning. . . . We all hide our cares betimes. And now, with the Torks within our borders, we can none of us be quite free of care, can we?" And the woodlanders, she added silently, have as much cause as any to

323

make them uneasy. Like Rendel, she knew that the Torks would despise woodlander ways and, given the upper hand, would not tolerate them long.

Gweynleyn sighed deeply. "I must not tarry, though I find more pleasure here in this hour than I would anywhere else in the city. I have no will to return to the crowds and to the parleys . . . and on this day it falls to Cassian Maris and myself to dine with the Tork leaders, for Jeron Rabirius will be otherwise engaged." Her tone made it clear that the task was one she did not relish. "You will know what to do if you see them?" she asked with a meaningful look, changing the object of discussion.

"Yes, my lady."

"Then I leave you to your watch." There were soldiers all along the ramparts, of course, but Gweynleyn had preferred that her own guard take turns among them. For the present, even among the Council Guard she trusted with certainty only Therin and Rostik . . . and Therin was nowhere to be found!

At the same time that Beth and her friends were settling themselves into Sereynel's small tent for a few hours of rest and simple refreshment, a magnificent feast was being set out in the Great Hall of Jeron Rabirius' castle. The meal reflected such bounty and such culinary skill as to cause envy among many who attended the Greyvic festival, but neither Gweynleyn nor the guest who sat to her right at table seemed to appreciate its merits. Farther down the table, Cassian Maris gave every appearance of enjoying not only the dishes set before him but also the company of his neighbor at table, Eustarius of the Torks. Gweynleyn would have preferred a different seating arrangement; she might actually have discovered some fitting topic of conversation had she found herself next to Eustarius, who at least was reputed to be a man of learning. And Cassian, who seemed to deal with all situations with remarkable equanimity and who managed to find suitable topics for easy conversation no matter who his companions happened to be, might even have enjoyed finding himself beside Myrmidon Tork for the hour. But that position had come to her. Throughout the interminable meal, she had made only minimal conversation with her adversary, whose varied attempts to charm or engage her had all fallen flat.

At last, Myrmidon gave in to baser desires and decided to nettle his cold and, as he perceived her, self-righteous neighbor. He knew just the topic that might do it. Leaning in and speaking confidentially, he said, "Perhaps you are unaware, my lady, that I am acquainted with you through another . . . in my own land. One who knows you well . . . and thinks of you often." In truth, he did not fully understand the connection between this refined and apparently soft-hearted lady and the stone-cold, single-minded, entirely ruthless individual of whom he spoke, but he knew enough of the connection to be certain that his dinner companion would not be glad to have the subject raised. As Myrmidon hoped, his words had an immediate and visible effect. Clearly, he had succeeded in discomposing Gweynleyn: her fingers faltered as they lifted her goblet, and he grabbed at it to keep it from spilling over.

Gweynleyn had no doubt of whom he spoke. Her connection with such a one cut at her heart – "one who has true evil in his heart," she had said to Luke in the courtyard of Arystar. One she had had the misfortune of knowing nearly her whole life and who now made his home among the Torks. Myrmidon watched with satisfaction the strain in the muscles of the lady's neck, but she regained her poise too quickly for his tastes. Soon she was responding warmly, attempting to divert the focus from herself, "And I know of you, sir, *and your family* through many here in my own land. Your reputation precedes you strongly."

Myrmidon did not like her turning of the conversation, but he responded with a smile that many might have deemed compassionate – provided they were not in a position to see the telltale clenching and unclenching of his left hand beneath the cover of the dinner table. "Truth," he answered in regretful tones, "the history of the two branches of our people – yours and mine – has not always been a pleasant one, but you know that I have denounced the despicable acts of my brother Karstidon against Gwilldonum." As he gazed at her, his head tilted slightly, smiling and unblinking, Gweynleyn saw with alarm that his attempt to convey sincere and amicable feelings was a skillful one, and she understood how many of her fellow citizens might be taken in by his manner and his deceptive eyes. He could put on a pleasing manner as easily as a tunic, it seemed.

"Lady Gweynleyn," he continued easily (even his hand was now relaxed enough to slip back into view – he almost dared to touch hers with it but restrained himself), "the interests of this land lie near to my heart, as I know they do to yours. Perhaps, by working closely together, we – you and I and the remainder of the Council of Ten – will be able to undo some of the harm that Karstidon did in his lifetime. I wish to make amends for his errors, if I can, and I flatter myself to think that I have some skills that would be of use to Gwilldonum if I might only have the opportunity to use them. I am, of course, grateful for the support the council has already shown me in inviting me to address the assembly tomorrow—"

Setting down her goblet a bit roughly, Gweynleyn turned fully toward Myrmidon in a resolute manner. "Let us dispense with pretense, sir; it sits on me ill. I will tell you frankly what you must surely know: I have no desire to see you take the throne. Indeed, the idea is entirely repugnant to me. Nonetheless, you and I both are aware that you have some support from within my land. The Council of Ten, legitimate rulers of Gwilldonum in the absence of a *princeps*, has chosen to honor our people by bringing this matter before a wider council for open discussion. In so doing, we honor the ancient ideals of *res publica*, a concept that may have carried down to you from your own ancestors.

"But make no mistake. You will be opposed – opposed with valor and vigor, opposed with the force of wisdom and of words, to begin, and then by any other force called for by your actions. I have great confidence in the peoples of Gwilldonum. We will not watch you succeed where your brother failed. We will not permit the throne of DarQuinn to be usurped. We will not sell ourselves to tyranny for a song."

She had spoken clearly but not loudly, and conversation and music continued around them. Myrmidon remained quiet for a moment (his eyes suddenly cold and dark, his throat tight, his left hand clenching once again) as he struggled to keep control of his person. When he did speak, it was in a low, menacing tone much different from before. "Very well. I understand you perfectly. . . . But since we speak frankly, *my lady*" – and he managed to fill those two words with great disrespect – "I feel compelled to inform you that my support may be greater than you allow yourself to believe. My informants (let us not call them 'spies' – such an unfriendly word!) have these many months made known to me the sentiments of these peoples in whom your great confidence resides.

326

And what are those sentiments, you may wish to know? Dissatisfaction. Unease. Fear. In short, the peoples of your land are not content, my lady – not content to let the present situation continue. They find themselves on a ship adrift in troubled waters with no captain at the helm. . . . " He caught his breath. "I mean no disrespect to your council, of course; I only repeat the sentiments that have been repeated to me." He was regaining his composure and was able to add in an almost casual voice, "In addition to all other troubles, they fear the goblins, you know. What great warrior-king will lead them if the goblins attack from the north, as might happen at any time? . . . Restless and unpredictable creatures, those goblins. Quite fearsome."

When Gweynleyn merely smiled (condescendingly, he knew) and reached again for her drink, Myrmidon returned to a more menacing tone as he leaned in close to her. He spoke in a quick but low voice so that she alone could hear beneath the cover of the musicians' tunes, for he did not wish to draw undue attention. "Gwilldonum wants a king of the ancient line. I am able to offer them one. Are you? There have been wild rumors that some great champion will appear to bring a royal heir, previously undiscovered, to claim the throne. But I see no champion and I hear no such claims. Surely I would have done by now if your precious council had any to put forth. My company and I would have been packed and dispatched the moment you had some pleasing alternative to offer the rabble gathered here."

Myrmidon would have done well to stop at that point, but he continued in a most self-satisfied way, raising again the question of goblins, dangling before her the possibility of attack as he described – in surprising and striking detail – their gatherings not far beyond the border. Both his words and a change in his manner snatched at Gweynleyn's senses, and a subsequent change in her own demeanor caused Myrmidon to break off mid-sentence. The lady's expression and, when she spoke, her voice were both calm – but it was a dangerous sort of calm. "You appear better informed concerning the goblins' activities and intentions than I," she said with a piercing look. "Have you some special intelligence on these matters you desire to impart?"

Myrmidon cursed himself for having lapsed in self-control in the way his brother had been wont to do. In his desire to provoke this infuriating lady, he had gone too far, even so far as to plant the idea that he was in communication with goblin forces. She had not suspected as much heretofore, he was certain. None of these fools had. "Not at all, my lady." He forced his tone to suggest that this topic was of little more import than the state of the day's weather. "I speak only of the situation as it is *perceived*. There are great fears and rumors about. I speak only of such things," he concluded dismissively, "not of any knowledge personally discovered." He returned to his meal in as casual a manner as he was able.

But he could neither retract his words nor undo the effect they had had on Gweynleyn, in whom strong suspicion was rearing up. After only a few moments, the lady rose abruptly, excused herself in a civil but cold manner, and made as if to retire.

She did not retire, however, but went in immediate search of Therin's second-in-command. Upon finding him, she demanded without preamble, "Swear to me, Rostik, that you know not where your captain has gone."

"I swear it, my lady," answered the undercaptain, bravest among the brave when in battle, but somewhat intimidated standing before Gweynleyn at this moment.

"He gave you no parting words, no commands to follow?"

"I-" He hesitated.

"*Tell me.*" Her eyes blazed. "Tell me now and tell me all."

"I- It is very little, my lady, and I swear on the life of my beloved mother that he told me not where he would go or what plan he had conceived, but— When last I saw him, he spoke to me quickly and urgently. He told me that, with or without him, I should lead as he would lead, be vigilant as he would be vigilant. He said" —this time the hesitation stemmed from embarrassment, though mixed with some pride— "he said that he had all confidence in me to meet what needed to be met until . . . his return. But, truth, my lady, he gave me no welcome to ask what he could mean by such words, and he was gone within an instant of saying them."

"Yes, yes, very well. I comprehend it." Her head neared bursting from the fever of unruly thoughts within it. In an uncharacteristically revealing moment, she pressed her hand hard to her forehead, but then dropped it again quickly. "Listen, then, carefully. The border along Ferinia must be secured. The Torks may have troops there unknown to us, awaiting some word from their commander. And, hear me, you must be on especial watch for goblin activity along the northland border. *You* know what to look for" – both his parents had been skilled goblin-hunters, as she knew – "but your troops may not. Inform them. Train them. And do it at once. I am well aware that we face problems of trustworthiness within our ranks, but I know that you will choose your confidants with care. And remember that there are many worthy ones presently at Greyvic who, though not trained with the rigor of soldiers, yet have the skills to act for you as scouts and trackers. Find them. Recruit them. Send them to the north. Send them in search of goblins and spies."

"All this has been done, my lady," Rostik answered with satisfaction, "at my captain's command."

"Has it? . . . *Has* it? . . . Yes, of course it has. Of course, though he spoke not to *me* of tracking goblins." Eyes turned aside, she addressed the last sentence to herself rather than to Rostik, but he responded nonetheless.

"Truth, my lady. My captain keeps his own counsel. It is one of his great strengths, I credit." The beginnings of a smile played at his lips for an instant, but there was no trace of one when Gweynleyn quickly turned her head to meet his eyes.

"Tell me," she said bitterly, "is there yet *more* I ought be told?"

"No, my lady," Rostik answered gravely, "only what you must know already – that there is a restlessness among the troops, that disputes break out among them easily, that few of them are trusted fully while the remainder resent that they are *not*. . . . And that we heartily wish our captain back among us."

With a sigh, she answered. "So do we all, Rostik. So do we all."

Mired in a frenzy of thought, Lady Gweynleyn retreated to the relative peace of her chamber, having requested that the undercaptain contact her there at once if any news of import reached him. Almost immediately after that, Rostik received a disturbing report from the north that took him directly out of the city, for the rumor that Sereynel would hear was true – a goblin party had been sighted close to the border.

Before leaving, Rostik sent word to Gweynleyn, who received it heavily. She had felt Harac's absence keenly, and then

329

Daasa was gone after him, and Therin, with little doubt, had followed close on her trail. Now, with Rostik gone too (and the council member Terilla with him, he had said), she feared for the security of Greyvic. What if this goblin report were a false one, of a purpose to draw the undercaptain away from the city? Jeron Rabirius remained, but his hands were full enough with the sorts of problems that always arose during festival days – problems that seemed greater in frequency and intensity this year. And the Tork was angered; she knew it. *She* had angered him. She ought not have indulged her contempt.

And into such a delicate situation the Anointed would come, even if all went as she had been hoping! Greyvic might be the most dangerous city in the kingdom at the moment! But surely the child would arrive in the protection of a valiant retinue, she reassured herself. Harac, Daasa, and Therin constituted a formidable company – pray they might be with the child even now!

If only Gweynleyn had known that Arandella's son no longer found himself in such illustrious company! If only she had known that at that very moment (as she sat alone in her chamber, distressed for the child's sake), the boy was entering into the somewhat less prestigious presence of Jeron Rabirius' kitchen staff!

"Let them enter through the main doors, if they have good cause! We're to let no strangers pass through here, and well you know it!" The gruff, bulky man who uttered these words was a master chef, but he was also a household officer, and he took both his sets of responsibilities seriously.

With the help of Sereynel's friend, a servant girl of the Rabirius household, Rendel, Beth, and Aron had made it as far as the large kitchen area of the Greyvic castle, but the hefty chef positioned himself to prevent their progress from that point.

The servant girl was of a timid sort and did not know how to answer her superior, but Rendel spoke up at once in most respectful tones. "We are here to perform the woodlander rites of peace before the great assembly of the morrow."

The chef narrowed his eyes. "I have never heard of such a thing."

"Truth, it is long, is it not, since they have been performed? But it *is* long since we have had an occasion of such import and consequence before us, as you must agree." Rendel turned his most innocent expression toward the chef.

"I know nothing of this." No immediate response to this statement was necessary for, as it happened, a minor crisis with the mutton stew called the chef away at that moment.

When he moved off to address that matter, having instructed the intruders to stay where they were, Beth asked quietly, "*Are* there such things as woodlander rites of peace?"

Rendel hesitated, then smiled, eyes glittering. "*Today* there are. They are very much wanted at present, do you not credit?"

"You're a much better liar than I am," Beth whispered, turning her head so that the sound wouldn't carry and her smile wouldn't show.

"I am glad to hear it. Your deficiency speaks well for your character, I am certain. As for my own part, I have of late been tutored in such matters by your friend Luke."

At the sound of Luke's name, a wave of anxiety passed over Beth, but all her attention returned to her own situation when the chef rejoined them. Before he could repeat that they must leave the way they had come and go around to the main gateway, Rendel spoke. "Forgive us our tardiness. We have been sadly delayed in our journey. Has Lady Gweynleyn been anxious on our account? And my friend Therin Mandek? Has he inquired after us, for he expected us this morning at the latest?"

"The Captain of the Guard? A friend of yours, you say?" He eyed Rendel speculatively before informing them, "Therin Mandek is nowhere to be found."

"What?" Rendel seemed taken by surprise and went on urgently, "Then it is her ladyship we must see, and straightaway."

The chef was torn between his two roles, for he ought not let these strangers pass (harmless though they might appear – woodlanders!), but at the same time that troublesome stew was not responding as it ought to the discreet addition of vinegar and saffron.

Sentinel and visitors seemed at an impasse. Rendel waited calmly, Beth not quite as calmly. Aron kept silent and still. He had been respectfully requested, on leaving Sereynel's tent, not to speak or make eye contact except as necessary. Uneasy as he was, his silence cost him no effort, and he reproached himself for his fearfulness.

The serving girl who accompanied them *wished* she could keep silent, but felt compelled to speak up. Hoping that she would not regret her words for any reason, she suggested hesitantly to the chef, "I could take them to the guard at the main entry, if you wish it, but it was Mariza of her ladyship's company who requested that they come to her at once by the most expedient route. And in any measure, we will pass another guard by this way, and he will approve the arrangement, I credit."

"Mariza? Why did you not say so to begin it all, you stupid girl? Of course, take them by the inner watchguard and be on your way." Then he added for good measure, "Get out of my kitchen at once!" This problem solved, the chef found himself free to turn all attention to the matter of the obstinate stew.

The serving girl did not take her companions by way of the inner watchguard, for the castle was full of passages and the household staff had its own ways of getting about. She led them through a veritable maze of corridors, and Beth reflected that the castle must be larger than she had originally thought. When at last they came to a spiral stairwell, the girl told them quietly, "Above us is the upper east corridor. The chambers of Lady Gweynleyn and of the Tork leaders are both found along it. The lady's door is the last before the main staircase; it is not far, but you must pass first by the Torks' quarters. Their chamber is always watched, however, so the corridor will be patrolled. Will you trust to the guards who are there to see you safely to the lady?" she asked hopefully.

"I regret it," said Rendel, "but we cannot. If we err, it must be on the side of caution. We will trust ourselves to Mariza or to the advice of Lady Gweynleyn. Can you get word to one of them to come to us or to instruct us?"

"I . . . I . . . if I must."

"We will not compel you," Rendel told her gently, "but I assure you that our cause is a great one. Are you willing to aid us in this way?"

"Yes," she answered, but the word sounded as much like a question as a statement.

"Sereynel tells me that you know all the secrets of this castle and might know how to conceal us close to the lady's chambers."

"Truth," said the girl nervously, "I do know the castle, for my family has served in it for generations and generations again, but I cannot hide you in a chamber for the festival has filled every room here." She considered briefly. "There is a recess above us where you may wait while I go ahead, though it is no perfect hiding place. Anyone passing close by might spy you. And," she added doubtfully, "I cannot say that it will hold three."

"We will do as you recommend."

They began their ascent of the narrow, spiraling steps, but stopped after the first full turn, when the servant girl motioned them toward a recess in the stairwell wall. Aron went in first and was able to conceal himself entirely, but when Beth followed, the best she could do was press herself against the wall and hope that no one could see her in the shadows. For Rendel, there was scarcely any room at all – a glance in the right direction would reveal him to anyone passing by. The girl hesitated before leaving them there – in part because she could see that the hiding place was inadequate and was unsure whether to suggest an alternative, in part because of reluctance to pass by the chamber where the three Tork noblemen were quartered, even if there was a guard on duty outside it. Knowing how easily sound would carry in the stairwell, no one spoke, but Rendel took the girl's hand and squeezed it, jerking his head in the direction she was to go. She continued up the steps.

Half a minute later, voices sounded above. The girl must have run into someone at once – probably the guards who patrolled the corridor, Beth thought, straining to make out the words. Two male voices seemed to be questioning the business of the servant girl, whose answers were barely audible. After a moment, Beth could no longer hear the girl at all, but the two other voices grew clearer as the men approached the stairwell entrance above. Beth pressed her tensing body even harder against the wall. She knew that only a few steps and the curve of a stone wall separated the unknown figures from them.

The men did not immediately descend. Paused at the top of the stairs, one instructed the other to go first to the main gateway and then to the lower corridor stations to inquire whether anything out of the ordinary had occurred. His subordinate assented. Immediately Beth recognized the sounds of feet starting down the steps toward them, and in the same instant she saw a shadow quickly grow on the wall opposite her. She looked to Rendel, but his face was turned away from hers and she couldn't catch his expression. Though Aron was close and faced her, she could not see his expression either, so well did the shadowy recess hide him. In a flash, Beth wondered if she and Rendel should step forward, as if just coming up the steps, so that the prince at least would not be discovered. Rendel had a similar idea, thinking that he alone might be able to go forward and turn the guard back with him. Before either Rendel or Beth moved, however, the footsteps halted.

"No, not by that way!" the first voice ordered gruffly. "Go by the main stairs." The heavy feet moved dutifully away.

Rendel turned his head back to Beth then, and the two exchanged what looks they could in the dim light. Both were relieved, of course, but also wary. Was there a particular reason that one guard had sent the other in a different direction? Was he suspicious of the girl and sending his companion to follow her? But he had said nothing of that. Or did the first guard plan to investigate this stairwell himself? If so, why hesitate? No footsteps were bringing him closer or taking him away.

Then, after the puzzling pause that seemed longer than it was, Beth heard the guard move away and begin a muted conversation with, she thought, a third person. *Maybe he sent the other guard in a direction that would take him longer,* she thought, *to keep him out of the way for a while.* "Something wrong?" she whispered to Rendel, barely audible.

The woodlander nodded, sensing trouble. He hoped it did not involve the girl who had risked herself for them. He considered their options, none of which much appealed to him. They could go back the way they'd come and do their best to stay out of sight until they were joined by someone trustworthy, they could remain where they were and risk discovery in a compromising position, or they could move ahead and take their chances with whatever (or whomever) they'd find in the corridor above. In principle, the guards of Jeron Rabirius' house should be their allies, but they could not depend on that.

"Come," he said decisively. "Something is amiss, but let us walk forward with confidence rather than be found cowering in a dark corner. And we cannot abandon the girl if she is in need." Beth missed the last words because Rendel was speaking quietly and had already turned to mount the stairs.

When they reached the landing above, Rendel knew which way to turn but stopped in an instant, Beth and Aron behind him. Ahead of them, where the corridor twisted, stood an unexpected and greatly unwelcome figure – the Tork captain, Rendel guessed by the uniform. Close by him was another figure – the guard. A *traitorous* guard, it seemed; guilt was written across his face. He hovered an instant, then quickly disappeared down the opposite hallway, leaving Rendel's company alone with the captain, Gydon Tork.

Gydon leaned back lazily against the stone corridor wall, but there was nothing lax about the gaze he settled on Rendel, Beth, and Aron. Though none of the three had laid eyes on him before, even Beth could guess that he was of the Tork company, and all three could see that he meant them no good.

Rendel smiled and nodded a greeting, beginning to walk again and not slowing his step when he neared the captain. Gydon, however, had no intention of allowing the strangers to pass by him uninterrupted. He stepped forward, blocking their way before they could turn the corner.

"I have not seen you in these hallways before," he said. His words and tone were casual enough; his manner was not.

"We are woodlanders of Greenwood," Rendel answered easily, "summoned by Lady Gweynleyn on festival business. We are to perform the traditional rites of peace of our kind."

"Summoned by the lady," Gydon repeated skeptically, "yet you come to her through some servants' hole rather than by the main entry as honored guests?"

"We are woodlanders," Rendel answered as if that explanation ought to suffice; he continued, though. "We have no need of great attention. We find no dishonor in entering in humble fashion."

Rendel's self-composure was unflawed, and Gydon changed his approach. "Rites of *peace*, you say? Then you have no objection to my assuring myself that you carry no weapon, for I serve a master whose safety I must ensure."

He watched Rendel carefully for any reaction, but the woodlander continued to speak calmly with no trace of distress. "I am surprised by the request, for this is the residence of Jeron Rabirius and I perceive that you are no Gwilldonian. It is an oddity that such a task should be given over to you by the lord of this castle, who, I am sure, has made his own provisions for the safety of your master. Yet I have no objection, nor will my apprentices, to your request. All measures that lead to peace are welcome to my kind." He opened his arms and let his jacket fall open for the captain's inspection. Rendel maintained his calm without difficulty, for he had no way of knowing that Beth carried with her a most deadly weapon.

Beth herself was far from calm. It would be bad enough if this Tork person took her treasured weapon from her, but its discovery was certain to give them all away! It was no mere utility knife like the small one that hung carelessly from Rendel's belt. It was a dagger like no true woodlander would ever carry, she was sure.

In a panic, she realized she was sweating. If he noticed, he would know! She tried to will her sweat glands to control themselves, and she hoped desperately that the Tork captain wouldn't notice as she took a quick swipe at the telltale droplets.

Myrmidon Tork was in a foul mood. He despised Lady Gweynleyn! He despised the lot of them, but she was the worst! Most galling of all was that he had allowed himself the pleasure of shaking her from that irritating self-composure. He ought to have held his tongue! The same blood ran in his veins that had run in his foolish and impetuous brother's! But he *would* keep control! On the morrow, when it mattered most, he would not misstep, he would be all felicity . . .

But at the moment, as he strode heavily down the upper east corridor, his anger sought an outlet.

The serving girl came out of the shadows where she had concealed herself. One guard had passed by, then in course another (that one had seemed as flustered as she felt herself!), and lastly, coming from a different corridor, the Tork leader himself – Myrmidon, they called him. He frightened her dreadfully! And he was heading in *their* direction. But she could do no good by trying to warn them and hoped only that they could remain safely hidden a few moments longer. She had been delayed but was nearly at the lady's door now.

When Gydon had assured himself that Rendel was armed with nothing of significance, he moved next to Aron – but not without first pushing hard into Rendel as he passed. "Pray pardon my clumsiness," he muttered lazily.

Rendel made no reaction beyond a slight inclination of the head. But Aron . . . How would *he* react if the Tork tried to test or provoke him in such a way? Rendel was uneasy about the answer. He knew the boy was afraid; it was only natural. But the young prince had been raised to a certain code of honor and of behavior and a sense of his own worthiness. He would suffer no insult lightly.

Without having previously met any, Gydon held all woodlanders in contempt. It had given him satisfaction to knock into the leader of this pitiable band. Finding no weapon on Aron, he further indulged himself by knocking the hat from the boy's head so that it tumbled to the floor. Aron clenched his jaw and a flash of anger crossed his face.

This one had a little spirit, at least; the boy was torn, as Gydon could see.

Beth could see it too and was afraid Aron might himself give them all away before the captain even got to her. "Sir," she said impulsively, trying to draw Gydon's attention at once, even without knowing where she might go from there. He turned to her inquiringly. "You seem very tense" was all she could think of to say. *What next?* "We woodlanders have ways of calming ourselves and feeling more peaceful . . . . We could help you." She sounded so stupid! But probably the Torks thought woodlanders *were* stupid.

The interruption worked. Aron forced himself to pick up his hat and return it to his head, pulling it down as far over his face as he dared. Gydon had not recognized him, he was sure, but there was no telling who might come upon them next. Surely *someone* should be coming soon. Aron felt as if they had been alone with the Tork captain much longer than ought to have been possible. Where were the guards? Surely there was treachery in the household. Bribery, at the least. But, he supposed, it must only

337

have been a few minutes, though it seemed longer, and it did sound now as if someone *was* coming toward them.

In the meantime, Gydon's attention had moved fully from Aron to Beth. He considered her carefully without speaking. In the silence, Beth heard footsteps echo around the corner of the hallway. Not slow or hesitant footsteps, but strong and purposeful ones. Could it be help for them? It *could* . . . yet she suddenly doubted it. She sensed that Gydon had not only heard but also recognized the footfalls. He knew who was coming, and a smile curled his lips.

In a moment, the newcomer reached them, stopping abruptly to survey the scene before him as Beth and the others took in the sight of him. His hair was jet black and his eyes dark. A purple band with gold trim encircled the crown of his head, and an elegant coat bordered with expensive damask covered his fine tunic. But this was a man who looked as if he should be attired in fighting rather than feasting clothes. This was a soldier and the commander of soldiers. Even Beth, who had never crossed paths with anyone like him before, could tell that. She saw in his cold, hard face what sort of man he was. She even knew *who* it was that stood before her.

This was Myrmidon Tork.

"Figure they're in Greyvic by now?"

"Yep, prob'ly."

"Figure they're safe?"

After a pause, Aynyxia answered, "Safer than us, prob'ly. But maybe not."

After a longer pause, Luke whispered, "Couldn't just lie to me, could you?"

"Let us move now," Daasa implored. "They are ours." The enemy was in clear view.

"Patience. We could overcome them, of course," Therin Mandek agreed, "but I have undertaken to return the boy and the walkabout in whole health. We will wait."

"To wait is a hard thing, is it not, Mariza?" Suddenly, Gweynleyn and her attendant both jerked their heads to face the door. There had been a knock.

338

"Sereynel? *Sereynel*, are you attending to me at all?"

"Oh, sorry, Steffeyn!" answered his sister. "My thoughts were away from me for a moment."

"And I can guess where they've been!" answered her brother teasingly. "With our friend Rendel, I'd wager!"

"Yes," she answered slowly . . . but she could not return his smile.

Rendel held his polite smile as Myrmidon stood and surveyed him. "What have we? These cannot be woodlanders, can they?" he asked Gydon with a sneer.

"They can be and they are," responded his captain in a similar manner.

Myrmidon had been pulling off one glove as they spoke; now, as he began to walk around the small group, he slapped it hard against his bare hand in a rhythmic beat. Beth found the movement menacing, as no doubt she was meant to. Where were the guards, she wondered, why didn't anyone come? This was supposed to be the house of a council member, wasn't it? And it was supposed to be filled with guests. To her as to Aron, the time spent in this corridor seemed much longer than the few minutes it had been!

"These are woodlanders come to perform rites of peace, they tell me," Gydon continued in explanation.

"Rites of peace?" Myrmidon seemed to consider the puzzling phrase before continuing coldly. "*I* am come to bring peace to Gwilldonum; did you know? I am Myrmidon of the Torks," he announced with pride and anger – anger that he would have preferred to direct toward Gweynleyn and Jeron Rabirius and the whole of the Council of Ten. A deep, full, radiating anger.

Beth was frightened. In fact, she had never been so frightened by any human being before, and Myrmidon's next words, though quietly spoken, only deepened the fear.

"Is it true," he asked Rendel, coming very close, nearly touching him, "that your kind are always peaceful, no matter what the circumstances?"

"It is our way to seek peace," the woodlander answered softly, but without timidity. Myrmidon did not attend to the answer, straining instead to hear any signs of approach behind him.

339

Then suddenly he raised his glove and struck it hard across Rendel's face.

Rendel made no sound, but Beth gasped loudly, drawing the Tork's attention. He moved close to her and stared.

She hated having him look at her. Anger and contempt were alive in his face, as fear was alive in hers. She dropped her eyes, but almost at once she raised them again, though she couldn't meet his gaze directly.

Her heart raced; her tongue wanted to lick her dry lips, but it didn't move; she knew he could read the fear in her. She thought he might hit her, hoped he wouldn't, didn't know if she could stand it if he did. . . . And if he did, then what? In days to come, she would remember that moment – remember it so well! – and wonder what would have happened next. But . . .

Someone was coming. Finally! Two sets of footfalls at least. The Torks heard them too and a frustrated Myrmidon willed himself calmer.

In an instant, two figures appeared – Mariza and the serving girl who had brought them into the castle, a girl whose name Beth didn't even know but to whom she would be forever grateful.

"You are here to perform the rites?" Mariza asked Rendel in a perfunctory way, ignoring the clear signs of the hostile situation she had interrupted. Rendel nodded. "Be on your way, then. Her ladyship awaits you." To the serving girl, she said, "You. Take them along, then return to your duties at once."

Immediately, the girl turned to go, followed by three very willing companions. The Torks made no attempt to stop them.

Mariza showed no sign of wishing to accompany the small party. After flashing a dismissive look in the direction of her adversaries, she continued on her way down the corridor, though she stopped shortly as if struck by a thought.

"Guard?" she called; then, in a more insistent voice that echoed in the hallway, "*Guard!*"

Hesitantly a guard came into view – the same guard that had sent away his companion and then hurried off himself, before thinking better of it and realizing that he should not be found so far from his post. He glanced briefly in Gydon's direction, but the captain did not meet the look or acknowledge him in any way.

"Ought you not be here at your station to attend to the needs of the council's guests?" Mariza demanded imperiously. If his conscience had been clearer, the guard (who held an officer's rank) might have thought to question Mariza's right to speak to him in such a way. As it was, he merely stumbled over disjointed syllables until Myrmidon's cool and sardonic voice answered her instead.

"You are most solicitous, but we have no need of any services at present."

"Nonetheless, I am certain that our host, the lord Rabirius, would wish for you to have assistance constantly at hand . . . but perhaps assistance of a more *dependable* nature is called for." She glared at the guard. "I will see to it at once." She turned and strode away, judging that she had given Beth and the others enough of a start to get safely to their destination.

The girl showed them into a tiny unfurnished room with a second door leading out of it and a small window high up in the opposite wall. "The lady said to wait here, rather than go directly to her chamber," she explained. "I . . . I had best leave you now."

"Yes," said Rendel, "but our gratitude is immense." Aron wondered if he should promise her some reward, then decided that that was a matter better dealt with later, once he was . . . king.

When she had gone, Beth, still shaken but now also incensed by the behavior of the Torks, burst out to Rendel, "How can you stand it?"

Her friend understood her. "I bear what there is good reason to bear," he answered evenly.

"But they were *horrible*!" She could feel herself trembling now, and she wasn't sure she could stop.

"They were," he agreed gently. "But why did *you* not then resist? You are no woodlander."

"Well, the odds weren't too good, were they?" she answered unsteadily. "I mean, those two were bigger than us and they were armed. And . . . and we had to get Aron away from them, even if it meant . . . well, whatever it meant."

"So then . . . you also bear what there is good reason to bear."

Beth thought that it really wasn't as simple as that and he knew it! But there was no time to tell him so, for at that moment the second door, not the one through which they had entered, opened, and Lady Gweynleyn walked through. She was followed by two Eyndeli, one of whom – Beth still could not tell them apart – went immediately toward the first door to station herself. But Beth scarcely paid the guards any attention. She watched a radiant and overjoyed Gweynleyn rush to Aron, kneel before him, rise again at once, take his hands, kiss his forehead, then speak to him in a flood of words of Gwilldonum and the throne, of his mother and of the father of his mother, of his people and the council, of peril and great promise. Her subjects changed with every other breath, but she expected no response from the prince. Her joy had released the floodgate of her mind.

Beth and Rendel watched the scene without, for the moment, feeling a part of it. On his end, Rendel felt great satisfaction and contentment, but Beth's feelings were more complex. She was delighted, she was relieved (*so* relieved!), but she was also still very much shaken by her encounter with Myrmidon. She'd never been in the presence of evil before, but *now* she believed she had been. And she never wanted it to happen again. Even if he were in a jail with guards and bars all around him, she wouldn't want to be near him.

She hoped, she wished, she prayed that she would never come face to face with Myrmidon Tork again. Ever.

CHAPTER TWENTY-FIVE – The Window of Light

Beth was to spend that night in the quarters allotted to Gweynleyn and her attendants. She doubted she would sleep much.

When the hour was late, Aron and Rendel had left her and accompanied Jeron Rabirius to the double chamber where the large Rabirius clan had been crowded together for the festival week. So Aron was just where he belonged. Everything was working out the way it was supposed to. Almost everything.

Where were Luke and Aynyxia? Therin *must* have rescued them by now, Beth told herself every hour or so of the evening. He would do what Aron had asked of him, she was sure; he'd save her friends whatever it cost him. And Harac – Harac wouldn't abandon his friends, even if they hadn't been his friends for long. He and Therin and Daasa certainly ought to be able to take on those other three. And unless Luke and Aynyxia had become actual prisoners, they would have their own weapons to add into the mix as well.

But was that a good thing? Had Luke ever even *seen* a battle that didn't have an electronic controller to go along with it? He could get hurt. She hoped he'd run for cover and let the others fight it out. But she doubted that he would.

Oh, they must *be all right!* Five against three with surprise on their side. And there'd been plenty of time. How long could a little battle like that take anyway? But she supposed Therin would wait for the right moment. . . . She just hoped he wouldn't wait too long.

If only she could forget about it for a while and make herself sleep. Then she might wake up in the morning to find that Luke and Aynyxia had already returned, safe and sound.

But Beth couldn't get to sleep at once. She wondered how Luke was, and if Aynyxia was all right, and whether Aron was too excited to sleep, and how Luke was, and whether Mr. and Mrs. Gribb had come to Greyvic for the festival . . . and how Luke was.

343

The day had been taxing, though, from the frantic horseride to the encounter with the Torks to the draining of so much emotion when Aron at last met with Gweynleyn, so, in due course, exhaustion overtook Beth and she slept, escaping the tangle of her thoughts.

She awoke to the sounds of trumpets and, in her sleepy state, couldn't understand why. Then she sat up with a jolt. This was the day. *The* day, the festival day when the Council of Ten would address the great assembly. The trumpets were probably announcing the special occasion, maybe even already calling the people together.

Rising quickly and taking in the flurry of activity around her, Beth wondered how she could possibly have slept through it. One messenger was leaving the chamber as another arrived. Gweynleyn, seated in a straight chair and dressed in a splendid gown of white with gold accents, was having her shoes laced up by one lady's maid while another decorated her hair with braids and ribbons. She looked amazing!

For a moment, Beth wondered if she herself might be loaned a beautiful gown for the day but then remembered that the plan was for her to remain in woodlander attire. It was a simple outfit (and she'd slept in most of it), so she was able to get herself entirely ready before Gweynleyn's hair was even finished.

An attendant pointed out food and drink that had been brought to the room. Enjoying the feast laid out in the Great Hall was out of the question, Beth knew, because she was to stay out of sight for a while longer. Aron, of course, had to lie low too – at least (they all hoped) until Luke was safely arrived.

Where *was* Luke? Beth asked Gweynleyn if there had been news, but she didn't really expect any reply other than the one she got – no report yet.

Beth was distractedly picking at her food when Rendel arrived, followed by a familiar figure in woodlander clothes.

"Aron?" Beth whispered, puzzled.

Rendel's companion came around from behind him and tipped back the wide-brimmed hat that had covered her beaming face.

"This is K'threen Rabirius," Rendel introduced her, "Jeron's daughter. K'threen, this is Beth of Fair Spring, a great friend of your father's newest guest." To Beth he added, "It was judged wise

344

that our company should not appear diminished, and so K'threen is to act as our third member."

"I am of a size with the Certain Someone whose name I am not to mention," the girl told Beth in a cheery, vivacious voice, "and so *I* was chosen to take his place in woodlander disguise. Father has *no sons*, but daughters *aplenty* to choose from, and *I* am the right size," she explained. "I have *five* sisters (may the stars shine brightly on me!) – *two* gemin older and *two* gemin younger as well as my sister Kelleyn, who is *nearly* as close as I to the Someone's age, but *I* was chosen over her, for I am a hand taller than she, though she is the elder! . . . Gemin run plentifully in my family," she added as an afterthought.

Beth, as yet, had said nothing, and it seemed late now for a "Hello" when so many other words had already sped by, so she forbore any type of greeting and hesitantly repeated, "Gemin?"

"Twins," Rendel explained, seeming a little puzzled. "I had thought the word *gemin* was of the ancient tongue."

"Oh, like Gemini, the constellation," Beth said, realizing instantaneously that the constellations of the Gwilldonian sky would be different. "And, uhm, I don't really know the ancient tongue. I never actually said I did, you know. I just know a few words. That's all." She felt unreasonably embarrassed.

"You have known what was needed," Rendel answered simply. "It is enough."

K'threen jumped back into the conversation. "*I* know words of the ancient tongue. *Many* of them. My family is of an ancient line," she informed Beth proudly, standing even taller. "The Rabirius *gens*. . . . Do you not think I fit well in these clothes? I saw the Someone-I-am-not-to-mention when he arrived in them – for I did not yet sleep. Father had been in such a state earlier that I *knew* something of *great* import would happen in the night, so I was watching for it from my bed, which I share with *too many sisters* – and I think I look much as he did then. The Someone, I mean, not Father."

The girl's face, Beth knew, could never be mistaken for Aron's, but it was true that she was as tall as the prince and anyone who had observed him only casually the day before might well be fooled. But if anyone had seen his face . . .

As if reading her thoughts, Rendel said, "She will keep her hat pulled down." He tugged forward the article in question and gave the girl a knowing smile, though she scarcely could have seen it, hidden as she then was. "*And* she will be holding her tongue!"

"I think disguises are *great* fun!" K'threen's voice announced with gusto from underneath the hat's brim.

"K'threen," Gweynleyn at last joined the conversation from the far side of the room, "this is no child's game. There may be risk."

"Oh, I *do* hope so!" the girl responded enthusiastically, tilting her head back so that her bright eyes showed in the shade of the hatbrim. "They *said* there might be, but I thought *perhaps* they had only said it to persuade me, though *I* was willing enough! I am *so* glad to hear *you* caution me as well, Lady, for I credit *you* speak only the *truth*! . . . What a wondrous day this will be!"

Gweynleyn had no immediate response to this exuberant speech, but the lady's maids (who had been provided by K'threen's father to honor his guest) exchanged amused and knowing glances.

It was time. They were to go to the Window of Light, from which Gweynleyn would address the crowd, already assembled. Beth knew little more than that, though Rendel seemed well enough informed. The "woodlander" party followed the lady out of the chamber, down the corridor in a direction that Beth had not yet gone. They were joined en route by two council members, Cassian Maris and Terilla (the latter having turned back from her expedition with Rostik when new, somewhat reassuring reports countered the one received earlier). Gweynleyn briefly introduced them to Rendel "and his companions" and then quickly claimed their attention with a discussion of what was about to take place.

The Window of Light, it turned out, was no window at all, but a long balcony looking out from the castle wall onto the open grounds of the enclosed city. Rendel and Beth took seats on a stone bench at one end of the balcony, K'threen keeping behind them, head lowered. Amazingly, she had not spoken a word since leaving Gweynleyn's chamber!

On the far end of the balcony were Myrmidon Tork (from whom Beth looked quickly away), Gydon, and a third man of their party whom Beth had not previously seen. He was not dressed in military garb, as the other two were, and she did not read the same cruelty in his face that she saw in theirs, but she didn't like the looks of him all the same. She didn't want to look at any of them and tried to pretend they weren't there. On the far side of the Tork party, close beside Myrmidon, a soldier in Gwilldonian uniform kept careful watch; nearer, on each side of the double doors that had led them all to the balcony, two more soldiers stood stiff and alert.

Looking above the open grounds to the parapets of the city wall, Beth noticed two of the Eyndeli among an assortment of guards. Their bows were lowered, but strung and ready. Though Beth was not in a position to see her, the third Eyndeli looked out from a window above her, studying the crowds closely.

Beth's gaze turned down then, and she leaned over the balustrade to see better what was below. The grounds of Greyvic were as thickly covered on this day as ever they had been. Everywhere, anxious faces turned upwards. Given the absence of microphones, Beth didn't see how those farther back in the audience could possibly hear anything said from the balcony, but then she realized that the most important members of the crowd (judging by dress, that is) were closer to the front or on raised platforms to the sides. She supposed the common citizens farther back could enjoy the spectacle as it happened and learn later on any details they'd missed, if they cared.

When Lady Gweynleyn stepped forward to the balcony railing, a great wave of cheers and whistles erupted from the masses. With a raised hand, she silenced them and then began to speak.

On behalf of the Council of Ten of Gwilldonum, she welcomed them all, hoped that their time in Greyvic had been pleasantly and perhaps even profitably spent, gave particular greetings to companies of travelers from the more distant regions, and ended with a special word for the Ferinians, whose alliance with Gwilldonum had for so long been strong and perfectly honored and had brought mutual benefits of great worth. Briefly but with apparent warmth, she welcomed Wastelanders and the company of the Torks, expressing hope that, despite the long period of estrangement and the sad history that had passed between their people and her own, harmonious relations could be established in time and that their children's children might look back to this very day as the beginning of that long process of change.

She did not introduce the individual members of the Council of Ten, as she might otherwise have done at that point, for she did not wish to draw attention to the continued absence of Harac and Daasa. She did, however, motion forward and introduce the council's newest member, Terilla of the Gilmarch, asking her to speak a few words to the crowd. While Terilla spoke, Gweynleyn used the time to search the crowds more thoroughly for any sign of Therin, Luke, or the others.

Gweynleyn introduced next Cassian Maris, who would bring greetings from and news of the coastal regions, whose contact with the more central regions of Gwilldonum was regrettably limited. Before Cassian could begin his speech, however, a voice from the crowd called out, "It's not him we want to hear. It's the Tork. Let *him* speak!"

"In time, sir," Gweynleyn answered with a dazzling smile in the general direction from which the gruff voice had come, for the individual who had called out did not make himself plainly visible.

Obviously amending what he had originally intended to say, Cassian spoke rather disjointedly and hurried himself along. Beth was sorry he did so; she wanted to stall as long as possible.

Nobody had *promised* to keep Aron hidden until Luke and Aynyxia appeared, though Beth had insisted that they ought to. Her friends would be under Therin's protection, Gweynleyn had told her; she need not fear. But what if something went wrong? What if the false guard still thought Luke was the champion and was keeping him alive only so they could use him to discover the anointed child? Once Aron had revealed himself . . .

Cassian concluded his speech and the crowd at once began to call for Myrmidon to speak. There were only a few voices at first, but they were dispersed throughout the assembly, giving the impression of a greater number. Soon, the number *was* greater and individual voices became lost in a clamorous sea.

"Peace," Gweynleyn called out loudly, raising her hand and saying no more until the crowd had quieted. While waiting, she looked discreetly toward Beth, who knew what the lady was thinking: she could not delay longer; she must introduce one or the other – Aron or Myrmidon. When her voice could be heard, she said loudly but calmly, "The Council of Ten is aware of the concerns of our peoples with respect to the seat of the *princeps*.

Rest assured that we share these concerns. We will—" She stopped, her attention drawn to some commotion off to the side of the assembly.

Many in the audience turned toward the source of the distraction (though only a handful could find it through the crowd) and wondered what had interrupted the lady . . . . Of course! It was the Captain of the Guard. *He* drew looks (even Lady Gweynleyn's, apparently) wherever he passed. And with him was Harac of the Council, whose absence had been noted by many. But the stranger between them . . . Who was that lad? A cheerful sort, it seemed, for his eyes could not have been brighter nor his smile broader, though closer observers guessed that the scratches across his cheek were fresh and that the bruise on his forehead must smart!

At the sight of Luke, Beth nearly jumped out of her seat, but Rendel's hand held her back. Quickly her eyes found Aynyxia, who seemed well enough, but not Daasa and none of the false guard. (Therin had, in fact, taken one prisoner, but that one was already safely on his way to the Greyvic dungeon.) Beth looked back at Luke. He had found her quickly, woodlander clothing and all, and as soon as he knew that she was returning his gaze, he lifted his hand high and gave a clear "thumbs up."

Myrmidon Tork, now leaning forward and fixing his attention on the lad, did not realize that Luke was looking at Beth; rather, he took the strange gesture as some sort of signal to Gweynleyn, who looked extraordinarily well-pleased at the sight of it. "This bodes ill, whatever it means," thought the Tork. His eyes returned to the newcomers and this time he spotted a walkabout, barely visible amongst the others. A walkabout in the company of Therin Mandek and a dwarf. She must be the one. And that meant that the boy must be . . .

"Show no surprise," Gweynleyn said covertly to Cassian Maris and Terilla, who looked surprised indeed at her words. She had turned aside to address them, but at once turned back to the crowd.

"My friends," she recommenced, and the murmurings that had rippled over the assembly during the pause now dissipated almost instantaneously. The stillness was remarkable; the anticipation, electric. "The Council of Ten knows and shares your concerns," she repeated, "and on this day – on this day to be marked and remembered in the history of our land – we shall answer them. I speak to you on behalf of all the council – Harac, son of Aracac the Swift and Harana the Victorious; Blom, daughter of Asiza; Daasa of the Great Wood of the Westmarch; Cassian Maris of the coastal regions; Quillin Q'en of the Meadowlands; Merk of the Nether Woods; Terilla of the Gilmarch; and Jeron Rabirius of this fine city." Gweynleyn was no longer stretching out her words in order to gain time and delay Aron's appearance; this recitation of names, delivered slowly, deliberately, and with a rising voice, was intended instead to build the anticipation of the assembly even further and bring the full weight of the great names of Gwilldonum into her momentous announcement. "And I speak on behalf of Rane of the Brenmarch, of cherished memory, who would stand proudly with us today had not the darkest treachery stolen him from our company and from the company of those *faithful* Brenmarchers whom he called friends. And I speak for myself, Gweynleyn Arana, daughter of Gwilldonum, when I say to you that the great day has come, the day you have awaited with patience *for ten years and more*" — a current vibrated through the crowd and loud gasps were heard, but voices were otherwise remarkably silent — "the day when all things will be made right. The day of the *princeps*!" She stepped aside and back, Cassian Maris and Terilla moving with her.

The wide double doors swung suddenly open. Through them burst Jeron Rabirius and a remarkably similar-looking young man (his nephew), both with swords drawn and held high. They separated and then between them passed His Highness – soon to be His Majesty – Aron Sterling, who strode at once to the edge of the balcony to show himself to the waiting crowds.

He looked magnificent! His clothes, of dazzling gold and the purest white, boasted the royal crest, having been brought from the wardrobes of Arystar by a hope-filled Lady Gweynleyn. His hair (which Beth had last seen in a dirty and matted state after their days of hard travel) was perfectly groomed and lustrous in the light of the morning sun. A golden braid of twine encircled his head like a crown. Everything he wore was new to him, save a ring on his hand (concealed within it were the finest strands of a white wolf's fur), an heirloom of his mother's on a chain around his neck, and the sword and swordbelt given him by Sir Alric (retrieved the night before from Sereynel of Newwood by one of Jeron's servants).

As he leaned forward in view of all, Beth worried for his safety, remembering Gweynleyn's comment days before about an assassin's arrow. But if Aron had any similar worry, she saw no trace of it. Neither fear nor hesitation marked his face. Gone was the vulnerable boy Beth had come to know in these last days, the boy who had confided misgivings and fears. In his place stood a king.

The crowd saw what Beth saw – the confidence, bearing, and splendor of a king – and it went wild at the sight. The young prince waited, smiling composedly, while the clamor of cheers, whistles, and victory cries grew before him. All the while, he did not look around the balcony itself, glancing neither toward his friends on the right nor toward his enemies on the left. Several minutes passed before he raised his hand and could at last speak into the quieted air.

"I am Aron Sterling," his strong voice rang out into the autumn air, "son of Arandella the Beloved, daughter of DarQuinn the Good, of the House of William Princeps, the Aethling, the Law-Giver.

"I am Aron Sterling, chosen and anointed to be King of Gwilldonum, High King of the Southlands, Protector of the Thessalyn Islands.

"I am Aron Sterling, and I greet you, my peoples, whom I swear to lead and protect with all my might, with justice and in accordance with the laws of our ancestors. Together, we will stand strong, we will cultivate peace in every region within our borders, and we will face unflinchingly any menace that comes to us from without. For a time our trials may be great, but our victories will be all the greater.

"I am Aron Sterling, and I am come this day to make all things right in the land of our fathers and our mothers, the land of our children and of our children's children."

The crowd roared.

The city had gone wild. Beth and Rendel (ostensibly followed by K'threen, though the girl stopped repeatedly to greet acquaintances) could barely make their way through the boisterous crowd, a good percentage of which had wasted no time in beginning to drink to the health of the *princeps*. After the first few minutes, Beth had taken over the lead, judging that she was

351

willing, in the present circumstances, to be a bit pushier than Rendel (and certainly more focused than K'threen!). The three were trying to find their way to the spot where they had spied Luke and Aynyxia.

After Aron had addressed the assembly from the Window of Light, Myrmidon Tork had been given, as promised, an opportunity to do the same, though the speech he made was certainly not the one he had rehearsed so many times in his mind. A clever man, he'd made his revisions quickly, but it had taken all his efforts to conceal the fury within him. He'd welcomed the prince of Gwilldonum (the *young* prince, as he'd stressed) and added his own expressions of joy to those of the crowd. How fortunate were the peoples of Gwilldonum, he'd proclaimed, to have before them *at last* the *princeps* they had so *long* desired and now so *desperately* needed in the face of the many trials known to them all! He trusted that it would not take much time at all before the prince had the experience necessary to steer his peoples well in such difficult straits. But the fickle crowd gave Myrmidon no chance to undermine their new favorite any more than this, interrupting his speech with calls of "Hail, Prince Aron!" and "The *princeps* has returned!" and "Long may he reign!"

After the speech, there was no question of Beth's having even a brief word with Aron, for his duties became his master at once, and he disappeared into the depths of the castle with Gweynleyn, Jeron, and the other council members, while the soldiers kept close to the Torks, watching them closely until Therin could get to them with further orders. The Captain of the Guard arrived, in fact, almost at once, having left Luke and Aynyxia behind (Harac had gone directly to the Great Hall, where he knew the council would assemble). Beth doubted whether her friends would so effortlessly be able to make their way through the mob and past the guards to reach the balcony, so she leaned over the balcony railing and signaled to them to wait where they were until she could get to them.

It was no easy task, but she managed it in due course. She reached Aynyxia first and gave her a big hug, but before Beth could tell Luke how glad she was to see him, K'threen, seemingly reappearing out of midair, careened into him, words rolling off her tongue at once. "Oh, my *apologies*, sir. You are Luke, are you not? I have heard *much* about you. They were waiting for you to arrive, as you must know, because you were claiming" —her voice dropped— "we-must-not-say-what" —her voice rose again— "and they wished to be assured of your safe return before the prince declared himself. Princes do not *always* wait on others in such matters, do they? *You* must be uncommonly esteemed . . . and you are very nice-looking, are you not?" she added, just struck by the thought. "He is, is he not, Beth?" Catching sight of Aynyxia, she grabbed her hand and began to shake it vigorously, exclaiming, "Oh, and *you* are the walkabout! I am K'threen Rabirius. Of the Rabirius *gens*. I am *most* honored to meet you, and you are *most* welcome to Greyvic! *Oh!*" she exclaimed suddenly. "You are not *offended* that I should take your hand, are you? I am *sadly* ignorant of the customs of your kind, but *most* desirous of being schooled by you in such matters. . . . Are you hungry?" This question she addressed to Luke, to whom she had unexpectedly returned her attention.

"I . . . uh . . . I'm starved," he answered, staring at the girl in wonder. He gave Beth a quizzical look, but she just smiled and said, "Hi!" She was too quiet and the crowd was too loud for him actually to hear the word (though K'threen's voice had somehow carried over the din), but Luke jerked his head upward in response, reminding Beth in a flash of the first day they had met.

"Then *surely* we should seek *sustenance!*" K'threen told Beth urgently, as if the two of them had been remiss in their duties. "We could go to the Great Hall where there will be food *aplenty*, but it will take us *an age* to get there (and no *doubt* the council will be talking over everything in great, boring detail), but *I* know every *inch* of Greyvic, so *I* will find us something *at once!*" Already she was leading them off, and they were soon ducking into the nearby and alliterative Tail of a Tenrec Tavern, where the crowd was even thicker indoors than it was out.

"I haven't a space for you and your friends, little miss," the proprietress told K'threen. "We're that crowded!"

"*I* know how we shall find a spot," the girl answered, undaunted. "Like thieves at night, we shall sneak into your upper room, unseen by any but yourself!"

"Oh, no, dear, not even for you," the proprietress replied hastily. "The reeve's insisted we close it off. The floor's all broken up in that room as you well know and could crumble right under your feet! I can't have your lot risking their necks in such a way, making no mention of what might happen to those underneath you in a fall!"

"Oh, Madam *Boss*," K'threen answered, dismissing the woman's concerns, "we are all *great* adventurers! A perilous floor is nothing to *us*! And we shall keep *well* over to the corner by the stairwell, so there will be *none* of your customers in jeopardy below even *should* we be fortunate enough to experience the thrill of a collapse! *Is* this not the best plan?" She beamed at her own ingenuity.

The proprietress hesitated, but apparently found firm refusal too taxing a task. "Oh, well, dear, I suppose. . .But, keep to that one corner, mind you!"

Soon Beth and Luke found themselves huddled next to each other on one of the safer-looking patches of floor in the corner of a dusty, ill-repaired second-story room of the tavern. Not an ideal spot for a reunion, but they could at least hear one another speak without shouting and there was no one to bump them, step on their toes, or spill drinks on their jackets (the latter had already happened twice to Luke), and, best of all, they were served food and drink with remarkable speed, despite the crowd below. (It was useful to be accompanied by the daughter of Jeron Rabirius while in Greyvic, Beth noticed.) Luke, who had not eaten since early morning, lunged for the food.

To no one's surprise, K'threen's voice dominated the conversation, but the pairs of friends who had been separated had a chance to hear a little of one another's adventures all the same. Beth told Luke about dressing like a woodlander to enter the castle with Aron. She learned in turn that Therin's company had delayed its rescue mission until quite late the previous day and that it had brought back a single prisoner to Greyvic. Presumably that meant that the other two false guards had been killed, but Luke didn't specifically say so. In fact, Luke seemed reluctant to discuss the details of the battle at all, summing up the events by saying, "Well, we made it here, didn't we?"

Rendel and Aynyxia said little, but K'threen never suffered a loss for words. "She just never stops, does she?" Luke whispered to Beth while the girl in question was distracted.

"Only when she has to," Beth answered, thinking of how silent K'threen had been on the way to the balcony. "I like her, though," she added simply.

"You like everyone," Luke replied before stuffing in another mouthful of food.

"Not everyone." Beth's voice was low and grave, and Luke cast her a quizzical look.

"I met him," she answered faintly. "Myrmidon Tork." She was spared saying more because K'threen's attention suddenly ricocheted back to them.

Before long, the five of them were out among the crowds again. Not long after that, they separated.

When only a few yards from the tavern door, Rendel caught sight of Sereynel and called to her. Somehow she heard him through the commotion and came running, throwing herself at him with a great embrace and an affectionate kiss. Beth watched the two with considerable interest, while Luke watched Beth with the same. Sereynel next embraced and kissed Aynyxia (though not quite so greatly or so affectionately), she nodded and smiled cheerfully at Beth, and Rendel made introductions for those who hadn't previously met. Almost at once, Sereynel begged leave of the others to take Rendel and Aynyxia away with her to greet mutual friends. Rendel suggested that they all go together, but by then K'threen had spotted three of her sisters in a different direction and the girl *mightily* desired that as *many* of her sisters as possible meet *both* Luke and Beth as *soon* as it could *possibly* be arranged. So the group split into two, all its members agreeing to meet again in front of the tavern in an hour's time.

K'threen's sisters spoke pleasantly enough to Beth when introduced, but in little time turned all their attention to her male friend; in moments, Beth found herself inadvertently squeezed out of a tight circle that had Luke as its focus. The oldest girls were fifteen-year-old twins and Beth couldn't tell them apart, not even by their clothes or the way they talked. She could only distinguish between them because of their jewelry – Kyrynn was the sister with a blue stone at the end of her pendant and Kerinna had a green; their rings were a little different too, but they matched in style and looked like they were meant to fit together like a puzzle (the design reminded her of something, but she didn't stop to think what). Both girls were clearly flirting with Luke and he was clearly enjoying it, though a few of the girls' comments flustered him momentarily. The scene amused Beth no end, and she couldn't wait to give Luke a hard time about it later. She could already hear in her head some of the things she could say.

After some minutes of this, Beth was surprised to find a young boy tugging at her sleeve and motioning for her to lean close toward him. She did, and he told her that she was to meet Mariza, her ladyship's attendant, by the gate of the Red Tower. He pointed across the wide square toward an entryway (raised on a slope and tall enough in any event to be easily visible over the heads of the crowd) that seemed to lead to one of the castle towers. Long red flags draped either side of it. "Go alone," he said. "You're not to draw attention." He spoke carefully, apparently having memorized his message. Then he disappeared into the crowd, not even hesitating when she called after him to wait.

Beth had watched too many movies not to feel some suspicion at the words "Go alone," but they were not, on the other hand, terribly surprising words under the circumstances. She could see that there might still be good reason for her to keep a low profile. She looked toward the Red Tower gate and saw nothing particularly sinister. It was so much higher up than the spot where she stood that she was able to make out castle guards stationed close by it and could see that the crowds were thinner there, but not too thin. It looked safe enough, she decided, and it was really very close. She'd probably even be able to see back to where Luke and the girls were. She'd make a point of being especially careful. She wouldn't actually go *into* the gate or stand in any shadows. She'd wait well away from the archway itself, out in plain view where Mariza could come find her. She wouldn't go anywhere with anyone else. That seemed reasonable enough. And it was, after all, broad daylight. (At home, Beth didn't even like walking around the mall alone, but she had grown into a somewhat different person here.)

"I'll meet you in front of the tavern," she said close to Luke's ear.

"Yeah, OK." he answered distractedly, not taking his eyes from K'threen's sister Kyrynn.

"The Tail of the Tenrec," Beth clarified, not sure he had registered her first words, "Right in front."

"Tail of the Tenrec. In front. Got it." He had half-turned his head while repeating the words, so she figured that was good

356

enough. After only two steps, though, she turned back to add, "I'm meeting Mariza by the Red Tower gate." Just to be sure.

That time, she caught his full attention. He turned quickly to ask whether he should go with her, but someone nearby yelled just then, covering his words, and someone else knocked Kyrynn into him (not that she much minded), and she needed an unreasonable amount of assistance from him to regain her balance. By then, Beth was gone.

Though the Red Tower was so near, the massive, shifting crowd kept Beth from being able to pick out Luke when she looked back for him. At a safe distance from the castle entry (but near enough to be in view should Mariza be watching for her from within), Beth looked through the open gateway but could not make out any figure awaiting her in the shadows. People periodically emerged and disappeared through the gate, but none paid particular attention to her.

Beth was resolved not to go through the gateway without someone she already knew and trusted. Even with people coming and going, she couldn't be certain that to do so would be safe. Her eyes were accustomed to the bright outdoor light and at present all she could see beyond the gates was darkness. She had hoped Mariza would be already here waiting, but the boy hadn't specifically said that she would be. He'd only said that Beth should meet her there. Maybe she simply hadn't arrived yet. Beth supposed she should just wait a while – not too long, though. She would still meet the others at the tavern as planned.

There were vendors and entertainers around, and Beth got distracted for a time by a juggler who was very good and told jokes that, though she understood only a few of them, must have been quite funny, for many people laughed heartily. Nearby, three cute dogs of unusual color performed clever tricks for a large, caped woman (who wore seven scarves that Beth could count and three times as much jewelry as Beth owned). When the tricks were over, Beth realized that several minutes must have passed since she'd last looked about for Mariza. Maybe even ten minutes.

Or more?

By now, she was fairly certain that something wasn't right about the message she had received, but, she reassured herself with satisfaction, she hadn't fallen into any trap. She hadn't gone through the gateway to find that someone besides Mariza had summoned her. *Go alone!* Those words were never a good sign! Despite her brave front, she'd been afraid that going off on her own had been a foolish mistake. But nothing bad had happened. She should have been watching more carefully, of course, not letting her attention get so thoroughly taken up by the entertainers, but no harm done. Nothing bad had come from her being separated from Luke.

But then the words repeated themselves in her mind. *Separated from Luke.*

Separated from *Luke!*

A flash of cold panic struck her. *Idiot!* Quickly, she began to push through the crowd back to the spot where she had left the others, reasoning furiously as she went.

If someone had laid a trap, maybe it wasn't for her! It was *Luke* who had claimed to be the champion. But, think . . . who knew that? Only the false guard, and they were all— That prisoner! What if that prisoner had gotten word to Myrmidon? Or maybe Myrmidon just guessed. So many people saw Luke arrive with Therin! What if the Torks believed Luke was the champion? What if they were trying to get *him* alone, not her? But why? Aron had already shown himself. Fear of something else he might know or do? Revenge? Revenge. The Torks certainly seemed like the vengeful type!

But Luke hadn't been alone. Rabirius girls had surrounded him. They'd been practically *glued* to him! But where? She should have found him by now. Everyone had shifted around, but she was pretty sure she was back in the spot where she'd left Luke and the sisters. She turned toward the Red Tower. It *looked* right. She *thought* she'd first seen it from this angle.

So, where were they?

"*K'threen!*" Beth thought anxiously. "You didn't leave him alone, did you?"

K'threen had not wanted to leave Luke alone and she'd told her sisters so. "You heard what the messenger said," answered her sister Kelleyn. "We must go at once. We are to be presented to Prince Aron!" It had already occurred to Kelleyn, who had learned of Aron's existence in the early hours of the morning, that although the prince was yet too young to be married, he was not too young for betrothal into a suitable family such as her own. He had the future of his kingdom to think of, after all. (Kelleyn was only about Beth's age, but had been very much influenced in her thinking by her elder sisters.)

K'threen, whose instincts were in many respects excellent, repeated that she did not wish to leave Luke alone, but her three sisters chided her for thinking her services so necessary for such an obviously capable young man. The young girl yielded, and took her leave with the others . . . but not before Luke asked which gate was the Red Tower one.

No one. There were people and creatures all about her, but not one that Beth knew. She made her way quickly toward the tavern. She could see the sign clearly. The Tail of the Tenrec. Then she saw the door. Next she should see Luke, waiting somewhere close by it. But she didn't. He wasn't there.

He couldn't have been there, actually, because by the time Beth reached the tavern Luke was no longer within the walls of Greyvic.

When the sisters left him, Luke had turned at once toward the Red Tower, certain by then that he should not have let Beth go off alone. (What had he been thinking?) He had been delayed immediately by a spontaneous parade of revelers who had linked arms and were singing slurred songs in honor of the prince. Anxious about Beth, he'd pushed his way through in a most uncivil manner. At once, he'd been held up again, this time by a tall figure that had barreled into him. Though the accident had not been Luke's fault, he'd muttered an automatic "Sorry!" and tried to get by, but the figure had blocked him again. Looking up, Luke had recognized the other's face and thought at once that this encounter was no accident. An instant later, feeling a sudden grip on his arm and finding the sharp end of a knife close to his chest, he'd been certain of it.

CHAPTER TWENTY-SIX – Myrmidon Tork

What was Beth to do?

She'd seen the direction Rendel and Aynyxia had gone. Probably Sereynel had taken them to the woodlanders' encampment outside the city walls. But with the crowd, it would take so long to get there and then even longer to find her friends. Maybe if she waited, right there in front of the tavern, Luke would just turn up and everything would be fine . . . but that's not what she expected. More and more she felt gripped by the certainty that Luke was in trouble.

Madam Boss, the proprietress, came out of the tavern door just then and recognized Beth. "Oh, it's you, dear one. Wanting to come in for a little something more? We're not quite so full now, at last. . . . Just came out for a bit of air, myself. They've been running me ragged all week, but today's been the worst. Not that I ought to be complaining! Sometimes I think we do more business during the festival than the whole rest of the year together!" She settled herself onto a wide windowsill and fanned herself with the hem of her apron.

"Madam Boss," Beth said, "do you remember the boy – the young man – who was with us earlier? Not the woodlander, the other one." With so many faces in and out all day, she didn't really expect the woman to remember, but Madam Boss did remember, it seemed.

"Yes, I've got a good eye for faces. Helps in my business. Fine-looking lad with a cheery smile. Looked like he'd been in a bit of a brush-up."

"Yes! Have you seen him? Since then, I mean."

"Aye, I did." Her tone had changed and there was something disapproving about it. "Didn't think he'd be the type," she muttered.

"What do you mean? What type?"

"Oh, nothing. Don't mind me. Not for me to judge, I'm sure."

"No, it's important," Beth insisted. "What type? What did you see?"

"Type to be cavorting about with them Torks! Can't abide them myself, though I've been serving their type same as the others all week, whenever they wander themselves i-"

"You saw Luke with some of the Torks?" Beth would have interrupted sooner, but Madam Boss's words had come as a shock. She felt sick in her stomach, like she might throw up.

"Aye. Went off with *one* of them, at least. One of them what was up at the Window with the rest of them. The captain, they tell me."

"The Tork captain?" Beth repeated. "*Luke went away somewhere with the Tork captain? Where? Which way?*"

"Through the East Gate." She pointed and Beth saw the gate in question. "Smiling and laughing, they were."

"Are you sure? My friend was laughing? Can you remember *exactly* how he looked?" Beth was so obviously worried that Madam Boss, a kindly soul, gave serious consideration to the question.

"Well . . ." A clouded look came over her face. "Now that you ask. . . . I'd have to say *he* wasn't laughing. Just the captain was, but in a way that made it seem they were sharing some good joke together. But your friend . . . well, he was smiling . . . but sort of weak-like, now that I reflect on it, as if he was forcing himself a bit. Looked kind of peaky, in fact." Even the proprietress was becoming troubled now.

"How long ago was it?"

"Not long. I'd come out to get some air, just like now. But someone called me back in with a question. I took care of it in just a minute or two and came back out, and there you were."

Beth was considering quickly. How long had they been talking? A couple of minutes? But you could get far in a couple of minutes! And she must have waited at least two minutes before Madam Boss had come out. She had to go after them now! She couldn't look for help first, or she'd lose them.

"Something was wrong then?' Madam Boss hadn't been very quick about the situation, but she'd worked it out at last. "Oh,

361

you're not saying the captain took him unwilling! And I watched him do it! Oh, the poor boy! The p—"

"Get a message to K'threen. Or Rendel or Aynyxia who were here with us." Beth rushed the words out. "*Please*. They'll pay you, if you want. Tell them what you told me. . . . Or Therin Mandek, or Harac – from the council," she called back, for she was already trying to run toward the East Gate, heedless of the number of times she pushed some unsuspecting bystander out of her way.

"I will, I will," promised Madam Boss. "I'm so sorry!"

Beth was too far to hear.

Two guards were stationed near the gate, but they seemed more boisterous than watchful, chatting and laughing along with the celebrating throng. Beth supposed that either the Tork captain had simply passed by unnoticed, or the guards had seen him and let him pass anyway. Neither scenario recommended them. Perhaps they were even supporters of the Torks, like the guard last night obviously had been. Beth decided not to approach them with questions, but to slip past while their attention was diverted. Probably they didn't even care who was going *out* of Greyvic, she realized as she moved beyond the city walls.

Once outside the east gate, Beth was confronted by a scene much different from the one she'd encountered on the west side the day before. No encampments here. A large barren expanse stretched before her. She could see far ahead and was fairly certain that Gydon and Luke could not have passed out of sight in that direction in the few minutes they must have had. Unless . . . what if there'd been horses waiting? She looked for fresh hoof prints and saw none, but she was hardly an expert in tracking.

But not all the guards that patrolled the walls of the city could be shirking their duties! Surely an alarm would've gone out if they had spotted Gydon riding away. The captain must know that his Tork clothes would stand out, even from a distance. He wouldn't have gone east, she decided, horses or no horses. Same applied to the south, where he'd definitely be noticed. And why go east or south anyway? But north . . . . The Torks had come in from the northwest, she knew, and no doubt they would be sent away in the same direction. Probably immediately, she realized suddenly. Now that the question of the *princeps* was settled, Therin Mandek would waste no time in escorting his enemy out of his land. Maybe that's why there were so few guards about; they were probably rounding up the Tork company or joining the escort unit.

She looked north. Myrmidon and Gydon would be leaving . . . and maybe they wanted to carry Luke away with them somehow!

North. It was the only reasonable choice. Facing that direction, she saw that there was cover there – a thick, wooded patch that might keep them out of view of the guards on the wall. As she looked, a flock of birds suddenly burst out from among distant trees and dispersed into the blue afternoon sky. Maybe it was only some forest animal that had scared them off . . . but maybe not.

Beth ran.

She discovered them in a gully where Myrmidon had impatiently awaited the captain. The Tork leader had smugly escaped Therin's watch, thanks to a diversionary tactic and knowledge of a hidden passage (his supporters, though suddenly fewer, were varied and useful), but he knew he had little time. Gydon had found him quickly, half-dragging Luke behind.

Beth was hidden, but she could view the scene well enough. Myrmidon and Gydon were on foot, their restless horses secured close at hand. Between the Tork cousins stood Luke, fear and fresh bruises on his face. His hands were behind his back, apparently tied. But he had turned his head to look squarely at Myrmidon, who was addressing him with angry contempt.

"I am well informed, you see. . . . Did it amuse you, leading them on a merry chase?"

Beth's eyes and mind worked fast. With darting looks, she took in the situation, searched for anything that might help. She ruled out immediately the possibility of going for help. She knew that whatever Myrmidon would do, he would do quickly. Certainly Therin Mandek would be searching for him, as he must know. If she'd had her bow, she'd have at least considered the possibility of an assault from where she hid – maybe trying to move about to make it appear that she had not come alone. But she had neither bow nor quiver, though the sword from Gribb remained safely concealed beneath her woodlander clothes. . . . Her woodlander clothes. They had already given her some protection, for, as she knew firsthand, the Torks scorned Rendel's kind.

"I would prefer to take you back with us," Myrmidon was now saying. "I am certain you would find our hospitality . . . noteworthy. But that is not possible, and our 'escort' wishes to waste no time in washing its hands of us and no doubt is already disturbed by our absence . . . so a quick penalty for your interference and your insolence must suffice." Myrmidon had held his rage in check since morning, but he intended to find it an outlet in Luke. From behind, Gydon gave Luke a hard blow to the head. Luke, hands tied in back of him, was unable to catch himself as he stumbled forward and hit the ground. He landed at the feet of Myrmidon, who kicked him away with the heel of his boot.

"*Stop it!*" yelled Beth, leaping up and rushing into open space.

Myrmidon's eyes found her at once, and his expression, momentarily altered, became quite smug again as he recognized her clothes and face. "I know you," he said. "The *woodlander* girl." He sneered, as if the words comprised an insult. He motioned to his companion, who began to advance toward Beth. "Am I to obey you?" Myrmidon mocked her. "A *woodlander*, unarmed, alone—"

As Gydon neared Beth, he raised his sword but not with haste, for the girl had not flinched – she would not run and he knew her kind would not fight. Cutting her down would be almost too easy to give pleasure.

He moved slowly . . . but Beth did not. As soon as he was in striking distance, she swiftly drew her sword – her beautiful, magical sword, which could be hidden in a sheath the length of a hunting knife – and she swung as hard as she could at Gydon's weapon, scarcely taking the trouble to aim. And then . . .

A wondrous thing occurred! Once drawn and set in motion, the sword found its own mark. As if pulled by a magnet, it flew to its counterpart, dealing it a crashing blow, liberating it from its master's hand, and sending it flying nearly a dozen feet away into the brush. The captain himself dropped to his knees as if struck, and he grabbed at his trembling swordhand, trying in vain to steady it. The man himself had not been touched, but when Beth's sword had hit his own, a great shock had shot from his fingertips to his shoulder.

Stunned, Gydon stared at Beth, and she stared back, trying belatedly to hide her own surprise, which surpassed his. That she would draw the sword this time and not the dagger, she had somehow known. That she would be able to wield it against another living being, she had been *nearly* certain. But that it would have a power all its own, that *it* would guide *her* rather than the reverse, that she would feel in her own body, when steel met steel, a shock like that of an electric charge . . . for any of that, she had been unprepared.

"I know that blade," breathed Myrmidon. She had forgotten him in the instant of her surprise and now turned quickly in his direction lest he come on her unawares. But he did not have the look of one about to attack. Amazingly, he was stunned, immobile, maybe fearful.

Though not understanding all that lay behind the fact, Beth saw that the upper hand was temporarily hers, and she spoke with confidence (or something that imitated it sufficiently well) as she responded to his earlier comment. "Actually, sir, I am *not* a woodlander . . . and, as you see, I am not unarmed." She aimed her sword in his direction, holding it with two hands and hoping to keep it steady, for his gaze was fixed on it and she understood intuitively that the weapon itself, more than what it had done, was the source of his fear. Then, inspired and pressing her luck, she tried a bluff. "*And,* I am not alone."

No one was more surprised than Beth to hear the subsequent whoosh of an arrow as it sped past her, well over Luke's head but not far from Myrmidon's, before sticking fast into a tree beyond. She steeled her expression and dared not look behind her. Myrmidon looked and saw no one, but his course was decided and he lost not a second of time. In an instant, he was on his horse, reins in hand, and his companion, still shaken, was hurrying to retrieve his own weapon and follow his master's lead.

Positioned to ride, some of Myrmidon's composure returned. "Have him! He is less than nothing to me." He gestured toward Luke, but looked toward Beth, his eyes darting between her sword and her face. Then, the light of understanding dawning for him, he uttered, "You! . . . *You* are the champion of Gwilldonum!" For a moment, rage flooded through him again and it looked as if he would advance on her, but he remembered the hidden archer somewhere beyond her. No doubt there were others as well. Prudence restrained him, but the muscles of his face and the veins of his neck reflected the effort it cost him. Fixing his dark, blazing eyes on Beth's face as if memorizing every line and hue of it, he spoke in a low, menacing voice. "I will leave here, for a time. But I assure you that my absence will not be a permanent one. . . . And I will not forget you," he promised. Then, slowly and intensely, "I will *never* forget you." With a fierce kick against his horse's flanks, he turned and rode off, followed at once by his captain.

Beth exhaled deeply and her whole body began to shake, as if from a strong feverish chill. With difficulty, she returned her sword to her sheath and somehow made her way to Luke, asking when she had, "Are you OK?" Only then did she realize that tears had begun to run down her face. She dropped to her knees beside him, shivering from emotion.

Luke had maneuvered himself into a sitting position by then, legs folded beneath him, hands still tied behind. "I've gotta say I've been better," he answered breathily. He looked pale, perspiration had streaked the dirt on his face, his forehead was scraped and bruised, and a trickle of blood ran from the side of his mouth. Even sitting, he swayed a little, but he managed to smile weakly. "And did I mention that I'm kinda glad to see you?" he added.

She tried to return his smile, recognizing the words that she had said to him some days – or an eternity – before, but she didn't have it in her to respond in the light manner he had then. She couldn't speak at all.

Her hands had steadied enough by then to allow her to work at his bonds, but she turned sharply when her eyes caught movement off to the side. It was the hidden archer, now in plain view. It was Rendel.

He had not made straight for them but had moved to a better vantage point for observing Myrmidon's retreat. "I expect they are joining the others," he concluded. "They would not be such fools at to defy Therin any further while their numbers are so few. We have no more to fear from the Torks at present."

When Rendel and Beth had between them freed Luke's hands and Luke had begun to rub at his wrists, Beth asked wearily, "Should we go after them?" She knew what she wanted the answer to be.

"No. We could not catch them on foot, but I believe it would be better in any event to get word to Therin Mandek and let him do what he deems best." Touching his hand lightly to her shoulder, he said gently, "Your part is over, Beth."

366

Then Rendel began to examine Luke's wrists, his face, and the back of his head. As he did so, Luke inquired, "So, *you* shot the arrow?" Rendel indicated that he had, though the answer was obvious; the woodlander had approached them carrying Beth's bow, which he had brought back for her from the Newwooder encampment. "And did you hit what you were aiming for?" Again, Rendel indicated that he had. "Glad to hear it," said Luke, beginning to sound a bit more like himself, "because for a second there, I thought maybe you'd been aiming for me."

"For a second there," answered Rendel, who some time before had come to appreciate Luke's sense of humor and wordplay, "maybe I was." Luke searched the woodlander's face but didn't find the trace of a smile. "Luke, Luke, Luke," Rendel laughed, imitating the way he had once heard Luke speak to Beth, "you should know me better than that by now." He stood, extended his hand, and pulled Luke up as well.

"Is it really over?" asked Beth, who hadn't spoken for a couple of minutes.

Rendel's eyes turned automatically to the direction Myrmidon had taken. The Tork would not so easily abandon his ambitions, he was sure; the day's events had marked a significant setback for him but not final defeat. The real battle still lay ahead—maybe months ahead, maybe years. But to Beth, Rendel said only, "Yes."

"Good," said Luke. "So, Beth," he begged his best friend, who sat immobile on the hard ground, "can we *please* go home now?"

They returned to Greyvic's castle and reported their encounter with Myrmidon to as many council members as they could find. Harac, Blom, and the bandaged Daasa had accompanied the Council Guard to see the Tork company (once its leader had rejoined it) safely out of Gwilldonum. Gweynleyn was also absent, and no one seemed to know where she might be found, but Jeron Rabirius and the remaining council members were present to hear Luke's story.

"A rider will be sent with a message for Therin Mandek," said Jeron, "but it may not reach him before Myrmidon and his company have crossed into Ferinia, for the border is not far. Therin was greatly vexed that the Tork escaped his company's watch for a time, but I credit that he will attempt no retaliation now, as mightily as he would enjoy arresting Myrmidon and his captain and throwing them both into a dungeon cell to rot. The snake has revealed his true nature, but it was no secret to any of us here, was it? And his offense against this boy," he indicated Luke, "was a minor one. The rough handling of a lad is slight pretext for the arrest of a ruling lord – particularly one who still has support among us and among our neighbors. No, the timing is not right for so weighty a step. Our first business is to purge our ranks; then we will be better equipped to give the Tork his due as the occasion arises." Addressing Luke directly, he added, "We all regret the incident, I am sure, but here you are, safe and sound. No real harm, was there?"

Easy for you to say, thought Luke, but aloud he said nothing. He was ready to be done with everything Gwilldonian and just go home. He hadn't felt that way all along, but he felt it now. No matter how minor an offense it seemed to Jeron Rabirius, Myrmidon's "rough handling" had added a new color to the whole adventure business, and it wasn't a pretty one.

When Luke raised the question of his and Beth's departure, which he did at once, all present agreed that it was Gweynleyn who should advise them, though the matter might need to be delayed until morning for she did not presently seem to be in the castle. "Advise us? *Advise* us?" repeated Luke to Beth when they were alone. "I don't want her to *advise* us, I want her to point us to the nearest transport system and hand us our tickets home!"

Beth regarded him thoughtfully and said, "It was pretty bad for you, wasn't it?"

He looked away, swallowed, and answered, "Let's just say that if I ever list the best afternoons of my life, today's won't make it into the top ten thousand! . . . And what about you?" he asked after a moment, looking back at her. "What was that he said to you?" He thought he knew but wasn't sure. His head had been spinning at that point and he'd only partially heard.

She knew what he was talking about, of course. Myrmidon's words, his expression, his piercing glare were etched into her memory – but especially the words. She didn't want to say them aloud; they had frightened her too much. She wanted to be vague about it or shrug it off. But she and Luke had just been through an awful lot together and it didn't seem quite right not to tell him.

"He said he'd never forget me," she repeated quietly.

"Well . . ." He hesitated, not sure how to respond. He knew the words scared her, and he couldn't pretend they meant nothing. "Well, of course, he won't forget," he said after the pause. "You brought him down practically single-handed, and he'd *better* remember that! . . . But we're going home. So it really doesn't matter what he remembers and what he forgets. It's all the same to us. We'll be there and he'll be here, and never the twain shall meet. . . . You don't have to worry about him, Beth. It's over."

She appreciated what he was trying to do, but at the moment she preferred not talking about Myrmidon at all.

"As long as we're on a roll with you giving straight answers," Luke said next, because in some ways he understood her pretty well, "let me try this one again – *where'd you get that sword*?" He'd asked twice already but she'd brushed the question off both times.

"It was a gift. . . . I didn't know—I *don't* know very much about it. It's magic."

"Yeah, no kidding! But why didn't you tell me?"

"I— It's hard to explain. . . . The magic is stronger if it's secret, I think."

"OK. Fair enough, though I don't think you're taking into consideration the best-friend exception for that sort of rule. But what are you going to do with it now? Can you take it home, do you think?"

"Oh! . . . I don't know. But I don't think I should. It belongs here. Maybe I should give it back to—" She stopped short and then repeated, "I don't know." And then after a moment she added, "He recognized it, you know."

Try as she might, she couldn't get Myrmidon Tork out of her head.

They were shown to rooms where they could sleep that night. Castle accommodations were not as luxurious as Luke might have hoped, honored guest though he was. Jeron Rabirius had arranged for a private chamber for Aron, but everyone else in the castle shared rooms with several other people and considered themselves fortunate to do so. Luke ended up with Rendel, among others. Beth was not sent to Lady Gweynleyn's room this time but to a smaller room where she knew no one. Though the young women there seemed nice enough and all showed great curiosity about her, she found a bedroll in a corner as quickly as she could and curled up for the night.

Morning came in an instant. Mariza awakened Beth out of a deep sleep and told her to come at once to see Lady Gweynleyn and to bring all her belongings, which had been fetched for her from Sereynel's. The woodlander clothes would be sent back on her behalf. (Beth didn't bother to ask whether Mariza had actually intended to meet her by the Red Tower gate the day before – she knew the answer.)

As soon as Luke joined them, the three went first to the stables and then, on horseback, beyond the walls of Greyvic. Gweynleyn awaited them on a nearby riverbank, her cream-colored horse tethered a few yards away. On the far side of the river stood two cloaked figures, faces hidden by dark hoods. While Beth stared at them, she thought she heard her name, though no one had spoken aloud. Then she mouthed the words, "It was you," for she recognized, though she could not have said how, the Silent One who had spoken to her in the Dark Rim.

Beth realized then that Luke and Mariza had already dismounted and were waiting for her to do the same. When she did, Mariza took her horse's reins from her, and Beth and Luke walked forward to Gweynleyn. By that time, the Silent Ones were nowhere to be seen.

"You are to return to your own land at once," Gweynleyn said.

"Well, okey-doke," answered Luke, returned to his cheerful self after a good night's sleep and a wash. "No offense intended, because you've got a really nice 'other' kind of a world and everything, but I'm ready to click *my* heels together and go home." With a look in Beth's direction, he added, "So, what do you say, Dorothy, shall we head on back to Kansas?" It was a rhetorical question. He was sure of her answer.

Pretty sure, at least.

And yet . . .

Beth remained silent as Gweynleyn continued. "I am greatly strengthened now" – she seemed to be addressing Luke –

"and I will be able to do this thing myself. But we must away in haste to the Stronghold of Arystar, to the Pool of the Ancients, while the door between our lands remains open."

"Great!" exclaimed Luke, while with markedly less enthusiasm Beth asked, "Now?"

Luke answered before Gweynleyn could. "Well, yeah, Beth . . . now! You know . . . while the door's still open. Wouldn't want to miss an opportunity like that!" He tried to speak lightly, but he felt uneasy. When he'd said to her, the afternoon before, "Can we please go home now?" she hadn't said, " Yes!" or "Can't wait!" or "We're outta here!" She'd just looked thoughtful and a little dazed. It couldn't be that— She wouldn't really— "You *do* want to go home, don't you?" he asked now, feeling a weight, like a heavy stone, form inside him.

She hesitated before answering in a quiet voice. "Of course," she told him. "But, *now*?" she asked Gweynleyn. "We . . . we won't be able to say good-bye to anyone?"

While smiling in a way that made Beth suddenly miss her mother terribly, Gweynleyn motioned to her to look back toward the city walls. When she did, she saw two lines of mounted horses approaching. A few of the riders she recognized at once, the others soon afterwards. On one end of the nearer line were Therin Mandek, tall in his saddle, and Harac, who was not so tall. On the other end rode Rendel, his curly, cinnamon hair mostly hidden beneath his woodlander hat, alongside Aynyxia, always unique in her riding style. Centered between those two pairs, Jeron Rabirius accompanied Aron Sterling, distinguished-looking and finely-attired, even if not quite as dazzlingly so as he had been the day before. Behind this company, riding three abreast, were Gweynleyn's archers, the Eyndeli.

Aron dismounted first and walked briskly straight to Beth, who beamed at the sight of her friends. "I am sorry, Beth," the prince began at once, taking both her hands in his, "that I may not accompany you. I must spend this day in consult with council members, among others, but I make for Arystar on the morrow or on the day after that at the latest. I am to take my vows and be crowned as soon as all can be arranged. I would very much like to have you with me. I suppose," he spoke hesitantly, dividing his glances between Gweynleyn and Beth, "that you are unable to delay your own return."

371

"It could not be done without risk," Gweynleyn answered. "Now, the time is right, but we cannot know how long it will remain so." She looked at Beth inquiringly, then asked, "Do you wish to delay?"

No, thought Luke. *No, she doesn't. She sure doesn't.*

"But Luke could go now?" Beth asked.

What? Why was she even asking that? Idle curiosity, Luke hoped. *Always a one for trivia, that Beth.* His heart beat rapidly as he waited for her answer.

Beth hesitated. "I'm sorry," she said at last.

Sorry?

She glanced at Luke, then faced Aron. "I wish I could be there." Relief overtook Luke.

"I understand," Aron answered. "Did you know," he went on, smiling and trying to disguise his disappointment, "that the lord Rabirius is my kinsman? On my father's line. I know little of that branch of my family and am anxious to remedy the deficiency. It seems that my father was not only a kinsman, but also a great friend of Sir Jeron's."

"The best friend a man could want!" confirmed Jeron, still seated on his horse.

Harac, dismounted, began addressing Luke, shaking his hand heartily. "You're a strange one," the dwarf couldn't help saying. "Truth, you are!"

"Yeah. Strange but good-hearted. I remember."

"Fare well, lad." Harac gave him an amicable slap on the arm.

"And you fare yourself well," Luke returned in friendly but slightly strained tones, rubbing his arm.

Harac then stepped over to Beth, who was hugging Aron affectionately. She supposed that that was permissible, since he wasn't officially king yet. She had already, under cover of Harac's booming voice, handed him the magic sword, saying only that it was quite special and asking that he keep it safe and unseen until Marcus Gribb could advise him about it. Rendel could introduce them.

While Harac exchanged good-byes with Beth, Aron did the same with Luke, who shook the prince's hand enthusiastically and clapped him on the arm in a spirited way, now that the matter of Beth's returning home was settled.

Therin Mandek came next, bowing deeply to Beth and thanking her for her service to his homeland. As for Luke, Therin could think of no better compliment than to say, "A year or two hence, I could find you a place in my guard, if you wished it."

"Thanks," said Luke, "but no thanks. I think I'll just head off to college in a few years, or something really low-stress like that." The majority of the company was accustomed, by that point, to Luke's saying things they could not quite comprehend.

Last of all, Beth looked to Rendel, then Aynyxia, then back to Rendel again. They had not dismounted. Rendel understood her puzzlement and said, much to her pleasure, "Did you not know? We are to accompany you to Arystar, Aynyxia and I. We will say our farewells there."

They rode two abreast, excepting the Eyndeli. One of those – neither Beth nor Luke could have said which it was – rode so far ahead that she was out of view a good part of the time; another led the main company, while the third followed behind. Between were Rendel and Luke, Aynyxia and Beth, Gweynleyn and Mariza. Beth and Luke found this arrival at the stronghold to be much different from the previous one. They were neither offered a meal nor shown to quarters where they could rest or otherwise refresh themselves. Walking purposefully and speaking little, the company – less the Eyndeli, who had disappeared at once – crossed the main courtyard and were nearly across the Great Hall when Luke was surprised to hear a familiar voice utter his name.

"Imre!" he responded, turning. "So, it looks like you made it back all right."

"Yes," said the girl, approaching him happily, "a messenger came to me in Little Down. And her ladyship's groom returned this morning to say that you were coming and to bring news concerning the prince. I *knew* you would be successful. I knew you would make all things right."

"Uh, well, actually . . . you know, it was Beth who—"

"Of course," Imre amended, "you both have done this thing for us. You have *all* done this thing." She included Rendel and Aynyxia, just to be on the safe side.

"Yeah, well, anyway, we've got to go now. Door's closing, and all that. . . . But it was really nice to meet you," he added quickly.

"And it was my deepest pleasure to meet you," she assured him.

"OK! Well . . ." He began to shake her hand vigorously.

"Good-bye, Imre," said Beth. "Thank you for your help. We really needed it."

"*Thank* you for saying such a thing," responded Imre with undue gratitude and a flushing face.

She withdrew then, and Lady Gweynleyn said, "It is best if the remaining farewells are said now as well. It is time."

These were the hardest good-byes. Beth was teary when she told Rendel that she would miss him.

"There is great sadness in my heart," he answered her.

"Mine too."

"Yeah, well," Luke chimed in, "I don't know about that 'great sadness' thing, but I've got to say that it's not impossible that I'll be missing you too . . . somewhere down the line."

Rendel grinned, eyes glittering. While Beth turned to speak to Aynyxia, remembering in time to give her a quiet message for Marcus Gribb about his "special gift," Rendel said to Luke, "So then, we are now all great friends together?"

"Yeah, whatever," was Luke's answer, but he took Rendel's extended hand and shook it warmly.

By the time Beth pulled back from embracing Aynyxia, her cheeks were moist and her vision blurred. "I'll miss you," Beth said.

"Yep," agreed Aynyxia quietly.

"Aw, come here, you over-emotional plant-thing, you," said Luke jovially, pulling Aynyxia into a tight, awkward squeeze and then releasing her. Watching through her tears, Beth smiled, but Rendel laughed right out loud. Then Luke turned to Gweynleyn. He wished he could think of just the right thing to say to her, but all that came out of his mouth was "I guess that just about covers it." Unaccountably, he blinked a couple of times. He turned away, then turned right back and said quickly and quietly, "What you said about needing a great good to rise up—"

"Your part is finished," the lady interrupted him.

"We could stay—" he surprised himself by whispering.

"It is not your part, Luke."

"But there's a traitor you still haven't found, right? Close to the council. Maybe we ought to—"

"Luke." She put her hand to his cheek. Then she pulled it back and, in a louder voice, addressed Luke and Beth together. "You have what you wish to take, and you have left what you wish to leave?" Both of them nodded. Actually, Beth wished she had her best pair of running shoes to take back so that she wouldn't have to explain to her mother how she had lost them, but they were still at the Gribbs' – unless, of course, Marcus had found a buyer for them. Her sweatshirt was there as well, but that hardly mattered since it was ruined (though the Gribbs had kept it because of the zipper). Her bow, quiver, and pack she had given to Aynyxia, but Luke had convinced her to keep the small (non-magical) dagger as a souvenir. The reed pipe that Rendel had given her for her birthday still hung on a string around her neck; she tried to return the hat he had lent her, but she was glad when he told her to keep that too.

So they were ready.

Leading them to an ordinary-looking wooden door, Gweynleyn opened it and walked through, holding it open behind her. Luke gave a quick wave to Rendel and Aynyxia, then went through the door. Beth followed, saying a quick good-bye to Mariza (whose presence she had forgotten) as she passed. Then, as if suddenly remembering something, she turned back to her friends. She wanted to ask Rendel how old he was and Aynyxia whether she had any brothers or sisters. But Mariza was already closing the door from within.

Beth and Luke found themselves alone with Gweynleyn in a small, entirely-enclosed courtyard, the existence of which they had not previously suspected. No windows looked out onto it, at least not from the lower floors. The sky seemed far above.

There was little in the courtyard – a few tended flowers, neat vines that crept up the castle walls, two stone benches, and a pool. Beth could not tell if the pool was natural or artificial, but, given its present use, she supposed the former was more likely.

"It was here that I first met you." Gweynleyn said to Luke, who looked surprised for an instant before comprehension dawned.

"This is where you were when you . . . appeared to me?"

"Yes. My affinity to this place is a strong one – so much so that I can sometimes wield its magic. I came here when the Silent One told me that Beth needed your assistance. He showed you to me, and I came here that I might call you. It fatigued me greatly, but, as I said, I am much stronger now. . . . I will be able to send you," she told them, "but we ought not delay."

"Thank you for everything," Beth said quickly, and Luke added, "Yeah, thanks."

"It is I and all those who are dear to me that owe our thanks to you."

Though she did not tell them to do so, Luke and Beth knelt by the water then and slowly extended their hands. They could see the reflections of their own faces and, above them, that of Gweynleyn. As they moved their fingers toward the water's surface, Beth suddenly grabbed Luke's hand so that the two of them would reach it at precisely the same instant.

Then they felt the cool water on their fingertips.

CHAPTER TWENTY-SEVEN – Back Again

Their fingers caused ripples in the water and for a moment they lost sight of Gweynleyn's reflection. Then it reappeared, somewhat altered in aspect. Its clarity had lessened, though a light now emanated from it. Their own reflections they could not find at all.

They knew they were home.

It was evening and they knelt on cold ground, reaching their fingers into well water that was even colder.

"OK!" Luke exclaimed approvingly, pulling back his hand.

Though less readily, Beth also pulled back, saying to the fading watery image, "Good-bye."

Even after Gweynleyn's face had entirely disappeared, the light remained, as did the water.

"So . . . we're home," said Luke, though not in an entirely satisfied tone. In fact, he sounded disappointed. "Looks like the door's still open, though," he added slowly. "There's still water in the well." Then he took Beth completely by surprise by saying, "But we probably shouldn't try to go back, right?"

"What? But you—"

"Yeah, I know. . . . Yeah, right. Just kidding." Or was he? He'd surprised himself as well as Beth. "I mean, I know that yesterday I couldn't wait to get out of there. (Can you believe it was only yesterday? It seems more like – oh, I don't know – maybe *forever* ago!) But now . . . well, it's funny. Now, even yesterday doesn't seem so bad. After all, it all turned out OK – you and that incredibly cool sword showing up like you did! What could be better than that?" By this point, Luke was upright and beginning to move about, noticeably warming to his subject with each new sentence. "I mean, no real harm done, right? Just as our buddy Jeron Rabirius would be the first to point out. And did we have some awesome adventures, or what? I saved you from those manic vines and that ugly little pig, and you saved me from . . . well, 'that *big* ugly pig' seems like a fair enough way of putting it! What a jerk that guy was! And we rode horses and slept in castles and went underneath a waterfall and . . . and we *saved* them, Beth. We saved them all!"

"We had some help."

"Yes, we did!" he agreed in a softer, more thoughtful voice. "We sure did! And that was pretty cool, too! . . . But, *MAN!! WAS THIS THE MOST AWESOME THING THAT'S EVER HAPPENED TO YOU, OR NOT?*" (The softer voice had zipped off into oblivion.)

"Luke—"

"Because if anything more awesome than *this* has ever happened to you, I'd sure like to—"

"*Luke!*" He stopped. "Don't you think we ought to find out how long we've been gone?"

"Oh, yeah. Right." A thought struck him. "My watch. It's got to be here somewhere, and it'll show the date." He started to feel among the fallen leaves for it. "I took it off and was playing around with it when I was trying to figure out what to do about you and just how long I should wait, and then I dropped it when I saw the water in the well and then the light—" He stopped short, and as one they turned to the well and realized that, unnoticed by them, the light and the water had faded completely away. "Well, that's that, then," Luke said a little sadly.

Beth found Luke's watch and said so without much enthusiasm.

"Check the date," Luke told her.

"It's too dark. How do you light it up?" She handed it to him and saw the blue glow as he lit and read it. "Same day!" he told her, almost triumphantly. "Looks like we've only lost about . . . twenty minutes. Or, I have. I guess you lost more. Anyway, I remember the time because I'd decided I'd wait until—"

Simultaneously, they froze, listening intently. They'd both heard the sound of a car, coming from the direction of Beth's house. The noise traveled easily enough in the quieted night, the heavy winds that had surrounded Beth on her way to the well having died out completely in her absence. "Are you sure the time's right? My mom shouldn't be back yet, and I don't know who else it would be." Even as she spoke, she began moving quickly toward the house, Luke right behind.

When they were nearly at the back door, Luke said, "If it *is* your mom, she's going to be a little surprised by some of your recent fashion decisions."

"My clothes!" She'd returned wearing her Gwilldonian jacket, shirt, and boots; Rendel's hat was clutched in her hand.

"Yep! That's what I had in mind. . . . Not to mention the fact that you're carrying a concealed weapon, and I don't think you used to."

They were close enough by then to recognize the voice from in front of the house, though they couldn't make out the words. "It's my mom." No doubt she was still apologizing to whoever had brought her home early from the meeting.

"OK," said Luke. "So you take the secret stairs and I'll go around front and stall. She's probably seen my bike anyway."

"What about *your* clothes?" And his bruises – he'd have to explain those too, though Beth noticed with surprise how faded they must already be. In the faint light from the back porch, she couldn't even see them.

"I don't think your mom's got my wardrobe memorized quite as well as yours. Besides, most of this is mine anyway. But, here. Take the jacket." He'd already gotten it off and was handing it to her. "Keep it for me. I kind of like it, but I don't want to have to explain it to *my* mother. Not to mention my new dagger!" He quickly handed her that too. "Now, go!"

She went. As she slipped inside, she heard him yelling as he rounded the house, "Hey, Ms. DeVere!"

It was a hard thing that circumstances kept Beth and Luke from seeing each other the next day, but the day after that they got together and went over their adventure in great detail. And they did much the same thing again not long after that, but in time . . .

They talked about Gwilldonum less and less. Every now and then, of course, they'd think of something new they wanted to discuss or just mention. Or, as happened on a couple of occasions, something happened that triggered similar thoughts in the two of them. Once, for instance, when they were with a large group of kids who were involved in a variety of conversations around Josh and Jordan Loo's family room – they were waiting for Mr. Loo to get off the phone and start science class – one of their friends said loudly and sarcastically to another, "Yeah, right! And then *one* day, plants are going to sprout teeny little hands and feet and start walking around and talking!" Immediately, from opposite sides of the room, Luke's and Beth's eyes found each other. The two friends smiled knowingly before returning to their own conversations.

Neither talked to anyone else about their adventure – this took little effort on Luke's part, but Beth did occasionally consider approaching her mother – and by Thanksgiving, they had more or less stopped talking to each other about it as well. This isn't to say that either of them stopped thinking about Gwilldonum, because neither did, but they kept the thoughts private, even from one another. Then, in late December, the subject came up again.

The homeschool group had rented the community center for a combined Christmas-Hanukkah-Kwanzaa party that night and a number of kids had volunteered to set up decorations in the afternoon. Luke and Beth were the last to get picked up (Ms. McKinnon was late again), and as they waited inside (it was literally freezing outside), Beth said after a pause, "You know, I wish we'd gotten to celebrate a holiday there." Although her previous sentence had had nothing to do with Gwilldonum, Luke knew at once the "there" she had in mind.

"Well, even if we had," he answered, as if that had been their topic all along, "I've got this feeling it wouldn't have been Christmas – or Hanukkah either, for that matter. But we kind of did see a holiday celebration – that Erasti-whatever festival looked like it was a pretty big deal."

"Yes, but we didn't really get the chance to enjoy it much."

Without thinking, Luke said, "Oh, well. Maybe next time."

Maybe next time. They hadn't talked about the possibility of "next time." Not once. They'd kept those thoughts entirely to themselves.

Even now, Beth chose to ignore the comment and respond instead to what Luke had said before it. "I suppose you're right about no Christmas or Hanukkah, but, you know, there are so *many* things that are the same in their world as in ours. . . . How much of it do you think could come from only a *few* people going from here to there every now and then? Because even if you figure that . . ."

And so began the longest conversation they'd had about Gwilldonum in weeks. It was at last interrupted by a phone call

380

from Luke's mother to say (unnecessarily) that she was late and (somewhat helpfully) that she'd be there in twenty minutes and (unnecessarily, again) to stay inside where it was warm.

Luke and Beth did not resume the thread of their previous discussion, but the conversation about Gwilldonum did prompt Luke to retrieve a present he'd stuck in his backpack to give Beth later that evening.

"Here," he said unceremoniously. "It's for you." She knew that, because there was a tag with her name in big letters.

"Thanks. Should I open it now?"

"Sure. Why not?" Actually, he was glad she was going to do it now while no one else was there to see. It might seem like not much of a gift to some other kids, but he felt pretty sure of her reaction . . . until she actually began to tear away the paper. *Then* he wondered if she'd like it after all, and he had to stifle an impulse to snatch it back out of her hands.

"I did it on the computer," he said when she'd opened the gift and was looking at the picture he'd made. "Well, duh! Kind of obvious!" He was talking nervously. He really wanted her to like it. "I used a landscaping program that lets you pick out the kind of materials you want – like, the blocks for the well and the walls – and you pick the different kinds of plants and put them where you want." He had restored the abandoned DeVere garden and rebuilt the magic well . . . virtually, that is.

She hadn't said anything. And then she laughed. "Luke, this is so funny!"

"Well, great!" he answered in a different tone. "But it wasn't really meant to be." He'd thought she'd be pleased, not amused. He even thought she'd think it was . . . pretty special.

"Oh, no! I don't mean it like that! It's . . . it's *perfect*! Really perfect! . . . No, the funny part is . . . Well, just look." She went to her tote bag and pulled out her gift for him. "I didn't want you to open it here, but since Mom and I are going away tomorrow, I thought I'd give it to you at the party tonight and you could take it home to open later."

While he removed the wrapping, she said, "I've been taking that art class from Ms. Stimms, you know. . . . I haven't done that many watercolors. I know it's not that great, but. . ."

"It's perfect," said Luke sincerely. After a moment of staring at it, he said, "And you're right. It's pretty funny!" He had made her the picture of the garden and the well. She had made him a watercolor painting of a magical pool in a lovely but somewhat eerie spot, full of wild beauty, dark shadows, and thick greenery. Her initials were half-hidden in a lower corner, but across the top of the painting she had written with small, precise strokes, "SANCTUARY."

"Look," said Luke, removing his computer-generated picture from its cardstock frame. "I gave mine a title too." On the back of her gift, he had handwritten the words "Open Door." "I didn't want to put it on the front," he explained, "just in case someone asked you what it meant. . . . You're not a very good liar, you know."

"I know." She slipped the picture back into its frame and stared at it, as Luke stared at his.

The same words drifted into both their minds. *Maybe next time . . .*

But all Beth said aloud was "Merry Christmas, Luke."

And all Luke said was "Merry Christmas, Beth."

Made in the USA
Middletown, DE
10 August 2019